MW00910080

13 Ghostly Tales and Yarns of the Navesink River

WHERE HISTORY AND FOLKLORE COLLIDE

Patricia Martz Heyer

Patricia Martz Heyer

ISBN: 978-1-4834-5766-6 (sc)
ISBN: 978-1-4834-5765-9 (e)

Lulu Publishing Services rev. date: 9/8/2016

Table of Tales & Yarns

Introduction

13 Ghostly Tales and Yarns of the Navesink River is a collection of ghostly folktales in which each story is based upon actual events or series of events from local history. Each tale included here provides the reader with the factual historical background and the circumstances associated with that event. It then goes on to mesh the historical elements with the paranormal and oral history accounts shared over the years by locals. The origins of these stories has been mined from the archives of local newspapers, as well as the records of local historical associations and libraries.

The local historical record of the Navesink is both colorful and lively. When folklore overlaps history one discovers phantom ships, peculiar old mariners, as well as giant sea creatures. There are specters of lost soldiers and glimpses of a cruel slave owner's ultimate punishment. The accounts include a war fought only on the Navesink, and a haunted house that once floated across the river. Others tell of a local valley where early American colonists refused to live, and an Indian wizard who could foretell the future. The collection includes an elegant Victorian party which goes terribly awry, and the front page story of a ghost once investigated by local police.

The collision of history and folklore creates savory reading. So sit back and relax and enjoy some of the many ghostly tales and yarns of the Navesink River.

Curse of the *Canis lupus*

One dark and windy night just as Oliver William Holton, his wife and two young sons sat down to dinner in their new home there was a loud demanding knock on the front door. Annoyed at being disturbed at dinner, Mr. Holton clutched his dinner napkin with one hand as he jerked open the door with the other. An old woman perched on his door step leaning inward, trying to avoid the rain. "What do you want?" he demanded.

The woman stared silently into his face. She was frail with olive canvas-like skin. Her large brown eyes seemed too large for her face, and her expression was that of one weary but earnest in their efforts. Her hair was tightly braided, over which a brightly colored shawl encased her face in vivid reds and blues. The remainder of her clothing was dark, ill fitting, and shabby. And if she wore shoes, they were mere scuffs hidden beneath her mud caked hem.

"Well," he demanded, "What do you want?"

Never taking her eyes off his she spoke in a low hoarse voice, "I am here to help, sir."

"Be gone with you, "he barked. "You cannot possibility be of any help to me.

The old woman's eyes were glued on his. "But I can sir, for the great spirits have sent me to you, for you have been cursed by an enemy. For only a mere five dollars I can removed the spell."

Holton was a God fearing Episcopal and a practical man with no patience for this foolishness. "Get out of here you thieving gypsy!" he roared. The old woman held her ground. The more he shouted insults at her the more intently she glared at him.

"You are doomed if you do not allow me to remove the curse. The cost is small; one you can well afford."

Holton lost patience with the old woman. "Get out of here before I call the dog out on you," he bellowed. He shoved the old woman away from the door. She toppled off the doorstep into the wet shrubbery.

As he turned to close the door the old woman appeared from the shrubs, "You scorn the gypsy. You are now duly cursed Oliver Holton!" She raised her arms skyward before sweeping them towards him. Her long fingers pointed at his face. "The malevolence of the *canis lupus*, the immortal one, will shadow you always, and will within five harvests moons, rip apart and devour what all is yours." Holton slammed the door and shook his head. When he returned to dinner he reminded his wife to be certain to lock the doors the following day as there were gypsies in the area. He thought no more of the encounter.

Oliver Holton was a man with an entrepreneurial spirit as well as an interest in exotic wildlife. It is likely this interest in unusual and peculiar animals that prompted him to purchase a 214-acre farm in Middletown, NJ in the early 1920's. It was located in the area now bordered by Twinbrook and Woodland Drives, on the south bound side of route 35. The homestead, known as Twinbrook Farm, would eventually become his pride and joy, Twinbrook Zoological Park. But Oliver Holton's life would be far from idyllic.

Shortly after his encounter with the gypsy he began a venture of poultry distribution. He began buying quantities of ducks, geese, chickens, and then reselling them to local framers. But the venture was short lived when a disease killed the bulk of his stock within a few months.

Holton quickly revised his business plan. He decided to open his dream attraction, a zoological park where exotic beasts from around the world would be displayed. He knew many such beasts were extremely popular at a larger zoo in New York City. His Twinbrook Zoo would enable people from all over the East coast to observe such creatures without going into New York. He knew it would be a success.

In early 1925 he began by purchasing a collection of wild game birds and a few exotic birds. Within a few days a pack of what was described as wild dogs broke through the enclosure and decimated the collection. Although a search was made, the culprits were not caught.

Not to be defeated, Holton built a sturdy compound in which to house his animal collection. He reinforced the structures and quickly began purchasing a wide variety of wild creatures. He bought specimens from other zoos, circuses, as well as made private purchases from well-known wild animal hunters and collectors. Despite three addition run-ins with the wild dogs in the area, the zoo opened May 1st 1926.

The public was enthralled and the zoo became an instant success. There were usually long lines of visitors waiting to see his collection of elephants, lions, tigers, monkeys, large Amazonian snakes, wolves, bears, flamingoes, and other assorted exotic beasts.

Within days more problems arose when several monkeys repeatedly escaped their cages causing chaos and destruction in the neighboring areas. Each time they escaped, Holton sent out search parties to track down the miscreants and quickly paid for the cost of their destruction. More than a few neighbors began to complain among themselves about the security of the zoo.

But then in July an extremely rare spotted leopard arrived from India. Unfortunately, the animal arrived earlier than expected and its permanent enclosure was not complete. Within an hour of arrival, the leopard had managed to escape from his travel crate.

To make matters worse, the leopard's absence wasn't noticed for some time. By the time the alarm was sounded the huge cat was nowhere to be found. Holton was beside himself with worry. Not only had the cat been extremely expensive, but was undoubtedly dangerous to humans and other animals in the area. He hired a search party which scoured the area with no success.

For a time, the only sighting of the cat was by a five-year-old girl, Margaret Ellison, from nearby Nutswamp. The girl saw the leopard and reported to her father that she had seen a big ugly dog covered with spots in the orchard. Despite an intense search nothing was found.

Initially Holton did not report the missing leopard to the authorities. He believed his hired posse would do a better job of tracking and capturing the animal than anyone else. It was not until several additional sightings of the animal were reported to the police that Holton confirmed that the cat was missing.

The local authorities never made attempts to capture the creature. They forwarded all sightings to Holton who checked out every report. With the missing leopard causing such a fuss Holton offered a $100.00 reward for the animal, dead or alive. That is about $1500.00 in today's money. Hunters from around the state joined the search in hopes of capturing the reward.

The missing leopard became front page news. The *Daily Register* reported reports of sightings in nearly every edition. Red Bank store keepers used images of a leopards as advertising, and it is reported that a road crew was once fired because they wouldn't stop talking about the missing leopard. The migrant blackberry pickers refused to go back to the field for a time.

Holton tried everything he could to capture the beast. In addition to his long standing search parties, he set live bait traps in the woods, and obtained special scents from the Department of Interior to bait the creature, but all were unsuccessful.

Despite his preoccupation with the missing leopard Holton continued adding more animals to his zoological park. After a few weeks without further sightings interest in the cat died down. Rumors persisted that Holton had invented the missing cat as a publicity stunt for his zoo.

Nearly four months after the disappearance, Willard Irons, a young farmer from Island Heights, began to find his ducks disappearing from his pond. He never considered a leopard as the culprit, as Middletown was over forty miles away. One day he heard his mother screaming from near the pond. He snatched his shotgun and ran to her. The spotted leopard had caught its paw in a beaver trap and was fiercely attempting to free itself.

Irons dispatched the leopard by firing both barrels of his shotgun into its head. He showed the dead cat to a neighbor and who reminded him of the missing leopard in Middletown. He telephoned Mr. Holton, put the animal in the back of his car, and drove it to Middletown.

Anxious to settle the capture of the animal, Holton arranged for Dan Dorn, a Red Bank photographer to photograph the return and display of the leopard. Using his new motion picture camera Dorn recorded the event. The matter died down and Holton's string of bad luck appeared to be over.

The zoo closed for the winter with most of the animals housed at the Steel Pier in Atlantic City. They were returned to Middletown early in the spring of 1927. Holton was anxious for spring and hopeful for a successful, and uneventful summer in 1927. But that would not be the case.

The summer at the zoo began without incident. The crowds were large, and the take impressive. In early July Mrs. Holton and their eldest son set out to visit relatives in Pennsylvania for a few days. Mr. Holton, his two-year-old son, and the family cook, Mrs. Mazza, remained at the zoo.

On July 20th Mr. Holton was working on repairs at an enclosure at the zoo. His son, Teddy, was playing with the cook's five-year-old son, Henry in the family's yard. Their trusted family dog, a trusted German Shepard named Duke watched as the children darted around the lawn. Duke was so well trained that he let himself in and out of the house by opening back screen door with his nose.

Suddenly Henry ran into the kitchen with blood running down his ear, "A big dog is biting Teddy," he sobbed." Mrs. Mazza dashed towards the door. She shouted at Henry to stay inside the house. She grabbed the first thing she saw, a broom, and ran out to confront the dog.

She gasped in terror. A large grey wolf was tossing little Teddy around as if he was a doll. She began beating the head of the wolf. Finally, the wolf let loose of the child for a moment. In that instant Mrs. Mazza snatched up the little boy. As she ran toward the house she saw in horror that own son had disobeyed and was standing in the yard watching the event. She held the bleeding baby in one arm and grasped her son in the other and raced back into the kitchen. The boy was bitten, but seemed not to be critically injured. She laid the boy on the couch and ran to get a gun .She found the shotgun, but there was no ammunition to be found. Then she heard her son scream, "No Duke, don't open the door."

The screams of the baby filled the house. Mrs. Mazza rounded the corner into the room. The wolf was in the house! As she raised the gun to strike the wolf it snatched the bleeding toddler and ran out.

Mazza chased the animal with the empty gun. The wolf was now tearing flesh from the screaming child. Mrs. Mazza bashed the head of the wolf with all her strength. Stunned, the wolf finally dropped the motionless child and loped to the side yard and lay down by the pond.

A worker hearing the noise alerted the crew at the zoo. Mr. Holton arrived and quickly dispatched the wolf. The children were taken to Woodley Hospital in Red Bank. Henry survived with a few bites and scratches. Teddy Holton, Oliver Holton's son, was not so lucky. The second attack of the wolf had punctured Teddy's lung in several places. Despite massive efforts to save the child, he died the following day.

The grey lobo wolf, *Canus lupus*, who keepers believed to be tame had escaped his enclosure and killed the child. Staffers who were later interviewed claimed that the wolf was so tame they could pet him, and that Duke the family dog could enter the wolf's enclosure without incident.

After the funeral Mrs. Holton and their other son returned to Pennsylvania. The zoo reopened for a few weeks. But Mr. Holton had lost his obsession for his zoological park. By October 16, 1927 the zoo was officially closed.

News of the tragedy spread across the area. The community became extremely vocal about their concerns for their safety. Holton was called to the town council meeting. He was so devastated that he made no defense. He informed the town council he was selling off the animals immediately.

Holton sold some animals to zoos or circuses. Large quantities of snake and poultry meat were purchased by a meat wholesaler. Soon afterward Oliver Holton put the farm, the zoo, and all the property on the market. The property was finally sold in May 1928. As if Holton need any more bad luck, his wife soon divorced him, taking their other son with her.

Oliver William Holton had combined his interest in exotic animals with his entrepreneurial skills in an effort to provide for his family. Despite his best efforts he suffered mishap after mishap in his business ventures. Finally, the devastating loss of his son and the resulting loss of his wife and family had annihilated his lifelong dreams. It had been literally devoured by the jaws of *Canis lupus*, just as the gypsy predicted.

The last we hear of Oliver Holton he left The United States bound for Central America. We can only speculate his destination. Was he in search of new exotic animals or was it in search of something else? Perhaps he was seeking the old gypsy, or anyone or anything that could remove the curse of the *Canis lupus.*

Dublin House: The House That Crossed a River

Many of the great old residences in the Navesink area claim to be haunted.

So it isn't surprising that a nineteenth century mansion with a history such as the Dublin House in Red Bank would have active paranormal activity. Not only does the building have a resident ghost, but a phantom witnessed by both staff and patrons. It is not a random haunting for sure, for the Dublin house phantom is none other than its former mistress, Roberta Patterson.

The adventures of the house began in 1840, when it was routed from its foundation in Middletown and floated across the Navesink on a barge. Little is known about it until it was purchased by Robert Allen Jr., who moved it once again. This time its destination was the west side of Broad street. Here at 60 Broad the small home would undergo a massive renovation which included the addition of second and third floors. The addition of unique architectural alterations resulted in the beautiful Mansardic mansion we know today as the Dublin House.

Robert Allen Jr., a prominent lawyer, real estate developer, and member of the New Jersey legislature supervised the transformations of his home with an eagle eye. He lived in the house with his wife and two daughters until his death in 1903. Upon his death the house was inherited by his eldest daughter, Roberta Allen Patterson.

Roberta and her husband George Hance Patterson moved the larger newly renovated house yet again. This time the task to move the mansion was more complicated. At last in 1905 the mansion came to rest in its current location at 30 Monmouth Street. The couple would spend the remainder of their lives here. Mr. Patterson died in 1938 and his wife lived many more years in the house, passing away in 1953. As the Patterson had no children Roberta Patterson's estate was left to a nephew and two nieces.

It was some time before the estate was settled, but by 1971 the building become commercial property. This began a new era for the old house. A series of businesses called the mansion home. As the "House on Monmouth Street" she held a number of shops including an ice cream parlor, chocolate and candle stores, two gift shops, and a restaurant. Other short term businesses included Longfellow's, Whiskers, and El Parador Restaurant. A coffee house too once occupied part of the second floor.

There have been claims that The Dublin House is haunted for many years. During the sixties youngsters approached the house with trepidation. Claims were made that a ghostly figure lived in the old house. After it became commercial, the allegations continued. Upstairs in the coffeehouse the coffee would sometimes brew all by itself. In the other shops lights turned on and off, doors slammed, and strawberry ice cream was frequently lobbed off tables.

In the late 1980's the Dubliner Pub which did business farther down the street, moved to 30 Monmouth with great fanfare. A parade of patrons and staff from the Pub, marched up Monmouth street officially opening the Dublin House.

In 2004 it was purchased by two Irish restaurateurs with new plans for the house.

Realizing the building had been neglected and poorly renovated over recent years, they undertook a massive rehabilitation and restoration project to restore the building to its former glory. This would not be an easy or inexpensive project for the house was sinking and in desperate need of major infrastructural work.

During the early days of renovation, the resident ghost seemed rather annoyed by all the noise and dust. She made her presence known by knocking over walls and equipment at will. It took some time for the ghost to become acclimated with Dunne and Devlin's renovation. But once she saw their determination to repair and preserve the beauty of the house, she seemed to be pleased with the arrangement.

The owners acknowledge her presence, happily greeting her each morning. Although some days go by when there is no contact between ghost and humans, others days are filled with interactions. She frequently unlocks doors and turns lights on and off. She likes a tidy household, and has been known to organize a messy desk or rearrange items out of place in the restaurant.

The resident ghost shows her mischievous side sometimes by sliding a bottle off the bar late at night. Other times she follows patrons and waitresses around the restaurant. Roberta is known to love music. Every night the staff turns off the radio system at closing, but frequently music is playing when they arrive in the morning.

Both staff and patrons report experiences with the ghost. Almost everyone reports amicable experiences with the ghost, although one patron reported an auditory experience with a highly peeved Mrs. Patterson. During the autumn of 2012 a female patron was alone in the ladies' room when she heard a harsh and irritated female complaining about the "dammed kids" who leave the bathroom messy. The tirade went on for some time. When the voice grew more agitated the patron quickly washed her hands and fled the room.

When Devlin & Dunne purchased the building they discovered it came with its very own local historian, TJ McMahon. As a regular at the Dublin House he spent many hours sharing his knowledge of the mansion's history and especially its ghostly mistress. After his passing in 2005 The Dublin House dedicated the downstairs dining room to his memory. An assortment of TJ McMahon's works, photos, and memorabilia are displayed in a large wooden display cabinet mounted on the far wall. On one occasion a few years ago just as a family was leaving their table beneath the case, it came crashing down to the floor. No one was injured but the case was broken and its contents scattered about.

The case was repaired and securely bolted to the studs to prevent any further problems. The memorabilia were carefully arranged so that a framed portrait of McMahon faced the room. Once closed, it was secured with special screws so that the case could not be opened without great difficulty. The next morning when staff arrived the photo of McMahon faced the wall. Since it was impossible for anyone to open the cabinet it was agreed that only Mrs. Patterson could have turned the picture towards the wall. Apparently Mrs. Patterson was displeased with the historian's constant discussion of the details of her family's life. The case remains unchanged in respect for her wishes.

So what does a modern business do when it has a resident ghost? Rather than flee from the idea the Dublin House has welcomed and embraced their resident spirit. Although the owners already knew they had a ghost, paranormal investigators have verified the existence of spirt in the building

The Dublin House ghost exhibits distinct maternal qualities. Just as any mother, she watches over the house and its occupants. At times she gets annoyed with those around her, and sometimes, just like any mother she is mischievous and teases us with evidence of her presence.

The cordial relationship of owners and their resident spirit may be the result of circumstance and coincidence. Mrs. Patterson never had children. As she grew older surely there may have been times when she wished she had a son to help her care for the old house. She needed not just any son, but a son who would love the old mansion as she did. Devlin and Dunne filled that niche. She has not one, but two sons, who respect and care for her home. They lovingly maintain and respect the great house while filling it daily with laughter, good food, and comradery. With people around all the time she can never be lonely. What more could a motherly ghost want? It is not surprising that she stays.

If you stop off at the Dublin House feel free to greet her and invite her to pull up a chair to your table or sit beside you at the bar. Who knows. you might meet her too.

The Serpent of the Navesink

The summer of 1889 would long be remembered by locals along the Navesink River for more than the soaring temperatures and unrelenting humidity. All along the river's banks discerning Victorian homes spread wide their windows attempting to catch a bit of a cooling sea breeze. Before the end of summer locals would have much more to gossip about than the weather.

On a scorching summer Sunday four Red Bank businessmen boarded the yacht, Tille S. heading out of Red Bank to enjoy a cooling afternoon on the Bay near Highlands Beach. It was nearly dark as they began the trip homeward. With a full moon providing ample visibility for the journey, the skipper, Marcus P. Sherman minded the tiller. His friends Lloyd Eglinton, Stephen Allen, and William Tinton settled in the bow keeping watch for floating debris ahead. They were in fine spirits enjoying the stiff summer breezes as they rounded the Highlands and headed for Red Bank.

Suddenly Eglinton leapt to his feet, shouting and waving his arms in warning to Sherman. "Hard to port," he shrieked. Sherman pulled hard on the rudder and the boat veered toward shore as he cut the engine. At that moment a huge dark mass, serpentine in shape, swam in a snakelike rhythm slowly through the water towards the boat. The men's attempts to speak were merely gasps and stifled moans. As the creature passed the bow it raised its head slightly and gave a mighty growl. In an instant it disappeared into the depths of the Navesink. Speechless, they watched as the wake from the creature eased slowly towards Hartshorne Cove. Then it disappeared into the dark water.

Once the men regained their composure they began sharing their descriptions with one another. They established that the head resembled a bulldog, with large eyes the size of silver dollars. On the very top of its head were rounded horns like growths jutting out just above the eyes. Bristles traced the upper lip of the creature and the nostrils were large and flattened. The men agreed that the tapered body was about fifty feet long and that had a pointed tail.

Although the four were reluctant to report the sighting at first, they discovered that many others had reported encounters with the creature. *The Daily Register* reported that over a dozen boaters recounted seeing the beast in the spring and summer of 1889. These occurred in both the northern branch of the river, known as the Navesink, as well as the southern tributary known as the Shrewsbury. Many locals called it the Shrewsbury Serpent, others insisted it was the serpent of the Navesink.

While this may be one of the most noted descriptions of the creature, earlier accounts from 1879 claim that a three-hundred-foot sea monster was sighted off Sandy Hook. This account is given credence as it was described in detail, complete with hand drawn illustrations in the December 1879 issue of *Scientific American*. Like the creature observed by the Red Bank crew the monster had a snake like body, a square head, with horn like projections on the top of its head. The Sandy Hook creature was described to be much larger, and for a time believed to be a giant squid. Over the next few years' sightings of unusual sea creatures abounded in this area of the Atlantic coast.

Throughout the following decades fishermen and boaters periodically claim to encounters with some sort of marine beast in the Navesink. In August of 1963 the *New York Times* reported that a serpent like creature was sighted near the mouth of the Navesink in Sandy Hook Bay. The eyewitnesses included Dr. Lionel Wolford, Director of U.S. Fish and Wildlife Research Center, who identified the creature as a forty-foot invertebrate, which moved through the water in an undulating fashion.

To this day local fishermen exchange tales and sightings, boaters scan the water on dark nights hoping for even a glimpse of the Shrewsbury Serpent. While no specimen has yet to be discovered, who is to say, what lies beneath the tidal waters of the beautiful Navesink River.

Beyond the Veil: A Victorian Ghost Party

The Navesink shores were bustling with activity during the Victorian Age. Local business and industries thrived as the demand for local agricultural products mushroomed. As transportation became cheaper and easier, the shore communities not only increased in population, but also gained a sizeable summer tourist industry.

Fashionable Victorian mansions sprouted along the river's banks as the populace became more urbane. Recreational and cultural activities expanded and locals joined in the growing spiritualism movement. Local interest in ghost stories and the supernatural is evidenced by the frequent paranormal accounts published in local newspapers. Nearly every edition contained at least one ad for a local medium or a clairvoyant. So it is not surprising that a popular entertainment during Victorian times was the ghost party.

Although such gatherings might be compared to modern Halloween parties, there were distinct differences. These parties were elaborate social events, using formal standards of Victorian entertainment and etiquette. Although they were mostly held in the autumn, they frequently occurred anytime between early October and the New Year. Those affiliated with the spiritualist movement emphasized communication with the dead, while admittedly others were simply social events.

Victorian homes all along the Navesink were sites for these elaborate parties. Homes were adorned with detailed and ornate seasonal decorations. Inside the homes, light from candles and small oil lamps reflected glittery lace chandelier sways. Rich jewel toned draperies flowed from ceiling to floor gathering in great puddles of fabric.

Equally formal was the extravagant bill of fare. A Victorian hostess took great pride in her menu and table presentation. Using her best linens, the refreshments were stylishly served on her finest china, silver, and crystal glassware.

Sometimes these parties included a formal sit down dinner party. Other times great buffet tables were heaped with both hot and cold foods. Appetizers, meats, seafood, potatoes, and vegetables dishes might be served. Other times elegant tea sandwiches, tarts, pasties, or nut filled breads graced the table. A separate, but none the less bountiful dessert table was always to be found. Beautiful crystal and silver serving pieces were practically buried beneath skillfully bedecked beautiful cakes, pies, eclairs, cookies, and other assorted sweets. To quench the thirst of her guests the hostess served liquors, wines, ciders, beers, as well as punch, teas and coffee.

As critical as the food was to a successful party, the entertainment was the indispensable ingredient. The entertainment was usually the purpose of the event. Sometimes the parties were masquerades, with guests arriving in sumptuous costumes and masks. Guests danced, enjoyed recitals, played parlor games, or exchanged stories of their own ghostly experiences.

Often professional story tellers recounted ghost stories while colorfully clad gypsy fortune tellers wowed guests with predictions of great love affairs or huge business successes. There could be palm readers, mediums, and psychics on hand to add to the colorful event. In some of the more elegant affairs a New York clairvoyant would conduct a séance.

Invitations to such parties were highly prized. Victorians could easily measure their social status by which invitations they received. At the same time a hostess measured her social status by the individual acceptances she received to her event. Parties could be serious business in Victorian times.

So it was with some trepidation that Anna finally agreed to hold a ghost party in her home along the Navesink in 1888. Anna and her husband George had relocated to Black Point from New England before the war. And as much as they loved their new beautiful house on the Navesink, New England would always be their home.

Anna's late husband George had been a prominent businessman, but that was before the war. When the hostilities broke out he promised Anna that when the war was over he would take her back to New England for a visit. When he volunteered for the local regiment, Anna was beside herself with worry, and when they carried him home in that wooden box from

Gettysburg she was heartbroken. Even after her formal mourning period had ended, Anna rarely participated in social events.

Her one close friend was Louisa, also a war widow. For a while now Louisa had been talking with Anna about the growing spiritualism movement. She brought her literature and took her to several meetings. Although Anna was skeptical she was enthralled with the possibility of communicating with George once more. She even began attending séances with her friend.

A few weeks earlier Louisa and Anna were invited to a ghost party at a nearby estate. They were delighted to find that a séance had been planned for the evening. Although they were disappointed that neither had been able to reach the spirits of their husbands during the séance, they agreed that it had been a most pleasant and enjoyable evening.

Soon afterwards Anna and Louisa were enjoying tea on the veranda overlooking the river. Louisa tried to persuade Anna to hold a ghost party of her own. Anna was skeptical, but Louisa insisted how perfect the beautiful house with its wide veranda be perfect for such an event. She even reminded Anna of much George loved entertaining in the house. Before they had finished the last of their tea, they had agreed to host a ghost party. In fact, it would be a masquerade.

The following month Anna was busier than ever preparing for the party. There were invitations to be sent, food and drink to be chosen and prepared, decorations to be gathered, and entertainment to be organized. The more time she spent planning the party, the lighter her mood became. It all took her back to her days as a young bride when she and George had first entertained in their new home. She felt content for the first time since George had died.

So it was on that warm autumn evening in late October her riverside home took on a dreamy gingery glow. Candles filled every window. Dozens of carved jack o lanterns traced the outlines of the long curved entrance.

Inside the entire first floor was awash in flickering lights. The buffet tables were glittering heaps of delectable treats. In one corner of the room an actress dressed as gypsy practiced with her crystal ball. An ensemble played softly in the background. The front parlor had been cleared for dancing, and across the marble mantel in the great room were mounds of pumpkins, gourds, corn, apples, and fall foliage resting amid tall pillared candles of gold and black.

Anna stood in front of the large mirror in the entranceway inspecting her costume. She wondered aloud if she had made a poor choice. Being a love of Vermeer's artwork she had designed her costume to be that of The Girl with The Pearl Earring. The painting had always been one of her favorites, yet she worried that some of her guest may not be familiar with the Dutch painter.

She purchased several yards of rich gold silk from which she had made into a full length evening coat. Beneath it she wore a white flowing linen sheath. Around her waist she tied a long royal silk blue scarf and tied a pale gold silk scarf around her head and tied it behind her ears. Finally, she created a wide head band from the same blue silk as her belt and layered it over the front edge of the gold scarf. It was perfect. All that was remained was a pair of pear shaped pearl earrings. She smiled to herself, satisfied with her efforts. She was ready for her guests.

Anna greeted her guests as they arrived. She was pleased that they had obviously taken great care and effort in choosing their attire for her masquerade. They were all superbly done, and their intricately detailed masks were obviously custom made. She chatted and laughed as George Washington, Benjamin Franklin, and a Grand Duchess arrived. They were soon followed by Gainsborough's blue boy in the most luscious blue silk Anna had ever seen. Then came several Van Dyke costumes, a Monet maiden, and even another Vermeer. Anna couldn't have been more pleased; her guests had truly gotten into the spirit of the party.

The chatter and laughter were suddenly interrupted by a loud shrieking voice. Anna spun around to face the sound. The fortune teller had abandoned her crystal ball and stood in the very center of the living room. She saved her arms in wide circles as she shrieked, "Woe, unto you who imbibe here this night. Within 7 weeks and 7 days, seven of those gathered here will cast off their living spirits and join the world of the departed. So says the gypsy." With that she flung her arms about one more time and hurried back to her crystal ball.

Anna took in a deep breath. This had not been in the discussion for the entertainment. She was about to go speak to the fortune teller when she noticed that the guests were all laughing and making light of the gypsy. She thought it best to leave well enough alone. The music resumed as couples hurried to the dance floor. The lively music and happy chatter drove away any concerns anyone had about the gypsy's prediction.

Anna scoured the room for Louisa, for she had not seen here since she arrived. Her eyes fixed on some white blotches mixed among the colorful costume. As she looked more closely she could tell that not just one, but six guests were dressed rather plainly, in long white sheeting. They had come as ghosts. Each ghost was talking earnestly with another guest. Apparently they were acquaintances. Anna couldn't remember greeting anyone dressed in that attire. Her invitations had clearly stated "elegant masquerade". She knew all her guests by name and could not imagine how anyone, let alone six guests, would display such a breach of etiquette.

Just as she moved toward one of the ghost figures a frigid breeze stung her cheeks. Startled, Anna stopped in her tracks. Just then one of the ghosts brushed against her without pausing to excuse himself. Instead she heard a low chuckle in her ear. Then he disappeared among the dancers. She lost her breath for a moment. "I know that laugh, why can't I place it?" Anna told herself she needed to concentrate on her guests and hurried over to inspect the buffet table.

Just then an old friend, Florence tugged at her sleeve, "Oh Anna, you do invite the most fascinating people to your parties," she said in such a happy whisper. "Who is the gentleman who came in the simplistic ghost costume? He is so knowledgeable. We talked all about the sailing ships, like my father used to captain. He recounted such tales. It was like he had once been aboard." She said excitedly. "Who is it" I must know."

Anne told he that she was unsure, but that Florence would find out when they unmasked at midnight." Florence scanned the crowd, "Well I don't want to lose sight of him, I must know who he is," she tittered as she headed into the crowd.

She had only taken a few steps when Sampson and Delilah approached her. "Ah," she said, "You two came as a Van Dyke, I see." Anna knew immediately it had to be George's friend Charles and his wife Margaret. Only Margaret would think of such a creative costume.

Sampson leaned forward and spoke earnestly in Anna's ear, "Where do you find such fascinating and interesting young chaps? We spoke with a most delightful young man, so enthusiastic, and his loves bicycle racing, just like our Benjamin." With that his wife put her hand on arm, "Please dear, I cannot bear to discuss Benjamin at a social engagement, he has only been gone two years." The man gulped and smiled weakly as he lead his wife away.

Anna felt her stomach tighten. There was definitely something going on. Just then Louisa appeared. "Anna, I didn't know you invited others that were not on the invitation list we drew up. But I am so glad that you did. I met the most interesting man. Not only is he charming, but he has been telling the most delightful tales." She paused and sighed," You know in some ways he reminds me of my husband Mark, he told such wonderful stores too. Although Anna tried to interrupt, Louisa chatted on," I can't wait for the unmasking, I do want to meet him formally."

"Louisa, I need to talk with you!" Before Louisa could protest Anna led her to the far side of the room. She recounted the six ghost guests that she didn't remember greeting. She told her of her encounters with Florence, and the couple dressed as Sampson and Delilah. When she finished Louisa gave her a quick embrace. "You worry too much; everyone is having a fabulous time. The ghosts are probably some of the men from the boating club playing a prank. It's nothing to be worried about. Go enjoy your own party, Anna." With that she hurried back into the throng of party goers. But something wasn't right, Anna could feel it.

The dancing was in full swing and the merry makers were having a wonderful time, eating, chatting, and dancing. Laughter could be heard throughout the house and across the large porch. As Anna gazed across the room she noticed that each ghost was once again conversing with another guest. Well this is not the time, she mused. Time to announce the unmasking. She made her way over the band leader and whispered in his ear.

The music softened until it was a soothing background for the announcement. With great fanfare he announced that it was time for the unmasking dance. He called for everyone to come to the dance floor and form two circles. Anna watched as her guests gathered around the dance floor. Something made her turn and look back towards the front door. She drew in a long deep breath, for each ghost had taken the arm of a guest and was leading them outside onto the porch. As she watched Florence, Sampson and Delilah, and even Louisa vanished onto the porch.

Someone snatched Anna's sleeve and pulled her onto the dance floor. The inner circle was mostly women, while men formed the larger outer circle. When the music began they joined hands and began spinning around in a circle. The inner circle danced to the right, the outer circle danced to the left. The music grew faster and at last it reached a crescendo. Shouts of "Unmask!" echoed throughout the house. Masks were peeled away or cast aside. People shrieked in recognition and laughter. At once the music resumed and the dancefloor was filled with swilling couples.

When Anna finally made her way through the crowd to the porch where she found the ghosts and their partners gone. Soon afterwards the guests began departing. There was a jumble as carriages were called for and farewells were exchanged. By the time Anna retuned to the porch everyone had gone. Louisa, too, was nowhere to be found. Although she found Louisa's behavior unusual, Anna decided that Louisa must had been feeling tipsy and accepted a carriage with a friend.

When all the guests had departed, Anna gave final cleaning instructions to the staff and announced she was going to bed. As she started up the stairs she caught something out of the corner of her eye, something white. Standing near George's pipe collection stood one of the guests still in his costume. Anna hurried back down the stairs and approached, "Excuse me, I didn't realize you were still here. We have all unmasked some time ago, You should…."

Before she could utter another word a low hoarse voice whispered, "You really don't know who I am do you?" And then, he laughed, not a snicker, or mere chuckle, but a loud booming laugh that echoed off the very walls of the house. The cleaning crew took no notice of the loud laughter. Anna gasped, she knew that laugh, that booming laugh could only belong to one man, her husband George.

The next morning the maid found Anna, still in her costume propped up in her bed. Her eyes were closed, and though she was certainly dead, her face was peaceful and relaxed. In her hand she clutched her diary with her final entry, "George finally came to take me home."

It has been said that six others from the party passed or simply vanished within 7 weeks and 7 days of the party. We don't know for certain, as no one is willing to speak of it.

The Ghost at the Greek Club

Despite sub-zero temperatures and relentless icy winds off the Navesink the Christmas season was in full swing in December of 1922. The storefronts and shop windows were clad in bright red and green, anxious to welcome shoppers. Men held on tightly to their fedoras as women shoppers clutched their parcels against their coats. It was a frigid Christmas shopping day and few residents took notice of a short article in the Daily Register on December 20th. It was a single column piece hidden far back from the front page. Buried deep within the advertisements for holiday gifts and treats it detailed a curious incident at the Red Bank Greek Club on Broad Street.

The Monmouth Refurbishing and Cleaning Company on Broad Street was owned by a popular Greek merchant named George Noglows. His Haddon Building shop catered to gentlemen clientele specializing in the cleaning and care of hats, as well as shoe repair and shining. His success grew from his serious and practical approach to business, his civic involvement, and his friendly nature. Like the majority of people in the early twentieth century, George did not believe in ghosts. But this was about to change.

On the second floor above his shop the Greek Club maintained a club room. All the members were Greek immigrants who would gather to play dominoes, cards, or share a drink or two with their countrymen.

Occasionally it would also serve as a bedroom in the event a member had too much to drink and need to sleep it off.

In early December a well-liked club member, Louis Caras, was killed in an accident. Members of the Greek Club were saddened and met frequently to reminisce about their old friend. They agreed that the club just wasn't the same without Louis.

One night was particularly frigid with temperatures hovering around zero. The Greek Club was not meeting that night, so George permitted his young shoeshine boy, Gus, to stay overnight in the clubroom instead of walking the mile and a half home in the cold. Gus readily agreed and that night happily snuggled beneath the quilts in the small bed.

About two o'clock Gus suddenly awoke. The room was dark and silent, but Gus felt as if someone was there. "Who's there?" he called. "Mr. Nuglows is that you?" There was no answer. The room remained silent and dark. The only sound Gus could hear was the beating of his own heart.

As he pulled the covers up around his chin the ceiling light suddenly flashed on! Gus choked down a scream. He was shaking so badly he couldn't hold the blankets in his hands. Wrapping the quilt around himself he reached for the iron poker from the fireplace. Ever so slowly he searched the entire room. There was no one there. As he returned to his bed the lights flashed off leaving him in the darkness. Gus shrieked in fright, pulled on his shoes, and without even grabbing his coat ran the entire way home.

When Gus reported the events to George the following morning, George couldn't believe his ears. He had always thought Gus to be a mature lad and had been truly surprised that the boy was so emphatic about what had happened. Attempting to make light of the situation George chuckled, "Well, maybe it's just a ghost." But Gus didn't want to talk about it and insisted that he would never sleep there again. So George promised Gus he would sleep there himself that very night.

After the store closed George took his supper up to the room. He ate leisurely as he reviewed the day's accounts. He made a point to be certain that the windows and door were securely locked. Then he crept into the bed and fell asleep. About two o'clock George was awoken when the lights in the room flashed on. After his initial startle, George inspected the room.

Finding nothing amiss he crawled back in bed. Thinking someone was playing a joke on him, he laughed out loud and turned off the lights.

A few minutes later another light flashed on. George got out of bed and turned off that light. A few minutes later, it happened again. Every time George turned one light off, another turned itself on. George was a practical man; he was convinced his pals were playing tricks on him.

Despite his attempts to figure out how the joke had been accomplished, he waited out the night and in the morning called for an electrician to come and inspect the wiring in the room. The electrician smiled as he handed George the bill, "There is nothing wrong with the electricity in that room, George, but I still have to charge you."

Now George was more convinced than ever that his buddies from the Club were playing pranks on him and decided to play along. That night he returned to sleep in the club room. As usual it was quiet until about two o'clock. Then once again the lights started to misbehave. George called out, "Come in, I'd like to speak with you. You are welcome here." There was no response. "Can I offer you a drink?" he asked holding a bottle in the air. Even now there was no response. The lights flashed on and off a few more times, and then stopped. George laughed and drifted off to sleep wondering how his friends had managed the hoax.

George cheerfully sought out his friends the next day to learn who had pulled such a complicated stunt. They all denied it, and began teasing him about being haunted. George began checking the room repeatedly. Nothing happened in the daytime. But each night about two o'clock the same events repeated. Lights would come on, and then suddenly turn themselves off.

When the nightly episodes continued George persuaded three friends to spend the night in the club room with him. One lightheartedly insisted that George bring his gun. The four men sat in the darkness, smoking cigars, and waiting. Two o'clock came and went. Nothing happened.

George's friends began to tease him mercilessly. The three men were laughing uncontrollably when the darkness was ripped away, every light in room suddenly flashed on. At the same moment a cloudlike face appeared at the window. George grabbed his gun and fired. But nothing happened, the gun misfired. Then the lights snapped off. The four men practically knocked one another over trying to escape the room. Chairs, tables, pictures were tossed about everywhere.

They ran down Broad street until they found a beat cop and brought him back to the room. They stuttered in dismay at what they saw. The room which they had left in such disorder was now neat and orderly with the furniture in its original position. On the bed lay a spent bullet. The bullet was distorted as it had hit something, but no damage could be found anywhere in the room. The next day Detective Sergeant Joseph Bray inspected the scene and found no evidence of either an intruder or the damage from a shooting.

After the newspaper reported the incident George was deluged with the curious wanting to visit the room, or from offers to exorcise the room-for the right price. George took it all in good humor, and finally interest in the specter died down. Now we are left to wonder if the current residents of the property have been graced by the ghost of the Greek Club, or was Louis Caras just wanting to say hello to his friends one more time

The Oyster Wars

Did you know that there was once a war fought on the Navesink and Shrewsbury rivers and only on these two sister estuaries? It's true. It is known as the Oyster War. It was a series of battles over a small mollusk, *Crassostera virginica*, the eastern oyster. Although the details of this conflict are not common knowledge, there is significant documentation of the lengthy legal and sometimes violent skirmishes that arose along the river.

The Navesink Indians had harvested the oyster for hundreds of years before the European settlers arrived. The protein rich oyster quickly became popular across the colonies and became a mainstay of the colonial diet. Soon there was demand for the oysters from nearby New York City. Using the Navesink as a highway, sailing sloops and schooners transported oysters by the bushel down the river and across the bay to the city.

Soon the little mollusks became a local specialty. Independent watermen, as well as local famers with water front property harvested oysters and shipped them from the Red Bank docks. So great was the demand that by the later part of the 1700's many of the natural oyster beds were nearly depleted. Those farmers with land touching the shore line began importing oyster stock and planting them in the water, allowing them to mature before harvest.

In the 18th century oyster plating was a lucrative business. Even in Colonial times arguments arose over the oyster beds. Those who planted the oysters claimed the rights to the oyster beds on their waterfront property; while the independent oystermen insisted that the river was public property and so was open to all.

Colonial New Jersey regulated a specific season for harvesting oysters as well as restricting harvest to genuine residents of the colony. After the Revolution the new state supported the right of farmers to private access to the oysters from their own shoreline.

In the early 1800's two oystermen were arrested harvesting 1000 oysters from a bed planted by a local famer named Leverson. They were required to pay restitution of three dollars for their deed. The oystermen appealed the ruling and with the support of many local watermen took the case to the new Jersey Supreme Court in February 1808.

The case polarized the local communities. Leverson demanded that the state uphold the existing regulation of the planter's rights to the water adjacent to his land. While the watermen reiterated their claim that the waterways cannot be owned and they are free to collect oysters anywhere in the Navesink as it is public property. Local newspapers took the side of the planters and referred to the watermen as pirates and poachers.

Court cases sprouted everywhere, but so did the raids of the planted oyster beds. Because the Navesink is a brackish estuary, the "river pirates" refused to acknowledge that the waterway was anything but common property of the people. The planters fought back to protect their investment and the "pirates" fought to maintain their livelihood.

The situation was made more complicated by the fact that the state did sell leases to the planters in other similar waterways in and around the state. For political reasons this was never done in Navesink or Shrewsbury. So the battle continued.

When shot gun diplomacy failed to quell the problem, violence resulted. There were on going feuds resulting in fights and actual killings. Usually the planters were acquitted of any crime as local authorities supported the rights of the land owners to protect their property. Planters were forced to hire armed guards who watched over their precious oyster beds.

Despite the hostile climate the raids continued. The raiders came at night in small rowboats. They tied up to the stakes which the planter had imbedded into the riverbed to mark his plot. Then they waded into the shallow water and harvested oysters, one by one, using an oyster fork. When they had gathered what they could carry away in the boat, they simply rowed away.

According to local lore this is about the same time that Sam Higgins fell into hard times. He knew it was his own fault, well partly his fault. The major part of the blame went to rum. If it didn't taste so sweet and make him so sleepy it would never have happened.

Sam found it impossible to hold down a real job. So when Nathan Johnson, a Navesink planter, offered him a post as a night watchman for his oyster beds, Sam jumped at the change. He knew Johnson was a hard task master and had a reputation for being a cranky old miser. But he didn't care, he needed the money.

On the first evening Johnson walked Sam to the makeshift shed by the water's edge where he was to keep watch. He gave him a lantern, some leftover meat pie from supper, and an old shotgun. Sam was happy for the food but a bit sad that it didn't come with liquid refreshment.

Johnson mumbled a litany of instructions which included, "If you see anyone in my oyster beds, you shoot them!"

Sam was an easy going fellow and offered," Don't you want me to just shoot over their head and scare them away?"

"No!" Johnson bristled. "Last month there were poachers, dammed water pirates, right here in my beds. One night I caught an old fisherman right here on the bank. I know he was about to steal my oysters."

"Really?" Sam croaked.

"He claimed he was just taking a walk at night because he had trouble sleeping. He even rattled off some old seafarer's legend. It was a bunch of superstition. He tried to walk away, so I shot him. Yep, shot right in the back."

"You did?"

"I sure did. Knocked him right into the water. Tide was going out and that is the last I saw of old Jack Campbell." Johnson snickered. "I spent a lot of money replanting these plots and they should be ready in a couple of weeks so they need to be guarded. You got that?" Johnson said.

"Yes, sir," Sam barked back.

As Johnson started walk back toward the house he stopped and turned to face Sam. "And Sam," he said, shaking his finger," No booze when you are working."

"Yes sir, no booze, not even a drop," Sam called after him.

It was quiet on the river that night. Sam gazed out over the glassy water and smiled to himself. He knew old man Johnson was sure to check up on him, but all he had to do was stay awake.

The snap of twigs underfoot and the rustling of leaves brought Sam to full attention. He peered along the river bank. Something was moving at the water's edge, and it was coming towards him. He picked up the gun and squinted to try and make out the figure.

"All is well, Mr. Johnson," Sam called out. The figure paused for a moment, then continued moving closer. Samuel saw that it was not his employer, but an older man, someone he didn't know.

"Hello there," the figure beckoned. "I don't mean to alarm you, sir." He reached out to shake Samuel's hand. "My name is Jack; I live up river. I just couldn't get to sleep tonight so I decided to take a walk."

The man was obviously a seaman. He wore stained canvas pants and a wrinkled work shirt. His craggy and scarred face showed his age. But it was a friendly face and soon the two were chatting like old friends. Within minutes they were calling each other Jack and Sam. Both had done some fishing in their day and both liked woodworking. After a bit Jack pulled out a jug from his canvas coat. He held it up so Sam could see. Both men smiled and soon it was like they had been friends their entire lives.

Leaning on the side of the old shed the two passed the bottle back and forth. Jack reveled Sam with sea faring exploits which were all tall tales, and Sam recounted his adventures traveling west where he had never been.

It wasn't long before Sam began to yawn, "Say mate, why don't you get some shut eye. Sleep for an hour, it will do you good." Sam started to protest but Jack reminded him," I've stood watch hundreds of time at sea. I know what to look for. If I see anything I 'll wake you.". So helped by the rum and the gentle waves lapping on the shore Samuel fell asleep.

It wasn't long before someone called out from the house," Is everything OK Sam?"

"Yes sir, everything is fine," a calm and sober voice that sounded just like Sam answered. The lights went out in the house and once again it was quiet.

Jack picked up a darkened lantern. He walked a few feet along the shore line and scanned the horizon. He uncovered the lantern and in a quick motion swept it up and down two times. He quickly covered the lantern, waited a few moments, then repeated his movements.

Within a few minutes the sound of oars and the gentle swish of water could be heard as a small rowboat pulled up to the river bank. Jack tipped his hat to the two men. In total silence the men wadded into the shallows. Each used a long fork like tool and began plucking oysters from the depth. When their baskets were full they loaded them into the boat. They tipped their hats to Jack and rowed away into the darkness.

For many nights afterwards Jack would walk along the river bank late in the evening to meet his friend, Sam. He never came empty handed, he always arrived with a bottle of rum. Jack told exciting yarns of the sea, and Sam chattered about this plans to someday visit California.

One night when the bottle was nearly empty Jack asked Sam if he believed in ghosts?

"Ghosts?" Sam laughed. "I'm a man who has to see it to believe it, no I can't say I believe in ghosts. I suppose you do, you ole seadog," Sam chuckled as he took another swig from the bottle. "How many have you seen?"

"Well," Jack said as he leaned over to look directly into Sam's face, "You know that mariners see things in this world that land lovers could ever hope to see."

Sam guffawed, "Go on! That's just superstition."

"Maybe so," Jack said. "I do know that when a mariner dies his spirit returns to the place of his death, and that my friend is a fact. Sometimes he comes back just help out another seaman in need. But if the old seadog, as you call him, met a violent end, he will always come back for revenge. Jack passed the bottle to Sam once more. "Would you believe it if you saw it?" When there was no answer he looked over and saw that Sam was fast asleep. Jack smiled.

One day two weeks later the planter sent his workmen to harvest the oysters only to find that the entire bed was totally depleted. They could find only a few oysters in the entire plot. Johnson flew into a rage. He sent a worker to get Sam, telling him to bring the watchman back even if he had to hog tie him. When the farm hand described Johnson's rage Samuel made a quick decision. He snatched his essential belongings and headed to the dock to catch the next packet out of town.

As darkness fell over the Navesink that night Jack approached the shed and saw that it was empty. He looked up to the sky and smiled. "Good for you my friend, I hope you like California," he murmured. He took Sam's seat on the bench and sat gazing out over the water. For a while it was quiet.

Jack knew the planter was near long before he saw him. The man's rage was like a stench drifting off a moss bunker left on the riverbank to rot. Johnson tore into the shed aiming his shotgun. "I'll kill you Sam Higgins, you miserable drunk!"

When he saw that it wasn't Sam he took a step backwards," Who in blazes are you" he demanded.

"Just an old seaman out for walk. I don't sleep well at night, you know."

Johnson made a gargled sound, "You?" he stammered. "You can't be Jack Campbell. I killed you when you tried to steal my oysters. I saw you float down the river with my own eyes."

"But I am here. I am the innocent man you shot in the back. I was just an aged seaman out for a walk that night. You should have listened when I tried to tell you that a mariner's spirit returns to the place where he died. It's true. Here I am."

"I don't believe it," the planter snarled.

The figure began to glow and rose slowly above Johnson's head and drifted over the shallow water. "I am here now, Nathan Johnson, and I will be here always. I am the new watchman for your oyster beds. You will never harvest another oyster from this river as long as you live." With that the figure began to spin about and then plunged into the depths of the Navesink with a great splash.

Locals say that Johnson tried in vain to replant his oyster beds afterwards. Each time his harvest was for naught. Finally, deeply in debt he sold his property and moved inland, far away from oysters and the specters that guard them.

The Heartless Ghost of Passage Point

If you had met Lewis Morris, royal governor of New Jersey in the 17th century, your opinion of him would largely be determined by the color of your skin. You see Lewis Morris was born into a family whose wealth was the result of being slave owners. In 1692 his uncle, also known named Lewis, died leaving him not only a prosperous iron works business in nearby Shrewsbury, but also a large plantation in what is now Rumson, New Jersey.

Consisting of more than 800 acres Passage Point Plantation was run by a staff of indentured European servants as well as at least 70 slaves. Its acreage included woodlands, farmland, a manor house, a shoreline, a commercial loading dock, as well as slave quarters and various shops and work sheds.

The plantation provided agricultural produce for use in the iron works settlement as well as the markets in New York City. Schooners docked daily picking up fresh produce and leaving behind goods for distribution along the Jersey coast.

The new master expanded the planation and ran his properties with an iron fist. Fellow land owners knew him as self- absorbed, serious, and unpleasant. His slaves knew him as harsh, unyielding, and cruel. With each passing year he became more ruthless and vicious.

The lives of the slaves on Passage Point were arduous and demoralizing. Morris devised more humiliating and cruel punishments for both real and perceived misbehavior daily. He perfected techniques for using punishments that resulted in disfigurement of the accused. It was often quipped that the master was indeed heartless. He once executed a slave who reported that one of the farm sheds was ablaze because he believed the man to be guilty of arson. The man was incinerated while locked in an outdoor toilet.

In the summer of 1695 Morris called out to a female slave who was working in the fields. When she did not respond he walked up to her, put a gun to her head and shot her. We do not know if she ignored his instructions or even if she heard him. He forced the other women to bring her body to the slave quarters where he hung her body from a tree for three days.

The frail woman was well liked among the others. Although the slaves attempted to get legal action against Morris, they were rebuffed by local authorities. Morris appeared to be in a constant state of rage, as tensions grew throughout the reminder of that summer and fall.

In October seven slaves attempted to speak with Morris about his extreme cruelty and the death of the unknown female slave. A scuffle ensued and Morris was shot dead by a bullet through his heart. At such a close range the heart itself was expelled.

The seven were arrested and tried within a few hours. Two were acquitted. Others including Oliver, Agbee and Jeremy were found guilty. Although Agbee escaped he was quickly recaptured. Oliver managed a lesser sentence, he was whipped so severely as to be totally disfigured.

Agbee and Jeremy, believed to be the ring leaders, were sentenced to death. They were first tied to a post while and their hands were sawed off. Bleeding and in agony they were forced to watch as the hands were burned. Then the two were taken and hung until nearly dead. Finally, they were pulled down and burned alive. The ghastly execution was forcibly witnessed by the remainder of the slaves at the plantation.

Agbee, Jeremy, and Oliver became heroes to the remaining slaves. Stories of their bravery and their courage to confront cruelty has been passed down by word of mouth for countless years as well as prayers that they may rest in peace. To all accounts, they have done so.

But the same cannot be said for their merciless master, Lewis Morris. For over the next hundred years reports circulated that an apparition of Morris was seen scouring Passage Plantation as if searching for something. The ghostly specter has a gaping hole in his chest so large one can see straight through it. Morris is missing his heart. For many years after his death, slaves reported that the ghost would sometimes approach a field workers and demand that they search for the heart.

Today sightings of the phantom are sporadic, although rather more frequent during the month of October. Some say he still searches Passage Point for his missing heart. Occasionally a resident calls the authorities about a suspicious looking character combing the neighbor as if in a desperate search for something. Mothers call in their children and fathers lock the doors against the unknown.

The phantom is harmless. Can it be that the former royal governor, Lewis Morris, will forever search for his missing heart? He doesn't realize his search is in vain. For just as his slaves knew so many years ago, Lewis Morris was heartless in life. So it is fitting that he is heartless in death.

The Ghostly Revenge of Indian Jack

By the early 1800's the shores of the Navesink were home to an assortment of farms, plantations and estates. The farm crews were comprised of slaves, indentured servants, as well as freed slaves who were often day workers on local farms. A myriad of folk legends and tales circulated among both the workers as well as the landed gentry. Stories of ghosts and supernatural phenomena were published in the *Daily Register* by such prominent people as Judge George C. Beekman. In February 1895 he related a peculiar event which occurred years earlier near his estate. The story is made more tragic by the fact that it occurred December 24, 1823, a day before the Christmas holiday.

The Christmas season is perceived by most of us as a colorful, fun filled period of glittering trees, gifts, and endless celebrations. During the early years of our history Christmas was no less important, but was observed quite differently. The religious significance of Christmas was paramount across all classes of people. The middle and upper classes celebrated the holiday season with sumptuous feasts, gift giving, and lively parties and games. For the poorer classes it was perhaps the one day of the year when food was plentiful. Families saved their pennies so they could at least have a bountiful holiday meal. It was perhaps the one day of the entire year when even a farm hand or slave might have a day of rest.

At dawn on the 24th of December 1823 the workers on a farm just north of the river in Middletown began their task of threshing wheat. At the time the job of threshing, or separating the grains of wheat from its husky covering had to be done by hand. It was backbreaking work.

After the grain was spread on the barn floor the farm workers beat the grain using hand held flails. These long poles attached to a heavy club by a short chain were difficult to use.

One of the workers, a freed slave named John Henry, was particularly skilled in his craft. It was said he produced nearly twice the amount of grain as other farm hands. As a result, he was always in demand at threshing time by local farmers. John was a quiet, hardworking family man who in only one year of freedom managed to build a small home for his young family in Red Bank.

John Henry was part of the threshing crew that December day. As usual he completed more than his share of the work before quitting time. It was the custom for the farmer to provide the workers with a hot dinner and sometimes a warm bed at the end of the days' work. On this day John Henry quickly finished his meal ahead of the others. He told the farmer that he would go back out to the barn and finish the remaining work so that he could spend the entire Christmas Day with his family. The farmer happily agreed.

As the other workers headed home they heard the steady echo of threshing coming from the barn. All through the evening the farmer could hear the unceasing thwack- thwack of John Henry's flail. It was well after eleven before the barn was silent.

The next morning as the farmer and his family prepared for their Christmas meal John Henry's wife appeared at the farm looking for her husband. He had not returned home that night. As it was unlike him to ever stay out all night, she was exceedingly distressed. A search of the barn found no trace of him. John Henry had simply vanished.

During the next week John Henry's friends searched for him, but to no avail. The only peculiarity in the area was a complaint that a row boat had been stolen from Compton's Creek. Yet no one could believe that he had run off and left his wife and children. He owned his little house and adored his youngsters.

The following week a bloated disfigured body was discovered floating in Compton's Creek. At first everyone thought the mystery had been solved and that John Henry had indeed taken off in the rowboat and somehow drowned. The crabs and eels had so mutilated the face that identification was not possible. But closer inspection of the body revealed that not only did the clothes not belong to John Henry.

The corpse was a much larger local man named Indian Jack. Now within a week there had been two mysterious deaths. Further it was known that the two men had once been slaves under the same master at a nearby estate.

Indian Jack had been on the estate several years before John Henry arrived. James was a reserved man who quietly did his work, caused no problems, and often helped others with their tasks. Indian Jack, however, was quite the opposite. He was outspoken, rebellious, and anxious to avoid his work, often pushing it off onto others.

Both men were promised their freedom after 7 years if they completed their tasks without issue. John Henry easily completed this requirement and was freed in 1822. Jack, however, was still a slave after 28 years of service due to his bad temper and belligerent manner. It was common knowledge that Indian Jack was outraged when John Henry gained his freedom while Indian Jack remained a slave. Although John henry had remained in the area it was not believed that they had any contact after he left the estate.

For nearly a full year the mystery went unsolved as no one believed the two deaths were related. In the days preceding Christmas of 1825 the same farm was in the middle of the threshing season. Just before Christmas day a local farm hand known as Harry hiked over to the farm eager to join in the threshing the following day.

It grew late and he didn't arrive at the farm until about eleven. Not wanting to wake the farmer and his family he decided he would just sleep in the barn and be ready for the next day's work. He climbed into the soft hay in the loft and covered himself with a horse blanket. Soon he fell asleep.

Sometime after midnight Harry was awoken by a loud thumping and a tremor that shook the planks of the hay loft. Tossing aside his blanket he crept over the edge of the loft to look down onto the barn floor below. A soft yellow glow from a lantern cast a dim light on the grain strewn across the floor below.

Harry couldn't believe his eyes, for there stood John Henry flailing the grain for all he was worth. Over and over his muscular arms raised the flail in the air and then quickly brought it down with loud thwack. There was no doubt, it was John Henry, the missing farm hand!

As Harry stared at the incredible sight the small barn door opened and a taller and much larger man entered. He wore tattered work clothes and in his hand he carried a large ax. Although his face was smeared in rage Harry recognized him at once. It couldn't be. for everyone knew that Indian Jack was dead.

In one swift motion Indian Jack crept up behind James Henry and buried the axe in his head. James Henry crumpled to the floor. A scream began in Harry's throat but only a gurgle escaped. The culprit took no notice of Harry, smiling at his achievement. He picked up a spade and moved to the far side of the barn floor and began ripping up the planks. When he had opened a space of floor about five feet by three feet, he grabbed a shovel and began digging a hole in the soft soil. When the cavity was about four feet deep he scooped up the body and dumped it in. He tossed the ax and James Henry's flail in on top. After spiting on the remains he refilled the hole and shoved the floorboards together. Tossing the tools aside he quickly left the barn.

Harry was frozen in terror and afraid to leave the safety of the hay loft. He lay shivering in the dark for hours. At the first streaks of dawn he ran to the house and told the farmer what he had seen. At first the farmer accused him of being drunk. But he knew Harry to be a decent worker, and not prone to storytelling or exaggeration. Finally, he accompanied Harry to the barn.

When the farmer inspected the barn everything was in its place until Harry called him over to the side where he had witnesses the burial. The farmer looked closely at the wooden floor, it had indeed been ripped up and re-laid. Using the same spade and shovel that Indian Jack had used the previous night they opened the floor and began digging in the soft soil. There they discovered a large rusty ax and John Henry's wooden flail resting on top of a decomposed body. The wound on the back of the head was a perfect match for the axe left in the grave.

As word spread of the grisly discovery, numerous sightings of Indian Jack were reported. Although none were substantiated, the farm soon acquired a reputation as being haunted. Local farm hands refused to work in the barn. In a few short years the famer lost the property and moved away leaving the abandoned barn.

The aging barn stood empty and deserted for many years. Locals maintain that each year as Christmas approached the sounds of threshing resonated from the barn. Although no one reported any visual contact with the specter, many swear to have heard the thwack- thwack of a flail on the barn floor. Believers contend that it is indeed James Henry completing his chores so he can be home in time for Christmas.

Perhaps you don't believe this tale. Maybe you are a person to needs to see it to believe it. You may want to locate the ruins of the barn and spend your Christmas eve waiting in the cold and dark for the threshing to begin. It would indeed be a most unusual Christmas adventure. You may even be witness to the ghost of John Henry as he works. If you do, don't forget to wish him a Merry Christmas.

The Graveyard Shift at the Oceanic Bridge

Just before the turn of the century the original Oceanic bridge was built connecting Locust Point with Rumson. It was an iron and wood planked structure with a pivot draw and a gray lattice work frame than ran the length of the movable span. On each end of the river iron and wood docks reached towards the middle of the river where they connected on each side of the moveable pivot.

The 123 feet long moveable part rotated on a central supporting axis ring. A center tower rose high above the water resting on a kind of artificial island. A turntable connected to a series of gears, clutches and wedges enabled the bridge to be rotated manually 90 degrees. The central tower housed the tender's station which enabled him to both operate the mechanism as well as keep watch for vessels.

There were mishaps on the bridge shortly after it opened in 1891. The first was that of a local man who rode his bicycle off the end of the bridge into twelve feet of water. Reports say he had downed a few pints that evening before starting for Middletown on his bike. Both the man and his bike were recovered.

In 1893 the schooner Emma Hendrix rammed the bridge on foggy morning. The tender didn't hear the warning whistle from the boat and said that the fog was so heavy he couldn't see the ship. The bridge was unscathed although the Emma Hendrix suffered considerable damage.

The most peculiar story is that one divulged by a young man and his uncle, an assistant bridge tender. The night was cold and it was drizzling rain when Jim and his Uncle Pete reached the tender's box. Jim had been here many times before of course, but it was always to bring Uncle Pete some supper or watch one of the large steamboats go up river. So when his uncle invited Jim to sit the graveyard shift with him, he was delighted.

By the time his uncle had checked the log book, adjusted the gear mechanism, and refilled the oil in the lamps, the drizzle had grown into a downpour. By eleven-thirty it was a full blown gale. The water had been blown into a frenzy by the winds, and the rain hammered the tender box.

"It's nearly 0000 hours," his uncle said." Are you getting hungry?" Before Jim could answer Pete swore under his breath," I left our supper in the shed on the dock." He grabbed his yellow slicker and fastened the hood snugly around his chin. "You stay here, there won't be any traffic tonight. I'll be back in jiff." He slammed the door behind him and slowly made his way to the shed on the far bank.

Jim had never been alone on the bridge before, especially during a storm. He felt uneasy but knew his uncle was right, there would be no traffic tonight. All they had to do was stay there until morning. He peered the length of span hoping to see Pete returning with the food. All he could see was darkness. The wind roared up the river and through the girders and Jim was certain he felt the entire bridge shake.

To calm his nerves Jim studied the inside of the tender's station. In the dim glow of the lantern the emergency horns and beacons hung on the wall ready for action. There were two wooden stools, a desk, and the mechanism panel for rotating the span. He looked back to the shore, still no sign of his uncle.

Jim walked to the window and gazed up river into the darkness. The rain pounded against the window. At first he saw only darkness, then something glimmered in the distance. Something yellow bobbed in the water upstream. He stared at the object but couldn't make it out. He knew it couldn't be a vessel, anyone would have to be crazy to be on the river on a night like this.

The goose bumps and the strange chill would not leave him. He peered anxiously to the shore, still no Uncle Pete. He snatched the binoculars from their hook and scanned the river. There was something there, all right, something big.

Jim couldn't take his eyes off the yellow bobbing. There was definitely something there, and it was moving. He leaned against the glass for a better look. Yes, it was headed straight for the bridge.

The uneasy feeling now became a loud thumping. Jim knew it wasn't the rain striking the window. It was the thumping of his heart. He stared frantically toward shore, still no Pete, where could he be?

The ship was close enough now that Jim could see that she was an old chipped and weathered schooner. There was no evidence of a crew. She was dark except for a yellowish glow that seemed to be escaping from the cabin. What should he do? Grabbing a warning lantern, he began waving it frantically. There was no response from the ship. He blew a warning blast from the distress whistle. Again there was no response. Finally, he stepped out into the storm and shouted, "Bridge to vessel, the bridge is closed, the bridge is closed!" There was still no response from schooner.

Jim ran back inside. Did he dare open the bridge? He had seen Uncle Pete do it a hundred times, but could he do it? He had no choice, the boat was nearly on the bridge. Lightning flashed just as he depressed the T-bar into the mechanism socket. There was a scrapping sound as the gears, clutches and wedges began to push against the turntable. It seemed like the bridge was not going to budge and then ever so slowly the great frame began to swivel. The wind whipped against the span and Jim felt the entire bridge rock. The bridge slowly swung to its open position.

The ship didn't hesitate. In an instant it sailed through the opening, never once acknowledging the tender. Jim pulled the binoculars up to his face the find the nameplate on her stern. It was the *Laura Maps.* Within moments she had sailed into the darkness.

The bridge vibrated uncontrollably in the wind. Jim had to close it again, before it was damaged. Ignoring the cold sweat that ran down his face Jim tried to picture exactly how Pete closed the span. He inserted the bar once again and the gears and clutches began to work, the bridge moved ever so slowly back into position. It made contact with the docks on each end and closed with a thud.

It was then he saw his uncle on the far dock. He was jumping up and down and waving his arms. His uncle took time to check the locking mechanism before sprinting across the span and racing into the tender box. His face was red, his eyes were bulging," What do you think you are doing?" he shrieked. "How dare you risk damaging the bridge? You could get me fired?"

"I had to, that ship would have rammed the bridge. "Jim blurted. "I tried to warn her but..."

"Ship, what ship?" Pete's voice was a squawk. "I didn't see a ship."

"It was the schooner, the *Laura Maps*." Jim said.

The color drained from Pate's face. "What? Did you say the *Laura Maps*?

"Yes, I read her nameplate, the *Laura Maps*."

"Jim, it couldn't have been the *Laura Maps*, she sunk off this spot years ago. It was a night just like this." his voice trailed off.

"What do we do? "Jim asked. "Do we put it in the logbook?"

"No," Pete said with a slight smile, "Let's just keep this between you and me, and the *Laura Maps*."

Strange Happenings in Ole Balm Hollow

Until the 19th century Bamm Hollow, the portion of Middletown just northwest of the Navesink, was known as Blem Hollow. If we follow Oak Hill Road from where it intersects with route 35 for two more miles westward, the road becomes Bamm Hollow Road. The route traces along the valley floor until it reaches Red Hill Road where it rises near Deep Cut Park. Today we think of it as one of the most desirable addresses in Monmouth county.

But this was not always the case. Few are aware of the mysterious happenings that occurred in the hollow ever since its history has been recorded. As early as the 1880's the *Daily Register* published accounts of strange events in the region. In 1887 Judge George C. Beekman, who was also a local historian, wrote that Balm Hollow was one of the most haunted places in all America. He noted that this had occurred even before the arrival of the European settlers.

The earliest passages through the hollow were mere footpaths used by local native American tribes. In colonial times it remained a single track with thick virgin forest on both sides. At many points the tops of the trees grew together forming a canopy over the path shielding the path in the daylight. At night it became a dark and foreboding place.

Before the arrival of the European settlers Monmouth county was inhabited by the native American tribe, the Lenni Lenape. Although the Lenape settled in the region they did not establish settlements within the hollow itself. They avoided hunting there or traveling the valley if at all possible. They insisted that the hollow was an evil place with malevolent history which threated anyone traveling there.

The Lenape told of an old Indian man named Cokonkqua a well-known hermit and wizard. He was the only person who resided in the valley. It was said that he recited incantations to an evil spirit who in turn gave Cokonkqua the gift of foretelling the future. But this did not come without a price. On certain nights Cokonkqua would sacrifice infants or small children and smear the blood upon a mysterious tree deep in the forest.

Cokonkqua gained fame for his predictions when he successfully predicted that a great canoe would come out of the water with men who had no color. He warned that these men would destroy the Lenape people. A few days after the tribe reported the arrival of the first settlers Cokonkqua mysteriously disappeared leaving his evil spirt to inhabit the hollow.

According to both Indian and early Dutch reports the sound of crying children reverberated through the woods on particularly moonless nights. The Lenape believed that should you hear the cries, then one of your own household would soon follow the crying child to the grave. While some settlers thought the Indian tales to be silly superstitions others confirmed of hearing the inexplicable sounds emanating from the deep forest.

Although the settlers began using the route more frequently, they avoided the valley at night. One report is of a farmer who was delayed doing business in the village and as forced to travel the route on his way home after dark. It was a warm summer night. Sounds of chirping and buzzing insects and the rustle of leaves echoed along the path. When the farmer's wagon reached the bottom of the hollow his docile horses stopped short. He tried repeatedly to force them ahead, but they refused. The farmer searched for what was frightened the horses but found nothing. He could find no reason for their fear. Even if he applied the whip the horses would not budge. They merely whinnied and snorted in fear. Even when he tried to walk the horses by holding their bridles they jerked away wild eyed and trembling. It was then he realized that all the sounds of the forest had been stilled. There was total silence, the wind had stopped, and the usual sounds of insects and woodland animals were no more. He finally turned the horses and retreated back up the hill until he was well out of the hollow. He rested the horses and slept in his wagon that night. After dawn he renewed his journey and passed through the valley without any further incident.

Another account is of a respected local physician who was called out one night to an emergency at a local farm. Although he did not normally use the path through the hollow at night, it was by far the shortest route to his destination and time was of the essence. As he hurried long the path he saw a lone man on horseback moving slowly ahead. He was surprised to see another traveler and pleased for the company through the dark hollow.

He nudged his horse forward to catch up to the rider, He called out but the rider did not respond. He tried again, "Hello, I say, it's a cold night for travel, don't you think?" But still there was no answer. The rider never turned to look back or pay any attention to his call.

Seeing that the path ahead was narrow and he could not pass the slow moving rider, he called out again, "Sir, could I pass please, I am a doctor on an emergency call?" There was no response. The rider made no effort to move aside to allow the doctor to pass.

Finally, in frustration the doctor stretched out his arm to the rider," Sir, I do need to pass," he said, as he tapped the rider on the shoulder with his riding crop. The crop made a swishing sound as it passed through the rider completely. Instantly both the horse and rider vanished. The startled doctor quickly nudged his horse into a gallop.

The rhymmic clopping of his horse's hooves on the frozen earth were reassuring to the doctor as he tried to concentrate on the sound instead of the strange phantom rider he had encountered. It was only when he pulled up in front of the farmhouse at his destination and his horse stopped that he remembered the horse in the valley had made no such clopping sound as it traveled the pathway. In fact, there had be no noise at all.

A few years later another tragedy occurred in the valley. In 1815 a freed slave named Samuel Herd, purchased a parcel of land in the hollow. He was pleased with his purchase as it was much cheaper than much of the land around his homestead. He was a hard working quiet man who built a cabin for his family near an estate where he worked as a foreman. One morning he was discovered two hundred feet from his front door, beaten and bleeding with a length of rope around his neck. There were no witnesses and the murder went unsolved. It would be two years before any clues would arise as to the mysterious death of Samuel Herd.

In the fall of 1817 two sailors came ashore after a lengthy sea voyage with plans to travel across the hollow to visit family on a farm near Holmdel. Daisy Dan, known for his flashy and colorful clothing and his stern and heavy drinking friend, Sam, were known as tough seamen. They were always looking for a challenge, and equipped for any brawl that came their way. Any tittle tattle of evil spirits or supernatural events only made them laugh.

As the pair traveled down the path that leads into Blem Hollow a sudden thunderstorm arose. The men were searching for shelter when they came to the abandoned cabin of Samuel Herd. They quickly started a fire and opened a jug of Applejack. Soon the cabin was warm and snug. Sam drank his fill and fell into a heavy sleep by the fire, while Dan leaned his back against the hearth and slowly sipped his ale.

Suddenly the front door crashed open. Dan felt himself frozen in place and could only gawk at the two figures in the doorway. He would later recount that one man was short, and the other much taller and wore heavy boots. Both had a grey-greenish expressionless faces. The taller man filled the entire doorway and the shorter one paused briefly at the door before shuffling across the room. A foul stench spread throughout the cabin as he walked noiselessly up the stairs. In a few minutes the apparition eased back down the steps and the two left the cabin.

Finally, able to move, Dan crept to the door and peeked out into the yard. About 200 feet from the cabin the men crouched behind a wood pile. Then a black man walked slowly down the path toward the cabin. The men leapt from behind the wood pile and began beating him. Within minutes they pulled a rope around his neck, the black man fell to earth and the two men fled into the woods.

Dan wiped his eyes on his shirt sleeve, he could not believe what he had just seen. He ran to the spot where the man had fallen, there was nothing there. He sprinted back to cabin and tried to wake Sam.

Dan was breathing so heavily he could hardly speak and it wasn't easy rousing Sam from his drunken sleep. Sam didn't believe Dan at first. He attributed Dan's story to too much of a good thing. It took Dan the remainder of the night to convince Sam of what he had seen.

When they finally arrived in Holmdel and shared the story, the locals laughed at them, considering it to be a tale of a couple drunken sailors.

This would not be the end of extraordinary events reported from the Hollow. Early 20th century reports describe that malevolent foxlike beasts were spotted on reclining fallen logs within the valley forest. Others recounted that red eyed creatures with fierce expressions followed unsuspecting travelers across the hollow. Other tales include the wails of a child in distress wafting through the woods. When anyone followed the sounds they are lead deeper and deeper into the woods until they are entangled in a quagmire of undergrowth causing the victim to wander helplessly till dawn.

Today the quiet of the Hollow is permeated by the revving of automobile engines, the drone of airplanes, and the inevitable ringing of mobile devices. So we must consider if the history of Bamm Hollow is mere folklore; or does the noise of modern America merely mask those echoes of the past. It is hard to say.

Shadows of the Great War

In 1920 Red Bank, like so many towns and cities across America, was still coming to grips with the effects of the Great War. Although many fortunate soldiers came home to their families, countless others would never return. The local newspaper, *The Daily Register,* reported a rash of paranormal happenings.

The descriptions of the phenomena, made by upstanding citizens of the day, were nearly identical. Although the phantoms were somewhat translucent, some nearly transparent, observers could see that each one seemed be wearing at least part of a uniform. Distorted pale faces were outlined by ripped and tattered wool military jackets. Still others exposed baggy canvas pants that bloused over mud smeared boots. The specters took no notice of the living, and never made a sound. They merely roamed the streets as if looking for their homes and families. Locals concluded these to be the spirits of local lads killed in the fighting searching for their homes.

Interest in these apparitions is not surprising. Spiritualism had grown into a popular obsession by this time. It's beginnings at the turn of the century were advanced by those such as Sir Arthur Conan Doyle who spread its popularity even further when he completed a world lecture series on the topic in early part of the century. London had its own well known Ghost Club back as far as 1862. Prominent members included Conan Doyle, Charles Dickens, and William Butler Yeats. It soon spread across

Europe and America with a ghost club arising even in Red Bank by 1920. The Scientific Savants, as they were known, were earnest in their efforts to investigate and explain the paranormal happenings. Yet little written evidence of their work or findings survives. It is assumed that the group eventually disbanded after a period of considerable ridicule from the press and religious community.

The advent of cable television had brought out an entirely new breed of ghost clubs, calling themselves ghost hunters, or paranormal detectives. One can rarely surf the television or internet without coming across these reality shows.

With so much attention paid to ghosts by the media, it is not surprising that once again interest in the paranormal happenings in Red Bank is thriving. As a result, our area has several such ghost clubs, one in Red Bank and others in neighboring towns. So we need not be troubled by ghosts, apparitions, specters, or even things that go bump in the night, Local ghost clubs are active and anxious to help you deal with any misbehaving spirit you may meet.

Civil War Silhouette

Unlike the American Revolution, where the Navesink area was at the center of military action, the Navesink region was spared any major battles during the Civil War. Yet the area suffered the horrendous loss of more than seven thousand brave young men. The fifty-two regiments from New Jersey fought in battles all across the nation.

The river too paid a toll for the war. As the war progressed the river commerce grew into predominately war related materials and equipment. Mariners, as well as their vessels, were conscripted into national service. Both sailing ships as well as the steamboats were either conscripted or leased to the government.

A total of thirty steamers from the north Jersey coast were drafted for military service between 1861 and 1865. Of these, at least six steamboats with regular Red Bank to New York routes became troop carrier vessels. Steamers quickly became workhorses for the navy patrolling the rivers and inlet waterways all along the coast as well as the great Mississippi.

Steamboats transported goods and troops towards the battles and afterwards they carried the survivors, as well as the dead and wounded away from the battle scene. After the war the ships which were not sunk or severely damaged were returned to the river. A few, with a fresh coat of paint courtesy of the military, resumed their original Navesink routes.

For half a century after the Civil War there were numerous reports of sightings of ghost ships on the Navesink. The similarity of the accounts over those years is quite astonishing. The sightings always occur at night when the river is quiet. The witnesses insist that the steamboat seems to be floating on the water, moving along without use of the engines or paddlewheels. The crafts have neither markings or navigational lights as if trying to avoid being detected.

One of the most notable accounts is derived from the journal of a local Dutch landowner of 1890's. His family had lived here since before the Revolution, and Lucas knew the river like the back of his hand. He had survived the Civil War except on nights like this when the horror invaded his sleep. On these nights he found solace sitting by the water with his journal and pipe.

The day had been hot and humid and the night promised nothing more. Lucas leaned against a barrel on the dock that jetted into the Navesink from his farm. He made notes in a small brown journal until the light faded away. He then turned his attention to the quiet of the dark night. Everything was so still it was if the heat and humidity had overpowered the river breeze. Even the tidal movement was imperceptible, leaving the river looking more like a lake.

Lucas glanced from the shore and across the river. How very different it was in the daytime with the steamboats and cargo boats hauling produce to the city. Yet tonight one could hardly ascertain that there was any life on or in the river at all.

Lucas looked down as a mosquito landed on his forearm. With one loud smack he knocked it to dock. When he looked up he noticed a faint glow on the water far upstream. It was no more than a twinkle, but Lucas found himself spellbound by the tiny flicker. He couldn't be sure at first, but it seemed that the tiny greenish light was moving downstream towards him. There was so sound, not even the flap of a paddlewheel. Most peculiar was that the greenish light didn't bob in the water like a boat, it seemed to be floating just above the waterline.

Lucas watched the light move slowly and yet steadily downstream towards him. He walked to the edge of the dock to get a better look. He could tell that indeed it was a vessel, in fact a steamboat. It seemed to be drifting with the tide. Lucas looked at the water, it was slack tide, the tide wasn't moving at all.

At last the boat drew near. A greenish hue hovered over the bow where groups of blue uniformed men sat huddled together in small groups. Some bent forward in earnest conversation, while others sat holding their head in their hands. A low murmur could be heard over the faint melody from a harmonica. Lucas rubbed his eyes, it couldn't be, it was Union soldiers. The war was over thirty years ago. When he glanced up he was suddenly over whelmed with exhaustion and uncontrolled tears trickled down his cheeks.

He had no time to compose himself before the mid deck of the steamer came into view.

Here the blue forms were lying in rows across on the deck. Others sat precariously leaning against the railing. A lone dark figure moved slowly between them, pausing for a few moments before moving on to the next. In the same instant the harmonica's melody is replaced with guttural moans and crying. The cries of anguish grew so loud they seem to be coming from the river itself.

Before Lucas could get his breath the stern came into view. Here the greenish hue faded to a sickening grey. The glow hovered over log shaped fabric parcels stacked in small pyramids stretching the width of the steamer. As he watched a gust of wind whipped away a covering here and here, and in the faint aura are the distorted faces of the corpses.

Lucas jerked his eyes from the scene searching for the nameplate on the ship. He gasped. It is the *Navesink*, a local steamboat named for the river, which was lost in the war. It had been sunk during a skirmish in a southern river. It never returned home.

For a few moments Lucas stood frozen in place. It is only when the ship disappeared into the darkness does the dreadful crying fade away. He heard rumors of ghost ships on the river, but never believed it, not until now. He scooped up his journal and hurried to the house to record his encounter.

Although Lucas never saw the phantom ship again, reports of the sightings continued for five decades. But then at the advent of World War I, they suddenly ceased. They have not been seen since. Who can explain the phenomena? Can you? Not me.

Tales and Yarns from Whippoorwill Valley

While many accounts of mysterious events in the Navesink region may be unfamiliar to many; longtime residents are aware of the peculiar reputation of Whippoorwill Valley Road in Middletown. About a mile north of the river this scenic country lane meanders through woodlands, rolling hills, horse farms, and great estates from Chapel Hill Road to Kings Highway. Until recently it remained heavily wooded, and generally a sparsely inhabited area. Although a few ruins of colonial structures could be seen, it remained a one lane dirt route through lush forest.

As in the recent past the road is a popular hangout spot for teenagers as well as a popular territory for paranormal investigators. There is a dearth of reports of paranormal activities reported by word of mouth, print, and now as internet postings.

One of the best known tales describes how "during the witch burning times" of the late 17th century a group of fifteen women were accused of witchcraft. Following a swift trial, the women were burned at the stake in a clearing along the road. As a result, whenever a driver passes the site he will experience a series of fifteen bumps in the road which jolts the car to a near stop. Inspection of the road reveals a flat road, without potholes or mounds.

A related account insists that the malevolent spirits of the burned witches have somehow reached across the centuries enticing modern day covens to the area. A few remains of old bonfires sprinkled with the residue of a few herbs and pieces of black fabric is given as evidence.

Research reveals that no one ever stood trial for witchcraft in New Jersey. No one was burned at the stake or even drowned. During the restless era of 60's-80's interest in Wicca and other witchcraft forms thrived. Although it is quite possible that local witch covens used the secluded areas, there is no evidence of their connection to any previous assault on witchcraft.

Yet we must remember that folklore can have an energy and spirit all of its own. And as we know, not all history is ever recorded. Who knows for certain if unreported accounts of cruelty among early settlers did not spur a malign energy on Whippoorwill Valley Road which periodically rises looking for revenge.

A second assertion is that the road is cursed because of a history of devil worship in the woods. Some reports insist that devil himself claimed the areas as his own, and he is said to roam the area protecting his tract for his followers. For some years' accounts circulated of satanic rituals, blood sacrifices, and the sounds of dissonant chants wafting through the forest.

Although no reliable account of observing the rituals exists today we do know that such groups did indeed utilize the isolated area. During the late 1970's ruins of an abandoned building gave evidence that some form of satanic activity occurred here. Multiple reliable sources identified the ruins of an abandoned building on which the remains of a worn wooden floor reveal a large pentagram within a perfect circle. On the adjacent wall two upside down Roman crosses flank the pentagram. Within the same area various satanic symbols, and numbers could be seen scratched or painted on the weathered surfaces. The site is now redeveloped private property and it is assumed that those markings have been erased.

Anton LeVay's Church of Satan originated in California gaining national notoriety in the 60's. While it remains an organized assembly, there is little evidence that it has a strong hold in this region.

Each of us must look within ourselves and our personal faith base to decide if Satanism is a provocation for these strange happenings on Whippoorwill Valley Road. Or is this just a colorful folktale?

Another legend of the Whippoorwill Valley Road is based on a dark period in our local history. One account maintains that on moonless nights an unsuspecting traveler may be waylaid by an opaque antique pickup truck. The truck suddenly appears in the narrowest section of the lane so that it is impossible to pass. Some reports claim that there is no driver at the wheel of the truck; while others insist that the truck is weighed down with dozens of Ku Klux Klansmen in full white garb. Of these reports a few insist they were able to outrun the truck, and others claimed they were forced to turn around and escape back the way they came.

As with much folklore these accounts have a correlation with historical events in the region. It seems that KKK was not so clandestine in our area The history of the Klan in our region is well documented. It is quite possible that in its early days when the Klan met secretly they may have used this secluded area for their rendezvous. By the 1920's and into the early 1930's the Klan was well entrenched and openly active in communities all along the Navesink. Large numbers of newspaper accounts as well a published photographs recount the meetings, cross burnings, and parades through the streets of local communities.

Although the KKK was adamant in their hatred of African Americans, Catholics, Jews, and any ethnic minority, the *Daily Register* provided sympathetic and detailed accounts of the Klan and their activities. The Klan was not encumbered by fear of the law or the church, they met openly in several Red Bank churches and civil buildings. Membership included all sectors of the public including town officials, law enforcement, the press, politicians, judges, business people, as well as the clergy. Although the organization still exists, in much smaller numbers, it exhibits no observable influence in our communities today.

In addition to the claims of KKK apparitions, a few individuals insist they have found assorted memorabilia or graffiti from Klan activities on Whippoorwill Valley Road. These artifacts have yet to be verified as authentic.

With our knowledge of the Klan's history in the area, we are left with a provoking question. What if the evil of the group was so strong that it managed to permeated the spatial energy on this 21st century road? Are these apparitions just the tip of a more sinister evil in our midst? And is the reason so many teenagers see the apparitions because the evil seeks out the young as a means to destroy all that is good?

Some of the best known legends of the road deal with bridges, babies, or sometimes both. Today the bridges along the road are so small as to be nearly undetectable. They are mere shallow platforms, covered in dirt and gravel over the small brooks. Yet the folklore is rich with accounts of assorted sightings at these spots.

One such tale is that of an infant thrown into the stream by a farmer who suspected his wife of having an affair. When she gave birth the farmer claimed the infant looked like his wife's lover and drown the child. One narrative claims that if you stand on the bridge late at night you can hear the helpless child crying. Another claims that if you stop your car on the bridge and get out, the baby will rise from its grave and push the car away from the grave site. Yet another related allegation is that if you stop your car on the bridge and then hear the baby cry, the car will not start again. Only after you have sung a lullaby to the baby will your car start.

We have nothing on the historical record of infanticide on Whippoorwill Valley Road or anywhere near the area. Yet history is not always accurate. Such an event would likely have not been reported or considered far too grisly to publicize.

Once again Whippoorwill Valley Road leaves us with unanswered questions. Who can say that if life is stolen from an infant in such a brutal manner, that its innocent spirit isn't given some sort of space in our sphere? Perhaps reality is a yin and yang, an ever changing balance of yesterday, today, and tomorrow.

In addition to the paranormal events discussed so far the road is recognized for a series of singularly peculiar occurrences and apparitions. Many of these have been passed down by word of mouth until recently when we find them cited in numerous paranormal web and blog sites.

Both web sites and popular regional magazines carry the reports of those who have claimed to have experienced paranormal events on

Whippoorwill Valley Road. Some discovered peculiar symbols carved on rocks or trees deep within the woods. Another describes seeing a handmade wooden sign shaped like an arrow with the word "God" scrawled across its length pointing into a dense thicket. There are countless claims of finding unidentifiable relics, symbols, and strange tools in the area. Still others insist they hear unearthly sounds and groans emanating from the road on more than one occasion.

There are numerous reports of ghostly creatures in a variety of forms. One is of a lone horseback rider who takes chase should any unsuspecting traveler try to pass through the valley at night. Other sightings claim to have heard what sounded like a large creature running through knee deep water in great haste. And one detailed testimony comes from a local man who claims to have seen Jesus dancing down the lonely road at dawn

Several witnesses have come forth with an interesting contention. They insist that the road contains some sort of mystical energy capable of influencing the human mind. Each describes experiences where normal individuals, who are not particularly interested in the paranormal or mystical, are suddenly overcome while passing along the road. Their feelings progress from a sudden sadness, to worry, dread, and fear. The afflicted individual flees the area in terror.

This bevy of occurrences and apparitions are impossible to either validate or rebuff as fabrications. The very volume of these reports must cause us to wonder if indeed the shadows of what has occurred along this aged road are somehow able to ooze into what we consider reality. Who can say?

One very recent report describes the discovery of a rather grotesque looking tree growing along the narrow lane. It is described as a tree whose trunk is twisted and gnarled as if nature was attempting to turn it into a pretzel. A closer inspection revels what appears to be an image of a human being devoured by the trunk of the tree. The bark of the tree is malformed and a rusty brown color. The upper foliage is scant and drab and the air around the tree is always damp and chilly.

When the same witness attempted to photograph the tree his cell phone simply would not work. Not only was the camera function disabled, but there was no cell service anywhere near the tree. The phone did not function again until he had driven some distance away from the area.

If we travel across Whippoorwill Valley Road on a beautiful sunny day we may be so taken by the rolling landscape, lush green woodlands, and exquisite estates that we may find it hard to believe the area holds such an eerie reputation. Instead we relax within the oasis of serenity and natural beauty nestled within hustle and bustle of metropolitan New Jersey.

Traveling across Whippoorwill Valley Road on a dark and moonless night is quite a different experience. With only the narrow beams of your headlights to guide you through the foggy darkness you can only focus on the scrawny path ahead. The forest creeks and groans and the trees themselves stretch their leafy branches out towards you from the darkened woods. There are unfamiliar sounds too, sounds you can't quite identify. So you tell yourself that it's just the wind, although you are not so sure. You find yourself depressing the accelerator just a bit more. Now the darkness rushes by. Your headlights seem to grow dimmer and you become acutely aware of this darkness. The oasis of the day is devoured by the darkness. There is something about this place, something that shrouds the secrets of yesterday while embracing the energy of danger. It is something, yet it is nothing.

So before we make final judgements about Whippoorwill Valley Road and its long history of strange and peculiar events, perhaps it is best to take that dark ride and then decide for ourselves.

Library of Congress Number: 2005902895
ISBN: Hardcover 1-4134-9179-0
Softcover 1-4134-9178-2

This book was printed in the United States of America.

To order additional copies of this book, contact:
Xlibris Corporation
1-888-795-4274
www.Xlibris.com
Orders@Xlibris.com
28337

In Transit

To the SPHS library
from an SPHS alumna
of 1945
Best wishes,
Virginia Brown

In Transit

A Memoir

Virginia Brown

Contents

For Ken

Out of a misty dream
Our path emerges for a while, then closes
Within a dream.

—Ernest Dowson

Excerpted from Vitae Summa Brevis Spem Nos Vetat Incohare Longam

An early photograph of the author

Family and Early Childhood

My journey began in Seattle in the boom year of 1928, with a stress-filled arrival that put both parents, Gladys and Arthur Stern, in hospital. My mother had sustained a difficult pregnancy and delivery, culminating in a breast abscess, and my father was briefly hospitalized with exhaustion. Our home at that time was on Mercer Island, accessible only by boat, and its rural location in Lake Washington may account for my lifelong love of water—to gaze at in all weathers, drink in prodigious quantities, and swim through whenever feasible. It was also the first of many circumstances establishing the American West as my heart's home. A year later, I was joined by a younger sister, Charlotte, who completed our immediate family.

We know little of the origins of our paternal grandfather, Edward Stern, beyond his emigration from Germany under circumstances never disclosed to his family. As a small child I became aware of my parents' concern for his mental stability, and indeed, as the years progressed, Grandfather's brilliance and originality of mind turned to fruitless invention and fantasy, eventually leading into a mental institution. We children scarcely knew him. But I knew and loved our paternal grandmother, Bessie Bunting Stern. A descendant of prosperous importers and businessmen, she counted among her ancestors the Marquis de Levis, for whom the town of Levis, Quebec was named, as well as Quaker colonists accompanying William Penn to the state bearing his name. Through many generations the Buntings have remained staunch members of the Religious Society of Friends, formal name for the Quaker church.

When my father, Arthur Bunting Stern, returned from overseas duty in the Army Signal Corps after World War I, he discovered the girl he had loved since childhood, Gladys Williams, had moved West with her family following financial failure of her Welsh father's horse farm near Philadelphia. A golf and country club now covers the lovely acreage where Morris Williams raised race horses as well as the sturdy animals required to draw carriages and plows at the turn of the century, before motor vehicles largely supplanted them. His wife, my maternal grandmother Charlotte Helmbold Williams, came from German and English stock and had been raised Episcopalian, converting to the Quaker religion of her husband when they married. Of my grandparents, she was the only one to survive into my adulthood and become well remembered by me.

Both of my parents and grandmother Williams suffered and survived the severe flu epidemic of 1918, which claimed the lives of an estimated twenty million victims worldwide, afflicting at least a billion more in what the *Encyclopedia Britannica* describes as "one of the severest holocausts of disease ever encountered." The death toll was exceptionally high on the battlefields in France, due largely to inadequate facilities for care and treatment. When my father became ill, he refused hospitalization, knowing the field hospitals were already full, with men dying on overflow cots set up outside. He also resisted efforts of his comrades to move him to an underground shelter for protection from enemy shelling, preferring to take his chances warm and dry in the signal hut rather than seriously chilled underground. His choice proved to be a good one for which my sister and I have reason to be grateful.

Just before the United States entered the Great War in 1917, my father had graduated from Lafayette College as a civil engineer and started working for the Pennsylvania Railroad. His job was kept for him until he returned in 1918, but by then, he had marriage on his mind, so he resigned and headed immediately for California. By the time he arrived in Palo Alto, he knew he had brought home from the trenches a highly undesirable souvenir. He had contracted amoebic dysentery for which there was then no cure, and although he eventually recovered sufficiently to lead a normal life, his digestion remained unusually sensitive. For several years, he was not expected to live, and because of his problematical health and ability to support a family, their marriage was postponed for two years.

During their first years of marriage, they struggled with his daunting diet, which seems to have smothered any latent desires of his bride to turn her hand to experimental cooking. Indeed, for a time, my father could digest only steamed clams and rice. Fortunately, his new employer, the Pacific Telephone Company, had transferred him to Seattle where good clams were plentiful. Many years later Mummy told me those clams nearly did her in; she could hardly stand opening the oven door, seeing "all those faces" staring at her from the opened shells. By the time I came along, Daddy's health had improved to the point where he could work full-time, commuting from Mercer Island to his office in downtown Seattle by ferry and cable car. Life there suited them, and they agreed to leave only because relocation to the parent company, American Telephone and Telegraph (AT&T), headquartered at 195 Broadway in downtown New York City represented a considerable promotion.

Their move began inauspiciously. The boss who moved him east died suddenly, and shortly thereafter the stock market collapsed, heralding the Great Depression that spanned our childhood years. This may have been a blessing in disguise for us girls. Our amusements were largely confined to home and consisted of simple games and radio shows shared with our parents and friends. In the evenings, we played Parcheesi, Concentration, or Canfield and regularly listened to favorite comedians and dramatic shows on the radio. Although we were spared the acute poverty experienced by many families at the time, we were taught early to be frugal and not to covet or expect luxuries. Unused lights were to be turned off promptly, outside doors kept tightly closed, and I remember being adjured to use as little toilet paper as possible.

We had settled into the first of our three houses in Fanwood, a New Jersey town of a thousand souls, characterized by a classmate as a "sweet little town." We rented for three years until I became ill with swollen glands, misdiagnosed at first and treated as mumps. When the doctor realized his mistake, he renamed it glandular fever and urged Mother to take me to a better climate before winter set in. Her widowed mother still lived on the West Coast, so she took Charlotte and me West by train to Grandmother Williams's house in Palo Alto where we spent the winter and part of the spring. It must have done the trick. A long time later, I was told my condition most likely had been mononucleosis from which I made a slow but complete recovery. The only lingering consequence was to postpone for a year my start in school, but after first grade, I skipped second to land in the unusually spunky class with which I went through the rest of my public schooling.

After another three-year rental, we became owners of a house situated on a hill, which now, to this Westerner, resembles a mere incline. Across the road a small woods separated the town dump from the home of my geographically closest classmate Janice Jensen, daughter of a retired Norwegian sea captain. Janice was a pixie, an inspired scamp who led us on many mischievous adventures brightening our young lives. The woods her family owned provided our first skiing experiences. Each ski was held to the foot by a single strap, slipped over to the instep. One or the other of these precarious straps threatened to slip off whenever I executed the small ski jump we optimistically constructed and tried to keep repaired.

The Jersey Central Railroad ran through a deep cut behind the Jensen property. My father had always loved trains and we girls picked up on this. We were located on the steepest grade between Jersey City and Philadelphia. Steam engines laboring up that grade with their heavy burdens of freight often made sleep difficult, for when they failed to make the hill, they broke down in huge shivering puffs, trying again and again before finally giving up and sounding their whistles to call a second engine from Dunellen down the line. All this took a little getting used to, but before long, Charlotte and I found ourselves straining with their efforts, rooting for the primary engine and welcoming the arrival of the pusher so we could go back to sleep. Indeed, those sounds became companionable to me, a fortunate thing since World War II brought longer and heavier trains, often requiring more than one pusher engine to help them up our hill. Those train tracks likewise provided opportunities for daytime adventure as did the nearby loading yard where Jan and I were bawled out and chased away whenever we sneaked in to jump into the inviting piles of various grains deposited in huge bins beneath the siding. Often, when we heard trains coming, we would scamper to a nearby bridge and lean over its railing to inhale the intoxicating puffs of sooty air that were belched into our faces. To this day, a train's plaintive whistle evokes feelings of nostalgia for many of us who grew up alongside those tracks.

Soon after we settled into our home, a piano materialized, leading my sister and me into music lessons for which I had little enthusiasm and less talent, but Charlotte quickly progressed to a level that satisfied Mother's frequent requests for Schubert's "Serenade." Though our father did not play particularly well, his touch transmitted character and feeling, and I treasure the memory of lying in bed and listening to his flawed rendering of waltzes from *The Merry Widow*. His hesitations, the missed notes, and corrected passages made his play seem all the more precious to me, possibly because my own was so hopelessly imperfect. My husband reminds me in a pun my father would have appreciated: "After all, the piano was never his forte!"

For the most part, we lived a small-town life, with our schools, markets, and library within easy walking distance. Many residents served as volunteer firemen, and I remember Daddy occasionally being called out in the middle of the night to the firehouse only a few blocks away. But it was also suburbia, a uniquely American form of living at that time.

Our nearby central city was New York, reached by train and the connecting ferry to Manhattan. At that time, no place on earth offered greater or more varied entertainment and cultural opportunity than New York City, with its abundance of museums, concerts, and theaters. Its cheap urban pleasures were legendary. Museums were free, subway rides cost a nickel, and Horn and Hardart Automats fed us from small glass-fronted cubicles where all manner of dishes were displayed, where nickels again were the coin of our realm. Riding double-decker buses was also great fun. Our favorite seating, in the first row of the upper deck on the open buses, afforded unimpeded views of that glamorous slice of America known worldwide as Fifth Avenue. Once a year, Madison Square Garden played host to Ringling Brothers & Barnum and Bailey Circus where simply visiting the menagerie made a trip into the city worthwhile. During major holidays New York was an especially festive place, and we tried never to miss the annual Christmas and Easter shows at Radio City Music Hall. My favorite part of the live show was the mesmerizing performances of the Don Cossack singers, blending glorious singing with inspired staging.

During the summers of 1939 and 1940, our family attended the incomparable New York World's Fair many times, traveling for a couple of hours each way by train, ferry, and subway, often making our way home well after midnight so as not to miss the closing fireworks. And there, in the famed General Motors (GM) exhibit, we first saw models of the freeways we would one day be traveling. I recall noticing how freely the traffic flowed, with no traffic jams to mar the utopian scene. One memorable day, the British royal family was in attendance: stately King George with his small matronly wife, Queen Elizabeth, and their two daughters, Princesses Elizabeth and Margaret Rose. This resulted in many onlookers commenting on the similar appearance of their family and ours.

Indeed, mine was a most happy childhood. In words of a later day, I was blessed with good role models: a mother who put home and family first, a father faithful to that family, and a sister who weathered our sometimes fractious siblinghood with loyalty and love. My father was a particularly dominant figure in building my future. A brilliant man, he spent much time with me, teaching me chess and challenging my mind with problems that encouraged logical and creative thinking. Favorites of mine were the endless variations of "nobleman and huntsman" puzzles in logic, in which one group always tells the truth while the other always lies. He also introduced me to geometry through play with poker chips after noting that as a very young child, I enjoyed mobilizing my dinner peas into rectilinear shapes, imitative of the military formations he had described to us from his army days.

With ingenuity and great patience, he overcame my fear of turbulent ocean swimming. This he did by digging a hole in the sand large enough to hold me, then filling it with water, and slowly lowering me into it with his supportive hands beneath me. As he gradually lowered his hands until I felt only water, I suddenly realized the thrill of floating on my own and have loved swimming ever since. We spent countless happy hours diving through waves and swimming from the beaches at Cape May, southernmost beach resort on the Jersey Shore. The entire town is honored among America's historic places.

Because of his own father's irresponsible behavior, Daddy was determined from early on in his life to set high personal standards. So he was no stranger to sacrifice and hard work, and during the depths of the Depression, he labored late into the night at home, entirely on his own, developing an invention that has saved AT&T millions of dollars over the years. Recently, I learned that his invention, sometimes known as Crossbar No. 5, or simply 5 Crossbar, introduced electrical switching into the mechanical telephone dialing system then in use, thus greatly speeding the dialing process and laying the groundwork for the fully electronic systems we have today. In fact, a latter-day engineer, with the Bell System, once told me that Crossbar No. 5 was the greatest contribution to the field of communication until that time.

After a ceremony at which he was awarded a check for $25 (half of 1 percent of his annual salary of $5,000), he requested transfer to Bell Laboratories in New Jersey, the research arm of the giant corporation that was conveniently located much closer to our home. His request was denied despite its appropriateness, given his demonstrated talents and loyalty to the company. When Bell Labs began making its mark with inventions like the transistor, which occurred during the halcyon period of postwar prosperity we all enjoyed after World War II, I asked Daddy why he hadn't been more aggressive in pursuing his own career. His reply was gentle and philosophical: "I suppose I should have been, Ginger. But you must remember it was depression times, and I had a family to support. I felt grateful to keep my job when so many around me were losing theirs."

Another striking feature of his attitudes toward humanity was his impatience with gullibility. To the extent I have developed discernment, I credit his attitudes and early training toward that goal, which subsequent experience has convinced me is by no means a common ingredient of parental guidance. It should be, though, for gullibility is what keeps a host of well disguised con games alive in this wily world.

Similarly, his emphasis upon safety precautions, including preparation for action and avoidance of panic in crises, was unusually adult fare for young children and has paid dividends in my adult life. He stressed preventive awareness and anticipation of possibilities, instead of worry, which so often turns counterproductive. He not only preached these measures but also lived them. Two illustrative examples: He bought and carefully erected for Charlotte and me a small acrobatic apparatus in our backyard, but before letting us use the rings or bar, he insisted we practice to his satisfaction the "safe" way to fall while hanging upside down, rolling upon the shoulders to protect the head and neck. With this approach, he showed us how risks can often be managed easily and effectively by practice of appropriate techniques. On one occasion, he demonstrated this philosophy more dramatically. On a Saturday while he napped on our raised porch, a fight erupted among the dogs playing with us children in the backyard. Daddy astounded me by flying off the glider with blanket in hand and vaulting over the porch railing onto the ground where he instantly broke up the fight by covering the pack of dogs with his blanket. When I questioned him later about this impressive performance, he explained he could tell from his experience with born fighting dogs, like his boyhood Yankee bull terrier Prince, that these snarling canines were unlikely to hurt one another seriously, but he was concerned that we children might rush in and be bitten while trying to "save" the doggies. So I learned many things from that demonstration, not the least of which was the importance of knowing how to do things right, in this case, plunging dogs into darkness to stop a fight.

With Daddy instructing me in what might be called the science of life, Mummy taught by example much of the art of living. During my childhood she was overshadowed in my eyes by the father whom I regarded with such great admiration and awe that her quiet acceptance of this circumstance obscured from me her own innate wisdom and resolve. Not until many years later did I realize the guidance she had given me with great subtlety. She excelled at making the best of what came her way. Of the countless words exchanged between us as we made our way through the days and nights of my growing up, I remember very little actual advice offered by Mother, and that little was usually in response to questions of mine. Three influential remarks have been her suggestion: (1) to smile for loved ones who prefer smiles to tears, (2) to spare them worries when they are too far away to help, and (3) "It's nice if you can keep a little romance in your life."

Mummy also possessed a distinctly doggy quality—liquid, friendly brown eyes, and a readiness for anything that was going. She was a good sport. At the beach, when my tall father would hoist me to his shoulders, she—though a head shorter and hardly sharing his enthusiasm for diving waves—would give in to my little sister's pleading and follow with Charlotte aboard. And up she would come, spluttering and smiling as she wiped her wet hair from her eyes.

She likewise embodied traditional Quakerism. Within our family, she always used the old "thee" and "thy" forms of address.

Her lessons of politeness and consideration were rooted in the Quaker upbringing she and my father had shared since childhood. My friends responded to, and occasionally commented upon, the peace they found in our home—the evident politeness and respect shown to one another, which we daughters took for granted. Most of that was Mummy's doing. Over the years, the firm but gentle ways she taught by example have often smoothed rough edges from unpleasant circumstances and sometimes even neutralized potentially dangerous situations.

Though my parents were spiritual, we children were never subjected to religious dogma or required to attend Friends Meeting regularly. As a matter of fact, my earliest remembered encounter with religious dogma occurred as a small child when a playmate asked me out of the blue whether I had been baptized. When I discovered what she meant by "baptized," I told her I had not, to which she responded with genuine concern, "Then you're not legally alive!" I could think of nothing to say except "Well, I'm *here*!" Looking back on that innocuous incident, I realize it represents much that I dislike about institutionalized belief systems. Their dictates can easily be implanted in receptive minds where equally easily they may germinate into confused and hardened conclusions.

The only time I recall receiving any formal religious instruction was when I was invited to attend evening meetings in the church of some of my Presbyterian friends. Daddy remarked that if we wanted religious education, he preferred we attend Friends' First Day School. Since my motivations had been social rather than theological, those sessions were short-lived.

My father's dislike of the "fire and brimstone" approach to religion, which he once expressed quite strongly during an adult conversation I overheard, has left a lasting impression upon me. Naturally that colorful phrase caught my ear, and I asked him to explain. He replied that threats of hell are used to scare people into doing what a particular dogma tells them to do. My distrust of religions using fear to keep believers in line undoubtedly stems in part from this early introduction to the more lurid postulates that have developed over the centuries.

In a lighter vein, both my parents shared an appreciation of simple family fun. Mummy had a lovely laugh. In what has become one of my golden memories, she once hurried from the kitchen to see why I was laughing alone in the living room. I explained I was reading an essay in one of Daddy's favorite books by the Canadian humorist and mathematician Stephen Leacock, and I offered to read it aloud. Still in her apron, she immediately sat down on the sofa and, as I read, she broke into peals of laughter. Together we could hardly reach the end of the story, and seldom have I seen such rejuvenation in a face as I saw then in hers.

That same long-ago sofa was part of another golden parental moment for me. Daddy loved music, and together one late afternoon we played a record of the lovely old song "Because," sung by a tenor whose name I never knew. My father, resting on the sofa with one long hand dangling on his forehead above his beautiful blue eyes, and I in my favorite chair watching him in the warm sunset light, listened over and over to that poignant song I'll always love.

I also cherish the memories of some of our family's philosophical moments—a night on the boardwalk at Cape May when we watched a full moon rise above the ocean and speculated about potential human travels to the moon, with my father wistfully remarking that such exciting possibilities would come too late for him, though maybe not for us. One evening we pulled off a highway to watch a particularly beautiful western sunset to its conclusion, another time just so we could listen on our car radio to the ending of a Chopin nocturne—nothing spectacular or pretentious, just quietly thoughtful interludes shared with us children.

Charlotte's and my extended human family was small. There were four cousins who lived at quite a distance from us. Three of them were too old to be anything but ciphers to me, and their parents—Aunt Mary and Uncle Will—only occupy a small spot in my memory. They lived on a farm, of which my chief memories center upon the large number of rabbits they raised and the rustling sounds I heard, reminiscent of a great forest, as I walked alone between rows of full-grown corn towering above me.

Two aunts, however, played significant roles in our lives. Mildred B. Miller, Daddy's older sister, was a much more distinguished artist than we girls realized. Endowed with an accompanying artistic temperament, she provided adventure by taking us on drives where she became "lost," consoling us with ice cream cones. Or we'd find ourselves lured to Cape May Point, a swampy bird sanctuary studded with osprey nests, where Charlotte and I spent seemingly endless hours swatting mosquitoes while Mildred patiently painted the landscape. We called her Auntie O because of the perfect circles she drew freehand for us. Only as adults did we learn how much farther her artistic accomplishments extended. As a student at The Pennsylvania Academy of the Fine Arts (PAFA) in Philadelphia, she was twice awarded European scholarships as well as two important prizes. Later, she taught at the PAFA Country School in Chester Springs, which she helped manage with her husband, Roy Miller. During those two decades, she exhibited to critical acclaim at major museums such as the Corcoran Gallery in Washington and the famed Carnegie International Exhibition of 1923 in Pittsburgh, where her work was especially well received and widely reviewed. Subjects of her commissioned portraits included distinguished members of government and the military, as well as relatives of the well-known artist Mary Cassatt. Decades later, my new husband and I would spend time with Mildred on her southern California ranch, but that lay far in the future.

Mummy's younger sister, Emeline Williams Mitten, was a splendid lady whose influence upon me extends well beyond her death. The wife of a professional naval officer, she and Uncle Bob had lived abroad for many years, bringing us girls exotic presents from time to time on their visits home from Europe and the Far East. Uncle Bob, tall and slender, cut a rather dashing figure. It was he who, at a more cosmopolitan drugstore than we girls usually patronized, introduced my sister and me to "lemon

Cokes," which represented to me the height of sophistication. For weeks afterward, I faithfully ordered lemon Cokes, though I never really liked colas. Uncle Bob also sported enviable balance; he could do a mean handstand on the beach, lowering and raising himself as I had seen in acrobatic shows in the circus. And he played a haunting version of "Waltzing Matilda" on the piano.

In his youth, Bob had served in China on the Yangtze Patrol, sailing aboard the *Monocacy* as First Officer and then Captain during his and Yine's early married years. On his lengthier trips, Aunt Yine sometimes followed aboard a Chinese passenger vessel where only Caucasians were allowed on the upper deck. On one trip, she was the only Caucasian aboard, gazing down upon masses of Chinese crowding the lower deck. They were caught one night in a terrible typhoon that most aboard, including the captain, never expected to survive. But survive they did, and although I was not there to see it, I am sure she emerged from the ordeal the quintessential lady she always seemed.

All that predated U.S. involvement in World War II. After Pearl Harbor, Uncle Bob was recalled from retirement to lead convoys along the eastern seaboard to and from South America. At that time, German U-boat activity was still strong in the Atlantic, and sinking ships were often visible from East Coast beaches. Whenever Bob's convoys departed from Brooklyn Navy Yard, Yine would stay with us after he was called to duty, and her quiet strength was impressive. One evening, after taking Bob's farewell call in Daddy's study, as she rejoined us in the living room, her emotion showed through her customary composure. When Mummy quietly remarked how hard these partings must be, Yine responded, "Think how much worse it would be if we didn't care!" After the war, Bob slipped back into quiet retirement in Virginia, with the distinction of never having lost a ship from any of his convoys.

Visits with Bob and Yine at their home in Alexandria seemed to Charlotte and me like exotic isles in the placid sea of ordinary life. I wish I could have gone back to one occasion during the war as I sat in their living room listening to Bob and my father discussing the Battle of Midway, a subject that strongly recaptured my interest half a century later. To us girls, Aunt Yine was inspiring. I watched her moving quietly about her domestic duties early one morning, wearing a soft maroon robe over an impeccably arranged lacy frill framing her serene face. That vision has remained for me the epitome of how life can be lived on its calmest shores. They had no children of their own, and she has told me since that *we* were her family, which fills me with pride and pleasure.

By 1938, when the Depression was easing and the new war was not yet on our shores, unknown to Charlotte and me, our father came close to nervous breakdown due to a particularly difficult boss. So that summer, on orders from his doctor, he went West to a ranch for two weeks. During his absence, Mother took us to Back Log Camp, a rustic Quaker resort in the Adirondack Mountains, where we lived in what I believe are known as Adirondack tents—canvas cabins open at both ends with cots on a wooden floor raised a few steps above the ground. One morning, I was awakened by a cat jumping onto my bed. Moving fast, he sat upon my chest and, before I got my eyes open, placed his left front paw on my right eye, followed quickly by the other one on my left eye, creating a potentially sticky situation for me. He received a tender lift straight upward. I think he may have used the technique before—an assured way to gain attention and cuddling.

Mornings were foggy. Charlotte and I started each day with a swim before breakfast, which included the eerie experience of diving through fog so thick we had to take on faith the water beneath it. The mosaic of impressions staying with me from that vacation includes an overnight canoe trip, complete with portages, campfire meals, and a handsome young college student romantically strumming a guitar while crooning "South of the Border" and "Begin the Beguine."

During the summers of 1939-41, we spent my father's last peacetime vacations at Bones Brothers Ranch, the working cattle and dude ranch he had discovered the previous year. Being a good amateur photographer, Daddy had been engaged by the

Alderson brothers—"Big and Little Bones," owners and operators of the ranch—to make movies for their advertising purposes. As compensation, we received partially discounted vacations for which we drove six days each way, feeling truly West upon reaching the Black Hills of South Dakota.

On one of our overnight stays in the Black Hills, I had an experience that has given me abiding comfort over the years. Mildly sick, I was confined to bed for a day. At first, I fretted at missing out on whatever the rest of the family might be doing. Soon, however, I began drifting in and out of sleep, slowly becoming aware of the soothing sound of the wind moving through the fragrant pine boughs outside the bedroom window. Decades later, when asked if there were any particular experience from childhood I would like to repeat, that is the one that came immediately to mind. The mere thought of it fills me with an inexpressible sense of peace. Those hours taught me that patient acquiescence to circumstances beyond my control could pay unexpected and enduring dividends. I had not yet become acquainted with the lovely Serenity Prayer, commending patience in accepting what cannot be changed, courage in changing what can, and wisdom in recognizing the difference.

We timed our arrival in Wyoming to catch the last night of the big rodeo held each summer in Sheridan, gateway to the Bones Ranch near Birney, sixty-seven miles north in Montana. At the rodeo, Charlotte and I were introduced to American Indians and traditional cowboy competitions in roping, bronc riding, and steer riding. It all seemed immensely colorful, and I recall looking down upon the scene from a fine vantage point atop a Ferris wheel, vowing to myself to remember the experience when immersed in my everyday activities at home.

Our ranch trips introduced us to wide open spaces, the glory of western sunsets, and startling phenomena not found in New Jersey. One spectacular rainstorm sprouted toads, thousands upon thousands of them covering the ground so completely within minutes of the storm's end that we could hardly walk without stepping on them. I remember one particularly appealing ranch dog, who tended to look puzzled most of the time anyway, standing at the top of a small rise, utterly confounded by this new life hopping about his feet. Those vacations made westerners of Charlotte and me, and to this day, when I smell the dust of paddocks occupied by the police horses in Golden Gate Park, I feel transported back to those halcyon days under the Big Sky.

In 1941, Daddy added an extra week to his vacation so we could visit Yellowstone National Park. I asked if we might do the same thing next year to which he replied he doubted there would be a "next time" for such vacations. When pressed, he said he feared our country would soon be at war, surprising news to one as protected as we children had been.

There was an amusing climax to that trip, perhaps emblematic of the last prewar frivolity our family was to experience. Against his better judgment, Daddy acceded to Charlotte's and my request that we spend our last night on the road in an advertised "wigwam"—merely a commercialized memento of the real West we had so recently and reluctantly left. Unknown to us, the wigwam's plumbing was incomplete. Water for Daddy's shower never made it to the bathroom, spurting instead through the wall directly into our bedroom, where we and our luggage were crowded into the conical confines of a tepee. Mother watched from bed as we girls began tossing clothes and luggage onto cots while hearing the angry and puzzled outbursts from my father in the bathroom. Suddenly, Mother began to laugh, and as the evening unraveled, she could not stop laughing. Of course by then, we girls had chimed in, and my father's outcries were intensifying in volume and vocabulary, further fueling our mirth. This is the only time I ever knew Mother to become hysterical. Decades later, I had the great good fortune to be in on another such episode, with my husband trapped in a bathroom in Katoomba, Australia. As he put it after being rescued, "Why can't *you* ever be trapped in a bathroom with me and the boys outside, unable to keep from laughing?" Daddy would have sympathized.

War Years on the Home Front

Although the United States was not officially at war until after the attack on Pearl Harbor late in 1941, signs of increasing U.S. involvement in the war were becoming apparent. When Congress approved lend-lease shipments to Britain earlier that year, freight traffic increased dramatically on our Jersey Central Railroad as more materiel made its way toward New York for shipment abroad. And late one night, our home experienced a surprise visit from a West Coast friend of my parents, who had become a pilot aiding the British in unspecified ways. He had suddenly been ordered to New York for passage to Europe the following morning. Banks were closed, and he did not have money to provision himself and travel to the city in time for his transport, so he rang our doorbell, rousing Daddy and Mommy in the wee hours of the morning. They gave him all the cash in the house, emptying our piggy banks for the cause. The two men met again several years later when Bill flew my father on a supply mission from Oran to Casablanca.

Early in 1941, I had entered my teens, thus beginning passage through puberty to the more interesting state of adulthood. My father's ominous prediction of war had wakened me to the wider world soon to encroach upon our tidy little family, and when events followed his premonition in December, he enlisted in the United States Naval Reserve and was sent to Tucson, where the navy had established an indoctrination school at the University of Arizona. Thus, our country went to war and I to high school.

Memories of those years remain a blur of old pursuits and new horizons. With gas rationing in effect, we children walked and rode bikes a great deal. In wintertime, we sledded on nearly deserted roads, and as the seasons revolved, we skated on or swam in nearby lakes and ponds. New in our lives was dancing to our recently formed and outstanding Scotch Plains High School band called The Moonglowers, still, half a century later, going stronger than ever.

At home, our trio of brown-thumbed females installed what was then known as a victory garden from which we gathered a rather pathetic harvest. Radishes were our main crop. Carrots were too stringy to interest anyone but our pet rabbit, and even he scorned all but their leafy tops. Good intentions had predominated over expertise, and we soon abandoned backyard farming. New Jersey was known as the Garden State, and its many fine truck farms supplied produce throughout the New York metropolitan area. As farmers left the land to enter military service or take more lucrative jobs in factories, farms became shorthanded, so a number of us worked after school helping to pick strawberries and the like, often paid in fruit and vegetables rather than wages as a contribution to the war effort.

On one memorable occasion, I was invited to join an impromptu hayride, a rare opportunity in our part of the country. Having romantic notions of the legendary hayrides of yore, I was somewhat taken aback by a peculiar odor I noticed as I clambered aboard. But no one else seemed affected, so I did my best to ignore it. As we settled in, the person next to me suggested I simply lie back in the hay and look up at the sky. Gingerly, I did so and found myself reclining on a dead snake that did much to extinguish any romance of the occasion for me.

Those of us expecting to attend college were becoming more serious about our studies. Mathematics and science were my favorite subjects, and I quickly discovered one of the hidden advantages to those areas of study, for often I was the only girl in the advanced classes. Accordingly, the boys "drafted" me to make the precisely folded airplanes they favored for aerial antics when a teacher's back was turned. I became quite good at this, though I can hardly claim any practical advantage beyond a transitory popularity. In retrospect, I think we gave one particular teacher too hard a time. I think ours was the unruly math class referred to in a northern New Jersey newspaper under a headline "What's Going on Here?" At a prearranged signal, we had all lowered our heads for a "minute of silence" to honor the memory of Flattop, a recently deceased character in the popular *Dick Tracy* comic strip. I heard that our mathematics teacher resigned shortly thereafter.

Occasional field trips provided extracurricular experiences. Especially provocative was a visit to Spanish Harlem led by our Spanish teacher. A spunky young woman, for days ahead of time she prepared us by flirting capriciously with one of my friends, demonstrating colorful Spanish dance steps in which she insisted he partner her. On the appointed day, we traveled to a cigar factory where our teacher was enthusiastically greeted in more Spanish than we could follow, then laughingly whisked off to a back room *con muchos amigos* while we were left to watch unsmiling employees wrapping leaves of tobacco around cigars. *Muy interesante*.

I recall only a few words of wisdom from those school days, but one bit of advice has proved applicable to many of life's transitions beyond the narrow one for which it was intended. It came from Mr. Gutknecht, our wispy-looking but firm science professor, who guided us through biology as sophomores, chemistry as juniors, and physics as seniors. He was an able teacher whose advice was characteristically direct and to the point. Toward the end of senior year, in the middle of a difficult physics lecture that had us groaning, he digressed to remark, "Incidentally, to those of you bound for college next fall, I have one bit of advice. For the first semester, skip the parties until you have your studies under control. Many students do it the other way around and fall behind in their work. Often, they cannot come back from that. Apply yourself pretty exclusively to your studies until your first exams prove they are under control. Then take on the extracurricular, and you'll have no trouble." It worked for me, and it has been helpful, with variations, in many challenging situations since then.

In music class I studied voice with Ms. Swetland. The first stanza of a song she assigned me has stayed with me. As a teenager, I thought the words were rather "dippy." Yet with the years and especially with subsequent changes in mores, their idealism and their applicability have appealed to me more strongly:

> *I would be true, for there are those who trust me;*
> *I would be pure, for there are those who care;*
> *I would be strong, for there is much to suffer;*
> *I would be brave, for there is much to dare.*

There were other verses that have escaped me, but its final line, sung twice, was lofty: *I would look up and laugh and love and live!*

I know few lines more inspiring to an idealistic young girl making her uncertain way through the teens. I wish I knew the song's origin, for I believe there are receptive teenagers today who would appreciate its message.

In 1943, my father was sent overseas. At the time, we knew only that he was working in "communications" somewhere in North Africa. Not until decades later did I discover he was using the newly developed forerunners of what have come to be known as computers, then dubbed Ultra by the British and Magic by the Americans. These machines had been invented to decipher Axis messages encrypted by the now famous Enigma machines used throughout the war by both German and Japanese cryptographers. During the war and for thirty years thereafter, information about these machines was protected under the Official Secrets Act, so I could never learn until after my father's death just what his wartime job had entailed.

In retrospect, I realize my father had an extraordinarily fine problem-solving mind. Whether concocting logical puzzles for my amusement, solving cryptograms and chess problems on his daily commutes into the city, or tackling the electromechanical challenges of Crossbar #5 and World War II decoding machines, he performed impressively. Some years later, when I was taking a fairly new graduate course in modern higher algebra at the University of Chicago, I sent him for his pleasure one of the intriguing problems assigned to us. When next we met, I asked him how it went, and with eyes sparkling, he remarked he had solved it but, in the process, had to invent a new form of algebra; effectively, he "reinvented" the matrix algebra I was then studying!

His stateside letters to me reveal that, while he was still in training, we sometimes composed and sent each other cryptograms (one of mine was difficult enough to keep him awake at night) as well as simple messages in the international Morse code he was learning. When he went overseas, we continued our correspondence (code free) on tissue-thin airmail paper and by single page V-mails. Many of his notes consisted of charming descriptions of the "blessed little donkeys" he encountered in dusty North African villages. Once, a letter came by regular mail, describing his invited visit to a nearby post of the legendary foreign legion. He recounted much of the history of the legion's battles in the world of "reality and romance," remarking that the men he met there did not seem like "the abused lot of people they are often represented to be. They look like fine soldiers, as they are. There are fifty-two nations represented at present. About one percent are Americans. The man at the gate was a Norwegian. The man who showed us through the grounds was a German. The man who showed us through the museum was a Belgian, and he was assisted by a Pole."

Early in 1944, I received a long personal letter setting forth many of a father's views he wished to pass on to a daughter just turned sixteen. I treasure that letter and find it fascinating reading from my current perspective as a septuagenarian.

As the war wore on with still no end in sight, his letters vividly conveyed thoughts about the reactions he was observing in himself and in his compatriots to the existence they shared so far from home. There were the thrills and satisfactions of certain activities he judged important and boredom and loneliness when such actions subsided. One particularly dull period led him to advise that if I ever found myself in such a boring place, I should do my best to keep an interest in the animal kingdom. The Mediterranean donkeys for whom he developed great admiration apparently inspired him to bear each trial with as sweet a temper as he observed in them.

During the war years, Charlotte and I had sole access to Mummy and promptly went to work on her to allow us a dog. She was in a poor position to refuse since at one time in her childhood, there had been no fewer than twenty-three dogs on her family's horse farm. In succession, we acquired Bo'sun, a rather insubordinate beagle, and somewhat later a couple of strays—Val, a lovely young part collie who soon died of distemper, and his successor, Provost, who survived to old age. I always felt Provost had the character of dogs depicted in sketches by the humorist James Thurber. Once while being walked on the dump across the street, he lunged toward a rat, yanking free his leash. Halting abruptly, he seemed to consider the situation for a moment, then carefully picked up the leash with his teeth, and brought it back to the hand where it belonged.

School life for me took an upturn when I successfully auditioned for cheerleading. During my junior and senior years, I helped turn our squad toward more acrobatic routines. Decidedly primitive by modern standards, with only a few cartwheels distinguishing them from the cheers of our opposition, nevertheless, they represented a breakthrough of sorts. An especially proud moment came when Daddy, who had been injured in a truck accident while on duty in Italy, was sent home on leave and attended our Thanksgiving Day game where I cheered my heart out.

Like many American high schools, ours had a school anthem to the tune of Cornell University's anthem. Of its words I have little memory, but I do better with our "cheer" song, sung to the "Fight" tune of Notre Dame:

Cheer, cheer for old Scotch Plains High,
Bring on the whiskey, bring on the rye;
Send a sophomore out for gin,

Don't let a sober senior in;
We only stagger, we never fall,
We sober up on wood alcohol
While our loyal team is marching
Onward to victory.

A heady bit of wartime romance came our way when a number of Australian flyers, on their way to England, were billeted in Fanwood for a few weeks. Wonderful dancing and parties ensued, and still in my memory is a soft night when half a dozen of us walked home singing "Don't Sit under the Apple Tree" after a jolly homemade doughnut party held in a neighbor's home. Somewhere among our souvenirs must reside the jaunty single-winged insignia pins sent later from England.

In our teens, Janice, my closest neighbor and pixieish playmate from childhood, shared two special occasions. On a double date, we were taken to see *Casablanca*, and I was swept away with its romance and intrigue. After countless viewings, it remains my favorite film. For me, it is transporting, a perfect blend of wit, character, and the high romance of adventure.

The second occasion was a truly joyous day three of us couples spent at Surprise Lake in the Watchung Hills, boating and picnicking. During wartime there were no new cars, and gas rationing restricted driving of any kind, so riding down the mountain in the "rumble seat" of my date's two-seater jalopy, into which the six of us crowded in various permutations and combinations throughout that "fun" day, was a rare and treasured treat. I was learning to drive then too, and since my father was away, the boyfriend of one of my best friends taught me how to drive. Moving ahead half a century, my husband and I have helped that couple celebrate their fiftieth wedding anniversary, and through those years some wry laughs have been exchanged over the fact that in our family I have the reputation of being the "fast" driver, and my erstwhile "instructor" has picked up a few speeding tickets. My husband's comment upon learning the latter news was "Suspicions confirmed!"

In August 1944, Mother rented a cottage on Cranberry Lake where a few of our friends joined us for a week at a time. We canoed, swam, slept late, ate much, and talked as only teenage girls can. Some of us shared an adventurous night when a bat got into the sleeping porch, and while squealing heads went under the sheets, Mother, wearing a shower cap over her hair, shooed the intruder out with a broom. One of our intrepid visitors that summer was my classmate Sada Thompson—among many other distinctions, the supplier of our little puppy Bo'sun.

Since grade school, Sada had enthralled me with monologues she performed during school assemblies. When she went into her skits, usually with no props, I quite literally lost track of my surroundings, feeling myself drawn into a world she was creating. She had studied acting very seriously since early childhood and, many decades later, earned the Tony Award for her unforgettable starring role in *Twigs* on Broadway. When that play went on tour, I flew down from San Francisco to catch a matinee in Los Angeles. We had a reunion in her dressing room, where once again, she captivated me with the almost imperceptible changes that came over her as she gradually began slipping into her role for the first act, essentially closing out the world and those of us around her. When I excused myself to go take my seat, she said softly, "All right, darlin'. See you after the show."

Her performance was extraordinary. At the end of act 2, there came a transcendent moment that took my breath away. Sitting next to me was a theatrical agent's wife who was attending every performance. She remarked she had never seen anything like it; it held the same spellbinding magic each time. She further commented that Los Angeles had not seen such a high level of acting for a long time—an appropriate tribute to a great lady of the theater.

During our light dinner between matinee and evening performances, the waitress asked us if we had seen the matinee, and we said yes. She then asked me how I liked it, and I replied with enthusiasm whereupon she asked the same question to Sada, who quietly replied, "I was in it." Since *Twigs* is a one-woman tour de force, the waitress was naturally surprised, for I'm sure at her table we both looked the matrons we then were. So I felt Sada's reaction was a further tribute to her natural and unassuming persona when offstage.

Attending my first play on Broadway with Sada, when we were schoolgirls, had been an eye-opening experience for me. She already knew a great deal about *The Barretts of Wimpole Street*—its author, history, and the careers of its cast. At its closing curtain, I was startled from my middle-class manners by her great booming "bravo" directly beside my ear. And her commentary was most intriguing when she opined that Brian Aherne, in his passionate love scenes with Katharine Cornell, "could certainly teach the boys in our class a thing or two!"

Sada joined us at Cranberry Lake that summer of '44, and Lois Archbold, who was Charlotte's classmate and a superb pianist, was there at the same time. I remember sitting with Sada directly beneath the room where Lois began improvising in the manner of her countryman Frederic Chopin. For once, talk was suspended while we listened to her music "for the duration," as the popular wartime expression had it—another of those special moments with which I feel my life has been blessed.

A singular event occurred early in our stay at the lake that summer, before our Fanwood friends joined us. One day, I accepted an invitation for a hike with five teenagers I barely knew. The three boys were what now would be called inner-city youth from New York City, obviously happy to be out in the spacious and pretty New Jersey lake country. None of us knew the area, but we confidently set off through the woods. Hours and many miles later, we realized we were lost. The afternoon was getting on, and we were beginning to worry a bit when, topping a hill, we emerged from the woods to a beautiful view below us. In a green valley lay a landscape so tranquil everything seemed unreal—meadows with white fences, a well-kept farm with horses, and a tall slender man quietly puttering around one of the fences. As we stood gazing for a very long moment, one of the boys breathed, "Oh wow!" Then we hurried down to ask directions of the farmer before he could disappear. When we reached him, one of the boys deferentially asked if he could tell us where we were. He replied, "Why, you're in Tranquility." We laughed, and someone said, "Well, we know that, but what's the name of this place," to which he replied, "That's it. Tranquility." Looking later on a map, we confirmed it. And a lovelier spot is hard to imagine. Our benefactor recognized our predicament and kindly arranged to have us driven back to Cranberry Lake before dark. We never learned his name.

Decades later, when reading a biography of Franklin D. Roosevelt, I was startled to read that his former mistress and lifelong friend Lucy Mercer Rutheford lived with her husband and family in the farm country thereabouts. Once during the war, FDR arranged in great secrecy to have his private railroad car diverted to Tranquility so that he might pay her a visit between his more pressing and publicized engagements. I can't say I blame him.

As graduation approached, I think we all felt a "sea change." There was nostalgia for what was passing and anticipation of what lay ahead. For many of the young men in our class, military service loomed. On May 8, 1945 the war in Europe ended, but the war in the Pacific continued and with it the draft. Upon graduation, some in our class were inducted into training for that war, winding up instead five years later in Korea. Our father had returned to North Africa briefly and was being reassigned to Miami in June. Mother, Charlotte, and I were scheduled to join him in Jacksonville, so we left Fanwood the day after my graduation to drive south to our rendezvous. Since Mummy was not fond of driving and I, with my new license, was eager to show my stuff, we made good time. One noteworthy incident took place in the Carolinas.

Breakfasting at an inn where we had spent the night, I noticed a comely young woman in military uniform seated alone at a nearby table. She seemed to be patiently waiting for arrival of her breakfast. But when it was finally put before her—delicious-looking bacon, eggs, and grits, with a side order of biscuits and a frosty glass of fresh orange juice—she continued to sit motionless, gazing downward as if she had lost her appetite. A moment later, a cup of coffee arrived, whereupon she picked up a knife and fork and bent toward her meal with zest. What made all this memorable was the way Charlotte and I simultaneously burst out laughing to Mother's complete bewilderment. Without a word spoken between us, we girls had each conjured up the same poignant scenario centered upon a bereaved young woman too sad to eat, and each of us understood instantly what the other had been thinking.

Our planned family reunion in Jacksonville took place on schedule but not without an event that impressively demonstrated Mother's quiet ability to defuse danger. Hearing a knock on the door to our hotel room close to midnight, we girls flung it open to a large drunken stranger who pushed his way into our room. Somehow, Mother, in her ladylike way, managed to talk firmly and soothingly while walking him backward and gently pressing him into the hallway. Our too-eager anticipation had led to a valuable and chastening experience, giving new meaning to the slogan Safety First.

Much of our summer was spent in Miami Beach, where we were billeted at the Flamingo Hotel, a predictably pink pile on Biscayne Bay that had been requisitioned for naval officers and their families. While Daddy toiled in the sultry heat of Miami across the bay, Charlotte and I spent our days on the ocean side of Miami Beach to which we walked a mile or two each way. Our suntans became spectacular, and we had a chance to have a taste of the more privileged side of military life. We took our first airplane ride in an Eastern Airlines DC-3, commercial version of the wartime C-47, and also shared the excitement of a hurricane that roared through the area one night, bending palms toward the ground and leaving fish stranded on grassy lawns. The eye of the storm passed directly over us, and during its lull, we ventured a few feet from our hotel to experience the eerie calm before the winds resumed.

At the beginning of August, Daddy was transferred to Key West, which was even hotter and more exotic. Despite our acquired tans, I suffered the worst case of sunburn of my life after a mere half hour swimming from our hotel dock. The evenings there were like nothing else—soft warm air; tropical skies; and a plethora of military bases offering dining, dancing, movies, and games alfresco. As the war wound down, all military bases opened to officers from all the services, which made for great variety of entertainment. VJ Day coincided with Mother's birthday, and our family opted for quiet reflection alone in the darkness at the end of our dock. With the help of Cutter's newly developed insect repellent, we were able to sustain a short reverie, but the mosquitoes soon penetrated our defenses, forcing an early retreat.

When Daddy mustered out, we started our drive north toward Pennsylvania, where I was to enroll at Swarthmore College on November 1. The opening date of college that year had been delayed to accommodate as many recently discharged veterans as possible, a circumstance that was to alter my life unimaginably. Keeping a leisurely pace northward, we zigzagged a bit to extend this carefree time before life would carry us in our different directions.

For me, a perfect evening toward the end of our wanderings took place at a small inn in Little Switzerland, North Carolina. Somewhat remote in the mountains south of the Blue Ridge, it was just the kind of cozy place one dreams of finding in such a setting. After dinner, we played several fast-and-furious games of four-handed Canfield in the lounge and soon became aware of other guests who were gathering to watch us, much as if we were dancers executing intricate steps on a stage. We poured it on, doing our best to entertain them, and there was much laughter and bonhomie. The next morning saw us firmly on our way once more, toward my college deadline.

Swarthmore College

My first and most enduring impression of Swarthmore is its beauty. The entire campus, including rugged wooded slopes lining Crum Creek, is encompassed in Scott Arboretum. The early buildings were predominantly "collegiate Gothic" in design and built of a locally quarried blue-gray stone with considerable aesthetic appeal. This stone is used in some of the modern buildings, and since my student days, the color of that stone has given the name "Blue Route" to a major highway cut through a vein of rock just beyond Crum Woods.

In 1864, Swarthmore College was founded by Quakers as a coeducational nonsectarian school, and it still adheres to historic Quaker ideals of educational excellence, rigorous intellectual inquiry, tolerance of differing views, and commitment to service. Having been raised as a Quaker, I found the values and atmosphere congenial, and this also appears to hold for almost all of the 1,500 remarkably diverse students in attendance each year.

Despite the well-known Quaker commitment to pacifism during World War II, Swarthmore College came to grips with the horrific fascism then dominant in much of the world by accepting military training groups at the college, while continuing to honor the conscientious objectors (COs) who chose nonmilitary wartime service. Consequently, 1945 saw naval cadets still on campus, along with many returned military veterans and a number of COs whose lives also had been on the line—one as a volunteer in the violent ward of a mental hospital, another as a front line forest firefighter. Thus, postwar Swarthmore invited great variety among its students and studies, while remaining united in its striving for excellence and commitment to service.

These values persist to this day. In the wake of what a Muslim professor of engineering at Swarthmore College has called "this monstrous act" of September 11, 2001, there has ensued on campus a solemn reflection and debate of the imperatives facing us in today's world. In some respects these are similar to the moral and practical dilemmas encountered during World War II. At times like these, I feel the Quaker heritage of Swarthmore College shines like a beacon for the future.

In what may appear quaint and restrictive to today's freer-wheeling students, we lived in single-gender dormitories with what seemed to me a reasonable weeknight curfew of ten fifteen for women. Rather than chafing at these restraints, I welcomed their simplification of my life. There were also widely understood rules of conduct, such as prohibition in the dorms of loud music or other noisy activities after 11:00 PM. If one wished to work late or socialize in the numerous late night bull sessions or bridge games, we girls could do so in the Commons, a large social room in our building that was used coeducationally during the day and on weekends for dancing and card games or ping-pong.

Fast-forwarding to the 1970s, I recall a night when our older son, a freshman at Stanford, was suffering from loud music booming unrestricted throughout his dormitory. He called to see if we could drive down and give him a few hours of relief. Upon arriving, we discovered a mammoth party nearly suffocating that sprawling campus with noise—fun maybe, if one is in the mood, but offering no options for those wishing to escape. I believe many students today would enjoy a more civilized environment on their campuses. I feel sure, too, that many would benefit both physically and spiritually from greater restraints upon noise.

One never knows what experiences may become useful. Having studied library science in high school, I was able to augment my small scholarship with work in the mathematics library. Nothing could have suited me better. The library was on the fourth and highest floor of Parrish Hall, the original college building which housed many of us girls in its dormitory wings. Additionally, it held lounges, the dining hall and administrative offices. Since the math library was atop the structure, it offered a beautiful view and was pleasantly quiet. Few people ventured up there, making it an ideal place to study while earning my dollar for each three hours "worked." My dorm room and the Commons were two floors down, with the dining hall only another flight below that—a most compact and convenient live/work situation.

For two months, I reveled in the stimulation of my new studies and friends. I had the good fortune early on to meet Elizabeth Urey through our shared math and science courses. She was the daughter of Harold C. Urey, Nobel Laureate in chemistry, and thus added a certain worldly luster to our science program. She and I often studied together in the basement of old Trotter Hall, home of our physics courses. On one memorable evening, we gave up on homework in favor of listening to the glorious voices above us rehearsing for a student production of John Gay's *The Beggar's Opera*.

Elizabeth's tales of the Manhattan Project fired me with enthusiasm for the level of science required for such a triumph. She had worked in her father's lab during the epochal summer of 1945, culminating in the August bomb blasts that ended World War II and changed our world. Many years later, this collegiate interest, largely generated by my friendship with Elizabeth and later her family, led me to one of the best books I have ever read: *The Making of the Atomic Bomb* by Richard Rhodes. It describes many of the processes and personalities engaged in one of the greatest scientific achievements of our time, and I felt privileged to have a personal connection, however tenuous, to those people and events.

All this formed the nucleus of my world until I returned home for the Christmas holidays. I felt independent and was unaware of having missed home or family for one minute of my new experience. Yet when I returned to college after vacation, facing my first final exams only a month away, I felt acutely the pressure from the unaccustomed intensity of study and found myself suddenly overwhelmed with homesickness. Charlotte wrote frequent notes, trying loyally but ineffectually to raise my spirits. For the first time in my life, I feared failure. When exams finally materialized and I could *do* something, my spirits improved. And that excellent advice received in my high-school physics class paid off handsomely the day I was stopped in the hall by my jubilant math professor, who congratulated me on the only perfect final exam in his class!

From then on all homesickness vanished, and I remember thinking two things: homesickness is an illness to which I have now acquired a lifetime immunity, and I will never again underestimate the pain to its sufferer. When I later took a summer job as swimming and canoeing instructor at a young girls' camp in Maine, one of my little campers was excruciatingly homesick, and I was able to help her greatly, simply by telling her I had gone through that experience as a "big" person and come out of it. She asked questions whose answers apparently satisfied her, and she became a changed girl for the rest of the summer. Simple reassurance can work wonders, especially when backed by personal understanding.

With finals behind me, I was dating and thoroughly enjoying parties and dances in the Philadelphia area. Then on February 16, Ken Brown, a veteran of the air war in Europe whose stylish dancing in the Commons had already attracted my attention and whom I had found myself running into frequently on campus, invited me to dinner in Philly. Everything seemed to synchronize between us before we even boarded our train. The feeling was warm and exciting, and even silences were entirely comfortable. During dinner, Ken talked interminably about reading a book on the fecundity of Russian women and the longevity of inhabitants of the Caucasus or the other way around. The facts didn't really matter to me; it was all so ridiculous for a first date and yet so dazzling.

Well before breakfast the next morning, I took a long walk in Crum Woods. When I returned, I learned Ken had called to suggest we meet for breakfast. As he explained later, he had not wanted that evening to end.

Both of us had recognized immediately that this was something different and very special. I was already impressed with his acute power of observation and his curiosity and interest about what he observed. These traits proved crucial to his career and have made him interesting company through more than fifty-eight incredibly rewarding years.

On one beautiful spring morning early in our romance, we climbed to the top of Clothier Tower where we could look out over the campus and the village of Swarthmore beyond. We were enjoying the views until Ken's expression suddenly changed to one of discomfort as we turned from the campus toward the town. When I asked about his distress, he said that particular view reminded him of the only time his crew had been ordered to descend from their bombing altitude to strafe the streets of a village. The town of Swarthmore, with its quaint buildings viewed from our high vantage point, resembled the German village and reminded him of that especially disturbing mission.

Though there was a joke on campus about "rehabilitating" the veterans, of course, this was no laughing matter. Some returned with horrible memories to incorporate into their ongoing lives. Ken was one of the more fortunate ones. We were young and alive, and we bantered about rehabilitation. Ken's war had been fought as a bombardier and lead navigator in B-26 medium bombers, the Martin Marauders which he greatly admires and that took so much heavy flak over Germany. Ken still retains an extreme startle reaction to sudden loud noises, diminished only slightly through all the decades I have known him.

From our first date onward, we met for almost all our meals. We also studied together and played together and were as inseparable as our schedules (and college rules) allowed. In fact, I quickly became so spoiled by the "perks" of this arrangement that after Ken graduated in 1947 and moved on to The University of Chicago for graduate work, Elizabeth, who had become my roommate, reacted to my query about how much a proposed movie in town might set me back by remarking, "Maybe we'd better ask Ken to send you an allowance!"

Once I had cleared away the required courses in social science disciplines in which I had little interest or confidence, my academic experience became everything I desired. All my courses were stimulating and well taught. In my sophomore year, I enrolled in astronomy and became hooked on the night sky. Junior year found me working and studying whenever possible at Sproul Observatory, which possessed one of the two largest refractor telescopes in the United States, after the great ones at Yerkes and Lick Observatories. Sproul's near twin was located at the University of Virginia where Emma Williams Vyssotsky, my distant cousin, and her Russian husband had both worked as astronomers for decades and which I remembered visiting as a child.

Of course our work in astronomy was low level, consisting mostly of measuring plates for Professor Peter van de Kamp. He was already beginning to excite interest internationally, with the possibility that one of the "double star" systems he was studying included large planets instead of invisible companion stars causing the observed perturbations in the star's motion. Though boring in one sense, our work was exciting in another—definitely "far out" to me. I loved the isolation of that seminar room. Usually, only one or two students shared it at a time, and among us developed a satisfying camaraderie which was limited to that quiet venue. In retrospect, I believe two of our "enlightened" society's greatest losses during the half century since then are silence and darkness. Indeed, excessive light and noise often overwhelm the quiet, mystical beauty of a night sky.

Astronomy and chemistry became my minors, with mathematics remaining my major. I was fortunate to have as advisor the chairman of the math department, Professor Arnold Dresden. A fine pianist, he once surprised me by sitting next to me at a piano recital by Rudolph Serkin. Dresden's comments between pieces were worth as much to me as the concert. Before graduation, he gave me two of the best bits of advice I have ever received, and they too became useful beyond the classroom. Expecting me to become a teacher, he told me, "Always stay ahead of your students, and never be afraid to say you don't know." How applicable to parenthood as well!

Like most colleges, Swarthmore had an athletic requirement. Having enjoyed my Western riding in a saddle that kept me more or less firmly in place, I elected horseback riding my freshman year. Apparently my mind was insufficiently focused on what I was doing, however, and the English saddle did nothing to contain me. Whatever the reason, my three falls—the first a throw over my horse's head, the second a gentle sideslip into a small stream, and finally watching the tail of my erstwhile mount recede as I slid to the ground behind him—soon led me to seek other sports more compatible with an unbruised body. I loved to swim and had never tried shooting a bow and arrow, so swimming and archery became promising alternatives. And I discovered an interesting thing. It is possible to achieve noteworthy successes that never make the record books. My sole triumph in archery was the fact that, because of my long arms, I was the only girl in Swarthmore's history who could not only draw and fire the longest bow and arrows in their collection, but also apparently did so with distinction at the correspondingly longer distances. On the instant I achieved varsity status which amounted to nothing competitively because I came down with measles before my only scheduled meet.

In swimming, I was put on the junior varsity team. My big triumph came on an occasion when transportation difficulties prevented our varsity from arriving on time for the competition, and we on the JV substituted in the varsity race. Our opposition was formidable, including a girl who the following year would set an NCAA record while winning the national championship in breaststroke. In those days we had no standardized height for starting blocks in our collegiate pools. Sometimes we dove from the lip of the pool and sometimes from a foot or more above it. In this particular case, the blocks must have soared a good foot and a half, and the race was only one length of the pool. I took off in my splendid racing dive and won with ease. Our coach was ecstatic. She greeted me as I came up for air, crying, "You covered half the pool on your dive!" Clearly, she foresaw great things for me, subsequently crooning in training sessions, "If only you could make your arms move faster" or "Kick!" But I knew better. I loved to swim but at my own speed. If we had ever met again, that future champion would surely have swirled past me on the first turn, as most of my junior varsity opponents already did. Still, it was nice to know I had once outdived her.

My voice teacher in high school had been disappointed when I went out for cheerleading, predicting it would "ruin my vocal chords." So when I auditioned for the Swarthmore chorus, I felt relieved and somewhat vindicated to be accepted. We sang the Messiah at Christmastime, an event I thoroughly enjoyed. But best of all by far was one extraordinary evening when we joined choruses from the men's Quaker college, Haverford, and the women's counterpart at Bryn Mawr, to practice together in Philadelphia under the direction of the famed choral director, Robert Shaw. Clearly a perfectionist, he was confronting imperfection.

Here we were, amateurs and not necessarily musical; yet the music he drew from us was thrilling. He drilled us firmly on small, difficult phrasings. Gradually he increased the pace of his demands. And he knew the value of laughter as a relaxant. After having us repeat one tiny phrase over and over at such a fast tempo that we lost all coordination and became frustrated, he applied the one further push that sent us over the brink into a complete cacaphony, dissolving into laughter. Next time it came out right.

Peter van de Kamp provided a special excursion to New York City to visit a facility of International Business Machines Corporation, where a small, highly energetic, and saturnine man showed us the remarkable new machines soon to take over much of our lives. Among them I saw card sorting machines of a type I would use a few years later while working on projects for the Aero-Medical Laboratory at Wright-Patterson Air Force Base near Yellow Springs, Ohio. After our rather awesome introductory visit to the computerized future, we repaired to a small spot below ground level where musicians played excellent jazz, another of Peter vdK's enthusiasms.

Small threads sometimes weave unexpectedly large patterns. As Ken's birthday approached, less than two months after our first date, I had wished to give him a small present. Ever mindful of my resources, I found in the college bookstore a slim volume of Edward Fitzgerald's *The Rubaiyat of Omar Khayyam*. Little could I have guessed the role that book would play in our life together. From the start it became one of his favorites, and he memorized many of its quatrains. His obvious admiration for this poetry has attracted gift copies from our children, now forming a respectable small collection in our home. Conceivably, its verses may also have inclined our sons toward the Middle East, but in the spring of 1946, such unforeseeable possibilities—not to mention grown sons—lay decades in our future.

* * *

Ken was two years ahead of me in college and graduated from Swarthmore in 1947. That summer, he worked at a laboratory in Massachusetts from which he could drive each weekend to Maine where I counseled at Camp Wawenock-Owaissa on Lake Sebago. He had bought a prewar Pontiac convertible with enough idiosyncrasies to dub it "Percy" which, he said, "is short for 'personality' because it has so much of it." I saved my time off for his visits, and we covered much of that lovely countryside in Percy. My only weekday excursion away from camp took me to Mount Moosilauke in New Hampshire where I led eleven of our young campers on a strenuous day's hike over the mountain while the other two counselors took a few hours off. The gains were not just physical. We spent that night at one of the fine Dartmouth Outing Club camps, where in addition to swims in their frigidly cold pool, we were given dinner, enjoyable companionship and the finest display of aurora borealis I have ever seen. Covering one half of the sky, pastel lights pulsated upward toward the zenith for hours, reminiscent of and vastly superior to the light displays in movie palaces of that era. There in the clear mountain air on a rustic wooden porch, we enjoyed front row, center seats for one of nature's most awesome extravaganzas.

Toward the end of summer, Camp Wawenock invited the boys' camp across the lake to join us for a picnic dinner, followed by an evening water ballet patterned on aquacades by Billy Rose. I was chosen to choreograph, practice, and lead our show. The participating campers performed beautifully. In fact, the only glitch, fortunately a small one, was mine. Near the end of our routine, which included synchronized swimming in various strokes interspersed with forward and backward surface dives and various popular patterns incorporating raised legs, we wound up floating on our backs in a star formation from which we were to dissolve into our final moves upon a signal from me. But by then the evening was growing quite dark, and I had become so beguiled watching the beautiful stellar show emerging above us that I let several bars of music slip past before suddenly realizing, "My goodness, they're all waiting for me!" I brought us in on the next available beat, and we finished without further incident.

For me, that summer marked the beginning of a period of restless sleep. My dreams in childhood had been pretty bland stuff, aside from one in early adolescence featuring a large cobra-type snake that reared up beside me and awakened me by roaring in my right ear. (I feel sure Freud would have had plenty to say about *that*). For the most part, I slept relatively undisturbed until the night a mischievous junior counselor decided to wake me from deep sleep "just to see what would happen." I am sure she meant no harm, but I was not amused and told her not to do that again. Still, for months after that capricious awakening, I found it impossible to lapse into my customary deep sleep. I can only imagine the lingering effects upon soldiers whose sleep has been broken nightly by shell bombardments or ominous small sounds in the darkness of a jungle.

At the end of summer, Ken left for graduate school in Chicago and I returned to Swarthmore. Some weeks into the semester, I awoke from the most beautiful dream of my life—so beautiful I wished I could remain in it. I was aboard a ship steaming into a placid harbor in what I knew to be a fjord in Norway, while in the background I heard strains of Edvard Grieg's "To Spring." It was sensational—the only time I have ever dreamt in sound.

Twenty years later, I was to relive its sense of clarity and peaceful beauty in a mystical experience aboard the Alaskan ferry, *Taku,* steaming up the Lynn Canal to Haines. At three in the morning, I had gone out on deck to watch our docking at Juneau, intending to go back to sleep as soon as I had seen Mendenhall Glacier. I shall be forever indebted to a crewman who told me, "If you can stay awake for another three quarters of an hour, you'll see not only Mendenhall but a sight you'll never forget." How right he was. The full moon illumined the glacier as our ferry exited Auke Bay, and as we turned north and began gliding up the placid Lynn Canal through that freezing cold northern air, the dawn alpenglow began creeping downward over the glacier-strewn, snow-capped mountains lining the waterway. All was indescribably beautiful: a feast for the senses. I remember giving silent thanks to God for the inestimable gift of sight, and I realized too that the experience could not have been so vividly sensuous without the bitter cold cutting through my inadequate layers of clothing. I remained on deck until five hours later we docked at Haines in full morning sunlight.

During my third and final year at Swarthmore, I had two roommates, Elizabeth Urey and Zlata Demerec, daughter of a prominent biologist at Cold Spring Harbor on Long Island. We shared a triple room in north wing of which I was elected president. One of my duties was leading the students on all floors of the wing to safety during fire drills. Half asleep one midnight, I distinguished myself by confusing the alarm code and guiding us all into the heart of the fictitious blaze. I like to think that in a real fire my attention would have been drawn to smoke and flames. But all I know for sure is that I had regained my habit of sleeping soundly. A few weeks later, I had the distinction of losing both roommates to the White House in Washington where they were dining with their fathers and the president of the United States, while I was downing chow in the cafeteria at "ol' Swarthmore."

Ken returned to campus just before Christmas, and we became engaged the evening he arrived. The previous summer had convinced us to accelerate our plans for marriage. Though my family had wanted me to finish college first, they accepted our decision graciously. By then, too, I felt inclined to leave my sheltered college environment for a large university in my senior year. Both Swarthmore College and The University of Chicago agreed to give me undergraduate degrees if I met their differing requirements, so during spring vacation I took a train to Chicago for a week's visit, staying with the Ureys and making preparations to transfer in the fall.

Toward the end of my junior year, I came down with a fierce case of measles and was moved into isolation in the Swarthmore infirmary with just a few weeks to go before exams. Sneaking a quick look at the thermometer a nurse had just put into my mouth seconds before, I was shocked to see it already registered almost 105 degrees. I began hallucinating and remember gazing sorrowfully at my engagement ring, imagining the stone was dwindling in size and "reasoning" that this must be due to my acidic sweat eating away the diamond! Evidently, my knowledge of chemistry could not withstand a high fever.

As I began to recover, I did a most foolish thing for which I paid in the long run. Pleading worry over exams, I persuaded the doctor to give me a "tonic" and let me go back to my room where I could study. This he did, and the night after taking the medication, I awoke trembling uncontrollably and sweating profusely. After what seemed hours, I finally managed to control the trembling by actively forcing my body to quiver fast, and then, ever so gradually, slowing the pace of that voluntary trembling until I could sleep. When I awoke and collected myself, I found I had sweated away five pounds in the night. The medicine turned out to contain a small amount of strychnine, so I threw it away immediately. All in all, it was a terrifying experience from which I was to suffer a few scary but lesser recurrences before it quit entirely. In retrospect, this was probably the first indication of my general sensitivity to drugs.

My years at Swarthmore were among the happiest and most influential years of my life. From the time we met, my feelings for Ken greatly enhanced my affection for the school. The periods of separation from each other had strongly underscored our desire to be together as lastingly as possible, wherever that might take us. So after completing my junior year, I left Swarthmore to marry Ken and become part of a wider world.

On the eve of my marriage, Daddy gave me a rather unusual counsel for a bride, but he felt it might someday become important to me. He had already acquainted me with Kipling's wise and inspiring poem "If," which had become a mainstay in my life. He now suggested there would likely be periods, perhaps lasting for years, when I would question how I could endure. At the time of his telling, I could hardly envision such a circumstance, but I paid attention. He told me he viewed life as an attempt to make one's way across a swiftly flowing river toward a goal on the opposite shore. The current carries you downstream, but the important thing is not to fight it. Go with it. Time to make your way back upstream toward your goal when high and dry again upon the far shore.

A Bride in Chicago

On June 30, 1948, Ken and I were married in the Plainfield Friends Meeting House. The ceremony began with a period of silence. Then we rose, joined hands, and spoke directly to each other, repeating traditional Quaker vows. My version stated, "In the presence of God and these our friends, I take thee, Kenneth, to be my husband, promising with divine assistance to be unto thee a loving and faithful wife as long as we both shall live." After Ken gave his reciprocal vow, we sat once again in silence. One person from the congregation delivered what I presume was an inspirational message, although I was too preoccupied with my own thoughts to remember a word of it. There followed another period of silence, after which we shook hands and kissed, thus closing the ceremony. We both signed a document to legalize our marriage in the eyes of the state, and I am amused and somewhat chagrined to see the contrast between Ken's good, strong signature and my emotionally shaky one. The reception was held in my family home in Fanwood after which we left for a wonderful summer honeymoon traveling the West.

Until then, Ken's West had been Texas, a state he understandably felt he had seen enough of during his wartime training. Thus, we began our trip on a northern route. With sleeping bags and a tarpaulin, we often slept overnight in the uncrowded campgrounds of our national parks. Rain that year was virtually nonexistent, and there were very few mosquitoes. Along our route to Yellowstone and the Grand Tetons, we passed through the Black Hills and

Badlands of South Dakota and then Wyoming's Big Horn Mountains.

What a drive across the Big Horns! The road was poor but passable, and it was ours for the day. Upon reaching the top of its climb, we found mountain meadows stretching in a huge plateau for miles on every side, with an occasional peak decorating the skyline. We visited an ancient Indian medicine wheel delineated by white rocks, but that was merely a side-show. Mainly we drove in silence through the quiet beauty of those high meadowlands. Approaching their western limit, just before a precipitous descent to the plains, we came upon a friendly Basque shepherd tending his flock. He invited us to his living quarters in a sheepherder's wagon and encouraged us to watch as he and his dogs herded the sheep. We spent much of the afternoon there, reluctant for the visit to end. Two decades later, with considerable trepidation, we repeated that drive and were happy to find the area much the same in its beauty and solitude. As we reached the spot where we had enjoyed such a peaceful afternoon, we again saw a sheepherder; however this time he seemed edgy and uncomfortable, retreating into his trailer and audibly locking the door. The times, they were a-changing.

As we proceeded through the Sierras we had our first look at Yosemite National Park and the giant sequoia trees, areas of enduring beauty and fascination, though ever more crowded with admirers like us. Upon reaching the Bay Area, we paused for an afternoon to visit David Krech, one of our former Swarthmore professors, at his home in the Berkeley Hills, above the University of California, where he then worked. We were not especially attracted to Berkeley as a place to live or work, but he and his wife gave us much appreciation for the Bay Area. From their garden, we had our first view of the white city of San Francisco perched upon its gracefully proportioned hills, garlanded with bridges and headlands. We fell in love with it immediately, but, of course, never guessed that ten years later it would become the home of our dreams. We spent the evening exploring Telegraph

Hill on foot and dining there at the Shadows, already a landmark and the Krechs' favorite restaurant.

A few days' drive south along the coast—much of it on Route 1—took us to my aunt Mildred's fruit ranch in Valley Center, not far from Escondido in San Diego County. Her style of living in that scenic desert land, studded with rocks and huge live oak trees, was agreeably casual. Rattlesnakes and coyotes also lived on her property, and she had once observed a mountain lion crossing below her patio in the moonlight, appearing for all the world as though he considered it *his* place, not hers. Never one for regular meals, my vegetarian aunt introduced Ken to the indifferent nature of meal preparation in my family. We often made dinner from an artichoke or the delicious avocados so plentiful in that region. Sometimes during afternoons when she was not teaching adult art classes, she and I sat outside listening on the radio to the Los Angeles classical music station, while she painted the portrait of me now hanging beside Ken's desk, and he painted the bedroom she had added to her cottage to accommodate us.

On days when Mildred attended to professional duties, Ken and I explored on our own. She lived along the road called "Highway to the Stars" which led upward to the great two-hundred-inch reflecting telescope atop Mount Palomar, where we visited early in our stay. We spent many lovely days on beaches north of San Diego and a few times crossed the border into teeming Tijuana. Once we drove south to Rio Rita where, on a deserted beach, we swam in intimidatingly cold water and rode along the beach on two beautiful Mexican horses, similar to those we had seen on the dismally poor properties we had passed on our drive from Tijuana.

When we left Valley Center, Mildred loaded us with local avocados and fruits from her orchard, thus sustaining us and a number of deer at the Grand Canyon who seemed to appreciate overripe peaches. Continuing east through Arizona, we received an unexpected job offer at the Meteor Crater. A lonely concessionaire manned what was then a tiny tourist facility, and he offered us his job for the balance of the summer. He was serious, and we felt somewhat complimented but not tempted, for by then we were eager to reach Chicago and get on with our studies. So we pressed on, camping only briefly at the Petrified Forest, which proved so petrified that we could barely scrape a place smooth enough for sleeping. I awoke frequently and lay on the stony ground gazing at that clear, star-studded sky following us eastward toward our hazier urban destination.

Relocating from the ivory tower of Swarthmore to the heart of Chicago was quite a stretch for me, but it was also invigorating to feel part of a great city as well as part of our team of two embarked upon adult enterprises. Because of The University of Chicago's unconventional two-year college program that led directly into its graduate divisions, my courses for a four year bachelor's degree at UC were necessarily taken at the graduate level among graduate students. All this was stimulating to me but less so for Ken who was starting his second year already fed up with the city and its living conditions. Years later, he summarized the situation in these words: "The honeymoon stopped at the city line."

From the beginning, I enjoyed being Mrs. Kenneth Brown, taking every reasonable opportunity to use my new moniker. As I went about arranging my academic course schedule, I discovered that in order to continue my minor in astronomy, I would have to move to Yerkes Observatory, a day's drive north in Wisconsin—not exactly a young bride's wish. Instead, I beefed up my chemistry minor with added courses in organic and biochemistry. And my math went into what was then known as modern higher algebra whose concepts are now taken for granted at the high-school level.

Veterans' housing had an impossibly long waiting list. Even though the remarkable GI Bill of Rights made higher education affordable for so many of us, housing costs stretched the budget. We first rented a bedroom in the apartment of a Mrs. Dennison, an elderly lady with heart trouble who lived in a fairly decent neighborhood two miles south of the university. Far from ideal, it served well enough for a few months and gave us some glorious memories. We could lie abed and hear (but not see) the wild geese flying south. How we sometimes longed to join them! And there, I heard for the first time the choral movement of Beethoven's Ninth Symphony, wafted in on the sunshine through our little window in that grim and grimy city. Although we had attended concerts in Philadelphia, most music for us in Chicago came through the radio—somebody's radio—which even then offered more choices of classical stations than we have today in San Francisco.

One memorable morning, I was slow in waking. To encourage me, Ken began playfully pulling me from bed. Thanks to the backyard set of trapeze and rings in childhood, I had become fairly acrobatic, and that morning, we wove a smooth almost-choreographic sequence in which Ken twined me around and overhead and eventually upside down. As I glided to within an inch of the floor, he assumed I was already there and released me. *Thunk!* A great way to get a head start on the day!

To augment our reserves, we took part-time jobs, Ken pumping gas and I packing candy and serving ice cream around the corner on Cottage Grove Avenue. I still remember the thrill of my first tips. Ken was working toward advanced degrees and a career while I was working only toward my college degree. So I had more free time and sometimes used it at the university swimming pool during warm weather. To my romantically attuned mind, hearing a student's baritone rendition of "M'appari" coming through the walls from the men's side of the locker room seemed emblematic of this glamorous new life I was leading in the big city.

When cold weather set in, I shifted to ice skating at the rink beneath the old football stadium stands, made famous by the world's first sustained atomic fission reaction performed there in 1942 in the laboratory of Enrico Fermi. A plaque commemorates that historic event, and I never passed it without a sense of awe at their achievement.

My skating as a child had been on ponds or lakes where frozen, windblown ripples undermined my stability. The smooth surface at UC was a joy, and despite wobbly ankles, I went often to skate by myself. One especially cold day, I put on my thickest socks and came home with a bad case of frostbite. Only then did I learn that multiple thin layers of clothing are superior to one thick one, especially when too much thickness can cut circulation as happened to me. From then on, I kept toasty and warm while spending many happy hours learning to stay upright.

Upon entering the rink, each skater signed a check-in sheet. One day, I scanned the few names above mine and saw a scrawled "E. Fermi." I thought there must be some mistake, but when I entered the rink, there he was, alone as most of us were. That day, another skater asked me to dance, and with the clear understanding that he would be holding us up, we proceeded to the best skate of my life. All of us were giving a wide berth to the imposing intellect standing near the center of the rink. As we practiced and I became more proficient and confident, we swept by him once quite swiftly. He looked straight at me and said admiringly, "You skate *very* well," surely, one of the most unexpected and most treasured compliments I have ever received. Although the previous spring I had attended a party at the Fermis' house, sparkling with some of the most brilliant people I have ever met, my only "meeting" with the great man himself occurred while skating past him that day on the ice.

Christmas Eve brought a crisis. In the apartment above us dwelt a big red-haired Irishman with his wife and several children. I saw him only a few times arriving or leaving the apartment house, and he seemed rather quiet and withdrawn, but nice. On Christmas Eve, however, we were awakened about 2:00 AM by furious noises from above—yelling, thumping, and children running around. We tried a few taps on the ceiling, but they could hardly be heard above the racket. Finally, Ken put on a robe and climbed the stairs to their apartment, knocking on their door as I watched from below. The stairs wound around a narrow stairwell and were two stories high at the landing where Ken stood.

Suddenly, the door was flung open and the doorway filled with a large man whose terrified wife pulled and pleaded behind him, their frightened children crying loudly. The man was clearly in a rage and began berating Ken who instantly became the proverbial "soft pillow." Putting his hands in the pockets of his bathrobe, he leaned back against the hallway wall and let the guy rant and rave. When the tirade had run its course, this man with the strength of a giant reached out and, straight-armed, picked Ken up by the shoulders, turned him around to face down the stairs, and said, "Now, you can go."

Fully expecting a kick in the back, Ken walked down slowly but very deliberately, braced for a kick that never came. As soon as he was safely in our apartment, we bolted the door. Of course Mrs. Dennison had been wakened by the commotion, and I was doing my best to calm and comfort her. But when I headed for the telephone, she begged us not to call the police because "it would spoil the children's Christmas."

Soon the raving broke out again and came out onto the stairs, the wife quite beside herself as her husband came down and tried to kick in our door. Ken realized the man wanted to beat someone to a pulp and was probably regretting he hadn't attacked while he had the chance. So he was challenging Ken to come out and fight. Suddenly, all became quiet, and we realized he might try the kitchen door, which opened onto a shared fire escape and was seldom locked. We made a dash for it, arriving just before he pounded down the back steps and assaulted that entryway, by then securely bolted. This pounding on one door or the other went on for about an hour, by which time he apparently ran out of steam. Presumably, the children's Christmas was saved.

Mrs. Dennison explained to us that, when sober, her neighbor was a model husband and father, but two or three times a year he got drunk and went berserk, throwing the hapless wife and kiddies around their apartment. We decided not to accumulate definitive statistics on this matter, and on Christmas Day began pounding pavements until we found a little tenement property that looked mighty good under the circumstances. Though shabby, it seemed peaceful and had an added advantage of being within walking distance of the university.

Although we were moving into what was generally considered a slum, we found it a welcome change. I had a number of laboratories that spring, so it was nice to be close to campus. I discovered, however, that crossing the Midway alone was not always a healthy enterprise as I had been warned by a friend whose husband would not allow her to walk there by herself, day or night.

I must have shared some of the defiant independence of my feminist Aunt Mildred, because one lovely spring morning I learned how dangerous the Midway could be, even in broad daylight, when I went there by myself to study. I had kicked off my shoes and was sitting at the base of one of the grassy slopes bordering each block-long rectangle of lawn when I heard a whoosh above and behind me. Without turning, I leapt to my feet and to one side as a man swooped onto the spot where I had been sitting. Red-faced, he leered up at me, refusing my angry request to toss me my shoes. That was enough independence for me. I walked home barefoot through the dirty streets, considering myself very lucky to have learned a valuable lesson so lightly. From then on, without fail, I accepted rides home from one or another of my partners in night labs.

Our new location offered many more opportunities for relaxation and entertainment, all within easy walking distance. We had the Mayfair Hotel where, for $1, we could eat from immaculate white linen in refined surroundings, a world away from the customary oatmeal breakfasts or fordhook lima-bean suppers taken in our room nearby. One morning I had the thrill of seeing my admired Don Cossacks milling about the lobby of this quiet old hotel which I viewed as a true "grace note" in the depressed neighborhood in which we lived. To think that the wide world of culture, as represented by idols of my childhood, could occasionally be found there on the south side of Chicago! Also, only a block away were the Dorchester Cafe, offering cheap full dinners at their quiet wooden booths, and a Hobby House, open at all hours, supplying the midnight cup of coffee and slice of pie to night owls.

We lived in a cramped room with a bay window overlooking an alley. There was a Murphy bed that folded down from the wall at night, then had to be refolded to its upright position before we could raise the leaf of our drop leaf table for our meals. The hall bathroom was shared with seven other tenants we never knew beyond the nodding acquaintance born of necessity. A cockroach-infested washbasin and gas burner occupied a tiny alcove beside the bed, and there we kept the eating and cooking utensils furnished by the landlady. Star attraction of that stuffy little room was the two sides of the bay window where we had an easy chair that allowed us to relax and catch any breeze managing to make its way down the alley on a sweltering summer's day. And, of course, it provided our only ventilation for sleeping. One of my self-imposed tasks each night was washing every visible roach down the sink just before going to bed. I knew full well, as Ken often reminded me, that the cockroaches would be all over the place again as soon as I hit my pillow, but at least then, I wouldn't see them.

Residing directly across the alley from our window was a beautiful white Persian cat. We never saw her owner, but she attracted many feline swains, principally one battle-scarred veteran of numerous fights who literally could not be touched—the quintessential alley cat—with ears chewed down flush with his skull. He was seldom seen during the day, being mainly a denizen of the dark during which he presided as the self-appointed and undisputed king of that alley. And part of his "turf" apparently included the Persian pussycat whose many alluring periods made our nights miserable. From several blocks away, we could hear his caterwauling approaching slowly, then passing beneath us and on down the alley to our right—but not for long. After a while, he always turned around and slowly made his way back, serenading all the way but always stopped about forty feet away. This was probably because the main street was close to our left, and he wanted to stay in a dark part of the alley. In any event, he always sat down there and proceeded with his incredible cat sounds that could only have been attractive to another cat of the female sex. Our landlady gave us permission to throw the china at him because it was dirt cheap, and she too hated being kept awake. But this had absolutely no effect, and neither did buckets of water slung in his direction. Ken's best efforts were in sailing small saucers, but he couldn't throw them far enough while keeping sufficient control to avoid putting out a window on one side or the other of the narrow alley.

However, our chance finally came. Late one night, the cat watched disdainfully as saucers fell a few feet short of him. Then, as if to prove once and for all whose territory this was, he got up and started walking beneath our window with a proud stiff-legged gait. Ken quickly unscrewed the light bulb from our nearby floor lamp and hurled it down at the fearless old tom. By great good luck, it struck the paving just behind his tail and shattered with a loud pop, which also shattered his composure. Taking off as if jet-propelled, he dashed headlong into the street, then stopped suddenly and looked back toward our window, emitting the loudest and most unmistakably outraged *meeeooooww* that either of us has ever heard. While confidently demonstrating supremacy over his domain, he had blown his cool completely and was letting anyone within earshot know that he did *not* like it.

That triumph did not end the periodic yowlings, but soon afterward, we returned home one evening after midnight. As we entered the outer vestibule of our building, the Persian femme fatale followed me in, rubbing against my leg. Bending down and starting to pat her, I glanced up at Ken. Simultaneously, we murmured, "Hmm!" Without another word, I scooped her into my arms, and Ken held the outside door open for us to go back to our car. Deciding that she deserved a better neighborhood, we drove out of our slum and, for the better part of an hour, cruised upscale communities, finally settling upon a comfortably familial-looking block of houses where we released her. Through all this, she seemed perfectly content even when she was released. Perhaps she was ready for a change. In any case, we like to think she won a good family, and we were never again bothered by the crooning from No Ears. Whenever we told friends about this episode, they invariably asked, "But what about the children? They must have missed her." I can't remember ever seeing a child in that area of housing, which may have been just as well. To me, one of the strange aspects of our immediate region was that, aside from Sixty-third Street, even the streets themselves seemed almost devoid of life, a far cry from neighborhoods in New York City.

Soon our social life improved to the tune of one dental student and his wife living in our building, with whom we sometimes escaped together for evenings in the neighborhood. Since our landlady had made clear she wanted *no* fraternization among her tenants, we worked out elaborate ways of staggering our departure times and meeting at a prearranged rendezvous, which lent a bit of illicit spice to our get-togethers.

Pathos on our street was provided by an elderly man living in a house directly across the street from ours. His bathroom arrangements may have been similar to ours and too challenging for his time of life. At any rate, he would unpredictably throw open his window and urinate from his third floor room onto the sidewalk, which presented another consideration for our nighttime ambles. But I never heard anyone complain. Though an air of dejection hung about the neighborhood, there was also a feeling of unspoken compassion. And we never saw the kinds of urban violence and abuse that have now become so widespread.

By contrast, at that time Chicago's reputation for official corruption and dangerous living was notorious. Street lights in our district emitted only the dimmest red glow, providing no protection, and police were so amenable to bribes that they were eager to arrest for infractions, however minor. Many motorists carried bills clipped to their drivers' licenses to buy their way out of such situations. In a hilarious case, a friend of ours was pulled down late at night on a deserted street for making an illegal left turn. When he found he had no paper money, he dug into his change pocket. The cop, undaunted, accepted our friend's only offering—a quarter—perhaps a record bribe for any city.

We had a few amusing adventures of our own. Walking home late one night, we turned into our dimly lit street and startled a probable thief prowling furtively among the parked vehicles. When he saw us, he bolted up a few steps into the vestibule of a house and stood nervously watching us. Trouble was, he was in our entranceway. Wondering what to do, we crossed the street, walked to the far corner, and looked back at him. He was still peering out, so I finally tried to indicate by pointing that *we* just wanted to be where *he* was. He looked at us inquiringly, ran down the stairs and up into the next house, whereupon we crossed purposefully without looking at him and entered our vestibule. For the moment, everyone seemed pleased—a not uncongenial experience which I believe we all enjoyed, once we caught the rhythm of it.

That spring we both had been working hard toward our degrees, culminating in the lengthy June graduation ceremony at which Ken received his MS in Biological Sciences and I my BS. UC required bodily attendance which spawned a brisk rental service whose cost we avoided by attending in person. Following a brief vacation with our families, we returned to Chicago just in time for the hottest Fourth of July I have ever experienced.

Job hunting in earnest, I tried door-to-door selling of encyclopedias but found I was no good at selling. On an introductory tour through our firm, I noticed a letter lying open on an unattended desk; it began, "While I was at work, one of your salesmen came into my home and persuaded my wife to buy an encyclopedia we cannot afford." All too soon, I found myself face-to-face with tired housewives opening their doors to me, and I couldn't bring myself to argue the importance of acquiring our books when I could see they needed other things so much more acutely.

An office of Illinois Bell Telephone Company was located just off Sixty-third Street about a mile east of where we lived. I was hired there as a service representative for what the company knew would probably be only a year, certainly no longer than two years. Because of that generous opportunity, I became acquainted with a different aspect of Chicago.

The previous year, I had been commuting north across the Midway to the UC campus. Now my work took me south and west, along a choice of city streets presenting quite different faces from those I knew. I tried public transport, but on one of my first days waiting for my bus beneath the elevated tracks of the IC (Illinois Central Railroad), a pigeon dropped his calling card smack onto the lapel of my only suit. From then on, I walked. And these walks were rewarding. Using residential streets, I acquired some unusual landmarks—a little dog that watched me solemnly from his window each morning and some energetic bagpipe practice a few blocks farther on. In general, however, the streets themselves always seemed surprisingly deserted.

For the trip home, especially on dark winter nights, I preferred walking along Sixty-third Street, our commercial avenue above which the IC tracks ran. Despite its tawdriness, it was also lively and colorful, occasionally offering unexpected pleasures and harmless surprises. A large painted model of the RCA mascot, His Master's Voice, sat in front of a record store I regularly passed. One night I heard for the first time the glorious bass voice of Ezio Pinza singing "One Enchanted Evening" from the musical *South Pacific*. The beauty of that voice, pouring out across the sleazy sidewalk, was magical to me. And there was a spring evening when two exuberant young men were coming toward me and one of them planted a quick kiss on my cheek as they passed. Somehow it all had an air of youth and innocence—the romance of a big city. Although Sixty-third Street had the reputation of being dangerous, and indeed my officemates saw a murder victim there early one morning, my experiences fell in a range between bland and charming.

Today, as I listen on the telephone to automated voices telling me how eagerly their owners want to serve me but "due to unusual caller volume" are unable to do so, I wish the standards of service demanded of us had prevailed down through the decades. No caller was to be kept on hold more than one minute; beyond that, a callback was required. One wonders whether such disciplined service is now extinct or merely dormant. Certainly it seems quaint and highly desirable.

The girls in my office were mostly native Chicagoans who kindly took me around town to see the sights. They showed me the old school once attended by Al Capone, apparently celebrated solely for that reason, as well as civic landmarks where I later spent much free time, including the Art Institute and the Museum of Science and Industry. Many of my co-workers were Catholic and introduced me to a phenomenon that has followed me throughout my life. When they discovered I did not share their religion, they questioned me and debated religious dogma during our coffee and lunch breaks. Upon learning that no priest or minister had officiated in my marriage ceremony, they stated flatly that I was not really married.

In our discussions, I was reminded of high-school geometry in which the logical development of a proof, if traced backward, always dead-ends in at least one axiom. Similarly, the religious arguments of these girls stemmed from their accepted maxims—scriptural and revelatory precepts proclaimed by their religion. We know how easily and effectively non-Euclidean systems of geometry can be developed by altering one or more of the basic axioms of our familiar Euclidean geometry. The plethora of religious systems suggests a similar process has been at work throughout human history, attempting to codify and logically support the enduring human quest for transhuman knowledge. I was to encounter this phenomenon again, many decades later, with far greater impact on my life.

Throughout our stay in Chicago, my college roommate's parents, Frieda and Harold Urey, were steadfast friends. They invited us to join them and their stimulating family and guests for every holiday dinner during those two years. Around their table, we met and listened to distinguished scientists proposing various problems thrown out for solution by the assembled brainpower. Most frequent among their guests was the young Willard Libby, soon to be awarded the Nobel Prize for his development of radiocarbon dating. His and Harold's exchanges were impressive examples of mental gymnastics—great minds at work and play, with often little difference between the two.

In the summer of 1949, the Ureys took a four-week family vacation and invited us to stay in their house while they were gone. We were delighted, for their generosity gave us a much appreciated respite from crowding and cockroaches. Their home was one of the so-called Gold Coast mansions north of the campus, in a green area of similar homes that had become something of a drug-on-the-market in the largely servantless postwar era. But they were ideal for large families associated with the university. Normally, six Ureys were in the main house, and a Canadian graduate student with his family occupied an apartment above the garage. But that summer, his wife and children had gone home to Canada, and he spent most of his time in the lab, so for a month, we were usually the only people on the property.

On the day of the Ureys' departure we moved in and late in the afternoon left to attend an evening concert at the Ravinia Festival on the north side of town. Carefully locking up, we did not think to leave a light on for our return after dark. When we entered the dark vestibule, Ken unlocked and started to open the front door into the house and *clank*! its safety latch suddenly caught, raising hackles on the backs of our necks, for we had exited by that door. We hastened to the nearest public telephone and called the police. Two officers met us on the lawn. After hearing our story, they removed the mounting for the safety hasp and opened the door. Then, with pistol drawn, one officer told Ken, "You go ahead since you know the house." Though uncomfortable with this arrangement, Ken led the officer through the house, floor by floor, while another officer guarded the door. When the graduate student returned home for the night, he was excited by the tableau and announced he would join in searching the house. But he was sobered quickly when the guard, with drawn gun, ordered him not to set foot inside. Ken at last emerged with news that nothing seemed amiss except for one unlocked window in the back of the house. When the police left, Ken told me the search had been too superficial for his comfort, so we returned to our room for the remainder of that night. The next day, he searched carefully through every nook and cranny to make sure no one had remained in the house.

We never learned what had happened. The police opined the safety latch had somehow gone on by itself as we closed the door behind us when leaving the house. But when they, and later we, tried to make it do so, the latch would not go anywhere near engaging. We felt quite sure someone had known of the Ureys' vacation and simply taken advantage of our departure that first night to sneak in from the rear, put on the safety latch to prevent being caught without time to get away, and then left by the back window when they heard us trying to enter the front door. The serious concern, of course, arose because Harold had access to many atomic secrets, and this occurred at a time when the Soviets were attempting to join the atomic powers as quickly as possible. We thought it likely someone was searching carefully and specifically for helpful information without leaving traces of his presence. Indeed, it had the earmarks of a highly professional job.

Of course, we told the Ureys immediately upon their return, and Harold assured us there would have been nothing to find since he never took classified materials home. Whether to make us feel better or from personal conviction, the family downplayed the possible significance of the occurrence. But they did tell us they kept one back window unlocked so the children could climb in if they lacked a key. Many years later, one of their children called me out of the blue to ask if I remembered the incident and her family's skepticism of our suspicions. Of course I did, and she said she wanted to apologize for their attitude, for they had recently read an account of such activities having been perpetrated by Soviet agents at just that time.

We have always treasured our friendship with that remarkable family. Over the years, Frieda and I have lunched together whenever she came to visit a daughter living in the Bay Area. In 1964, when I inherited Aunt Mildred's desert property in Valley Center, Frieda and Harold came out from their home in La Jolla to visit. It was heartening to see how enthusiastically Harold embraced the life there, reminiscent of his own rural boyhood in the Midwest. As he watched our sons fabricating all sorts of things from a sawhorse and miscellaneous articles scrounged from the outbuildings, he commented that he thought this the finest kind of environment for boys. Since he seemed especially appreciative, I have to think this kind of rural background had probably been good for him as it certainly had for Ken.

In the aftermath of World War II, there was an understandable revulsion toward war and its implements, most notably the atomic weapons that ended it. Yet many easy and false conclusions have been drawn. I remember the first time I entered Harold's office. Stretching across most of one wall was a picture of an atomic bomb blast, and I was stunned. Seeing my expression, he said gently, "Beautiful, isn't it?" And I realized not only was it beautiful; it also represented the fruit of years of effort when he and other scientists scarcely saw the light of day, leaving for work well before dawn and working long into the night that we might prevent being victimized by the same technology then under development by our enemies. Dreadful as those bombs were, historic evidence makes clear that on balance they saved more lives than they took by forcing an end to the already disastrously long and destructive war, by then killing Japanese and American soldiers at a ratio of 10-1 in battle, while thousands upon thousands of Japanese civilians were being destroyed in saturation bombings of their cities. An estimated one hundred million lives had already been lost worldwide. Enough had already become vastly too much.

From my experience, atomic scientists are no strangers to spirituality. But they are also realists. The simplistic image of the unconcerned or unfeeling scientist overlooks the fact that, in cruel times, hard decisions have to be made and forceful steps taken to defeat obvious evil. The men and women who rise to meet such challenges often have given much harder thought to the consequences than those of us who may benefit or suffer from their decisions.

The fact that many children of prominent atomic scientists turned to careers in biology has been taken as a sign of rejecting their father's work. In some cases, this may be so. But I submit that their values also stem from those of their parents. And better than most, such children know both the sacrifices required and the excitement to be experienced on new frontiers. When new technologies arrive on the scene, they alter that scene and will—for better or worse—remain a fact of existence. If down the line ethical doubts become publicized, as certainly happened in atomic physics and is now happening in biology, this does not necessarily indicate the scientists involved have not already met and indeed grappled with these concerns for some time, evaluating their moral cost/benefit ratios.

After the war Harold turned completely away from his research that had helped win it, taking up study of the moon which he assumed would remove him from politics and controversy. Technology quickly ended that dream, however, and within a few years placed him as a consultant to our incipient moon projects. So goes life, which so often has that "life of its own" ultimately sweeping us along with it.

* * *

That summer, Ken and I swam a few times in Lake Michigan, a fine big body of water which often behaved like an ocean, but I could never quite get used to emerging from so much water without the taste of brine on my lips. We had better luck with movies. It was an age of "art theaters" in which were shown the great postwar films coming from England and the continent, and we lapped up frothy stuff like *Tight Little Island* and *Passport to Pimlico*.

The classic film *Les Enfants du Paradis* led to a special night. We went to a small theater in Hyde Park and afterward, in the lobby over coffee, ran into college friends. Sweethearts since schooldays, they had married shortly after graduation and were studying toward their PhD's in physics at UC. Still reeling from the emotional and artistic impact of that great Jean-Louis Barrault film, we were looking for an extension of the mood, and they suggested a drive around the city. As I recall, we started at one of the beaches where we cavorted briefly, moved on to the Loop and North Shore, working our way inland to Skid Row where we found a small dive for refreshment, then on to our South Side for breakfast around six o'clock in the morning. It had been a glorious evening, reminding me of a touching short story entitled "Young Man Axelbrod," authored, I believe, by Sinclair Lewis. Our adventure became one of my most cherished memories. When Ken and the others went home to bed, I went directly to my office and was on such a "high" that I felt energized until nightfall.

Near the end of my second and Ken's third year in Chicago, Ken's thesis sponsor, Austin Riesen, arranged for him to finish his research and write his thesis while working as a civilian in the Aero-Medical Laboratory at Wright-Patterson Air Force Base at Dayton, Ohio. Plagued by an allergy to something in Chicago's air, Ken was desperately eager to leave the city, and though I still found pleasures and a lingering exoticism in the big city life, I was also much relieved at the thought of leaving our slum. Indeed, we both felt we had been pressing our luck and were happy to put those particular streets behind us, exchanging them for the relative bucolicism of Ohio.

"Four Years on the Floor"

On a sweltering morning in June, we packed our car and headed, via Canada, to my home in New Jersey to await the beginning of Ken's job in Ohio. Surprisingly, we soon found ourselves reaching for sweaters as we stopped to bid farewell to the Riesens on our way out of town. We had encountered one of the famed sudden temperature reversals in Chicago. How blissful it soon felt to be driving through cool country air north of the city, with miles of space in our future! We were on our way to Quebec City for a reunion with my sister who was to sail aboard the *Volendam* to France for a summer's study at the Sorbonne.

Several restful days were spent walking and bicycling on automobile-free Mackinac Island, situated in the straits between Lake Michigan and Lake Huron, before continuing our drive east through Canada. Tire trouble forced a stop one afternoon in Sudbury, Ontario, where a garage owner offered to take us in his truck to a nearby lake to give his Labrador retriever a swim. As we neared the lake, the dog began whining softly and when released, shot out the door and plunged into the water. We watched him dog paddle to the center of the lake, where his paws splashed continually and apparently aimlessly. He seemed joy incarnate. His owner told us the ice had melted from the lake only a few days earlier, and as soon as the dog took his first swim of the season, he had actually turned somersaults in the water! As we left the lake, he ran behind the truck while we drove slowly back toward the garage. When tired of running, he whined, and a nearly dry dog was let aboard for the rest of the drive.

We spent that night in Ottawa. The hotel we tried had no rooms on their tourist floors, but we were tired and rather insistent that we would take anything, so we were given a room on a floor that seemed to serve as a discreet brothel, not far from the seat of the Canadian government. Next stop was Montreal, where Percy boiled over on a hill while taking us through a pleasant residential area. A reluctant housewife lent us a saucepan for scooping water from her fishpond to relieve our dry radiator, watching us suspiciously from inside her house. In Quebec, we settled into a small hotel, a stone's throw from the Château Frontenac.

When Charlotte arrived, we three toured the city in Percy, soaking up the ambience and sunlight while Charlotte practiced French, and we jointly shared news. After her sendoff to Europe, Ken and I began exploring more of Quebec Province on our own. My astute father, knowing that a part of me would wish to be aboard a ship plowing toward Europe, had sent us some money to extend our travels in Canada. Immediately, we headed north to Laurentides National Park in the Laurentian Mountains, where we found tent cabins in a campground on a tiny island in Lac des Islets, one of the many lakes there. We had the campground entirely to ourselves and devised our most luxuriously satisfying wake-up routine ever. Each night before retiring, we set the makings for a fire in the stove next to our sleeping bags, placing our prepared coffee pot atop the stove and making sure our matches were within easy reach. Upon waking in the cold mornings, one of us simply leaned out, put a match to the kindling, and rolled over again until the coffee was perked and the cabin warm and fragrant. In all our wanderings since, we've never known simpler or more satisfying bare-bones comfort.

In a few days we turned north again, driving to Chicoutimi on the banks of the Saguenay River. As we stood looking northward across the wide river, we began a love affair with the North. There is a mystique about northern lands, and we were drawn to it—so much so that we even toyed with the idea of ferrying across the river and driving a long dirt road up to Chibougamou, much farther north. But we had "promises to keep" and turned south, eventually turning up at my family's home in Fanwood to await the unpredictable call from Wright-Patterson Air Force Base that would inform us when they wanted Ken to begin working there.

While in the East, we sold our problem-prone convertible, bought the 1940 Ford that had been used by Ken's family for its first ten years, and settled down to serious waiting. Uncertainty extended through half the summer. On a midsummer Saturday, a postcard arrived, telling Ken to report for work Monday morning at eight. I was determined to attend the wedding of a close friend late the next afternoon in Scotch Plains, a town two miles west of Fanwood. So with our car fully packed, we witnessed the marriage, skipped the reception, and continued driving west through the night, arriving with the sun on the rolling landscape just east of Dayton.

We had decided we'd rather live in a college town than in Dayton or its suburbs, and since we had no time to detour into our chosen target of Yellow Springs, I asked Ken to let me out at the closest junction so I could walk into town and begin apartment hunting while he was reporting for work. The morning was bright and promising and the walk through the farm country lovely but miles longer than it had looked on the map. So I gladly accepted a ride from a woman on her way to work in the cafeteria at Antioch College. She gave me useful information as well as transportation. Antioch's campus appeared restfully green and spacious and definitely "laid back." Everyone I met was friendly and helpful, and within a few hours, I had rented a room above a store on the main street of town. Living there that first week introduced us to one of the town's true gems just a few steps from our door: the Area Theater. Over the next four years, we enjoyed great cinematic entertainment there, thanks in large part to the responsive collegiate audiences.

The town of Yellow Springs was a small village serving surrounding farms and, as its name implies, had once been a health resort for people coming to take its waters, laden with minerals that conferred the color. I liked the town immediately, but soon discovered a darker side to those waters that took many newcomers by surprise, requiring several months of internal adjustment and generating relentless jokes.

Within the first week we found a three-room unfurnished apartment, which comprised the second floor of a house situated near a small undeveloped town park. We liked the rural nature of the place and also enjoyed the realtors' ads in which "modern" meant "with indoor toilet facilities." This was mid-twentieth century in the heartland of America, and we felt pleased to realize a level of premodernity still coexisted with our more up-to-date accommodations of 1950.

Two jobs at the college quickly came my way. I worked full-time on the Wright Field Project, contracted by Wright-Patterson Air Force Base fourteen miles away. My desk was next to one of the new IBM card-sorting machines I had first seen at IBM Corporation in New York City, and all too quickly I discovered what thunderously unpleasant office companions those early computers were. Not until I developed tinnitus a few months later was my desk moved to a quieter corner. I had also lucked into a small but high-paying position for one year as head of a two-year statistical project whose director was temporarily hospitalized with tuberculosis.

Ken commuted by car pool to Wright-Pat while I usually walked to my jobs on campus. Later we bought Schwinn three-speed bikes so we could explore the surrounding countryside and nearby Bryan State Park. Mine became a beloved treasure for I used it to commute in all kinds of weather, learning to handle even the treacherous frozen ruts on winter roads. The route between our apartment and one of my jobs crossed a five-hole golf course and was a delight to ride in good weather, for the narrow paved path followed the gentle contours of hills and curves and took me right to the door of my office. As winter deepened, however, only one other biker rode the ruts. One frosty morning, he and I approached each other with great concentration, each shakily raising a hand in salute.

Antioch had been a collegiate pacesetter from its inception. Founded in 1852 by Horace Mann, an educational idealist, it was known originally as Antioch University. In the early part of the twentieth century, the college achieved distinction in innovative education when Arthur Morgan introduced a work/study program: every student spent half the school year studying on campus and the other half on jobs, sometimes located quite far from Ohio during an era when travel was not so easy as it has become.

Though this system was beneficial to some students, it could be annoyingly wasteful. The year was chopped into quite small segments. One autumn I tried to audit a math course, but I gave up after three weeks passed without discernible instruction. In a somewhat typical maneuver, the teacher had effectively abdicated, allowing students to talk away each lecture period debating what they *wanted* to study during their eight-week academic period on campus. Predictably, obstruction replaced instruction, and while this may have enhanced the "self-esteem" of some students, it probably robbed more of them of any constructive basis for it.

In any event, Antioch attracted many bright students who would have succeeded with or without classroom instruction. One of America's best cartoonists, Ed Fisher, was a graduate of Antioch. He poked fun at the self-consciously introspective aspect of the college long before he became famous for tweaking the foibles of our wider world in the *New Yorker* and *Punch* magazines.

An upperclassman in chemistry once told me he had learned the hard way that Antioch only had one chemistry professor who presented challenging lectures to his students, and his courses were always oversubscribed. Serious academic desire certainly existed, but the college failed considerably in its educational mission to those students whose priorities rose above "reevaluating their basic assumptions"—as an Ed Fisher cartoon so succinctly presented Antioch's emphasis at the time.

In retrospect, Ken and I were witnessing at Antioch the small beginnings of a trend toward student domination of universities that reached a disruptive peak at Berkeley in the mid-sixties, seriously shaking academia nationwide. A small but significant group of teachers who default on the hard work of teaching will always find "takers" among students trying to avoid the hard work of learning. And worse, those who exploit their tenured positions to advance private political agendas may well disable the educational process they are honor-bound to provide to the society paying for it.

For me at that time, Antioch campus was an agreeably casual place to work. One hot afternoon, I nearly tripped over a large Irish setter flaked out on the cool tiles of a ground-floor ladies room. And townspeople as well as dogs were drawn to campus. For several years in the mid-fifties Antioch hosted extraordinary summer theatricals when the Yellow Springs Area Theater held an annual Shakespeare Festival on a makeshift Elizabethan stage erected against one wall of the administration building. Aspiring young professional actors came from New York and were joined by talented amateurs from town, presenting the most enjoyable Shakespearean experiences Ken and I have ever had.

There was the night an enterprising cat began climbing the ivy on a darkened portion of the building. A spotlight following the action on stage suddenly caught him in its beam, freezing him as he looked frantically over one shoulder at the audience erupting in laughter. Another drama saw a spear-carrier miss his footing and fall into the bushes between the platform and the wall. One of our finest professionals, Jack Bittner, who was portraying a king, solicitously leaned over and helped bring the fallen actor aboard, while asking in his unforgettably rich bass voice, "Art thou all right?" An all-time favorite occurred when an actor dashed onto the stage, slipped, and fell flat. There was a stunned moment of silence after which the man he had been rushing toward declaimed portentously, "Stand, thou Greek! Thou art a fair mark for any man!" We rushed home to our volumes of Shakespeare and sure enough, the line was there. There were glitches on rainy nights when the tarpaulin refused to move smoothly above the bleachers, stopping in spurts and dumping accumulated rainwater on portions of the audience below. One spectacular mishap occurred when a pulley system jammed as Mark Antony was being hoisted aloft on a litter to the balcony where awaited an impatient Cleopatra. Her tragic mien soon dissolved into boredom as the soldiers below began shouting "Pull! Pull!" while her delayed Antony became canted at ever more precarious angles.

But the Antioch Shakespeare Festival was not all laughs. It presented moments of surpassingly great theater. When Jack Bittner as Enobarbus in *Antony and Cleopatra* gave his beautiful soliloquy describing Cleopatra traveling down the Nile upon her barge, time stood still for me and all the beauties of a distant land were spread before me. It was one of the greatest moments of Shakespeare that I have known. The company also brought us plays seldom produced at that time, notably the harrowing *Titus Andronicus*, a bloodbath in which a horrifying number of hands were hacked off.

Two of the professionals throughout these triumphs and tribulations were William Ball and Ellis Rabb, fine actors and codirectors who later founded the American Conservatory Theater in San Francisco and the APA Repertory Company in New York City respectively. Sada Thompson, my friend from high school, starred in some of Bill Ball's productions at ACT during the '60s and '70s. Once when Bill was out of town, Ken and I spent an evening with Sada in the Russian Hill apartment he had lent her. From its balcony we gazed out over our city through a screen of branches while sipping predinner drinks—a long distance in space and time from New Jersey via Yellow Springs to San Francisco.

Prior to Yellow Springs, we had lived only in single furnished rooms. There, with some discretionary income at our disposal, we literally "went to town," driving into Dayton on weekends to buy furniture and tableware for the first unfurnished apartment we had occupied. Approaching the Rike Kumler Department Store, our list of "high" to "low" priority pieces was intimidatingly long and topped by a bedstead since mattress and springs were still on the floor. As I read the list to Ken on our drive to town, I remarked, "Well, at least we don't need a desk." Of course, the only item we took home that day was a desk, and it is in use today as I write. Its graceful design attracted us to the line of Willetts cherry furniture called Transitional. We gradually rounded out our collection, but, of course, our bed stayed on the floor until we bought our very last piece of Willetts much later while living in Baltimore. Ken sometimes characterized our period in Yellow Springs as "four years on the floor."

These excursions into Dayton sometimes delivered a bonus. On the way into town, our road rounded a wide curve and descended a slight hill while crossing the line of a runway at Wright-Pat. If we were lucky, we might see a B-36 taking off or landing. The B-36 was the largest bomber ever built and the only plane with six propeller engines mounted as pusher engines on the trailing edge of the wing, to which jet assists were later added. It had great range and was used as an intercontinental bomber, serving in SAC (Strategic Air Command) during the height of the Cold War. I understand it never fired a shot in anger and thus came to be nicknamed the "Peacemaker."

To me, it is still the most thrilling plane I know. It had an unmistakably "different" sound—a drone I could always recognize from afar. It was so large and appeared so slow on landing approaches that it seemed to hover motionless above our road. Along that stretch of highway were signs prohibiting stopping, and consequently, traffic slowed to a crawl as motorists gawked at that beautiful bird settling slowly to earth. Very few of those great planes remain. I understand the last one to fly went to the Air Force Museum in Dayton in April of 1959.

The first time we had learned of the B-36's existence was while sauntering along Michigan Avenue one day in Chicago. Noticing an unusual sound above, I turned to look, as did a few other pedestrians, and we were awestruck by this great contrivance, so out of scale with any plane we had ever seen. The most precious part of my memory was Ken's reaction. As the rest of us gazed skyward in quiet awe, Ken danced around excitedly, crying, "Ginnie, look at that. Look at that! That's an A-26! Isn't it a beauty?" And sure enough, flying circles around the B-36 was a lovely sprite of a plane with only two engines, darting hither and yon, examining its big relative from all angles as a bird might have done. During the war, Ken had flown in medium bombers, primarily the B-26 Marauder, but as the war in Europe wound down, he also flew bombing missions in the sleek new A-26 Invader. Devoted to both planes, he had often described to me the relative beauty of the Invader, and indeed it had lovely clean lines as it circled Big Brother above us. The A-26 went on to distinguished service in Korea and, for reasons that are still unclear, was redesignated B-26, an unprecedented move producing much confusion in the history of aviation.

During a short vacation at Christmastime, we discovered Cumberland Falls State Park in Kentucky. This became our favorite spot for R&R. We always stayed in the big old inn, surrounded then by snow. Often we were practically its only guests, yet always enjoyed full amenities of food and service. Hiking trails were beautiful and uncrowded. We went back several times, returning either to masses of blooming dogwood in the spring or flaming fall colors, and always the same gratifyingly uncrowded inn.

Driving farther afield, we made our first trip to New Orleans, arriving the last day of Mardi Gras. Just as well for we found the celebration of Fat Tuesday almost too fat for comfort. By the time we arrived, streets in the Latin Quarter held so many drunken revelers that an early evening downpour sending them indoors came as a relief to us. We could settle down then to enjoying the city without the bedlam. Our bedroom and balcony had been burned in a freak fire the day before our arrival, so we were allowed to stay only that first night with orders not to set foot on the charred balcony. Through a native, we found lodging in the pleasant residential section along Bayou St. John, and from her, we also found Galatoire's, favored by many locals over the more famous restaurant Antoine's. When we made our first trip back to New Orleans a quarter century later, the doorman at Galatoire's greeted us as if we had been there last week. When Ken told him we now lived in San Francisco and had last dined at Galatoire's in 1952, his expression changed to concern as he exclaimed, "That's a long time to go without dinner!"

At the end of our first year in Ohio, Ken returned to Chicago to take his orals and fortunately survived some last-minute obstructionist dramas, finally receiving a PhD in physiological psychology. For weeks thereafter, we each had nightmares of ill-defined obstacles tossed into his path.

Although most of our travels in those days were by car, we occasionally flew back East to visit our family, and I want to pay tribute to the commercial planes that flew us. My favorites were the Martin 202s and 404s, two-engine and four-engine versions of a human friendly, comfortable aircraft built by the same company that had employed my aunt as draftsman and had manufactured Ken's sturdy B-26s during World War II. They flew so low we could look down into the blazing Pittsburgh furnaces, and on the fifty-mile hop from Columbus to Dayton, we could "navigate" by familiar gas stations and roadside restaurants along old Route 40. Just this past spring I learned from a former B-26 pilot who later in his commercial flying career flew the Martin 202s that the 202s were the civilian versions of the wartime B-26.

One memorable flight on a stormy night caused many people to become airsick, and the stewardesses were run ragged, replacing passengers' vomit bags. When I began feeling queasy myself, one of my father's tales suddenly popped to mind. Seasickness had assailed him as he talked on deck with the captain of their naval vessel in convoy to North Africa, and just when he thought he would have to disgrace himself as a navy man by dashing to the rail, a large crane broke loose on deck, swinging wildly at great danger to the men and ultimately to the ship itself. They had to drop out of convoy—not a comfortable situation since they carried explosives as well as troops. But several courageous seamen, "true heroes," finally made a coordinated rush into the swinging tons of metal and brought the crane under control. This took the better part of an hour, and only as things began to settle down did my father's seasickness return. He realized it had been kept at bay entirely by the distraction of their crisis.

In my case, I asked a passing stewardess if they could use some help, and she accepted eagerly. I unbuckled and joined them in replacing full bags with empties, to and fro in the bucking plane. All my airsickness vanished in trying to keep my footing. Such an occurrence today, with corporate liability concerns, seems unimaginable.

* * *

We spent the summer of 1952 in Europe for which I had saved salary and Ken had hoarded vacation time. Our tour began in London and was rather eclectic. Perhaps its character was captured some weeks later, when we were trapped briefly in a narrow-gauge rail car that broke down on its way up the Jungfrau in Switzerland. While stopped for repairs, we became acquainted with Britishers who began asking us whether we had seen this or that in London. Answering quite often in the negative, we heard a woman remark that, goodness, we had missed a lot to which Ken responded brightly, "Oh, you'd be *amazed* at how much we can miss!"

Even so, of course, there was much we did not miss. Celebrated cities were visited, but also the small thousand-year-old walled town of Dinkelsbuhl that we had admired in a lovely old print hanging in the apartment of Ohio friends. We spent several days there, walking its walls and watching storks nesting on its towers, washing down our strenuous activity with "*viertel* liters" of the local liebfraumilch. A Rhine steamer from Mainz to Koln took us through country Ken had seen from the air during the war. The bridge at Neuwied had been especially attractive, and in his memoir *Marauder Man*, he wrote of our Rhine trip that

> passing Neuwied was an emotional experience for me because the bridge was still in the river. Though I

> had exulted in destroying it, thus completing our assigned task, that seemed a hollow victory in 1952 as the bridge still lay in ugly rubble, so I deeply regretted the necessities that had brought it down. Such are the ironies and mixed emotions made inevitable by war.

In Belgium, Ken took me to meet the Hanot family who had been exceptionally kind to him and his wartime buddies when they were stationed nearby in Asch. The Hanots were no less welcoming to me, gathering relatives and friends from miles around to meet us. Most haunting of all was a visit to his old airfield, once vibrant with noise and action, eerily silenced beneath a tall sea of grass.

Later we visited with Dutch friends who made sure we tried raw herring, swam in the North Sea, and took our lives in our hands while pedaling bikes around The Hague and Schreveningen. While in Holland, we were also taken to the great dike, a most impressive sight, and a small exchange there tickled me. When I asked if this was the dike into which the legendary little boy reportedly stuck his finger—thus, saving the country—I was told no. They named a smaller dike some distance away. Surprised at the seriousness of their reply, I asked if such an event *had* ever occurred, and again, they answered no.

We stayed briefly with a French wartime colleague of my father in Perigueux. He and his wife drove us to the caves at Lascaux where we marveled at the stunning artwork on those living walls, vivid with ancient action. That section of France is also considered a gourmet paradise, its sumptuous cuisine incorporating the famous local truffles. Paris also gave us artistic and gastronomic treats. Though the Louvre overwhelmed me, the marvelous sequence of Monet paintings lighting up a wall of Jeu de Paume Museum—a famed series depicting the facade of Rouen Cathedral as lit by the sun at different times of day—was enchanting. We savored flawless croissants each morning at a neighborhood cafe, superlative onion soup along the Champs-Élysées, lunches of bread and camembert in our room, and cheap steak and pommes frites in sidewalk cafes before finally heading south to the Riviera.

Three times in my life, I have felt my breath taken away. The first occurred at Silver Springs in central Florida, where my family had stopped for a swim on our way north from Key West. Accustomed to three months in the sun-warmed waters of southern Florida, I was unprepared for the physical shock of diving into the crystalline sixty-eight-degree water. When I surfaced and my father called from the dock, "How is it?" for several seconds, I found I could not draw breath to answer. The wind had been knocked out of me, and I felt as though I had been socked in the solar plexus. Three decades later, I felt a similar visceral shock when I stepped into the overpoweringly great nave of the Cathedral of Yorkminster.

And in between, during our time on the Riviera, I experienced a very different but equally stunning experience in Monaco. Ken and I had just entered a small, unprepossessing cafe when we saw a breathtakingly beautiful woman, simply but exquisitely gowned. She resembled Ava Gardner or Cyd Charisse but was neither. As she sat across the table from a surprisingly ugly man, she appeared radiantly happy. She must have been aware of her beauty for she obviously took care with her presentation, but her attention never strayed from her animated companion and she seemed totally unselfconscious. We found the sight strangely moving, and she remains the most beautiful woman I have ever beheld.

In Italy we spent a week divided between Florence and Venice. Florence is so stuffed with art treasures that we fagged out one day while searching for the famed Ghiberti doors. Sitting down upon the steps of the Duomo to rest, we suddenly spied them across the street, far more satisfying an introduction than if we had followed a map. We walked the hills to Fiesole, learned to pronounce "septente due" so that our playful concierge would reward us with the key to our room, and lunched daily in a nearby restaurant whose garden held a turtle. Already too hot to consider going on to Rome, we headed for Venice where we rode vaporettos more than gondolas, for the latter were expensive for us, and strolled delightful back alleys and squares. We squeezed in a swim on Lido Beach and a brief visit to the historic glass-working city of Murano before entraining to Brunnen on the Vierwaldstattersee in Switzerland.

Highlights there were a schmaltzy afternoon spent in Morschach, which we happened upon while hiking halfway up a mountainside from the next ferry stop, and a picnic lunch in Altdorf, made interesting by one of Ken's observations and subsequent experiments. A yellow jacket had alighted on the ham at the edge of his sandwich, and I was about to shoo it away, having been painfully stung a few times by the black variety of wasp as a child. But Ken stopped me by saying, "Let's watch him and see what he does." And indeed, he did an interesting thing. He moved around a portion of the ham small enough for him to carry, in such a manner that he completely severed it from the main part and flew away with it. Sure that he would return, Ken saved his sandwich. Again the yellow jacket took a manageable portion, repeating the process several more times. We could not be sure whether he was somehow managing to "chew" the meat off or was softening it with chemicals from his mouth, which we thought more likely from the moistened edges of the meat. In any event, I became sufficiently fascinated by this little investigation that I lost my fear, acquiring for the first time a bit of composure around creatures of the stinging persuasion.

Eventually, we wound up again in London where Ken received a cable from his lab at Wright-Pat, requesting that he stay over for an indeterminate period to do as yet unspecified work for the Air Force at the American Embassy. Needless to say, we were more than happy to oblige. And since there were precious few duties, we spent another four or five weeks on assignment in one of my favorite cities, occupying digs near the London Zoo where we spent many an hour awaiting calls to action. These days gave us chances to explore and sightsee in leisurely fashion. On an excursion to Cambridge University, we visited the esteemed Dutch ethologist, Nikolaas Tinbergen, who generously gave us several hours of his time. Slender, almost wiry, he impressed me with his interest and energy. The talk was mostly scientific, exciting to us and made all the more inspiring when we considered that his war years had included near-starvation. I recall his dismissive laugh while describing the effort he spent trying to lure, and capture by hand, birds coming to his windowsill during those desperate times.

One day—in line of duty, of course—Ken and I attended the first postwar Farnborough Air Show at which jets of the future were unveiled to the public. These included military jets and the British Comet, first jet airliner into service on routes connecting England with India and South Africa. A feeling of renewal and promise infected the crowd as one plane after another flaunted its stuff. The entire show conveyed a sense of power intensified by noise: a sudden blast from a jet turning straight upward drove Ken down onto one knee in a reflexive avoidance maneuver.

This idyll in London finally came to an end when Ken was recalled to the states. We enjoyed a last elegant dinner in the dining room of the American Embassy on Grosvenor Square, and on our appointed day of departure, we were picked up by a spiffy black Humber Pullman limousine. Naturally enough, the chauffeur drove us to the first class section of the terminal, and after such a pleasant and refined ride, we did not have the heart to disillusion him. So we waited until he was out of sight to find our way back to coach class.

* * *

Fresh from the theatrical riches of London, I was more keenly aware of the comparative leanness of live entertainment in Ohio. Aside from occasional visits to campus by fine string quartets from New York City, few top-drawer performances came our way. But I was able to hear the bel canto tenor, Ferruccio Tagliavini, in recital in Dayton. George Cuttino, my history professor at Swarthmore, had served in Italy during the war and was among the U.S. servicemen who "discovered" and helped bring Tagliavini to international fame. So hearing him was a satisfying occasion for me.

We did occasionally drive to Columbus or Cincinnati for special events, sometimes giving students a ride with us. The return drive from a summer performance of Rossini's *Barber of Seville*, held in a park along the Ohio River, was made especially memorable for me because at midnight I acquitted myself rather commendably when Ken fell asleep at the wheel. As our car drifted down onto the right shoulder of the road, I quietly steadied the steering wheel while gently waking him. Coming to with a start, he then carefully brought us up onto the road, while the two passengers in the back of our car slept on undisturbed.

By far the most notable theatrical event I attended in Ohio was a performance in Columbus of the play *Don Juan in Hell* with its extraordinary original cast: Tyrone Power, Agnes Moorehead, Charles Laughton, and Sir Cedric Hardwicke. The play was splendid, but the unexpected greatness of the evening lay in an extraordinary reading given by Laughton before the performance. A friend and I had driven the sixty or so miles from Yellow Springs through the beginnings of a blizzard, and as the storm worsened, the props needed for the play were delayed in transit from the railroad station. Mr. Laughton stepped out upon the stage and told the capacity audience of the enforced delay, which he offered to fill with readings—*if* we desired. Applause was thunderous. He began with spellbinding passages from Thomas Wolfe's novels. And again, I was transported by great theater. He read from a wide range of authors, topping off with a local son, James Thurber. This last choice brought down the house, filled as it was with loyal devotees of Thurber's wit. The whole thing was a tour de force, never to be repeated and never to be forgotten.

One spring, I caught a bad flu that left me with a stubborn middle ear infection, eventually bursting an eardrum. Once a week, I dutifully visited the doctor and his array of tiny bottles from which he extracted and gently dabbed this and that, here and there, among my nasal and Eustachian tissues, before sending me back to work. Progress was slow. Apparently none of his concoctions was an antibiotic, and as summer approached, he recommended I go to a "high altitude," which he said would do more to cure a condition like mine than any of his potions. So we headed west to Colorado where we visited in Pueblo with Swarthmore friends, Joe and Betty. Joe had grown up there and knew the country intimately. He suggested we go to a ranch near Westcliffe in the Sangre de Cristo mountains, and that did the trick. We spent a recuperative week with Mr. Hemenway, an old-timer who had lived on his ranch for decades. Since we were his only guests, and we so obviously enjoyed everything about him and his place, he took us riding, told us tales of the old days, and paid us a high compliment when he remarked, "Oh, you two would have loved it here back then!"

Change was in the air for us as the academic year of 1953-54 began. Ken was hoping to advance from research in the psychological aspects of sensory perception to more basic research in the physiological functions underlying those sensations. To this end, he applied that fall for an NSF (National Science Foundation) fellowship to do postgraduate work at Brown University in the laboratory of Prof. Lorrin Riggs who, though a psychologist, had made an important discovery in the physiology of vision. He had found a small continuous tremor of the eye that proved essential to vision as we know it, a discovery that elevated him to the National Academy of Sciences and a few pages of coverage in *Life* magazine.

For that last year, I took a new job as lab assistant to Dr. John Lacey at Fels Research Institute, adjacent to the Antioch campus. Lacey had been doing interesting longitudinal studies of the measurable physiological responses to various imposed forms of stress. He discovered that the physiological response pattern of an individual remains essentially constant throughout life, regardless of the nature of the stress, whereas these lifetime response patterns differ widely between individuals.

Late that year, I participated in a prophetic occurrence that came back to haunt me at the height of the hippie era here in

San Francisco. In Lacey's lab, we used sophisticated equipment that enabled us to measure heart rate on each beat of the heart and skin resistance continuously. The latter is an especially sensitive indicator of physiological reaction since it essentially measures the presence or absence of sweat on the skin. Because of our technical capabilities, John was asked to participate in a special experiment that had to be conducted after hours, presumably for liability and insurance reasons. John's wife, Bea, and I volunteered to return one evening to be technicians for the experiment.

Our subject was a man in early middle age who had voluntarily taken a dose of a fairly new synthesized chemical whose effects were little known—diethylamide, then called lysergic acid, later to become famous as LSD. When he entered our lab, he was already quite voluble, and another technician began recording his subjective experiences as the drug took further effect. Bea and I hooked him up to our monitors and began watching the physiological results unfold. As the subject described ever more colorful mental phenomena, we began looking at each other in concern, for the measurements of his bodily reactions were jumping all over the place, and there was no way to stop these alarming results since the lysergic acid was already taken. Skin resistance especially worried me, for it swung wildly, soon moving entirely off our charts. At that moment, I remember thinking, "I hope this drug never catches on." A decade later, a colleague's son whom we had known as a little boy became a victim of LSD when he tried to fly from an upper-story window of his Harvard dormitory.

That year also produced some other dramatic disturbances. Driving home from our trip to Colorado, we encountered an increasing amount of debris as we neared our apartment. Thus we learned that during our absence from Yellow Springs, a small tornado had ripped through town, touching down at only one place: our building, from which it tore off a large portion of the roof above our apartment and deposited it next door, shearing off our neighbors' porch. Rain followed, and friends had kindly moved most of our things out of harm's way, but our coffee table still bears a scar from that occurrence. A bit later, while away for a weekend, we learned from the radio that in our absence, a dormitory at Antioch College had burned to the ground, fortunately with no casualties—unless you count one student's hundreds of wedding invitations, stamped and ready for mailing, left in her room while she went to dinner.

In April, we learned that Ken's NSF fellowship had come through, a great relief to us both, for the town of Yellow Springs and the college dominating it had begun to pall. Most of our friends had either left or were soon to do so. My father was recovering from lung surgery, so as soon as my job ended, I flew East to be with him and Mother. And as soon as Ken could get away, he joined us by car for the move to Rhode Island and the fellowship awaiting us there.

Upon settling in Providence, we took off on vacation before the school year started and returned to find our new home, this time on the top floor of a three-story house, had lost its roof to Hurricane Carol. Amazingly, we had little damage, considering the torrential rains accompanying that storm, but the same coffee table received another gouge, and we began to feel we should never leave home, regardless of where "home" might be.

In a game of Canfield, the author and her parents hold as still as they can for an old-fashioned time exposure taken by her sister.

The Stern family posing with their prewar car, a Packard.

My high school graduation picture.

On Magill Walk, the historic front entrance to Swarthmore College.

My husband, Ken Brown, while a graduate student at The University of Chicago.

Ken and I cavorting on the shore of Lake Michigan.

Riding our new bikes through Yellow Springs, Ohio.

Our top floor apartment in Yellow Springs with the bedroom roof torn off by a tornado and deposited in a neighbor's front yard.

Back East

Our apartment in Providence was the springboard for a trip north to Baxter State Park in Maine, then on into the Atlantic Provinces of Canada where we found the finest part of our vacation on Cape Breton Island in Nova Scotia. We drove the Cabot Trail counterclockwise around the northern part of the island, spending time in the appealing fishing villages of Dingwall—with its salty docks and ocean-going vessels of varied type and registry—and Neil Harbour where evening strollers passed us with polite nods and friendly greetings of "good night!"

There was a primitive road leading northward from the town of Cape North to a geographic feature of the same name at the tip of the island. While driving this road, which closely followed the coast, the Atlantic Ocean was never far from view. At one point, we came to a farm between the road and the ocean, and with an exclamation, Ken stopped at its entrance gate. Getting out of the car, we spoke little while gazing toward the ocean, awed by the beauty of the entire scene. And we slowly realized that the far right corner of the farm, directly between us and the sea, was almost unbelievably idyllic.

This corner comprised only one or two acres, yet seemed to contain all the elements of natural beauty one could imagine in such a small site. The beautiful rolling grassland of the large meadow was almost treeless. But within that small corner were three trees, shaped and located upon gently rolling hills as if designed by a supreme artist, which they undoubtedly were. Years before, we had been greatly impressed by a Rembrandt etching called *Three Trees*, and this scene strongly reminded us of that artistic masterpiece.

Ken wanted to look up the farmer and see if he would sell us that parcel. Thus we met the owners of the property, John and Bessie Buchanan, who gave us permission to examine closely that corner of their farm. When we walked upon the site, just the two of us, what we found challenges description. Eastward toward the ocean, a sheer rock cliff dropped about forty feet to a sandy beach running the full length of the ocean front of the farm. To the left was a beautiful farmland graced by a distant farmhouse, attractive enough to enhance the view while also sturdy enough to have withstood for decades the worst storms the North Atlantic had thrown at it. To the west, behind us, the land rose rapidly to a wooded mountain called Sugar Loaf, and to our right, as we had already seen from the road, the south side of the site was densely wooded with virgin forest. Almost unbelievably, there was a delightful narrow stream of crystal-clear water bubbling and trilling its way from the forest, ultimately angling toward the ocean and dropping unimpeded from the cliff top to the beach.

The Buchanans owned a total of several hundred acres, including Sugar Loaf, and were happy to part with that one small parcel for a very reasonable price. But first, their deeds had to be found and a survey conducted. We agreed to pursue necessary negotiations by mail and then were invited to enjoy the rest of the afternoon on their farm.

Mrs. Buchanan had nine grown children from a former marriage. One son, Rory, still lived and worked there. He gave me my first taste of raw buttermilk, a delicious treat scarcely obtainable in our pasteurized society south of the border. Upon leaving the farm, we discovered that the commercial food service in Cape North had been suspended early that day to allow the locals to attend a “milling frolic” in their community hall that evening. Our motel hosts kindly offered us dinner in their kitchen and invited us to accompany them to the frolic.

What a festive event! Along one wall stood a long table symbolizing the old days when women, sitting side by side, spent evenings communally smoothing bolts of handmade fabrics by kneading them in long tubs of water as their menfolk and youngsters cavorted around the hall, keeping them company and occasionally taking a turn. By the time of our visit, fabrics were no longer milled by hand, but happily, the celebration survived. The milling tub lay on one table, and a band played rousing music for dancing. Food was plentiful, and everyone seemed to have a grand time. When years later I heard Burl Ives sing "The Killigrew Soiree," I knew whereof he sang.

During our year at Brown, Ken began moving from physiological psychology into straight physiology, a transition from relatively "soft" to technically demanding "hard" science rarely achieved in those days. Our new associates in Providence were mostly childless young couples like ourselves, and we had some great times together socially as well as professionally. We cheered our Brown University Thanksgiving Day football game and shared turkey dinner afterward. There were enough of us to field weekly volleyball games in the gym, and during the winter, we took occasional weekend ski trips. In the spring, we headed for the New England hills and lakes. One early summer weekend a friend lent us his cabin on a small lake, and during a night much too hot for sleeping, Ken and I rose at midnight for a cooling swim shared with a musical loon.

We enjoyed a civilized year in New England, at the end of which Ken was offered a postdoctoral position in the laboratory of Stephen Kuffler, a prominent neurophysiologist in the medical school of Johns Hopkins University in Baltimore. So we bade farewell in fierce summer heat, with our aging Ford loaded to the gills, and all too soon, we were stalled by a vapor lock while climbing the winding approaches to George Washington Bridge during rush hour. Echoes of honking horns reverberated in our ears as we nursed our car southward, arriving in Baltimore well after midnight.

* * *

The Kufflers had offered us their house while they were in Woods Hole, where Steve spent his summers at the Marine Biological Laboratories. He had instructed us to contact their next-door neighbors Bud and Betty Clemens to acquire house keys. Somehow, we felt our request might not be welcomed in the wee hours of the night, so we dragged lounge-chair pads from the garage onto the lawn and slept there until sunup. As it turned out, the Clemens were not especially enthusiastic when disturbed at seven thirty on a Sunday morning after a party, but subsequently, they became our closest friends during and well beyond our Baltimore years. For the record, I learned everything I ever knew about giving dinner parties from Betty. Their New Year's Eve parties were unmatched and unmatchable.

Baltimore was unusual in that rental apartments were almost impossible to find and prohibitively expensive. Houses, however, could be bought relatively cheaply. With a loan from Ken's parents, we bought a row house in Northwood for $13,000, selling it to friends for exactly the same amount when we moved to San Francisco three years later. The first of only two houses we have owned, it was pleasantly situated a fifteen-minute drive from Ken's work and within easy walking distance of a shopping center and a park. Both of the latter became especially important to me after we acquired a puppy and our first baby, in that order. I quickly learned home ownership ties one down more effectively than either pets or babies which, in a pinch, can be packed into a car. Our weekends soon became devoted to home maintenance, a kind of physical work Ken enjoyed as a balance to his mentally demanding research at Hopkins.

Life among the row houses and back lanes of Baltimore was a lot of fun. Each string of houses had backyards opening onto dirt lanes, and ours was a lively lane where tradesmen hawked their wares, including the best tomatoes of my life, fresh from the Eastern Shore of Maryland. Occasional knife sharpeners honed their musical sales pitches along our lane, and ice cream carts helped us—especially the children—through the hot summers.

Quite early on, a number of teenagers gravitated toward us via the back lane. In their canny way, they discovered our university connections and therefore our potential usefulness in shortcutting their homework. Quite often they stopped in after school for answers to questions they had been assigned that day, and I was impressed with their zealousness until I belatedly asked them how they were *supposed* to acquire their information. They replied, "By looking it up." Thereafter, I tried to play by the teachers' rules, but the children, undaunted, simply waited for Ken to return from work, gleefully intercepting him in the lane and dancing about firing questions which he answered good-naturedly. I once heard one of them shout triumphantly, "I got it!" as off they ran, delighted at having tricked an answer from "Dr. Brown." Done in a spirit of fun, it was enjoyed by all.

One afternoon a year later, these youngsters shared a comic incident that could not have been improved upon by Hollywood scriptwriters. Ken had grown up on a farm in Northern Virginia, fifty miles west of Washington, DC. For the first time in two decades he lived within striking distance of his family home, so we often visited his parents on weekends. Fortunately we told them early of the new grandchild they could expect the following summer, for early in 1957 Ken's mother died. Her death occurred so suddenly that the period immediately afterward passed in a blur for me. I remember Dad Brown clinging hard to my hand throughout the memorial service and burial at Goose Creek Friends Meeting in Lincoln, Virginia. And Ken and I then began making regular trips down to the home place to assist Dad Brown and Ken's sister, Ruth, in disposing of Mother Brown's property. From his mother, Ken inherited a grandfather's clock made by a remote ancestor and restored by Ken in his early teens. That clock has ticked companionably through our lives ever since, now standing just outside my study where it calmly paces my work.

Ruth had an established household, including a television set, but Ken and I had been traveling light, so when Dad Brown declared he no longer wished to live there and would dispose of the furniture, we acquired our first TV. When we carried the large and cumbersome old set into our living room, the neighborhood children quickly assembled to watch. Television was still relatively new, and they peppered Ken with questions as he doggedly wrestled with wires and twirled unfamiliar knobs. When our phone rang, I shushed the kids so he could hear, and we were treated to a one-sided conversation that went something like "Yes, we do . . . Well, yes, it's on—uh, I don't really know . . . we-e-ell, we're looking at a lot of *different* channels . . ." As he hung up, we all burst out laughing. In half a century of television ownership, we have never since been bothered by any of the TV rating surveys and conclude we must have been placed firmly in the "mindless viewer" category.

In basement quarters occupied by Kuffler's neurophysiology lab, Ken began a careful analysis of the electroretinogram, a complex electrical response of the retina to light. The lab was small, with only four scientists: Steve, Charles Edwards, Ken, and Torsten Wiesel, who worked with Ken and later won a Nobel Prize for work with David Hubel at Harvard. Within those three years in Baltimore, followed by work in his own lab in San Francisco, Ken rose to international prominence in the field of retinal neurophysiology. With a procession of research postdoctoral students and associates, he separated the various components of the electroretinogram and elucidated their cellular origins, later identifying the two basic receptor potentials that initiate the sensation of sight. These achievements placed him among world authorities on the elemental processes of vision, which resoundingly completed his transition from psychologist to physiologist.

We knew many fine people in Baltimore. Through our friendship with the Clemens, we met Peter and Eva Safar, a Viennese couple who have remained steadfast friends through the decades. Peter became a world authority in anesthesiology, widely known for his work in emergency medicine. While still in Baltimore, he developed the system of mouth-to-mouth resuscitation accepted by the Red Cross and now used worldwide. In later years, he has been called the father of CPR. Bud and Betty also introduced us to Joe and Cassie Lilienthal from whom we learned about Bethany Beach in Delaware where they had a cottage. Several times, we slipped down to Bethany for shore getaways, staying in a room near the ocean. Each morning, we walked along the boardwalk to breakfast at a most appealing restaurant, rather like an airy tearoom. The moment we sat down, demitasse cups of coffee appeared before us as eye-openers, a perfect regimen for me, since I could have the gratuitous little "wake-me-up" before ordering tea or hot chocolate with my meal.

One morning at Bethany, we witnessed a spectacular migration of dolphins porpoising southward just beyond the breaking waves. There appeared to be hundreds, and we walked parallel with them until we broke off for breakfast. Still, we stood and watched for some time, not wanting to miss any of the spectacle. But we needn't have worried. There must have been thousands of the graceful animals, for when we emerged from the restaurant, they were still coming at the same stately pace, two or three abreast, rising and falling to their own rhythm, sunlight streaming from their glistening bodies—a stirring sight.

For some time, poetry had been an enjoyable diversion for me. My attempts began with informative doggerel in Chicago. Ken and I worked varying schedules, and I would leave notes posted to the door of our room, telling him what I was doing and where. Perhaps mercifully, only one effort from those days survives in either of our memories:

Lost my mind
But kept my head;
You will find
I've gone to bed.

In Baltimore, this questionable pastime expanded into limericks, a couple of which still give us pleasure. After departure of guests from an unusually late party, we toppled into bed, awakening before dawn in some discomfort. While lying there, my muse kicked in and produced, for a sympathetic audience of one, the following lines:

At one the party's a revel;
At two it's naught but dishevel;

By three I'm in bed
With a terrible head,
And by four I feel like the devil.

Encouraged by Ken's response, the rest tumbled out:

I've a hangover, if you please,
I can tell it as easy as ease;
My stomach is churning,
My eyelids are burning,
And my head aches right down to my knees!

In the spring of 1956, on a day when we had planned to leave for Tangier Island in Chesapeake Bay, we went instead to the emergency room at Johns Hopkins Hospital. Before dawn, I had awakened with abdominal discomfort and an associated distinct bulge I hadn't noticed before. It proved to be a large ovarian cyst but had given no previous discomfort, which amazed both the doctors and me. Emergency surgery removed the ovary, and as I recovered I was told that if I ever wanted children, I'd better start soon since my condition could prevent conception. How important that advice was to us all! Until then, Ken and I had enjoyed things the way they were, but to my amazement, as soon as I heard our options might be severely limited, I knew I very much wanted children and was soon pregnant with our first son. This initiated me into what I think of as the golden period of my life. Though I had never cared much for babies, I must have been born to be a mother. Many years later, when Ken and I returned from an obligatory adult trip east, he watched me sitting with our sons in our San Francisco garden, and the erstwhile farm boy in him observed that I looked "like a mother hen who has just been put back on the nest!"

Following up on our trip to Cape Breton Island, we had been corresponding with Mr. Buchanan about the proposed sale of that beautiful parcel of land. The first blow to realizing our dream came when an old plat of the region showed that the Buchanans had never owned that corner of their meadow. Instead, a very long time ago it had been designated by the Canadian provincial government as a fishing preserve, which had been abandoned for that purpose and used as part of their farm as long as they could remember. So it was not theirs to sell. They took all necessary steps for legal acquisition, and just as we were about to close the deal we received a letter from a distraught Mrs. Buchanan, telling us her husband had died in an appalling accident. He had bought a fine new tractor which he was trying out in the meadow, and she was watching from the kitchen window when he put it into reverse. As it rolled downhill, he was frantically trying to get it out of reverse gear but couldn't, and as she put it, "he probably was too Scotch" to jump clear and lose the machine. Instead, he rode the tractor backward over the cliff to his death.

His widow was quite elderly and without him was no longer interested in keeping the farm. So she did not want to sell just a part of it but offered to sell us the entire property. The price was so reasonable that we considered her proposal seriously. Ken wanted to go back and assess its possibilities, but with me pregnant and under instructions from my obstetrician not to travel because "we don't want to lose this pregnancy," I was unable to go with him. Ken's father was languishing following Mother Brown's death, so Ken invited him along, which proved a fine arrangement. My father came down from Fanwood to watch over me and keep me company while Ken's father accompanied him to Cape North.

There was a bonus for me when they returned from Canada. I have always been fond of Maine lobster, and they brought home a few live lobsters for a welcome feast. My father and I had been battling unusual heat—103 degrees daytime down to the 90s at night—and lacking home air-conditioning, we had migrated daily to the coolness of the Hecht Department Store for slow lunches of salad and luscious lime sherbet, followed in late afternoon by resting on the slightly cooled tiles of our basement floor. Those lobsters became our first real dinner in several weeks.

Buying the Cape Breton farm proved hopelessly impractical for us. But Ken and his father helped Mrs. Buchanan dispose of a few pieces of old furniture and memorabilia by buying them and bringing them home. These included a cobbler's bench with moose-hide seat that we treasure as well as pieces we sold to Harry Kirk, an antique dealer who had bought the Brown homeplace primarily for its large and historic barn where he could store and display his ever-growing stock of antique furniture. Thereby hangs an instructive tale.

When Ken began arranging the sale of his family home, he contacted both a realtor and the president of the local bank. Both advised him to raze the barn. This was on the theory that no buyer would want the barn since the surrounding farmland was not being sold with the house. Ken thought this sounded crazy and did not follow the advice. The barn was large, strong, and in good condition—in fact, an antique itself constructed of hand-hewn timbers. Ken felt someone surely would have a use for it. Harry and his wife lived nearby, and their antique business had so overflowed their house that when they learned the Brown home was for sale, they snapped it up *because* of the barn, which soon became well-known to Washingtonians traveling the antique circuits in Virginia. Never be intimidated by the experts!

And never underestimate the power of a dream. During the spring of 1957, Ken had been investigating several job opportunities advertised in the East and Midwest but had turned up nothing appealing to either of us. We still had our dream of San Francisco; however, for the half century following the great earthquake and fire of 1906, the San Francisco Medical School's first two years of basic sciences, including Ken's field of physiology, were taught at UC—Berkeley while the last two clinical years had remained in San Francisco where the pool of patients was larger. That spring, Ken wrote to Ben Libet, the only colleague he knew in the physiology department at the University of California who, like Ken, had worked with Kuffler and also taken his PhD from that "other" UC, the University of Chicago. Ben replied, giving Ken the name of the chairman of physiology, Dr. Leslie Bennett, and also telling Ken that for the first time since 1906, UC was consolidating its first two years of basic sciences with the medical school still on the slopes of Mount Sutro in San Francisco. To that end, several members of the physiology department, including Ben, were moving from Berkeley into the new Medical Sciences Building on the University of California San Francisco campus now known as UCSF.

Not expecting much, but with nothing to lose, Ken wrote to Dr. Bennett inquiring about possible new faculty positions on the enlarging San Francisco campus. Back came a cool reply saying they had two new openings, one of which was already filled by Dr. Julius Comroe, director of what has become the world-renowned UCSF Cardiovascular Institute. The other position would be in neurophysiology—Ken's field. Bennett went on to say they expected to have a great many applicants for the latter appointment since so many people want to live in San Francisco. When Ken showed me the letter, I reacted in high dudgeon—what an insulting implication! Does he not know you would be a great addition in building their new department? Do they not look "outside" to find the best trained and qualified candidate, etc.? Ken listened to my outburst, calmed me down, and went off to work. A few hours later, he called from the lab and asked, "How does this sound?" Always the Virginia gentleman, he had composed a marvelously forceful yet diplomatic letter distilling the thoughts behind my earlier explosion and adding salient points of his own. Apparently it worked since Bennett's next letter was much more respectful and offered a recruiting visit to San Francisco, which resulted in a job offer. Leslie visited us in our Baltimore home shortly thereafter, beginning what became a long and congenial friendship with him and his family. When later he became vice-chancellor for academic affairs, he remained one of Ken's strongest supporters at UCSF. A Westerner who is very loyal to his alma mater, I think Leslie saw from the first a "Western" quality in Ken, both as an academician and as a man.

With the birth of Stephen Kenneth Brown late in the summer, I began to learn life at an elemental level since layers of civilization cannot entirely cloak the animal nature of pregnancy and birth. When my surgeon first confirmed my pregnancy, I had taken a long walk through downtown Baltimore, marveling at the miracle within me that so transformed those gritty streets. More compelling was actually feeling the miracle evolve as hormones took over. My mother had complained so much about her difficult first pregnancy that I resolved mine should be pleasant, and with very good fortune it became so. For the better part of nine months, I not only bloomed but felt competent and important. Midway through I had a flutter of panic, wondering what I was going to do with myself as a mother, for I had no experience with babies. My mother put this qualm to rest with the statement, "Well, I think when the baby is born, you'll find out." How simple and inescapably true!

When the baby came, all my reactions felt primitive. Almost every aspect of the experience partook of wonder and surprise. Nursing was an experience both sensual and serene. And I felt animalistic in my protectiveness, ready to attack anyone rash enough to harm this child. That particular feeling persisted for months. Once, when a man I did not know knelt down to talk to Steve in his stroller, I was amazed by the melodramatic thought racing through my mind: if this man tries to grab the child, I'll jump on him and scratch his eyes. It's hardly a Quakerly or ladylike sentiment but perhaps legitimately maternal in a jungle, even an asphalt one. Twenty-one months later in San Francisco, these primal instincts were aroused again with the birth of our second son, Laurence Bunting Brown. I remember watching as the doctors performed a perfectly routine check of a newborn's reflexes, lifting Larry slightly from the bassinet, holding onto a doctor's finger with one tiny hand so recently liberated from my womb. Weak though I was, I envisioned leaping from the delivery table to catch my baby if he should let go.

Such irrational reactions take some getting used to and may be easily dismissed as hysteria or paranoia. I had indeed been blessed with a husband who was not only tolerant and lighthearted about some of these aberrations he found in the wife he thought he knew, but who also made me feel capable and desirable, no matter how absurd the circumstances. There can be no greater gift a new father can give to an uncertain new mother than the reassuring encouragement that she will somehow find ways to do whatever needs doing. A few weeks after Stephen's birth, I had my only postpartum period of panic, wondering how I was going to cope each and every day on my own with my suddenly acquired new responsibilities and restrictions. Ken stirred me with a marvelous statement. Looking me straight in the eye, he said earnestly, "You *have* to do it. I can't be here; I must work in the lab. You wanted a child, and you will have to be responsible for most of his day-to-day care." Those no-nonsense words, so sensible and true, somehow bolstered my resolve and confidence for which I've always been grateful. I felt that by taking my concerns seriously and responding with an implied assurance that I could do it, he had helped lift me over a hump of doubt that had momentarily stopped me in my tracks. I have never forgotten those words, increasingly helpful through the years.

Often, just before Ken returned home from work, I propped little Steve against pillows in the middle of our bed, ready to greet his father. One day, after bending over and offering his usual greeting, Ken extended the index finger of each hand to the baby. With a big smile, Stevie, always good at recognizing a new game, reached out and took hold of them, one tiny hand curled around each big finger. As Ken gently raised him a few inches, Stevie gave a joyous little cry and my heart turned over.

Page Hunter was one of our favorite neighborhood "imps." It was she who had persuaded us to take a puppy from a neighbor's litter, thus introducing Ruffi into our household. And in the weeks preceding Steve's birth she visited often, helping me prepare for the baby's arrival. Once, thinking she must be finding much of this boring, I asked her if she minded. She gave me the dreamiest look, wordlessly conveying her answer. When Ken and I returned from Johns Hopkins Hospital with our precious new bundle, there stood Page waiting to greet us with the gift of a fine diaper bag that I used for both children. I no longer rode my bike, so I sold it to her for the allowance she had been saving for that purpose. Her mother later told me Page polished that bike every day.

When a year later we moved to San Francisco, Page joined Steve and me to spend a week at my family home in New Jersey, where Ken left us before starting west on his solo car trip across country. Unburdened by wife and child, he set what still stands as our family record—nine hundred miles across the Great Plains in one day, driving the small used Mercedes we had bought during our stay in Baltimore.

On the last day of Page's visit, Daddy and I took her across New York Harbor on a ferry, showing her the spectacular sights that countless tourists travel from afar to see. Almost stumbling over each other in our efforts to point out the Empire State Building, Statue of Liberty, and various fine bridges during our brief voyage, we suddenly heard Page chuckle, "Dig that crazy bird!" Through our bombardment of words, she had been watching a pigeon trying to keep its footing on the pitching deck of the boat. Exchanging smiles, we subsided, letting her have the rest of her New York experience on her own terms before entraining home to Baltimore.

The Far-Out West

In 1957, the year before our move West, San Francisco experienced its strongest earthquake since 1906. Naturally, this was reported back east, and a friend asked me whether the news changed my mind about moving. I replied that I only hoped the city would hold together long enough to allow me to do some living in it. Thankfully, it has.

When Ken reported in from California, Steve and I boarded a plane for San Francisco. An hour out of New York we quite visibly lost one of our engines, so the pilot feathered the propeller and headed back to LaGuardia airport, jettisoning fuel over the ocean before landing. Our scheduled flight time was increased by a number of hours. When Ken finally met us about three in the morning, he remarked upon never before seeing me looking so tired. Steve had been awake throughout our adventure, happily entertaining one and all who came to see him standing in the bassinet mounted on the front wall of the cabin. Only as we neared his new home did he topple off to sleep, presaging the formidable schedules he would keep as a child.

How lovely our new city looked when once again I was rested enough that my eyes were open! One of our first evenings here, we rode a cable car to Fisherman's Wharf where we dined at the Franciscan Restaurant, enjoying views of the great San Francisco Bay spread before us while becoming acquainted with local abalone and Grey Riesling wine. Returning to our hotel in a nearly empty cable car, we were charmed to see an attractive couple who seemed very much in love—he Caucasian and she Chinese—

so comfortable, so natural, so San Franciscan. A few nights later at the famed Cliff House, then quite a dressy place, we noticed a middle-aged couple wearing old fishing clothes. They had been given one of the choicest tables overlooking the ocean and appeared to have just come from Sutro Rock, a popular fishing spot below Cliff House. This welcoming of legitimately casual dress—so unlike the exaggerated slovenliness that has disfigured the city since—appealed to us, typifying the West of those still-early postwar years.

The university typified the West in another way. A surprising number of social events were essentially "stag," for they were limited to professionals, which in those days amounted to much the same thing. It was still a man's world, following traditions from a more rugged era. After enjoying the graciousness of the Johns Hopkins University Faculty Club for three years, UCSF required some social adjustment for us, mostly for me.

Many academics enjoy opportunities for periodic moves and new beginnings, especially when developing their careers. And the academic schedule often allows time before each "beginning" to unload one's possessions into a new abode and take off on a short vacation prior to starting the new job. In that respect, San Francisco proved no different from Providence or Baltimore for us. Early in June, we had found new digs, and Ken's contract did not begin until July 1, which gave us time for a week's holiday in Carmel, surely one of the world's loveliest resorts, well remembered from our brief visit there ten years earlier.

Near Carmel Mission at the southern end of town is Mission Ranch, then a sleepy resort with swaybacked beds and gas stoves, whose oven, in our case, was home to a resident mouse. Since we were still reeling from West Coast prices (often described in those days as "slightly higher West of the Rockies") and had a baby in tow, the run-down cabin and its surroundings suited us perfectly. And the owners' teenaged daughter was eager to babysit! This was great for us, and over the next few years we effectively financed a pair of riding boots she coveted. At the restaurant on the premises I tasted my first California salad with green goddess dressing and became hooked forever on this state's agricultural treasures.

That hostelry now has been greatly upgraded by its new owner Mr. Clint Eastwood, and I am profoundly grateful to him for saving the uniquely beautiful property from developers who wanted to cover its hills and meadows with "progress." Thanks to that one individual who used his wealth well, the public can still enjoy unsurpassed views across fields harboring four or five grazing sheep, down past a lagoon to a scenic sandbar, beyond which endless waves crash against the headlands of Point Lobos across an inlet—a lovely legacy from Dirty Harry.

We returned to our newly rented house in the western part of San Francisco, half a block from Golden Gate Park, and exulted in the remaining June days with their cloudless blue skies and distant fog horns lulling us to sleep at night. Steve, Ruffi, and I spent hours in our sandy backyard or walking trails in the Park. Then suddenly July clamped down with a dense layer of fog, and for a month we saw the sun only three times at our house. I was ready to head back East. Fortunately for me, Chuck and Jean Blevins, friends from graduate school days in Chicago, showed up four blocks away. They knew California well, Chuck having graduated from Stanford and then taught for some years at a junior college in the East Bay. They had moved to San Francisco for Chuck to complete his PhD in anatomy at UCSF.

Jean saved my summer, often driving Steve and me across the bay to the sunshine of Orinda, where they had kept their home. While Steve and the Blevins girls played with their friends, Jean and I recharged our spirits in one-hundred-degree warmth. Upon returning home from these excursions, I always felt glad to slip back under our cool blanket of fog, surprising myself with how quickly I was becoming San Franciscan.

I also was becoming a devotee of the Pacific Rim, a term then emerging to designate the largely volcanic and earthquake riven countries ringing the Pacific Ocean. Signs of volcanism and quake were plentiful and rather thrilling to this Jersey girl accustomed to more placid terrain. Perhaps embedded in my psyche was a prenatal trip I had made with my parents to Paradise Inn on Mount Rainier, where my mother (and, perforce, I) waited for several days while my father joined a group climbing the great mountain. Since early childhood, I had known the ascent of Mount Rainier had been one of the cardinal experiences of my father's life, and I remember his sadness upon learning that Rainier's volcanic status had been downgraded from "dormant" to "extinct." It would please him that, with more recent evidence of increased heat, his mountain is again upgraded to "dormant." Surely, he would be delighted that his grandsons, aged two and four, were successfully coaxed and carried up California's Mount Lassen, southernmost of the volcanoes in the Cascade Range which includes Rainier and stretches north to Mount Baker just south of Canada. I was won to Lassen country by that first unforgettable view across the gently smoking crater of Lassen Peak to the snowy cone of Mount Shasta, California's taller volcano, rivaling Rainier in altitude, if not in bulk, ninety-three miles to the north.

We had been given excellent advice by Leslie Bennett before our move West. While visiting in Baltimore he warned us not to make the mistake of many new Californians, namely, buying a house immediately. There are many factors easterners are likely to miss in deciding just where to live. Earthquake fault lines are an obvious example, but some others are less well-known. Cool redwood forests, so inviting on dry summer days when mere shafts of blazing sunlight penetrate their towering branches, become dank and moldy during the rainy winters upon which those trees depend for their impressive stature. And houses near the beach may offer spectacular sunsets in winter but are likely to be buffeted by fierce winds in the spring and shrouded in fog all summer, as was our first house in the well-named Sunset District of the city.

Following this advice, we rented for our first year while studying the terrain and deciding what we might want for the long run. Like many newcomers, we were attracted to Marin County and almost bought there. But being separated from work by a bridge, even one as thrilling as the Golden Gate, appeared problematical as we watched the Bay Area's population already expanding explosively. And Ken was complaining about the commute from two miles west of the medical center, not a good omen for the much longer commute from Marin.

After many months of discouraging weekend house hunting, Ken happened upon a one-time ad for the house that has now been our home for over four decades. Although it clearly needed much work, it was that rarity—an affordable house within walking distance of UCSF, either by city streets or more fragrantly through a sizable eucalyptus forest located just a block above it. I think we both realized instantly we could be happy here.

And so we have been. We live in Parnassus Heights, on the eastern slope of Mount Sutro, around the corner from UCSF, which faces north from Parnassus Avenue to Golden Gate Park and the Presidio. The streets here are hilly, and ours is an uphill house requiring two flights of stairs for entry. But once in, we are on a level with the garden in back. The early years here were extremely busy, and the convenience of being around the corner from UCSF has been immeasurable as when Laurence Bunting Brown was born atop Moffitt Hospital within weeks of escrow.

Our house was built in 1902, before the great earthquake of 1906, so it needed considerable updating and remodeling to our needs for which we hired a contractor. For six weeks, Ken worked each morning in his lab at UCSF while every afternoon he used vacation time to work on the house. Having learned carpentry as a teenager, he worked alongside a professional carpenter on weekdays, continuing on his own through many an evening and weekend. With this schedule, the house soon became livable, after which he continued working on it in spare time for the better part of a year.

We had wonderful next-door neighbors who took all our new ventures in stride. They allowed a temporary sluice to be built through their backyard for pouring cement into our patio. And in a city that didn't seem especially welcoming to strangers at that time, Muggy gave a much appreciated tea, introducing me to the neighbors. She and Stan remained our close friends throughout the rest of their lives.

A large fuchsia plant grew on our side of the wall separating the two backyards. Raccoons foraged in the garden, helping to keep our yard free of snails—and also becoming adept at extracting cookies from us. Soon, however, we discovered our fuchsia plant was being damaged by use as a highway connecting the various backyard buffets. So to prevent the plant from being destroyed, Ken built ladders on the garden walls to provide alternate access. Muggy told me that one day a socialite friend interrupted a phone conversation to ask, "What's that hammering?" to which Muggy replied, "Oh, it's just the new young doctor next door, putting up raccoon ladders!" There was a pause, followed by a brief "I *see*."

Those ladders led to a fascinating discovery. To train the raccoons to the ladders, I placed bits of cookie on the rungs. Learning was quick. Then one night a year later, I heard a noisy commotion out there. On the south wall stood a large mother raccoon squawking at several little ones—I couldn't see how many but at least three or perhaps four. Immediately, one little body hurtled down the ladder, raced across the backyard, and scurried up the north ladder onto the top of its wall. More chattering and a second baby followed, and so it went until all had moved from south to north, whereupon their mother raced to where they were obediently waiting on top of the fence and made off with her brood. Quiet returned, and I was so excited I hurried to tell Ken I had observed evidence that animals can, and do, transmit information generationally by "verbal instruction." Though this conclusion may seem a bit of a stretch, all subsequent generations have used those ladders the same way, so for me, this hypothesis has stood the test of time.

During their preschool years, the boys and I often walked in the eucalyptus forest above us or in Golden Gate Park a few blocks away. Sometimes, we spent sunny mornings on Ocean Beach, three miles west of our home. One such day, Larry seemed especially exhilarated and soon initiated another of those heart-stopping moments for me, similar to Steve's little cry as a baby "riding" his father's fingers for the first time. Racing across the sand, he suddenly bent forward and scooped to his bare chest a large jellied mass lying at high-tide line. Remembering painful jellyfish stings from my childhood, I was aghast. But with a huge smile on his face, he spun around once, threw his arms wide, and flung the mass into the air, then raced onto some other flotsam or jetsam. Again, I felt my heart turn over, this time partly in relief, but mostly at the personification of pure joy I was witnessing. Years later, I saw a replay when his oldest daughter, so like him, spun with arms outstretched in the sunlight of our garden on her first visit here since infancy.

As our children grew, I began reading to them about Ishi, California's last surviving Yahi Indian. He lived the last five years of his life in the anthropological museum atop the California Affiliated Colleges located where UCSF now stands. A rock outcropping in our forest is called Ishi's Cave, where Ishi is rumored to have gone frequently to escape the city into an approximation of the wild Lassen country of his origin. Steve and Larry became two of the many boys who have "explored" and chipped away at those historic rocks.

Our location near UCSF allowed Ken and me to share lunches as well as dinners each day. We now lived far enough east and high enough on our hill to avoid much of the city's famous fog. The lotus life beckoned so appealingly that frequently I set up a card table on our patio for white-wine lunches, an idyll that would have persisted had we not discovered our afternoon efficiency declining precipitately. We continued with wine-free lunches, however, and I often think how much we would have missed without those times together. They assured Ken wholesome exercise walking up and down our hill, in addition to the thirty steps to our front door. They also gave the children and me his daytime company and brought to our home many fascinating colleagues visiting his lab from around the world, a treat I wouldn't have missed for anything.

I met two of my best friends for the past forty years in the nearby parks. On the daily walks that Steve, Ruffi, and I took in Golden Gate Park when we lived in the Sunset District, I met Eva, a former actress who had a daughter a year older than Steve. Her husband, Bill, half Chinese, had grown up in a prewar Shanghai that surpassed, in wry humor and exoticism, anything I could have imagined. We still see each other, though they have moved out of the city. After Larry's birth, I met Ann Gilliam over our respective baby carriages at Grattan Playground near our new home. She was the wife of the *San Francisco Chronicle* environmental columnist Harold Gilliam, whose many books about this unique Bay Area became influential in my life. Ann and I remained close friends until her death in 2002.

Shortly after moving into our new home, Page Hunter flew from Baltimore to join us for two weeks. She was then a young lady of sixteen, eagerly embracing everything about our new life. I love the thumbnail description of our environs that she gave to her parents on a phone call soon after arriving, "You should *see* these crazy hills!" Ruffi, the pup she had insinuated into our family in Baltimore, was the only one who did not adapt to our new situation. He was languishing, having acquired a skin condition the veterinarian thought resulted from something in the forest that disagreed with him. His coat lost its fluffiness, and he became irritable and peevish, sometimes even nipping at one of us. So we gave him to a family on a large property in the rural outskirts of South San Francisco who had wanted to give their teenaged son a full-grown dog for Christmas. It proved a good arrangement. A year or so later, while in that neighborhood with a friend, I saw Ruffi on leash, walking jauntily along the sidewalk with his owner and two or three other boys. He looked wonderful—all fluffed out again. I felt a tug at the heart, but gladness too at seeing him well.

When we moved to this city, the Top of the Mark reigned supreme on the skyline, offering 360-degree unobstructed views of the Bay Area to its patrons. I feel chagrined that initially I missed the skyscrapers and canyons of New York City and wished for a bit more verticalization here. This proved to be an example of the old adage "Be careful what you wish for; you might get it." Before long, Manhattanization swept through downtown San Francisco, cutting off the tiny views from our house of Bay Bridge and the UC Campanile in Berkeley. As with pregnancy, evidently there is no such thing as "just a touch" of high-rise.

In 1960 we were visited by my sister and her husband taking new jobs in San Francisco. They moved to an apartment on Washington Street along the cable car line. Charlotte worked in an office at the old P&O Orient Lines on Union Square, and she and I sometimes met for lunch at an old-fashioned tearoom on the third floor of a building along Maiden Lane. Breezes blew in lightly through its open windows—everything was light about the place—and I would often bring Char a bouquet of pink roses from an old bush revealed when Ken cleared our backyard jungle with an ax. Those soft, lovely roses invariably drew admiring attention. I have never seen them elsewhere and never learned their name.

During my sister and brother-in-law's six months in San Francisco, we often made a foursome at Scrabble or anagrams in our patio, and her husband proposed a nifty "handicap" system: whoever was ahead in whatever game we were playing would have to ride herd on our superactive Larry. These were among the most enjoyable times we ever spent together. During our calmer talks at home and especially on a brief stay the boys and I had with them in Los Angeles, I came to appreciate some of the wisdom born of wartime sufferings my brother-in-law had endured as a teenager in Europe. He was perceptive and had a fine aesthetic sense; he gave us much appreciated advice in decorating our home. Yet over the years, his considerable artistic talent was dissipated, and he became a tragic figure, quite possibly a belated casualty of his terrible war.

Late that spring, my father became terminally ill, and he wrote an extraordinary letter in which he bade me not to come back for a last visit or memorial service. As a family, we had never been much for funerals, and in this case, Daddy's reasoning seemed impeccable. He and Mother had visited us once in San Francisco, and Steve had been the apple of his eye from the moment of their first meeting in Baltimore. Although he never met Larry, he cherished the tales I wrote about the two of them and said he didn't want me to leave my "little family," for if something should go wrong while I was away, he would never forgive himself. I was grateful for his consideration, but the impending finality made it hard to honor his request. I was never entirely sure he meant it until after his death; Mother emphatically affirmed those wishes, adding his one fear had been that I might disobey him.

Ken's widowed father had become clinically depressed and after successful shock treatment recovered enough to travel west. He came to live with us for six months, and during that period he and I became good friends, which proved therapeutic for us both. We had many wonderful long talks and were able to give each other comfort and perspective on our lives. He spoke of some of the mental distortions he had suffered in his darkest days, describing how he could not even understand a cartoon I had sent to cheer him during that period. But he had saved the cartoon and could understand it easily after his shock therapy, which he took to be a promising omen for his eventual recovery.

Being with his two healthy grandsons also seemed to help. He had noticed how busy Ken and I were each day, and he helped us in many ways. One morning, while he and I were walking together in the park with the very active boys, he remarked, "You know, sometimes you and I have trouble getting through the day but for very different reasons!" His sense of proportion and gentle humor were returning.

Dad had moved back to his old family home near Appalachicola in the Florida Panhandle following his wife's death. There he met again a teenaged sweetheart from whom he had been separated when her parents moved away so many decades ago. In one of our many talks, Dad asked me how he might renew their old friendship, and I suggested he invite her out on a date.

On his next visit some months later, I noticed he kept beating me to our mailbox each day. This handy delivery service stopped abruptly after I found him on our patio, chuckling over a letter he had just received. Absence had made his heart grow fonder, and he had so missed Gertie (the same name as Ken's mother) that he had written to her, proposing marriage. From his seventy-year-old bride-to-be came the acceptance along with a report of the reaction of her ninety-year-old mother with whom she lived. Mother Harms thought it was nice they were such good friends but suggested, "Why don't you wait? After all, you have plenty of time." As Dad put it, "That's the one thing we don't have!"

Gertie flew to San Francisco, and we took them to Carmel where we witnessed their church wedding and gave them a minireception at the Pine Inn. We also bought a bottle of champagne with which to toast their happiness, but I don't think either of them had ever drunk champagne, each taking only one sip. We left them in a Carmel cottage to begin their traveling honeymoon that ushered in what became the happiest five years of their lives. We and the boys sped homeward through the inland heat with an unfinished bottle of champagne naively capped and propped upright between our seats. Of course it blew, capping our festivities by spewing bubbly over us.

Ken's early work on components of the electroretinogram had brought him to the attention of Japanese scientists, who at that time were trying to catch up after the losses of the war years. So his first postdoctoral fellows came from Japan, soon followed by others from England and Germany, as well as U.S. postdoctorals holding either PhD or MD degrees.

Those became our halcyon years, filled with harmony. Our social and professional lives expanded into an invigorating group of congenial individuals from whom we learned much. And I was experiencing an adultly aware "second childhood" that injected masculine preferences of our sons into my own inventory of feminine interests. I was fascinated by how boys' interests seem directed outward toward the world of things rather than inward toward the personal, as I observed among their female playmates. I have yet to hear a little boy ask, "Have you seen my new shoes?"

For the first time, I was reading literature my father had loved as a boy—and I had ignored during my childhood. In our sons' early years, together we read Jack London's *Call of the Wild* more than once. On the last occasion, a new period in the life of our family began. Steve brought the book to breakfast, saying, "Listen to this. It's *so* beautiful!" and began reading where I had left off the previous night. We all sat spellbound, for he read with great feeling a passage describing a fight to the death that established Buck's dominance over the other sled dogs. As he read, I felt tears flow down my cheeks and hoped they might go unnoticed if I didn't move. But when Buck's rival was about to expire, Ken glanced my way and remarked rather wonderingly, "Oh look, boys, Mommy is leaking!" to which Larry responded, "Why are you crying, Mommy? It's only a story."

I sometimes felt affirmations of wonder and love all around me. Our older son was always tender toward babies and young children, and I especially remember an occasion when we were visiting with friends in their kitchen, and the wife momentarily left to answer the doorbell, leaving her infant lying on the sideboard. Ten-year-old Steve immediately rose and stood beside the baby, making sure she couldn't roll off, while he entertained her quietly with hand motions. It was all done so considerately and unobtrusively. The mother had momentarily forgotten her baby and came rushing back into the room, effusively grateful to our young boy.

Larry showed similar tender feelings toward animals. Years later when I visited him in a lab where he had a summer job, I found him writing notes with one hand while dangling his other hand down toward a cage with a kitten in it. To my question about this he replied he felt the kitty had a hard enough life, so he had moved her cage near his desk to offer amusement to brighten her day. Looking more closely, I saw she was playing with his fingers through the wire meshwork.

His affinity for animals extended to the very small. From him I learned that what I had taken to be a dry leaf was instead a marvelously camouflaged moth. Similarly, he introduced me to the remarkable diversity of spiders and their distinctive webs on a walk in Vancouver's Stanley Park, known in our family as the Spider Walk. On a weekend trip to tidepools at Asilomar, Larry busily inspected insects in the chaparral while Steve and I watched the sea otters. Not until he reached second grade and complained he couldn't read the blackboard did we discover Larry was nearsighted. So it was little wonder he noticed and studied the small-scale world around us much more intently than we did.

The children grew more challenging. When once too often I preached my mother's mantra "Moderation in all things," Larry quietly added, "Including moderation." And one day during the sixties, Steve responded to my usual request that he carry my groceries up our stairs with the startling response, "No!" When I confronted him with a menacing "What did you say?" he announced, "Revolution begins in the home."

The sixties ushered in a huge increase in public activism. In our small area, a neighborhood association had already successfully defeated a proposal to extend their dead-end street through the forest to a major highway. This group, the Edgewood Avenue Improvement Association, then fought other such proposed measures as they arose. Chief among these, and just getting under way when we arrived, was the state's attempt to build a freeway through San Francisco connecting the Golden Gate and Bay bridges. Furthermore, the link would have cut through a corner of Golden Gate Park and threatened to force a disfiguring and quite possibly dangerous second level to Golden Gate Bridge to handle the increased traffic. Several beloved landmarks of the city were endangered simultaneously, and opposition mushroomed from many quarters. This was the first time I ever participated in any political activity, and my contribution was small—determining and publicizing, to the extent I then could, the largely neglected fact that trucks could not legally be kept off such freeways.

Effectively, the proposal would have diverted long-haul trucks from north/south freeways in the East Bay to a shorter route through Marin County and San Francisco, in the process threatening to overload Golden Gate Bridge and destroy many qualities of this city that keep it so livable.

I watched on TV the final vote of the board of supervisors and was thrilled with its dramatic outcome in our favor. Underlying emotions ran so high that heroes were created and political careers ruined upon that one vote. We saw what knowledgeable citizens with a good cause could do against entrenched political interests.

Activism on a large scale has become commonplace in recent times, but it was quite new then. That first victory became known as the Freeway Revolt. Shortly thereafter, we received a letter from a British scientist who had just returned to London after two years in Ken's lab. He enclosed a clipping from the *London Times*, telling of a similar proposal in a residential part of London quashed by local opposition, citing as their precedent the historic Freeway Revolt in San Francisco.

Ken came due in 1964 for his first sabbatical leave. Already leaning westward toward the Pacific, he applied for and obtained a fellowship from the Commonwealth Fund. This supported his work in Japan for two months, principally with colleagues at Keio University in Tokyo, and in Australia for nine months with Sir John Eccles at the Australian National University in Canberra. In a nice bit of timing, between the time Ken was granted the fellowship and our departure a year later, Dr. Eccles was awarded the Nobel Prize for Physiology and Medicine. We left California early in October, stopping first for a week in Hawaii, where we stayed in a Waikiki Beach hotel owned by the father of a neighbor on our block. When we entered the dining room that first evening, the band struck up "I Left My Heart in San Francisco." We have returned to the Hawaiian Islands through the years. Even the prominent presence of transients like ourselves cannot bury their essential loveliness. Their varied and dramatic natural beauty continues to set them apart as truly blessed isles.

Sabbatical

Carrying swimsuits still damp from an early swim in Hawaii, late at night we reached Tokyo's Haneda Airport where we were welcomed by the Watanabes and a number of colleagues from the Keio Physiology Department who taxied us to our hotel. Steve was wide awake, making continual observations beginning with "Look, Mommy." The bicycles were "backward," and traffic went the "wrong" way. Meanwhile, Larry nestled against Mieko and slept. When we reached the Hilltop Hotel, our home for the next two months, so much attention was focused on moving Larry to our rooms (he was a very large five-year-old) that we neglected Steve who sleepily leaned against and circled a thick pillar as though it were a wall leading to his room.

Each morning after Ken left for the university, the children and I set off to explore our surroundings. We spent much time in a nearby playground where the boys were accepted instantly by their Japanese counterparts. Children rushed up to them, calling hello, to which they responded *ohayo*, settling quickly on aloha as the greeting of choice. A special day began for us when three teenaged boys, clearly practicing their English, invited us to join a fair at their high school. We followed them through back streets to Meiji High School, where we represented a triumph of sorts for the young men who had brought us. Teachers and students gathered about to give us formal demonstrations of their culture— a tea ceremony, many Japanese arts and crafts, and several martial arts. In karate, a young black belt chose Larry for his partner. After showing him various moves, he engaged Larry in "combat," at the end of which he made it appear Larry had "thrown" him over a shoulder onto the mat. Larry brought down the house by stating accusingly, "*You jumped*!"

We enjoyed a marvelous few hours with these enthusiastic hosts, and I tried to think of a gift to leave with them in gratitude for the gift they had given us. I had with us an illustrated book about American Indians, so with the boys' approval, I inscribed it as a gift to the Meiji High School Library. I like to think it still resides there. We know that American Indians are of interest to many Japanese and vice versa. There seems to be a common bond. A young Japanese artist in San Francisco told us he has hitchhiked several times through our southwest, often obtaining rides from American Indians whose first question is "What's your tribe?"

Our big blond Larry charmed the Japanese everywhere. Whenever he asked me for some little trinket in stores, the clerk, with a smile, simply offered it to him, absolutely refusing payment. Steve's immersion into the culture was more subtle. He caught on fast to Japanese ways and became a favorite with the Keio graduate students who romped with him at parties. He also learned enough Japanese to startle the students upon occasion, and he responded appreciatively to the Japanese women's tender regard for children. Looking at photos from that time, Ken and I feel he almost "became" Japanese during those weeks, even to the cast of his eyes.

Wherever we went, especially when accompanied by Ken and our hosts, children rushed up to ask our sons two questions: "Where do you come from?" and "How old are you?" In one of the stores near our hotel, an English-language tape ran continuously with the first question answered, "I come from San Francisco." Upon one occasion, Steve and Larry were engrossed in conversation when a crowd of children asked their ages to which Steve replied absently, "San Francisco."

Refreshing to me was discovering the relative freedom from street crime in Tokyo. Friends had warned me of the only section of the city I should avoid with the children. For the rest, crime was virtually nonexistent. Near the Watanabe's home late one night, I was amazed to see a middle-aged woman hobbled by a slender kimono yet strolling alone in a dark park. Upon inquiring of Mieko, I was assured that even such a woman was quite safe.

This circumstance proved reassuring the night Larry lost a shoe as we hurried through Tokyo Station during rush hour. Such shoes were hard to come by, so after the boys were in bed, I returned by myself to the nearly deserted station and, after some searching, located the stairway where his shoe had come off. At first, I was dismayed to see the empty steps; then my eye was suddenly caught by the little brown oxford, carefully placed at eye level on one of the stone slabs beside the stairs.

Midway through our stay, we made a circuit of Honshu on Ken's intensive lecture schedule. Like most Westerners, we were overwhelmed by the gracious hospitality of our hosts wherever we went. Each day there were things laid on for the boys and me and, during the evenings, for the whole family. Especially memorable was a Genghis Khan banquet, the local version of a barbecue, held in a tent during a snowstorm in the mountains between Morioka and Akita. And in our favorite city of Kanazawa, we were treated to an exotic dinner and evening, which included refined geisha entertainment appropriate to the occasion. Also particularly appealing was a night spent at a superbly quiet, remote marine biological station on an island in the Inland Sea where I felt I could live happily for months. For our boys and us, it was all fascinating, and they adapted amazingly well to the adult aspects of that kind of travel. Indeed, we were treated like royalty, and they played perfectly the role of little princes.

After three weeks on the road, the boys again had us to themselves when we spent three days on our own at the historic Minaguchi-ya, memorialized in Oliver Statler's book *Japanese Inn*. On our first morning, I settled down onto a pebbly beach, where the boys immediately joined me and began constructing their games. Ken—who was wandering the shore, looking for photo opportunities—excitedly called to me, "Ginnie, you must come see this!" I asked what it was, and when he replied, "It's a beautiful view of Mount Fuji," I scrambled to my feet and started toward him. Instantly, Steve protested, "Oh, sit down, Mommy. Why don't you just wait and see it in the picture?" Luckily, I did not wait, for that roll of film disappeared in development, and we learned we had been at one of the most desirable spots from which to view Japan's most revered mountain.

When we again reached our rooms in Tokyo, Ken and I almost literally fell into each other's arms, and he laughed heartily when I remarked, "We couldn't have done it if the boys had been one year younger or if we had been one year older!" During this second stay at the Hilltop ("Yama-no-Ue" in the language of our hosts), friends arranged for us some other fine experiences. An especially close friend, whose family had lived in Kamakura for many generations, gave us a great local tour. Arranging for our boys to play with a Japanese youngster in his home, he then introduced Ken and me to several out-of-the-way places. In a small museum, I was struck by a lovely small portrait of a Chinese girl, apparently highly regarded by the Japanese, and several wonderfully humorous works by Hokusai, painted when the artist was in his eighties. Our afternoon culminated in a powerful rainstorm, catching us at a teahouse located in the middle of a lovely—and suddenly noisy—bamboo forest through which we departed soaking wet and exhilarated.

In Japanese homes, we saw very small boys doing homework, glued to their desks until late at night. Our friends explained that such effort was necessary to advance in the Japanese educational system. One mother and son had missed a chance to accompany the father during his two-year appointment at Yale because the three-year-old son needed to qualify for the elementary school feeding into the chain of schools leading eventually to Keio, considered the best private university in Japan. Again, a premonitory thought: "I hope it never comes to this in our country."

With visas expiring, we left Japan on the afternoon of Christmas Eve. Our flight gave us superb views of smoking Mount Kagoshima, in eruption on Kyushu Island south of our flight path.

Later, during early darkness, we flew into Hong Kong over its thrilling harbor, gazing down through wispy clouds upon a fantasyland of ships strung with decorative holiday lighting. After a week on our own exploring Hong Kong and Macao, we moved on to spend a boisterous New Year's Eve in Bangkok. On New Year's Day, we were privileged to accompany our host, a professor at the Chulalangkorn Medical School, inside the royal palace where, in a private audience, he presented his holiday greetings to the king while we waited in an antechamber. In humble contrast to that opulent venue, our hotel room overlooked a field where we could watch a water buffalo grazing.

We had been scheduled to stay in Thailand for a week, but one evening in an outdoor restaurant, Larry spotted a dish of condiments on a table and, quick as a wink, popped a red pepper into his mouth, swallowing it immediately. That evening, he was terribly sick to his stomach, and Ken distinguished himself as a family clinician. We had two adjoining rooms. Realizing that an upset mother was more hindrance than help, he suggested I take a bath in our room while he helped Larry get rid of the offending pepper. So there I lay, listening to gagging sounds in the adjoining bath while Ken patiently coached Larry in the art of inducing vomiting. Finally rid of the pepper, Larry was eager to impress me with an account of how everything had been accomplished. We couldn't help laughing as he lectured from a high stool upon which he sat clad only in his underwear, one leg crossed over the other, in a casual professorial pose quite familiar to us.

We realized we had been pressing our luck and therefore decided to head Down Under a few days early. Our hosts sympathized and were probably relieved to have us away from their red peppers and attendant complications. So the next day, we left the sweltering winter heat of Thailand for the dry midsummer heat of Australia, and I still carry with me the memory of three lovely Thai girls waving us into the sky, looking for all the world like a tropical bouquet in their slim silk sheaths of opalescent pastel hues ranging from apricot to aquamarine.

Many hours later, we touched down in Canberra and were impressed by the apparent friendliness of a crowd of Australians waving from the roof of their small terminal. As soon as we deplaned onto the stairs, however, Ken and I looked at each other in dismay, wondering aloud what we had gotten ourselves into. We too were waving briskly, having been assaulted by a swarm of the all-too-friendly bush flies, pesky little summertime beasts ubiquitous in the Australian bush. As far as anyone knows, bush flies do no harm except perhaps worry a person to death. They are attracted to moisture on the skin, and I never became used to seeing them plastered around the eyes of children at the swimming pool. I soon learned bush flies shun the dark. Stores and cafes at our nearby shopping center at Manuka often had only Asian style, beaded curtains hanging in their doorways, yet remained comfortably free of flies despite the throng waiting in the sunlight outside.

We were billeted in housing provided by the Australian National University (ANU). Our compound was located within easy walking distance of Manuka and the boys' elementary school. From the first evening, when we walked from our unit in Forrest Flats to the beer garden at the Hotel Wellington, the evening light struck me as different from that of early twilight in northern skies. The sky above looked lighter than at the horizon, a reversal of what I recalled from home. During the months ahead, we were to notice many dramatically colorful sunsets associated with a recent large volcanic eruption in the South Pacific.

Australia impressed me immediately as a land of enchantment, its beauty less heralded than that of its spectacularly scenic neighbor New Zealand, yet more alluring to me because of the vast, often-stark spaciousness. Its bush and its birds were magical. A forest not far from us rang with the raucous calls of sulphur-crested cockatoos bickering among the gum trees, and in early morning and late afternoon, kookaburras tuned up with laughter so human we often laughed along with them. I think of Australia as the greatest South Sea Island with the most beautiful beach I have ever known at Moruya Head.

This in no way contradicts the other side of the coin: the extreme lethality of some of its fauna. In addition to its justly famed sharks, the tropical seas of Queensland and Northern Territory contain numerous saltwater crocodiles, while insignificant-looking but deadly toxic cone shells and stonefish inhabit their coral reefs. And on the sea floor, giant clams camouflaged with sea growths, which render them hard to identify, await prey, occasionally closing upon and drowning an unwary diver. Farther south, one can meet equally deadly jellyfish. On land, Australia harbors some 120 species of snake, twenty of which are extremely venomous and one, the taipan found in the tropics, very fast and aggressive as well. Though the great majority of species are nonpoisonous, it is generally agreed that most of the snakes one might meet *are* poisonous, probably attesting to the survival value of this feature. In nine months of bush walks, the only snake we encountered was a red-bellied black snake, certainly poisonous, riding the riffles of Paddy's River into which we had startled it.

Before leaving this intoxicating subject, I must mention that some small fry—spiders and such—as well as flora, like stinging nettle trees, can seriously injure, if not kill, their victims. Even the shy and inoffensive duck-billed platypus, rarely seen in the wild because it lives in mud banks beside rivers and is exquisitely sensitive to vibration is equipped with poison glands beneath two sharp claws with which it inconveniences attackers. Even the cuddly koala bear comes lightly armed, as do an astonishing number of innocent creatures in this land of "Oz." To the convert, however, the hazards add spice to that fascinating continent.

We arrived in Canberra halfway through summer vacation, so the boys had a month of fun-in-the-sun dodging bush flies. Steve learned to swim there at Manuka pool, and minimal household duties allowed me to join them frequently. Early in February, I walked them to school on opening day. One look at the spacious green lawns surrounding the sprawling building made me wonder if I could ever entice them back to their cement home schoolyard in San Francisco. I needn't have worried. Some weeks later, when I asked how they liked their new school, Steve replied it was all right but somewhat boring. When I asked why it was "boring," he said all the children were "so white." So much for the "white Australia" policy, officially known as the restricted-immigration policy.

Perhaps significantly, Steve and Larry's closest friends at school were two brothers from Ceylon (now Sri Lanka), whose father was in his country's diplomatic service. As the relatively new capital of Australia, Canberra hosted many resident diplomats from consulates and embassies with more arriving all the time as embassies moved up from the former national capital at Melbourne. Our apartment complex contained mostly families of foreign academics working temporarily at ANU, and our children attended the same public school as the children of many of the diplomats. Accordingly, our sons' playmates had worldly interests; I once overheard Steve assuring his Ceylonese friend that tigers do not roam the streets in San Francisco.

Our kitchen looked out on a communal area where the children played, surrounded by two-story flats. I particularly enjoyed watching a little Japanese boy strutting about with a play sword while wearing a paper-bag costume resembling Sidney Nolan's popular depictions of the Australian outlaw and folk hero Ned Kelly. Kelly was a thoroughly vicious and despicable piece of work; nevertheless, he had been mythologized by Australians, much as Bonnie and Clyde were in the United States. In Nolan's paintings, Kelly was portrayed with the upper part of his body resembling an elongated cube, thus, inspiring new uses for old grocery bags at Forrest Flats.

Among our sons' closest neighbors and friends were the three sons of a delightful Norwegian colleague in Sir John Eccles's lab. Jan was Steve's age, and Dag and Tom, known as the Terrible Twins because of their relentless mischief in concert, were Larry's classmates. Steve had always enjoyed a good fight, but Larry never had. However, his large size for his age invited fights, for he was always the "guy to beat" in any new setting. So the feisty little twins, half his size but working as a team, took him on daily and so intimidated him that he and Steve came to me for ideas on how to stop the bullying.

Remembering Ken's tales of similar victimization as a boy, I had learned something about the psychology of bullies (Ken considers them essentially cowards trying to build up their egos). In any case, I felt this particular problem could be nipped in the bud. I suggested to Larry and Steve that they go out and sit quietly, talking on the lawn. When the twins approached, as they were sure to do, our sons should wait until one of the twins attacked Larry, whereupon both boys should leap up and each take on a twin, not actually harming him but hurting him enough to make him cry. For successful completion of the campaign, I offered a trip to Manuka for soft drinks, ice cream, and candy. I watched from the kitchen as they followed orders to a *T*, racing home shouting "We did it! We made 'em cry!" After congratulating our boys and making good on my promise, I contacted the twins' mother, my opponent in exciting squash games and an enjoyable friend. She had heard the news already of course and, far from being angry, thanked me! In her words, the twins had become too aggressive, completely terrorizing a four-year-old Danish girl. The boys' mother and I became even closer friends, the little Danish lass became one of Larry's admirers, and our five boys initiated an informal club that eventually included a number of other children at Forrest Flats. Would that all international problems could be dealt with that simply!

* * *

Late in the Australian fall, Ken was invited to present a paper at the annual Cold Spring Harbor Symposium on Long Island and departed in June for what became seven weeks in the states. Winter clamped down on us in Canberra with temperatures dropping to a record 19°F. This would have posed little problem had our flat been heated. But there was only a difficult and very small coal stove that created more smoke than heat. The situation was further complicated by the laws of New South Wales (NSW), which mandated continuously open spaces about two inches wide above all bathroom windows. Thus, the windows were built that way, appearing to newcomers as examples of grossly incompetent construction. Ironically, though we lived in the Australian Capital Territory (ACT), for some unexplained reason we also had to abide by NSW laws. Anyway, ingenuity had led to all sorts of ways to seal the required openings against the cold, all of which were unattractive and ineffective. We bought a small electric stove that warmed us to the knees as we sat in the evenings huddled over books and homework. And for several weeks, I wore my one set of ski underwear night and day, unable to launder it during the cold spell because laundry froze on the clotheslines.

The boys and I got around to see the country when we could, and when a week of winter vacation occurred during Ken's absence, we took the train to visit friends in Melbourne and see the sights in Adelaide. At that time travel was cheaper by Pullman than by air and lots more fun, with tea served morning and evening in each compartment and occasional stops where we could briefly leave the train. The boys had been wishing for a train ride behind a steam locomotive, since such engines were still occasionally used in Australia. So we signed onto a waiting list for a compartment and hoped.

We had just about given up when early Saturday evening we were called and told we could have space on a 9:00 PM departure that night. Packing with haste, we gave our cat what was left of our rather lousy fish and chips (at which even she turned up her nose) and headed for the station. Our train, alas, had a diesel engine but was otherwise satisfactory, and the trip was wonderful though not without complications. Steve came down with chicken pox, and our Melbourne friend, who happened to be a pediatrician, told me to set the alarm each night to assure Steve regularly received a pill to help keep him from scratching while asleep. I put him in my bed so I could monitor his restlessness, but it probably wouldn't have mattered, for one night while bumbling around after the alarm went off, I popped *his* pill into *my* mouth.

Highlights in Melbourne included a drive up into the Dandenongs, home of the famed lyrebird. Though we failed to find him—hardly surprising because he's reclusive—it was a privilege just to share his domain for an afternoon. Another special treat was the cream taken from the tops of milk bottles. In Australia at that time, dairies delivered milk to the door as in my American childhood. The cream floating on top was thick enough to whip, and cream spooned from a small bottle of pure cream was already as thick as whipped cream, making it the ideal topping for a luscious Australian dessert, Pavlova, consisting of baked meringue covered with cream and fruit. (Back in the United States, my attempts to make Pavlova failed because the whipped cream fell down within minutes.) The cream in Melbourne was undoubtedly loaded with cholesterol, but it did not contain the controversial growth hormones and antibiotics that have caused so much trouble in our country. Later, I happened upon a depressing three-line filler in our Canberra newspaper, to the effect that consultants from the U.S. dairy industry were on their way to Australia, so the continent has probably been well homogenized for a long time now.

Another overnight Pullman took the boys and me to Adelaide, capital of South Australia, which has a refreshing spirit all its own. Unlike its neighboring states of New South Wales, Victoria and Tasmania, which had been founded in the late eighteenth century as English penal colonies, South Australia was established somewhat later as the continent's first "free state." Descendants of those original nonconvict settlers exhibit considerable pride in their voluntary settlement of South Australia.

Adelaide seemed a lovely place. Its parks, strung out along the Torrens River, were pretty, and the rowing parties there looked vigorous and picturesque. Cream teas with delicious scones were to be had, and evidence of empire also remained in the Southeast Asian influences in the heart of the city. All in all, Adelaide seemed a refined and fortunate British outpost basking in Austral sunshine.

The day before our departure, we took a tram down to Glen Elg, a resort town on Spencer Gulf south of Adelaide. Scrounging its beaches, we amassed an exotic collection of oceanic debris that filled the boys' pockets. Then toward evening, we joined throngs on the pier to watch an awesome sunset that spread across the sky, slowly deepening in color to a deep red just before dark. Upon returning late to our room, we carefully washed our treasures, laying them on towels to dry for packing the next morning. Sometime after midnight, I was wakened by a massive stench that so completely permeated the air I could not localize its origin without sniffing each item in turn. The source turned out to be an unfortunate sponge, which we had failed to realize was still alive—a mistake unlikely to be repeated.

The last segment of our return trip to Canberra was broken late at night in Goulburn, where our car was detached and shunted onto a siding as the rest of the train continued on to Sydney. I was dimly aware of the shiftings, finding it pleasant to be moved about with so little disturbance and no effort required from me. When I sat up in bed for tea the next morning, I was overjoyed to see great puffs of white smoke drifting out across the beautiful Aussie landscape from our speeding locomotive. My exclamation brought Steve and Larry down from their berth, and our trip was complete as we hove into Canberra under steam.

When Ken returned from the States, we finished our sabbatical in a spurt of activity beginning with participation in inaugural events at the new Performing Arts Center in Canberra. Most memorable was a stunning performance by the Australian Ballet Company. We also managed a ten-day car trip north, including a visit to a wildlife sanctuary at Gosford, a wakeful night listening to a lovesick cow in the otherwise serene Bellinger River valley, a ramble in a rain forest on the Dorego plateau, and a visit to a sugar cane plantation in southern Queensland, topped off by an overnight in the Blue Mountains en route home—a good score, but time was growing short with our desires remaining long.

Eventually, the day came to bid farewell to Manuka, Moruya, and the Murrumbidgee, to Brindabella and Coolangatta and the irresistible kookaburra. All those musical aboriginal names and their tangible manifestations had to be put aside for another day. Behind us, we were leaving unfinished business, and we hoped to return someday for further explorations of that great land.

A final delight awaited us on the way home. A jetport had just opened on Tahiti, and our Qantas flight to Los Angeles made a stop there. We stayed for ten days, occupying a grass-roofed hut in an old resort on the outskirts of Papeete—total relaxation. The open-air market offered grapefruit the size of volleyballs, and they were delicious. Many foods tended to be expensive, but French imports such as brie and wine were surprisingly cheap. Augmented with the local fruit and breads, our meals taken alfresco at the little native-style cottage became feasts.

A narrow cement walkway ran alongside the cottage and bifurcated halfway down a slight hill below us. This provided the boys a setting for new games, the cleverest of which was Steve's, using the two paths as "runways." When he ran down the longer path, he did so with arms swept behind as befits a proper jet, but when he took the shorter path, his arms were held straight out to the side, like wings of a propeller plane, as he carefully explained to his brother.

Larry learned to swim in Tahiti, using his own ingenious method. The pool at our resort had no shallow end, so at first, he used an inflated plastic tube to stay afloat. As Ken and I lazed around talking, Larry kept calling, "Look at me. See how I'm swimming." We dutifully responded without paying much attention, failing to notice that he was periodically letting air out of the tube. In exasperation, he finally tossed the empty tube onto the grass then pointed to it. That time we showered him with praise, both for his success and his method of achieving it.

One day on a hike in the hot, humid inland hills, we turned a corner and encountered scruffy-looking men on military maneuvers. Rumor had it the foreign legion was training in those hills toward action in the wars of Southeast Asia. They were taciturn and unwelcoming—their appearance differing greatly from that of the legionnaires my father met in their headquarters twenty years earlier during war in North Africa. Time had marched on, the world obviously marching with it.

Our evenings often included joining residents gathered on low hills to watch the exquisite cloud patterns as the sun set over the island of Moorea, eleven miles away. And toward the end of our idyll, we swam with frangipani blossoms tucked behind our ears. At one point, Ken looked at me sheepishly and remarked, "Better not let *this* get back to UC!" It was a wonder-filled year, and on its last night, we heard from afar the faint strains of "I Left My Heart in San Francisco," the same song that had welcomed us to Hawaii just one year earlier. It was indeed time to return home.

The Golden Gate Bridge, symbol of our new home, photographed by a friend, Hans Dieter Oestreich.

Motherhood and my golden years.

Introducing the boys to a swimming hole on our first family camping trip.

Family portrait taken by Kosuke Watanabe, an artistic postdoctoral fellow in Ken's laboratory.

At Valley Center in Southern California with a favorite painting by my aunt, Mildred Miller.

In the gardens of Kenroku Park in Kanazawa, our favorite Japanese city.

Our son, Steve, with Professor Tsuneo Tomita, Chairman of Physiology at Keio University in Tokyo.

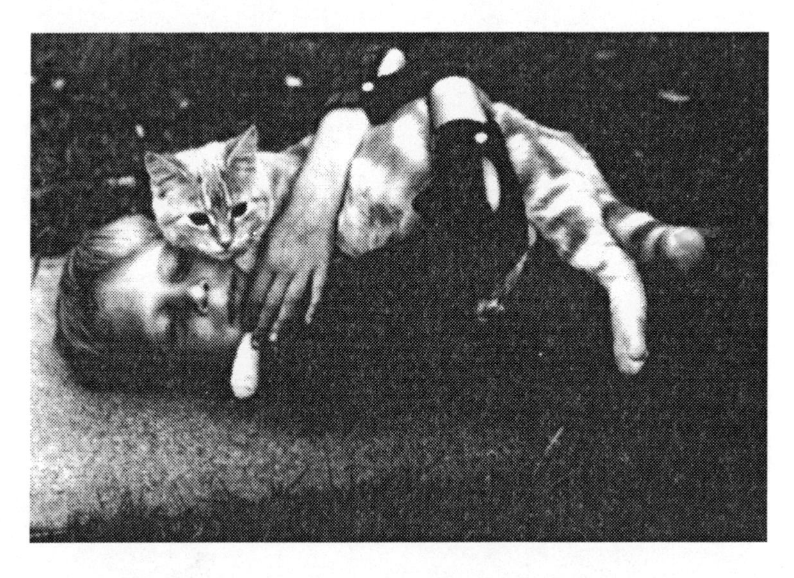

Our son, Larry, and pet cat, during our sabbatical in Canberra.

Back home in San Francisco,

Our Green American House

Soon after returning to what Steve called "our green American house," we drove to Valley Center, bringing home some of our favorite paintings by Mildred Miller, my aunt, which I had inherited from her just before our sabbatical. The bulk of her works remained stored until we had time to arrange their disposition, and Bob Williams was happy to continue indefinitely as caretaker on the property, which we used for several years as a retreat. Since a truly clean cottage was never an option, we could entertain there with rustic ease. The Riesens and Ureys, then living in Riverside and La Jolla respectively, enjoyed soaking up the sun on Mildred's patio, and together we examined paintings and speculated about their future. Helen greatly admired *Sunflower Girl*, one of Mildred's large canvases now in the collection at Swarthmore College. And with the Ureys, we spent lazy hours watching Larry and Steve as they bustled about the property with wheelbarrow and implements cadged from the outbuildings, rekindling memories of our own childhoods.

The boys reentered Grattan School two months after the school year had begun, and I walked them there to register. As Steve's class filed past on the way to homeroom, one of the boys remarked, "There's Steve," whereupon his classmates made room for him in line, and away they went. Larry slipped in too, though having been just a kindergartner when he left, his bonds were not so strong as Steve's.

With both children in school, I volunteered at UCSF hospital for several years. UCSF is one of the best tertiary care centers in the country and as such attracts a large number of seriously ill patients. My medically untrained presence could do little substantively, but I could raise spirits by providing company for those far from their families. Perhaps my greatest contribution was devising a simple method for reducing a time-consuming clerical task required of the nurses, thus releasing them for more productive activity. That simple improvement gave me much pleasure for it was not "down my alley." By now, it has surely been superseded by computerization, but my satisfaction remains undiminished. Other volunteer efforts included ushering one year at Thursday matinees of our San Francisco Symphony and working for a time at our zoo where the most interesting project assigned to me was monitoring "swimming lessons" given to a newborn sea lion by its mother!

During our year's absence, changes had occurred in the Bay Area, and these dominated the local scene for decades, spreading quickly across the country. The UCBerkeley campus had been commandeered by the Free Speech Movement (FSM—soon dubbed the "Filthy Speech Movement" as its emphasis became clearer). And in San Francisco, the first hippies moved in to our Haight-Ashbury District. Initially, these "flower children" brought a revitalizing force into a deteriorating neighborhood. They introduced fresh ideas, youthful joy, and a sense of fun, creating fine poster art and cheerfully sprucing up the city with their colorfully decorated houses and fire plugs. Many of these innovations survive including painted rainbows over tunnel entrances north and south of Golden Gate Bridge and a natural food store established two blocks from our house.

The boys and I joined throngs of young people streaming on foot through Golden Gate Park to the first "Human Be-In" held at the Polo Fields in the western end of the park. Goodwill overflowed. Alas, the hippie scene quickly turned sour, with organized drug interests moving in and actualizing my fears first engendered by the LSD experiment I had monitored a decade earlier in Ohio. Many of the original hippies left San Francisco for enclaves in the felicitous northern California countryside. We have them to thank for contributions to enduring improvements in our lives—the organic food movement, sustainable agriculture, and a resurgence of arts and crafts. But the remaining presence in the city did not deliver on its early promise. Over the years it has attracted generations of alienated malcontents who form a disillusioned constituency perennially ripe for political exploitation.

In our year away, a new concern had arisen very close to home when a high-rise office building went up in Parnassus Heights despite strong objections from the residential neighborhood. This introduced us to its builder, a Marin County real estate investor, who over a period of years had been buying up a residentially zoned block of houses and wished to replace them with a hotel. We were to experience several confrontations with him over the next fifteen years, culminating in a citywide political contest that cost him virtually all his former support, as described in chapter 11.

Meanwhile, Ken undertook a project of benefit to our block. For years, PG&E (Pacific Gas and Electric Company) had slowly been putting overhead power lines underground. In this city of spectacular views, the list of neighborhoods awaiting undergrounding was already long. To get on the waiting list, an area of the city had to form an "undergrounding district." This required a petition signed by a substantial percentage of property owners since each property owner would have to pay for connections from the undergrounded wiring into his own property.

During our sabbatical, the Edgewood area, just above us, had submitted such a petition, but our adjacent block lay outside its boundaries. Ken and I had a powerful incentive to have our block of wiring also undergrounded, for just outside our prime view window stood a power pole loaded with almost everything imaginable either electrical or telephonic. In addition to a large transformer and bulbous old streetlight, it bore multiple crossarms from which wires radiated to every house in our vicinity. So Ken undertook to form an undergrounding district for our block by obtaining the necessary signatures during evening hours, then convincing PG&E to underground our block at the same time as the Edgewood area.

Our block looked more difficult than Edgewood for acquiring the requisite signatures because we have several apartment houses, and so absentee property owners are mixed with the resident home owners. Of course, Ken knew about this but set out in good spirits, prepared to persist with a little daytime help from me. His first excursion was successful but not very efficient. After dinner, he headed for the people we knew best, our "uphill" next-door neighbors who we judged would be the softest targets. When he returned a couple of hours later, I asked how things had gone, and he said, "Just fine." Stan and Muggy had signed immediately then offered him a drink, and he spent the rest of a pleasant evening with them with only two signatures and a happy face to show for it.

Eventually, we had well over the required number of signatures and were ready to submit our petition, but Ken was striving to come as close to a hundred percent as possible. A dear old lady, Mrs. McMonegal, lived in a house with a charming conically roofed turret on one of its front corners. She seemed to enjoy Ken's repeated visits and always stalled, claiming she had to contact her son who lived elsewhere, didn't know how much she could afford, wondered how disruptive it would be, etc. For Ken, this became a challenge—plus he enjoyed visiting her. And he had the satisfaction that when she *did* sign, she was enthusiastic.

We had to wait until 1970 for the actual undergrounding to begin, but the result has been worth all the effort and waiting. Neighborhood reaction is well expressed in the story of an old-timer who said their teenage son had just left for school one morning when he raced back into their house, crying excitedly, "Why haven't I ever noticed before that we can see the Golden Gate Bridge from here?" That young man is now an architectural photographer.

The sixties brought San Francisco two murderous crime sprees: the Zebra killings and the Zodiac murders, each of which spread uncertainty and fear throughout the region. There was little the average citizen could do but be wary and wait. To his credit, Mayor Joseph Alioto somehow put a stop to the racially motivated Zebra killings shortly after he took office in 1968. We don't know how he did it but suspect there was behind-the-scenes maneuvering, for that often seems the way difficult things are accomplished. For a time, speculation continued about the Zodiac killer who has never been identified publicly, but his killings also ceased abruptly.

Of less renown were our school crises. In a neighborhood as diverse as ours, busing of children in and out of this neighborhood to achieve some sort of racial parity aroused parents of all colors and backgrounds in objection to the proposed forced commuting. Prior to this controversy, I had watched numerous parades in the schoolyard on holidays such as Halloween, and often, they brought tears to my eyes. All unconsciously, they represented a United Nations in microcosm—black, white, and everything in between—natives of the Americas, Europe, Asia, Africa, and Pacific Island nations. Their fathers and mothers were laborers, academics, artists, musicians and writers, businessmen and lawyers, longshoremen, doctors, nurses, and housewives. No way could busing increase the diversity already achieved naturally in such neighborhoods.

Predictably, busing led to an exodus from the city by many who could afford to leave, thereby skewing the population ratios used to determine future busing. This guaranteed a vicious cycle for the next round of mindless meddling. Indeed, it represents "wheel-spinning" in every sense of the word, and the effort continues today. A third generation of San Francisco students has been threatened with hours of bus riding despite strenuous objections from their parents. While such machinations, often promoted by entrenched bureaucrats, serve an obvious political purpose by creating constituencies increasingly dependent upon government, the price to individuals is the loss of personal control of their lives and families. Alternative schools have been instituted by those who cared enough about quality of education and could afford the effort. Meanwhile, the city has lost a lot of its middle class. Left behind are the wealthy who can afford private schooling, the poor with few options, and a city full of problems inherent in a society with such severe dichotomies.

In the case of our sons, I sometimes felt during the late sixties that bridges were falling behind us. I have always favored public schools, especially at the elementary level. Yet I was seeing our younger son suffering from the disruptions that were interfering with both teaching and learning. Classes that had been orderly and educational when Steve took them two years earlier were becoming hopelessly unruly despite being taught by the same teachers. In talking with some of those teachers I admired, I learned they too were suffering from the "degradation of education." One of them told me Steve's class was the last satisfying class she had taught.

Within a few months of our return from sabbatical, Larry was complaining of headaches from noise in his classroom, so one day, I obtained permission to observe his class. Within *half an hour*, I had a headache, and the teacher was visibly stressed. Afterward, when I asked her how I might help, she said *anything* I did would help, a pretty desperate statement considering she knew almost nothing about me. So I went to the principal and offered to work as a volunteer. Bureaucracy then stepped in; for reasons of liability and insurance, I would have to be part of an established volunteer program. Since none yet existed at Grattan, I became its founder and director. I acquired administrative responsibilities as the program grew and, though minor, these were annoying because they took me farther from the pupils. As the national election approached in 1968, for example, I was informed that one of our new "volunteers" hardly stepped into a classroom, spending most of her time politicking for her candidate in the faculty lounge. When we called her on this, she departed that day.

Usually, teachers asked me to work with either the troublemakers or the top students, thus separating the children to give motivated pupils and teachers a chance. The best students were particularly satisfying for there were a lot of talented and intelligent children eager to move faster than the system allowed. Much of this has changed by now, hopefully for the better; but persisting troubles threaten the stability and the value of public education to its most important clients—America's future adults.

Ken's lab was operating in high gear and morale there was high. So this was an exciting time for us and fun into the bargain. We sometimes held lab lunches in our patio, serving either a ten-foot-long subbie sandwich, its bread baked in a stovepipe oven by a local supplier or during bass season a large striped bass caught by Ken or Larry. Some of our best dinner and holiday parties were given during those years. Thankfully, Ken shared with me both his work and his reactions to it. I remember when he discovered the "late" and "early" photoreceptor potentials (in that order). These times were so exciting that for some time afterward he reported a mild but distinct burning sensation in his abdomen, a phenomenon he thought could easily have given rise to the well-known phrase "fire in the belly."

New members in the lab included an Australian postdoc whose second child was born here. When he and his family departed, they invited us to join them for dinner aboard the P&O Orient liner *Himalaya*, sailing later that night. After dinner, we wandered out on deck and stood at the rail reminiscing about times here and in Australia. As I looked up at the great Bay Bridge above us, I felt a sudden surge of joy to be staying in *this* port instead of sailing off into the night.

Observations of our sons as they grew older fascinated me. In each of the boys I caught striking reminders of their father and two grandfathers. And I felt I was witnessing an intellectual analogue to the embryological principle of "ontogeny recapitulates phylogeny." Steve at age three asked, "Why do cars and trucks and buses have wheels?" And a somewhat older Larry, watching a fire in our fireplace, asked, "Is fire alive?" In the latter case, I began to answer no but quickly realized fire does possess many characteristics of life such as motility, reproduction, consumption of food and oxygen, and eventual death. So I later put the question to Professor Leslie Bennett whose eyes lit up with delight. He pointed out fire lacks cellular structure, an essential feature of living beings. Fire and the wheel—surely among primitive man's earliest forays into intellectual inquiry, questioned eons later during our sons' early mental development.

For me, those blossoming years had a fine balance. To be sure there were problems, but all the essentials for basic satisfaction were there. During the late sixties, we began family vacations in the northwest, driving to the Canadian Rockies in the summer of 1966. And fall of that year took Ken and me to UCLA for the dedication of the Jules Stein Eye Institute where Ken was one of the scientists invited to speak. Though Jules Stein was an ophthalmologist by training, he is more widely known as the president of MCA (Music Corporation of America) and head of Universal Studios. In actuality, this gala affair turned out to be more social than professional, and we had the pleasure of joining some of Hollywood's glitterati at cocktail parties, luncheons, and a one-thousand-seat banquet. Ken later sized up the affair as "academia in la-la land."

Wives were royally treated. Before the grand banquet, we were given the full treatment by makeup men from Universal Studios. At a luncheon for wives, Cary Grant topped a roomful of lesser lights. Heading my lunch table was a cowboy actor who seemed especially pleasant and communicative. When telling the boys about him, I couldn't recall his name, but a short time later, while watching a Western together, I recognized him cantering across the screen and exclaimed, "That's him—the guy at lunch." Steve and Larry seemed properly impressed.

We were given a visit to Disneyland and a tour of Universal Studios, which was more entertaining than many movies. But, of course, the real showstoppers were the glamorous gatherings of movie folk. At the welcoming cocktail party, I noticed the largest clump of guests were gathered not around Zsa Zsa Gabor, Cary Grant, or Gregory Peck; the largest group surrounded Peter Ustinov.

For us, the Jules Stein affair was the most glamorous scientific meeting we had attended since an international convention held in the Hague some years previously, whose highlight for me had been a private evening reception in the Mauritshuis museum—wandering about, champagne glass in hand, among exquisite small Rembrandts hanging on the walls lining a vast staircase. Those years in the sixties and seventies were the best of times for scientists who then enjoyed better support for their work and related travel than most previous academics had ever known.

* * *

During the summer of 1967, we took the trip of a lifetime to Alaska for which Ken had saved almost eight weeks of vacation time. We drove a thousand miles up the coast to Vancouver Island, visiting Victoria briefly before continuing north to Kelsey Bay where we caught the newly established British Columbia ferry to Prince Rupert. We spent an interesting day there before boarding the Alaska ferry that evening to go up the Inside Passage. This culminated in an ethereal moonlit ride up the Lynn Canal in the wee hours of morning, for me an incarnation of my hauntingly beautiful dream twenty years earlier while still at Swarthmore. We disembarked at Haines into a sparkling day and were in the best of spirits as we started the long drive up the Haines Highway toward Haines Junction where we would join the Alaska Highway.

A tiny northwest corner of British Columbia and then a sizable portion of the Yukon Territory had to be crossed on unpaved road. But the sun was shining over a vast and glorious wilderness, and we were exulting in the scenery and the great open space all around us. Ken exclaimed he thought we should do this *every* summer. A couple of hours later, the sky darkened, and rain began to patter, then pelt; the road turned slippery, and we longed for the paved "Alcan" ahead. Finally, we made the left turn onto asphalt and, greatly relieved, pulled into a muddy parking lot at a warmly lit, inviting little restaurant that promised civilization. As our engine was turned off, we listened to the gentle but persistent *pssssssss* of a tire going flat, whereupon Ken turned to me and remarked, "Well, maybe every *other* year!"

In Alaska, we experienced cold glaciers and hot springs, camping and fishing and panning for gold, swatting mosquitoes while trying to light a fire in a cold drizzle, and being blown out of a campground south of Fairbanks in the vanguard of one of the worst storms ever to hit that city—the flood of '67. We drove many roads so poor that our top speed was reduced to twenty-five miles per hour, and traffic was limited to very few cars. The worst of these led to Mount McKinley National Park where we devoted a week to exploring and enjoying its animal-watching opportunities. And we spent one day just outside the park, gathering blueberries for the best pancakes I ever made, complete with hot blueberry syrup over berry-studded cakes.

On a particularly precious afternoon, we waded to a small island in a shallow lake and watched as a determined beaver plodded up a gentle slope, gnawed down a sapling, then sank his teeth into the cut end, and dragged the tree to his beaver house. There he dove, presumably to attach the cut end to the foundation of his home. Each time he surfaced, he nibbled a few of the floating leaves before heading up the slope again for another sapling. We were entranced. He had to know we were there; indeed, on the last trip, I had the inestimable pleasure of watching a small procession wending its way solemnly down the hill—led by the furry little creature followed by his tree and then, at a respectful distance, Ken, Steve, and Larry in single file, hands clasped behind their backs, heads down, looking thoughtful. These are the images with which mothers paper the walls of their memory banks.

Robust challenges to us and to our car were also presented by the road leading from Fairbanks to Circle, northern limit of the connected highway system of pre-pipeline Alaska. The character of this bumpy road was well defined by a hand-lettered sign, which, nailed to a tree, proclaimed, "Beer and Sandwiches—15 Miles." At Circle Hot Springs, we stayed in an old resort hostelry where we quickly learned, to our surprise, that the plumbing in the cabins delivered nothing but boiling hot water directly from the springs.

Our trip concluded with a drive down the Alcan Highway. On a detour to Dawson City in Yukon Territory, we encountered another memorable sign. Our dirt road sloped down and vanished into the Yukon River, a mighty waterway whose surface was covered with intimidating, swirling eddies. While waiting for the ferry to take us over to Dawson, we noticed at water's edge an official highway sign reading Stop!

By chance, we had arrived on the eve of Discovery Day, an annual celebration of Carmack's 1897 discovery of gold in the Klondike. Celebrants from as far away as Whitehorse were coming down the Yukon in more than a hundred boats, including four amphibious vehicles, the first I had ever seen, that suddenly departed from the flotilla and rolled up onto land.

We literally landed the last room in town—a tiny affair on the ground floor of the Flora Dora Hotel where our boys camped on the floor between our cots. In the lobby outside our door, sourdoughs in town for the occasion bedded down on sofas, chairs—whatever they could find.

That evening, we attended an act by a magician who turned up late—and very drunk—aboard a tethered riverboat where his puzzled audience awaited him. He tried to include in his act our eight-year-old Larry who was especially quick at analyzing spatial problems and unobtrusively upstaged the magician by placing his hand slightly differently from the magician's instructions with comical consequences. Over the next two days, we received laughing congratulations from people who had inadvertently attended our son's theatrical debut.

During Discovery Day itself, we explored the town, taking in a sprightly revue at the opera house. If memory serves, it was put on by a talented group of young performers from Vancouver. We spent that evening in what seemed to be the liveliest bar where we met a friendly Indian (drinking nonalcoholic beverages) who offered to take us on his boat leaving the next morning. He had just concluded his annual trip "outside" to bring supplies for the winter to Old Crow, his village on the Porcupine River. It sounded a fascinating and exotic experience, tempting the romantic in us. But it would have seriously interrupted Ken's career since the trip took weeks of traveling down the Yukon and up the Porcupine, after which we would have had to winter over in Old Crow until the spring trip outside.

The day after Discovery Day is aptly known as Recovery Day and was extremely quiet. The following day on our way out of town, we took advantage of another invitation proffered at that same bar, this one much more practical for us than the trip to Old Crow. A stooped and ancient miner named Pete Brady had asked us to visit him on his claim in the Klondike. As a small lad in Ireland, he had been smitten with gold fever and scared his mother daily, spending hours after school mixing Irish earth with flakes of precious gold sent him by a brother in the Yukon; he would then practice "panning" them out in a nearby Irish stream. In the early years of the twentieth century, when he was eleven years old, Pete joined his brother on the goldfields, and, with the exception of overseas service during World War I, remained in the Yukon the rest of his life.

The track into his place was quite difficult for our Dodge Dart, so the boys and I walked to prevent our car from becoming hung up at his claim. When we arrived at his cabin, he was still in bed from Discovery Day. I noticed a coffee pot on the stove, and as he sat on the edge of his bed, I offered to brew some coffee. He seemed amenable until he saw me start to empty the sludge in the bottom of the pot. That really woke him, and he shouted, "No no!" Ken rebuilt the dead fire, and I reheated the dregs in the pot to revive him. He then spent several hours showing us his claim. He had dug out by hand a long section of stream bank and had built a hand-operated rocker to separate out the gold. Each summer he earned enough from his small operation to support his winters in town. Indeed, a tiny vial resting on my desk holds some coarse Klondike gold that he washed out while we watched and gave us as a memento.

No words can do justice to that marvelous trip. Its effect on Ken was so strong that when we returned home he devoted much time to finding a place within easy driving distance of San

Francisco where we could at least camp on unsettled land. On weekends, he would head north, usually finding that others with similar ideas had been there ahead of him, inflating prices accordingly. Finally, near Boonville in Mendocino County, he came upon wooded acreage that had long ago been logged of its redwoods and now had a lovely second growth of evergreens, madrones, and chaparral. The boys and I also loved it, and it became our rural getaway. We used only tents for which Ken built a platform, and had no running water except from a distant small spring. But we also had a swimmable pond and soon a rowboat. We spent many fine short holidays there, glorying in the quiet, starry nights and gleaming white morning fogs which often blanketed the valley below us.

I had an exhilarating surprise while using our primitive facilities there very late one night. I sat entranced by the predawn sky until I noticed what appeared to be a searchlight extending straight up into it. The light did not extend the other direction, however, down to the ground—and I realized with a start that I must be looking at a comet. I roused Ken and together we managed to coax our sleepy boys out of their pup tent for the cosmic spectacle.

We no longer took daily newspapers, which Ken had opined were too dreary a way to start the day. (Indeed, he had made clear that either the paper or he would have to go, which I reported verbatim when canceling our subscription.) Thus we no longer knew much of what was happening in or out of the world. So when we returned home, I called the astronomy department at UC in Berkeley and learned that, yes indeed, there was a bright comet, Comet Bennett, best seen about four in the morning in the eastern sky. Bingo! My only "discovery" of a comet and full-blown at that!

Teenaged Larry was the last member of our family to use the Boonville property, and on his final trip, he found poachers had come onto our land, done some illegal hunting, and cut down several madrone trees. The handwriting seemed on the wall, so we sold the place to people who could protect it better than we.

Late in the sixties, I performed a service unusual for me. Rental property was hard to find in San Francisco, especially near UCSF, and houses to rent were almost impossible. But we had three requests for rental houses for the academic year of 1969-70, all preferably within walking distance of the UCSF campus. I lucked into one on Willard Street and two on Edgewood Avenue, each of which proved ideal for its occupants. The first went to the family of Roy Steinberg, coming to work in Ken's lab for an indefinite period of time. The second was for another colleague on sabbatical, and the third was to accommodate our old friends, the Safars, also coming to UCSF on sabbatical although in a different laboratory. I was able to place the latter two on Edgewood Avenue with Peter and Eva right against the forest. From their backyard, Eva walked daily up the forest trail with their year-old son riding on her back. Their older son was Larry's contemporary, and together the boys often walked through the forest to and from school. Many years later, when walking up there by myself, I received an unexpected gift. There on a metal light pole beside the path were the barely legible scrawls of their names, lightly covered by a skin of green fungus or mold that had formed over their signatures during the intervening decades.

As Ken became more prominent in his profession, he traveled more, though by choice keeping professional trips to a minimum. With our boys still young, I seldom accompanied him on these business trips, but that year Eva urged me to go with him to an annual meeting of ARVO (Association for Research in Vision and Ophthalmology) held in Sarasota, while she kept Steve and Larry in their home. I'll always be grateful, and so are our sons, for Peter took them with his older son to the Sierras for their first ski lessons.

Meanwhile, Ken and I were staying on the Lido. For me the whole week passed as an idyll—swimming every day, sometimes so early that my only companions were pelicans flying above me or herons observing from the shore. Austin Riesen, whom we hadn't seen for years, was also attending the conference. He and Helen had lived many years in Florida, and he was an accomplished sailor whereas Ken and I were mere recent graduates from a sailing course at Lake Merced in San Francsisco. Austin, Ken, and I rented a Sunfish one day for a thrilling sail in the Gulf of Mexico. Since the boat was intended for only two adults, I spent most of the time sitting on the bow deck with legs extended in front of me, plowing through the blue-green waves. Eventually, we overdid our maneuvers and capsized, and through the clear water, I watched as our floatable gear and lazily flailing arms and legs rose to the surface. We righted the boat, sailed it back to shore without incident, dropped it at the beach, and dove into the waves for a swim—a totally exhilarating experience. All in all, this was a wonderful year for me, but I decided to quit my brief career in real estate while it was so agreeably successful.

My childhood experiences on a ranch appealed increasingly to the males in our family. When our boys were very small, we had spent a few horseless holidays at ranches in the Salmon Mountain-Trinity Alps region of Northern California, but now it seemed time to saddle up in earnest. In the summer of 1968, we eased into things at the appropriately named Greenhorn Ranch, near Quincy in the Sierra country, north of Lake Tahoe. Mindful of California's litigious environment, riding there was limited to nose-to-tail trail rides—at a walk. The next summer, we ventured farther afield to Tepee Ranch in the Big Horn Mountains of Wyoming, recommended to us by a young man who had worked there. Tepee turned out to be as beautiful as he had described—well above seven thousand feet in elevation, with a shimmering blue lake on the property, and miles of country we were allowed to ride by ourselves. I was given a palomino called Champagne, who had lovely soft gaits, and Ken was aboard a powerful animal named Murph. Sometimes we rode with the boys, and sometimes they went by themselves as did we.

We returned the next summer and probably would have continued doing so had it not closed for guests the following year. We can only speculate why such a well-established ranch, with quite a few annual "regulars," would discontinue their successful dude business, but a credible surmise is the ever-rising costs of liability insurance required to protect against the catastrophically high legal settlements that increasingly cripple our society. The next year, we tried Eaton's Ranch, also in the Big Horns. The Eaton family is distantly related to the Aldersons of the Bones Brothers Ranch and thus formed a nostalgic connection with my childhood. Theirs is probably the best remaining guest ranch in that part of the West.

A legacy from Eaton's Ranch is a recipe we found in a book in our cabin. *Gold on the Desert* describes a year that the author, Olga Wright Smith, spent prospecting in the remote southwestern desert with her husband and his father. She tells how she made her own sourdough starter, and I copied her simple recipe. When we returned home, I bought a tall thick-walled porcelain crock. Into it I mixed the recommended quantities of flour, water, yeast, and pinch of sugar; placed the heavy lid over all; and left the crock on top of our stove overnight. When we came down next morning to see what we had, I saw one thing we had was a problem. The mixture worked so well that it had pushed up the lid and oozed a drying, sticky trail down the side, spreading out over the stove top. Once under control, however, that starter gave us some of our best breads and pancakes for the better part of a decade, and I wound up baking loaves for a neighbor who longed for the "old" San Francisco sourdough—really sour, with a crisp crust outside and soft bread inside.

At the turn of the decade, Ken was named faculty research lecturer for 1970, the highest academic honor UCSF bestows on a faculty member. And in typical Ken Brown fashion, he set a precedent by requesting that I be invited to the celebratory luncheon following the lecture. All wives of honorees since have been beneficiaries of that small but significant action of his.

Projects

During the early seventies, I undertook two projects that had been germinating since shortly before our departure on sabbatical in the fall of 1964. That year, my aunt Mildred had died in September, leaving me her property in Valley Center, including all the paintings stored there. And one month later, San Francisco suffered a bad smog attack. These two events invited action on my part.

Clean air had long been a large factor in our appreciation of San Francisco as a place to live. Well before coinage of the word "smog," referring to photochemical air pollution, Ken and I had experienced it on our honeymoon in 1948 when his eyes became so irritated by air in the Los Angeles Basin that we had to leave the area immediately. At that time the haze was barely visible, but the world has since become all too familiar with smog's distinctive brownish color. A few weeks before our sabbatical began, smog hit San Francisco while Ken was trying to complete a research paper. Although that episode lasted only a few days, it was severe enough to drive us to the top of Mount Tamalpais in Marin County so he could finish his writing. That makeshift tactic worked, but, of course, the growing smog problem concerned us greatly for the future.

Strong prevailing winds from the ocean had led longtime San Franciscans to declare smog an impossibility here. Yet here it was. So I began taking considerable interest in this phenomenon threatening not only our future, but that of the entire area. I learned an oil refinery had been built in the East Bay shortly before our arrival (a number more have been added since), and I knew from my childhood near the infamous Jersey Meadows what consequences could come from those enterprises.

Upon Aunt Mildred's death, we had arranged for safe storage of her paintings with the help of her devoted pupil, Juanita, who introduced us to Robert Moore Williams, a science-fiction writer living nearby in a trailer. He moved on to the property and became its caretaker, regaling us with beautifully written letters describing life there on the "ranch" with its resident dog. Dino was a formidable animal, part Great Dane, acquired by my aunt as a puppy. Bob actually saw Dino chase and kill a bobcat, carrying the cat off and burying it so quickly that Bob could never find the remains. Apparently, Dino considered the bobcat a mere "varmint" not even worth eating.

Mildred had loved both nature and art, and during our first few weeks in Australia, I tried to imagine her reactions to Australia's eminently paintable landscapes as well as the incomparable light infusing them. I studied works by late nineteenth and early twentieth century Australian impressionist artists who rendered their land so well: Sir Hans Heyson, Sir Arthur Streeton, and the immigrant New Zealander Elioth Gruner, whose crisp blue Aussie air could almost be breathed. In the idiom of a later day, a large vigorous oil by Tom Roberts called *The Breakaway* simply "blew my mind." These antipodean painters were probably unknown to Mildred, for Australian art is never mentioned in the notebooks where she describes works of European and Japanese artists that influenced her. Yet like the Australian impressionists, she had painted from nature, loved light, and excelled in the use of color; one of my favorites among her works is an oil painting of eucalyptus in southern California. I imagined her enjoying the art and landscapes I was observing in her stead.

An observation of a different sort began an informal investigation we believe helped to motivate subsequent research in air pollution. While standing atop Black Mountain, enjoying the clear views of nearby Canberra, I noticed and remarked upon a small patch of brown haze hanging over just one small area near the city. Canberra was not industrialized; that brownish area overhung the airport, which had only recently introduced "jet prop" planes of the kind we arrived in. Already suspicious that characteristics of jet fuel contributed a great deal to smog, I found this observation potentially very significant.

While gazing from Black Mountain, we realized smog in the United States was already so widespread that identifying new sources and studying their interactions was nearly impossible. On the other hand, there in clean Australia, we could plainly see newly generated smog, distinct from ambient air pollution of large urban and/or industrialized areas. In Ken's phrase, we were looking at smog formation "in embryo." Upon returning to California, this experience on Black Mountain became central to initiating and guiding my first serious foray into what might be termed scientific activism.

Thus in the early seventies, I undertook the first of three projects for which I may have been uniquely qualified. For starters, I had free time to spend on them. I was also reasonably well informed in chemistry for the concomitant pair of projects dealing with air pollution. And in the case of my aunt's biography, I was the sole repository of her voluminous journals and diaries, potentially converting me into the best-informed surviving authority on the American artist Mildred B. Miller.

The air pollution study—particularly my concerns about the stratospheric sulfate layer—resembled a detective story. It also posed considerable challenges, since I lacked both the expertise and facilities to evaluate definitively within this important field. Nevertheless, to me its incipient problems were so compelling that I hoped my informed instincts, supported by insights derived from observations I was privileged to make, would have value for scientists who could move research in that field toward definitive conclusions.

In the late 1960s, I had begun gathering and filing evidence implicating jet fuel (used in both jet turbine and jet-prop planes) as a crucially important factor in air pollution. Jet fuel is a relatively crude fraction of petroleum, akin to kerosene, and we all know how kerosene smells when burned, noticeably demonstrating the presence of smelly by-products of combustion that are left behind in the air. Families living near airports noticed early in the jet age that, during and immediately following take-off, planes spewed conspicuous trails of black carbon particles—soot. Steps were taken that effectively reduced the *size* of these soot particles and therefore their visibility, but the carbon particles were unavoidable by-products of combustion and could not be eradicated. Ironically, their reduced size makes them even *more* significant in catalyzing reactions as discussed later in this account.

When I became actively involved, publicized research into the generation of smog still focused almost entirely on analysis of *homogeneous* gas-phase reactions, without considering possible interactions involving the nongaseous components—aerosols or particulates that are also present in smog. To me, the sudden widespread emergence of smog in areas previously free of it argued strongly for a newly introduced agent, perhaps catalytic, rather than simply an incremental growth of car traffic. In any case, studies of *heterogeneous* interactions between gases and other components of polluted air seemed overdue.

A further suggestive point: at Greenhorn Ranch we had met a native Los Angeleno who had lived in the Los Angeles area all his life. I asked him if he could remember when "Los Angeles—type smog" first appeared in Los Angeles. He replied, "I can tell you exactly when it appeared—when refineries in the Los Angeles Basin began using the catalytic cracking process just before World War II."

Remembering our own Jersey Meadows, I did some checking and in June 1970 received letters from Mobil Oil Corporation and Sunoco Oil Company indicating there had been a by-product from early catalytic cracking processes, petroleum coke (no longer used) that was burned as part of the cycle regenerating the catalyst used in the cracking process. The flue gas generated by burning coke could then be used to drive the blower that supplied air for the combustion, so the process in a sense was self-supporting. Of course, efforts were made to contain these useful products, but inevitably a small fraction escaped into the air. From a representative at Standard Oil Company, I learned that adsorption on the surfaces of such particles speeds the reactions forming photochemical smog from its necessary ingredients of reactive hydrocarbons, nitrogen oxides, an oxidant, and sunlight. In a polluting sense, jets are somewhat like moving refineries.

The problem became of greater concern when jets routinely began flying in the stratosphere, because the stratosphere lacks mechanisms for self-cleansing provided in the troposphere by wind and rain. What reaches the stratosphere tends to stay there a long time. Witness the longevity of sulfur species injected into the stratosphere during large volcanic eruptions.

The lower stratosphere contains a layer at variable altitude, higher over the tropics, lower over the poles, averaging about twelve miles above the earth's surface. It is a natural layer heretofore fed principally by volcanic injection, and it was called the sulfate layer because of its high content of sulfates. That content has roughly doubled in the three decades since studies began, and many scientists now believe anthropogenic sources account for half this doubled sulfate content of the sulfate layer. This is at the altitudes where military and long-range passenger jets have flown for nearly half a century.

Sulfates are a relatively stable oxidized state of sulfur to which reduced species of sulfur gases such as hydrogen sulfide and sulfur dioxide progress in the presence of active oxygen. Since the sulfate layer comingles with the contiguous ozone layer above it, likely connections between ozone depletion and the increasing presence of sulfate in the sulfate layer are now under investigation, but that has not always been the case.

By 1970 I had learned the following: jet fuel contains more sulfur than higher fractions of petroleum, such as the high-octane gasoline used to fuel propeller planes and cars (other than diesel).

In 1965, I had observed the telltale smudge of smog over the airport in Canberra's otherwise clear sky. At the beginning of that year, we had flown into Canberra aboard one of the new jet-prop planes just introduced into daily service in Australia.

About the same time, friends at Dartmouth College told us they were noticing for the first time occasional Los Angeles—type smog wafting over their small rural town of Hanover, New Hampshire. When I asked whether they had jet service yet, they replied that jet-prop service had begun about *four months earlier*.

A neighbor who grew up in Honolulu told me they were starting to experience smog there despite their famous trade winds.

Then, on the cusp of a new decade, a sad front-page story appeared in San Francisco's *Examiner* of Sunday, December 21, 1969. Datelined Scotia, New York, it bore the huge headline READ THIS AND CRY. Stating "there's no more clean air in the United States," the story followed, describing scary predictions for the troposphere. I'm happy to say these were largely averted over the next few years due to strong measures that dealt successfully with many smog problems at ground level.

However, the article went on to state the "last vestiges of clean air" found near the resort town of Flagstaff had disappeared *six years before*[italics added]. According to Alfred Hulstrunk, director of the Atmospheric Sciences Research Center, air pollution from California had finally reached Flagstaff in northern Arizona. Perhaps so, but consider this. A letter of mine, dated five days later to the Chamber of Commerce in Flagstaff, inquired whether they had jet or jet-prop service yet and drew this somewhat proud-sounding reply: "*This service started about six years ago* with the Convair 340, which was converted to jet/prop." [italics added] When I related this story to a friend piloting for United Airlines, he said he had wondered for several years why he no longer reveled in the clear views of our country he had previously enjoyed while flying his transcontinental routes. The entire country, coast to coast, seemed to him to have become "veiled by haze."

In 1970, I began writing letters to A. J. Haagen-Smit at Cal Tech in Pasadena and Richard D. Cadle at the National Center for Atmospheric Research in Boulder, two prominent authorities in the field of pollution research. I had begun reading their papers in *Science*, the AAAS (American Association for the Advancement of Science) publication coming to our home, as well as articles in the engineering library at UC—Berkeley, where many research papers in the burgeoning field of air pollution were available. I also wrote to Willard J. Libby at UCLA, whom I knew slightly from Chicago days. In these letters, I laid out in detail my findings and hypotheses, especially my conviction that the homogeneous gas-phase reaction studies then being conducted were not enough to explain the mechanisms of smog generation. So I urged undertaking studies of heterogeneous reactions including particulates—often called aerosols in those days. I further asked them to consider the possibility that sulfur exerts an effect disproportionately large for the relatively small percentage it represents of contaminants in polluted air, perhaps even assisting reactions catalytically by providing surface areas on sulfate aerosol particles. Particulates—be they water droplets, soot, or sulfate particles—on whose surfaces reactions are facilitated catalytically are often called condensation nuclei, an apt term to describe their function; for they seem to attract and concentrate reactants.

At that time, Cadle was head of the chemistry department at the NCAR (National Center for Atmospheric Research) Laboratory of Atmospheric Sciences in Boulder, Colorado. In 1966 he described experiments confirming the existence of the sulfate layer in the stratosphere, as well as the gathering of samples there by means of direct flow impactors on U-2 aircraft flying at 20 km altitude within it. He added, "By a happy coincidence the 20 km level is right in the center of the layer." As subsequent decades have passed, and the sulfate loading has doubled, I have wondered, as I wondered when I read it, just how coincidental or happy this fact really is, since that is an altitude favored by jets. Representative of my handwritten letters in that first round of correspondence is this quote from a letter to Cadle, dated January 23, 1970:

> It seems . . . highly likely that there is in the emissions from jet-fueled aircraft some ingredient which produces effects enormously disproportionate to its quantity. There may be a component which acts as a *catalyst* in some of the photochemical reactions (such as those you mention involving ozone) which take place on many of the exhaust products from automobiles.

My boldness in all this surprised me, and the replies were even more surprising. Libby, Haagen-Smit, and Cadle all indicated they took my suggestions seriously, with Haagen-Smit declaring, "I am transmitting to my technical staff your idea of irradiating a mixture of jet and auto exhaust. I know they have many irradiation experiments in progress, so it might be sometime before they get around to the tests you propose, but they will give your ideas full and careful consideration." Libby responded, "I found your letter on air pollutants from jet aircraft very interesting. I would like your opinion of an article in the current issue of *Astronautics and Aeronautics* on what we may expect from the SST."

Concurrently, I had become involved in the fight against a proposed fleet of SSTs which would fly in the stratosphere. William A. Shurcliff, an MIT physicist, founded the CLASB (Citizens' League Against the Sonic Boom), which led the opposition. He raised many issues on which he was well informed, and he welcomed my additional speculations regarding jet fuels at sulfate layer altitudes. I wrote numerous letters to legislators, top officials of airline companies and, of course, aircraft manufacturers, adding my arguments to his. A treasured note from Dr. Shurcliff at the top of an enclosure he sent me reads, "Dear Mrs. Brown: My goodness! Those letters you wrote to airline men were simply top notch. Beautifully written! Vigorous clear yet polite & winning. And the replies you got back! Amazing. Most people get back little of interest. Many thanks." The evidence against fleets of SSTs became so overwhelmingly strong that the proposed Boeing project was scrapped, and Concordes were limited to very few in this country.

On these two projects, dozens of letters had been exchanged, and I felt my job was done. But with publication of a seminal article by T. Novakov, S. G. Chang, and A. B. Harper in *Science*, 18 October 1974, a whole new round of communications began. The Novakov paper and its follow-ups presented strong scientific evidence for catalysis on carbon particulates—specifically oxidation of sulfur dioxide to sulfates on the surfaces of soot particles, abundant in polluted atmospheres. Entitled "Sulfates as Pollution Particulates: Catalytic Formation on Carbon (Soot) Particles," the authors described in detail laboratory experiments in which sulfur dioxide was oxidized far more quickly on soot particles than by means of the "solution chemical and photochemical mechanisms" that had been studied in the past. Furthermore, experiments showed the homogeneous gas-phase oxidation of sulfur dioxide to sulfate was of "relatively minor significance" in the system—meaning that studies limited exclusively to homogeneous gas-phase reactions of contaminants, without considering possible catalytic contributions from particulates, would yield little knowledge about the important oxidation events taking place in polluted atmospheres.

As mentioned earlier, there is an irony here: soot particles are an unavoidable concomitant of combustion. Yet reducing the number of large visible particles results in an increased number of small invisible particles, and these provide a greater total surface area per total quantity of soot on which catalyzed reactions can take place.

I called Novakov and learned he could see no reason why reactions occurring in plumes from jets in the stratosphere should differ from those coming from turbine plumes in his laboratory. The same mix is there—reduced sulfur gases, carbon (soot), oxygen, and high temperatures. Additionally, the Novakov team found "there was an increase in the number of very small, high-surface-area particles produced in oxygen-rich flames." I couldn't help wondering about the situation near a plentiful supply of that highly reactive form of oxygen known as ozone—found abundantly in the layer of the stratosphere bearing that name.

A week later came a rather comprehensive research article whose authors, Allen L. Hammond and Thomas H. Maugh II, remark in passing, "There may, moreover, be other reactive components of the stratosphere and other reactions—especially those occurring on the surface of particulates—of which we are unaware." Then the authors conclude their article by quoting a Dr. Michael B. McElroy at Harvard, and I quote from my letter to him the next day: "By your question 'What the hell else has slipped by?' with which the research article on Stratospheric Pollution (*Science*, 25 October 1974) closes, you have opened the door and my foot is in it. May I respectfully suggest *sulphates*?"

In this second round, I also sent a letter to Libby, saying of Novakov's work, "It is pretty persuasive and revives my curiosity about whether sulfur compounds, in this case, sulfates themselves may exert catalytic effects upon smog reactions either upon their surfaces or by some direct chemical involvement." Furthermore, I quoted Rowland and Molina's acknowledgment that their recent work on chlorofluoromethanes was "based entirely on reactions in the gas phase, and essentially nothing is known of possible heterogeneous reactions of chlorine atoms with particulate matter in the stratosphere." I then went on to say, "Yet the soot and the sulfates are there and seem to me to be crying out for inclusion in stratospheric study as well as general atmospheric air chemistry."

In his reply, he stated, "Your points . . . certainly must be considered" and passed my letter on to his former graduate student Frank S. Rowland, who passed it on to his graduate student Mario J. Molina. Soon Rowland and Molina were to become famous with their work on chlorofluorocarbons and the ozone layer for which in 1995 they were awarded the Nobel Prize. As we know, that issue turned political when proposed protective measures threatened large economic interests. I had a very interesting telephone conversation on this subject with Molina. I wanted his opinion of my suspicion that, in addition to the CFCs he and Rowland were investigating, sulfur from jet injection might also be an important factor in ozone depletion. Things were still at a speculative stage then, and he did not answer that question directly. But he did remark I might be surprised to learn that, in certain quarters where their research on chlorofluorocarbons was becoming inconvenient for economic reasons, the sulfate layer was being put forth as a "good guy," the argument being that sulfates might remove the threatening CFC molecules on their way up through the layer to the ozone above it. Through subsequent decades, Molina has become prominent in ongoing studies of the sulfate-ozone layers of the stratosphere.

In a letter to Haagen-Smit, I asked, "Mightn't these sulfates, particulates themselves, act as condensation nuclei for photochemical reactions [or dark reactions] in smog formation? Surely, the possibility of such surface reactions or more direct chemical catalysis from sulfates should be studied if it hasn't been done already."

That was in the 1970s. It seemed to me then that a wall of resistance prevented zeroing in on jet traffic at the altitude just below and contiguous with a reservoir of reactive ozone ready to oxidize sulfur gases to the sulfates initially giving that stratospheric layer its name. And my letters on that round sound a bit combative. Of course, I cannot know whether my efforts had any effect on subsequent research in this highly complex and technical field. I believe they did, but progress has seemed slow. Not until the late 1990s did I begin to see mentions of a likelihood that had seemed evident since Novakov's work a quarter century earlier. For instance, the 1998 Geophysical Research Letters lists among its titles, "*First* direct sulfuric acid detection in the exhaust plume of a jet aircraft in flight" [italics added].

There is now much research on heterogeneous reactions occurring both in the lower stratosphere and the upper troposphere, and I see an occasional conjecture that aviation may be an important factor in ozone depletion. As previously mentioned, a doubling of sulfate has occurred in the stratospheric sulfate layer during the past thirty years and is now generally attributed to anthropogenic sources, though principally attributed to the tropospheric burning of coal.

The importance of stratospheric sulfate is increasingly recognized, although not so publicly as the growth and spread of ozone holes with which I believe it to be connected. A paper published in *Geophysical Letters*, November 2002, volume 29, number 22 is entitled "Climate Forcing of Subsonic Aviation: Indirect Role of Sulfate Particles via Heterogeneous Chemistry." It speaks to the role of sulfates as condensation nuclei supporting heterogeneous reactions upon their surfaces. The authors G. Pitari, E. Mancini and A. Bregman state, "The present modeling study focuses on an additional indirect effect of aircraft-generated sulfate, namely heterogeneous chemistry on liquid sulfuric acid particles." I see this as a vindication of the surmise expressed in my question to Dr. Haagen-Smit three decades ago, and I welcome use of the term "aircraft-generated sulfate."

According to Mr. Jim Scanlon, Marin County journalist whose special interest is ozone holes, an anomalous hole began showing up some years ago along the Atlantic Flight Corridor, one of the most heavily traveled jet routes in the world. Because jets there are flying at high latitudes, they are often in the stratosphere rather than the troposphere. Much work is still in progress and will undoubtedly unravel some of the remaining unknowns. Meanwhile, an aeronautical engineer has told me he thinks scientists today are well aware of serious problems associated with jet transport but simply don't know what to do about them. With that straightforward dilemma, I can empathize, for until an alternative can be found we are surely going to keep jet travel.

And who knows? There's a nice recent twist to the concept of sulfate perhaps turning out to be a "good guy" after all, by helping to offset global warming. In the 2001 book *The Greening of Conservative America*, author John R. E. Bliese points out that sulfate aerosols "affect climate in two ways. They reflect the sun's rays (a direct cooling effect), and they also act as nuclei for water vapor to condense and form clouds." Reflection of the sun's radiation back into space acts as a "negative forcing" of the climate, in opposition to the warming trend resulting from greenhouse effects.

At parties back in Ohio, I often heard young women complaining that their college educations were wasted in the lives they subsequently lived as wives and mothers. I submit no education is wasted. An early intimation of this came with motherhood when my knowledge of simple chemistry guided me to the weak base, baking soda, to prevent stains from the correspondingly weak acid, urine. As we progressed toward adulthood in our family, more and more uses came for the education Ken and I had acquired in the ivory tower. Indeed, I feel that my life has been a vindication of the value of a liberal education. Of course, one cannot know what is going to be useful in the future, but I have found that if we stay alive to possibilities, we may well find good uses for almost anything we have learned. There is an old saying, "A little knowledge is a dangerous thing." Indeed it can be. But if insights born of such incomplete knowledge are forwarded to responsible parties possessing greater knowledge, it can help alter directions and accelerate progress.

A further point: from my experience working on projects of potentially great consequence, it is important to approach correspondents cooperatively rather than combatively. As soon as oil-company executives learned I was not agitating with some group antagonistic to them, they gave me all the help they could. After all, they don't create the demand for petroleum; they try to provide what we have grown to feel we "need." We're literally all in this together.

* * *

My next project was personal: a biography of my aunt.

MILDRED B. MILLER

Portrait of an American Painter

Mildred was a remarkable woman, an individualist living in an era when women were beginning to enter the mainstream of American public life, yet still remaining largely on its sidelines.

She was a serious artist with high aspirations. Though her life was far from smooth, she felt near its end that she had been living "in paradise." Among those who knew her, she left a refined and touching personal legacy. One of her ranch neighbors credited Mildred with teaching her "how to truly *see* the country" where she had lived all her life. And a workman, young enough to be her grandson, found his visits with her in her rustic cottage restful and comforting. She had a calming influence on others, though she felt far from calm within herself. In her youth, she was a distinguished participant in the vibrant Pennsylvania art scene of the early 1920s. Yet she chose to live her old age alone in desert ranch country, far from the green landscapes of her youth.

Her greatest legacy was a large body of artistic works of rare beauty. As a professional artist, she had sold countless commissioned portraits and paintings. In her collection at the time of her death were several hundred works on canvas and paper—paintings she had refused to sell—as well as a few that she probably never could have sold. I inherited the best, worst, and much in between, plus an abundance of journals and writings informative of her life and thought from 1911 until her death in 1964.

By the time I began compiling material for her biography, we knew her paintings well. They had been shipped to our home in San Francisco within a few years of our sabbatical, and we filled many an evening and weekend working with them. Most of these sessions were pure delight. The heavy work fell to Ken who, fortunately, had always admired her art as much as I do. He spent untold hours wrestling canvases in and out of bins, which he constructed for them in our garage. A number of them had suffered from neglect in the outbuildings where Mildred had stored them, so necessarily, we also learned much about cleaning and restoration.

Over the years, we have worked with several fine conservators. Saturdays were often set aside for choosing frames for those works we wished to hang in our home, and we had the great good fortune to find three successive framers who were artists themselves as well as fine craftsmen. One night we hung a recently framed group of watercolors along our main stairway. The following morning, Steve came flying down the stairs, calling, "Mommy, Daddy, I *love* our new museum!" We were delighted by our boys' enthusiasm, for we intended these artworks to be theirs someday.

Eventually, my biography was finished—and rejected by a few of the big well-known publishers in New York and Philadelphia where I had optimistically and naively sent it. At the suggestion of my friend Ann Gilliam—whose husband, Harold, is well published—I then submitted the manuscript to a small but respected publisher in Palo Alto: Pacific Books. Its editor, Henry Ponleitner, accepted the manuscript with the proviso that I add significantly more information about the art scene in which Mildred moved and that I undertake substantial editing. I did not feel knowledgeable enough to satisfy the first stipulation and had little heart for the second, so the project languished a few months. On our next contact, I learned he was moving to a new location, and soon afterward, he went out of business.

I could not have guessed there would someday be a use for that unpublished biography, yet today, there is. Interest in her work has grown as Swarthmore College has made available some of her paintings to collectors and dealers who wish more information about the life and times of this rediscovered artist.

The Younger Generation

The seventies also ushered teenagers into our lives, and we found them good company, fun on excursions, challenging at games. They were bright and considerate and their energy overflowed. During junior high and high school, our sons explored their city on bikes with friends, and on one occasion Steve invited me to ride with him on a circuit he had devised solely for my ease. Magically, it seemed to be downhill all the way—through Golden Gate Park and the Presidio, pedaling uphill so briefly or gradually that I hardly noticed, then coasting down long, steep hills for a thoroughly satisfying ride. They also worked during summers on volunteer jobs in laboratories at UCSF, good background for the medical doctors they eventually became.

Meanwhile, our northwestern vacations continued until the boys protested the long drives. Some of our finest experiences have occurred in Canada. There was the night of the tree frogs when Larry and I were wakened by a cacophony outside our cottage. Slipping out the back door at around two or three in the morning, we sat above a railroad cut, listening to the immense sound made by the little creatures. Every now and then a train passed, adding to that feeling of mystery that night in unfamiliar places evokes. As we bedded down next evening on the outskirts of Vancouver, Larry wanted a repeat of the previous night's adventure—alas, beyond our reach near the bustling city. But Vancouver's Stanley Park was eminently accessible, site of our "spider walk" along trails draped with an astonishing variety of spider webs and their distinctive occupants.

A few years later, Larry and I shared a thrilling encounter with a grizzly bear on a hike in Canada's Waterton Lakes National Park. At that time, the Canadian park was thought to contain only about seven or eight of the great bears, for its terrain is much less wild and mountainous than that of our Glacier National Park with which it is contiguous. In those days, an estimated 90-100 grizzlies roamed Glacier, and in 1967 two campers in the back country had been killed by grizzlies in two separate incidents on the same night. Backpackers were warned especially against camping overnight if any member of the party were menstruating. Ken wanted to backpack at least one night in Waterton Lakes, but since I was hors de combat and felt no confidence that grizzlies would honor international boundaries, I opted out. We all rode a ferry to Ken and Steve's trailhead where Larry suddenly decided to return with me to our inn in the town of Waterton Park for the night.

Before our anticipated rendezvous with his father and brother the next day, Larry and I set off on a local hike and were rewarded with a thrilling and thankfully calm encounter with a grizzly no more than twenty-five to thirty yards from us. We had stopped and were preparing to turn around when we heard a loud crack from behind a knoll. I thought the sound was made by a large animal stepping on a fallen branch and suggested we remain quiet to see what would happen. Instead of the anticipated elk or large deer, a beautiful bear rounded the knoll. Our eyes followed along the hump of his shoulders, which instantly put our senses on high alert with keen attention paid to every detail of our situation. There was a slight dip in the terrain separating us from him, and that was psychologically comforting. We remained silent and still, and there was no wind to carry our scent, so as yet the bear was unaware of our presence. For years I had both wished and feared meeting a grizzly in the wild, and I recall a quiet thrill running through me as I thought, "Here I am at last!"

Larry softly asked what we should do, and I opted to see what the bear would do. This whispered exchange caught the bear's attention, and his astonishingly prehensile nose, so unlike the "Roman" nose of a black bear, began twirling in an effort to pick up our scent (grizzlies have poor eyesight but acute senses of hearing and smell). After a long moment, he calmly lowered his head and began ambling diagonally down the slight declivity toward us, as though to say, "I am curious and coming to investigate you, but I won't mind if you are not there when I arrive." We knew you never want to catch a grizzly's eye with sudden movement, and since our grizzly seemed peaceably disposed, we did not want to change that. As he negotiated the little dip, I whispered instructions to Larry, and when the bear's head went behind a particularly thick tree trunk between him and us, Larry and I zipped back around the corner we had turned before the bear arrived. Thus, we were able to backtrack out of his sight.

Fascinating to me was how instinctively my six-foot son had followed my instructions with no word of argument. Afterward, I was on such a high that it took Larry's reminder to walk, not run, down the trail to avoid spraining an ankle. I have been a grizzly fan ever since that awesome experience and recommend to anyone with a similar affinity a fine book, *The Grizzly* by Enos Mills, founder of Rocky Mountain National Park and an early twentieth-century Colorado author and devotee of the great bear.

The grizzly, sadly, has passed from many places, but not yet from memory. Our bear struck me as a majestic animal, his fur riffling with each step as he moved through his domain with a flowing grace entirely dependent upon freedom from confinement. Encounters with animals in their home territories have always seemed to me to enrich human experience out of all proportion to any intrinsic significance of either the animal or the encounter.

There was an amusing aftermath to our adventure. At trailhead, an official Park Service sign asked hikers to report all grizzly sightings. Additionally, someone had posted on a tree a hand-lettered warning that a grizzly had been sighted on a kill located several miles beyond where we had gone. That lettering was so badly smeared by rain that I thought the sign had perhaps been left over from a previous year. On our way back to town, we stopped at the park station to report as requested. The ranger on duty was a young fellow recently transferred to Waterton Lakes and frankly envious of our experience. He asked for every detail, and when I started describing the bear's prodigious nose twirling, he tried but failed to suppress a huge smile. I have always tended to talk with my hands, and apparently, in this case, that tendency extended to my nose. Of course, the ranger knew of the hand-lettered warning sign and told us it applied "very much to this year's bear" who was known to have been staying up there for ten days near his kill. I asked how long bears usually stay on their kills, and with a mischievous twinkle, he replied, "Oh, I'd say about ten days!"

On one of our trips in western Canada, we visited Kaslo and, farther west, the Chilcotin country. On the road to Kaslo, our gas tank was punctured by a rock, which resulted in sporadic trouble for the rest of the trip, necessitating an extended stopover for repairs in the Chilcotin. There I had another delightful animal experience, this time with a golden retriever who lived at the cabin complex on Nimpo Lake where we stayed for a few days. He shared my fondness for canoes, and we had several fine travels together while the boys were out fishing with Ken. Mac provided me company as well as ballast amidships, but he endangered our craft every time a loon popped up to taunt him, first from one side of the boat and then the other. At those times, I corralled him between my knees, tightening my grip on his shoulders each time I felt his muscles flinch preparatory to jumping overboard. (When I had asked his owner for permission to take Mac with me, he replied it was fine as long as I wouldn't mind hauling a wet dog into a canoe!)

Out by myself one day, I paddled into a small cove where I stopped to watch an eagle making repeated attempts to capture a baby loon. The eagle operated between two trees on opposite sides of the cove. Each time he swooped down to make a pass at the chick, the parent birds shielded the baby. They made no attempt to hide it from me, though they surely knew I was there. The eagle was their paramount threat, and naturally they knew that. Time after time, he swooped, and they evaded. Finally, the eagle gave up and flew away. Immediately, the parents' attention shifted to me, and the one I took to be the male began swimming toward me, uttering what I understood as instructions to get out of there. His mate, meanwhile, positioned her body in such a way that I never again caught the slightest glimpse of her baby. Needless to say, with the insistent loon as escort, I paddled promptly from their cove, knowing they had already put in a hard half hour.

With the advent of lightweight camping equipment, we began backpacking vacations that brought us closer to wild animals. In the North Cascades, we wandered for the better part of a week, once sharing a mutually surprised meeting with a mountain sheep on the trail. Late one afternoon, Steve and I watched through binoculars as a large group of mountain goats frolicked on a mountainside opposite our campsite. The kids played roughly, and there appeared to be one or two supervising nannies standing near them as if to prevent them from tumbling down the bank. Suddenly, a large eagle flew in and landed below them. Instantly, the nanny who appeared to be in charge advanced toward the eagle, placing her feet firmly above him. Thus began the staring down. When the eagle moved threateningly, she planted herself directly in its path, so after a few feints, the bird flew off empty beaked. We were skeptical an eagle could handle an animal the size of a young mountain goat. Yet I remembered a particularly compelling passage from that versatile book, *Gold on the Desert* which, among other things, had furnished the recipe for our sourdough starter. Its author, Olga Wright Smith, states that in the more lonely parts of the southwest, where her husband and father-in-law mined, human toddlers had to be closely guarded at all times from those capable predatory birds cruising high above the desolate landscape.

A short backpacking holiday that Ken and I took in Lassen Volcanic National Park also provided one of my favorite bird encounters. After a hot hike, we made early camp on Horseshoe Lake, where I took a swim to cool my sore knees. Sitting on a rock in the sun to dry, I began watching a distant osprey who seemed to be flying the lake from one end to the other in leisurely sweeps, bringing it ever closer to me. Thinking the bird was probably quartering the lake for fish, I gradually changed that opinion when he appeared to become inquisitive about *me*, perhaps due to the sparks given off by my engagement ring as I waggled it in the sunlight toward him.

Before he reached me, however, I headed back to our campsite and began describing my newest avian adventure to Ken who, as a thoroughly responsible scientist, questioned my hypothesis that the osprey was approaching me out of curiosity. I argued the bird had watched where I went and would probably fly right over our campsite, which it obligingly did as the words left my mouth. This was an altogether satisfying event for me and I hope for that interesting and interested raptor as well.

On a more distant journey, we drove to Prince Rupert, left our car there, and donned backpacks for another trip up the Inside Passage, staying a few days each in the salmon capital of Ketchikan, the Indian village of Wrangell, and the Norwegian settlement of Petersburg. Each of these towns has a distinctive character, and no roads extend far out of town, so a car is superfluous for the short-term visitor.

The day of our departure from Wrangell, I felt ill, and while waiting for the ferry to Petersburg, Ken took the boys sightseeing so I could rest on the grass in a nearby park. Soon several little Indian children approached me slowly and respectfully, keeping their distance until I made them welcome. At first, I resented this intrusion on my malaise, but their visit quickly made its way into my memory most endearingly. For they were dear children. All they wanted was to investigate this new intrusion into *their* world. They had a bundle of questions, and when I answered, more followed. They wanted to know about schools in the Lower 48. One little boy with bright eyes, and IQ to match, was interested that I tutored math. He asked so many questions that I began quizzing *him*, and he went to the top of our impromptu class.

In Nevada, some years later, while swimming alone in a large and rather old-fashioned pool at a Winnemucca motel, a similar small group of dusky children gathered at its edge. Since they were all in wet bathing suits, I asked them why they didn't join me, which they seemed eager to do. They replied that their parents worked for the motel and had hurried them out of the pool when they saw me coming. I regretted being the cause of their disappointment and invited them in. We had a delightful few minutes, before the motel owner rushed over to order them out and scold me for violating motel policy. How we Americans sometimes cut ourselves off from exotic experiences in the name of protecting our bland, risk-free ideal of life!

Closer to home, we had stopped several times for the summer Shakespeare Festival in Ashland, Oregon. Somehow, Ken and I could never quite reconcile those impeccable performances with the unpredictable ones we had so enjoyed in Yellow Springs. But there were compensations. On one occasion, we overlapped the stay of our erstwhile neighbors, the Blevins, who knew the countryside and its attractions well. They led us to a great swimming hole on the Applegate River where we adults appropriated the boys' floating tubes to help us glide down a small canal without scraping bottom. To this day, decades later, we occasionally reminisce long distance on the phone about that fabulous afternoon, Chuck recently remarking, "I don't think the boys ever forgave us!"

Those "boys" were growing up. In 1975, Stephen graduated from high school and moved to Stanford University that fall. We celebrated our last vacation as a family with a week in the Selway-Bitterroot Wilderness Area where I had the thrill of saving a young Midwestern woman from serious injury. Mary Ann joined Ken and me on a hike with Everett, the proprietor of Selway Lodge where we were staying. She had not hiked for years and was somewhat jet-lagged; additionally, our hike lasted longer than expected. So in order to make it back by dinnertime, we took a shortcut along a narrow trail on the side of a steep bank. Walking behind Mary Ann, I noticed she looked sleepy, so I began watching her closely, recalling a tale from my father's climb of Mount Rainier where he had narrowly avoided death. During a rest break he had fallen asleep for an instant, coming awake sharply when he started rolling down the mountain. In a flash, he realized that unless he could stop his slide on the next roll, he would gain so much momentum he would roll to his death. So he held his ice axe at what he hoped was the right angle and plunged it into the ice as he came around. It held, and he lived to tell the story.

With that in mind, I observed the bank we were walking on had soft soil, and I knew my walking stick was very sturdy, so I felt ready if needed. Amazingly, on her next step onto her downhill right foot, she continued leaning outward, and her arm began to separate from her side. As it dangled limply, I jumped forward with my own right arm catching her under her armpit, planted my right leg, and drove my walking stick as deep as possible into the soil. The stick held beautifully, supporting her body weight and a good part of mine, since the lower part of my arm rested on my bent right leg. She awoke with a start, looked down at the pile of rocks below, and exclaimed, “Ginnie, you saved my life!” I was immensely pleased, for how many times does one receive a chance like that? Needless to say, she was wide-awake the rest of the way, and Ken and Ev never knew until we told them what had occurred, with minimal commotion, behind them.

In the fall of 1977, Larry, the one member of our family who is a native Californian, headed east to college at Cornell University. On the day of his departure, we all drove to the airport and sat around, making small talk. When his flight was called, Larry rose to his six-foot-six-inch height, saying, “Well, Mom, your baby’s got to go.” With that, we all stood and watched him on his way. On the drive home, Steve sat in front with his father, holding and softly squeezing my hand over the back of the seat the whole way. Shortly, he was off to visit friends, and just like that, our “nest” was empty.

On the heels of Larry’s departure, Ken and I traveled to Tohoku University in Sendai, where Ken had been invited by the Japan Society for the Promotion of Science to be a visiting scientist for six weeks. This went a long way toward assuaging any empty-nest syndrome. We lived in a university building in the nearby hills of Yagiyama, and I was very happy there in our small apartment with its tiny balcony, and I thoroughly enjoyed the nearby shopping area where I used my microscopically small Japanese to purchase what we needed. All the tradesmen seemed glad to encourage and teach me, and when desperate for understanding I sought out a clerk in the local five-and-dime who was the only salesperson I knew in the village who spoke enough English to rescue me.

On days when I joined Ken at the lab, I usually rode the bus to and from the university, but men in the lab gave me tips on a portion of "old" Japan lying between Tohoku Daigaku and our district of Yagiyama. One day, I walked that route home. I passed no other Caucasian that afternoon, and I happened into a remarkable shop in a private home where exquisite bows and arrows of great expense were crafted by hand. Most enjoyable was a stop at a hole-in-the-wall junk shop run by a Filipino who traveled the Pacific, acquiring thousands of items crowding the two levels of his corner store. He was eager to have company and, furthermore, to converse in English. In the midst of our spirited conversation, there came a sudden explosive burst of squeaks and scrambling on the wide shelf above the desk at which he sat facing me. Above him were two good-sized rats chasing each other among the copper kettles and assorted knickknacks, occasionally biffing into something and ricocheting into each other. I burst out laughing as the owner, in an attempt to indicate he had not known they lived up there, ordered silence. They complied, and he apologized to me, but when I let him know I liked it, he relaxed and let them romp during the rest of my visit.

Our last night in Sendai, Ken and I were wakened by the sound of wolves howling. Curious and excited, we dressed and hurried out to track the sound. Not until we had walked a long way along wooded streets did we realize we were approaching the zoo. All became clear, and we rather sheepishly returned to bed for what was left of the night.

The next day, we departed for Fukuoka on Kyushu, the most southern of Japan's four main islands. There, our hosts had arranged a physiology department picnic atop Mount Aso, a large and active volcano. When we reached its rim and gazed down into the fiery crater, with flames visible and smoky steam rising, I felt as close to volcanism as I cared to go. On the barren land around the crater were a number of strong concrete huts or bunkers, which we were told had been erected many years ago, after a disastrous surprise eruption had killed many children on a school outing. We retired some distance down the cone where there was grass for our picnic, then slowly drove down the mountain, aware as we descended that the present cone lies within two other volcanically shaped craters, each larger and older than the one it encloses. Finally, we were driving on flat land. Our host pointed out that what appeared to be distant low mountains surrounding the roughly circular plain on which we drove, are the remains of the rim of an enormous ancient crater in which small settlements and rich farms now dwell at peace with their troublesomely rambunctious, centuries-old neighbor.

Alongside the road, near Fukuoka, were fragments of the wall erected nearly a millennium earlier when the Japanese were bracing for one of the attempted maritime invasions of this southernmost Japanese island by Mongols. The last attack in 1281 is legendary, for the thousands of invading ships and boats were turned back by a famed kamikaze, "divine wind," of a typhoon, which destroyed the greatest armada of its time.

From there our itinerary took us back to Kanazawa, our favorite Japanese city, situated on the West Coast of Honshu between the Japan Alps and the Japan Sea. Kanazawa's lovely mountainous setting along the crystalline Ishikawa, "Stone River," in which kimono silks have been rinsed for centuries, its ancient and evident tradition of superb crafts, and exquisite Kenrokuen, the park for which Kanazawa is famous—all somehow combine to lift the heart and quiet the soul—not a trivial achievement in such a crowded and bustling country. Our first morning there, we received an excited phone call from our Fukuoka hosts who reported that early in the morning of the day after our picnic, Aso-San had exploded in a large eruption, hurling boulders over a wide area. Fortunately, no one was up there at the time, and all of us who had been there the day before the eruption were exhilarated by learning of our close call.

En route home, we stopped for a week in Kauai and Maui, continuing our love affair with the Hawaiian Islands, which culminated years later upon visiting the Big Island and its active volcano, Mount Kilauea. On Kauai, we were privileged to stay at Coco Palms, one of the last two hostelries of "old Hawaii" then remaining in the islands, both long gone by now. Across the road was a beach where I took the greatest swim of my life.

* * *

By the late 1970s, our old political antagonist was trying to persuade the city of San Francisco to allow him to upgrade a residentially zoned block in our neighborhood on which he proposed to replace the existing houses with a commercial hotel adjacent to his office building. The community responded magnificently. As has been discovered throughout the world, people who have never previously been activists become so to protect something they cherish. In our case, it was our unique residential neighborhood—and the precedents allowing us to retain such neighborhoods in a large city. This first opposition was spearheaded by local residents, including a lawyer who had once worked for the city and gave me, by her assertive example, a crash course on how to lobby city hall. Also, on the early team was a fine UCSF scientist living nearby. Soon we had an impressive group of supporters: a few supervisors, some politicians, and the dean of a prominent law school, as well as scores of neighbors with varying talents and connections. Although the proponent (a Marin County resident) had started with a lot of support from our city agencies, it dwindled as evidence and legal arguments were amassed and officially presented. In March of 1979, the board of supervisors voted against him, and we prematurely thought we had won.

The next and final round of battle opened in 1982, when catching us by surprise, a last-minute initiative—Prop. M—was accepted onto the ballot, making it subject to a citywide vote on what was essentially a local proposition. Realizing we could not fight the promoter financially, we set about the uphill battle of citywide education and gathering of support from as many agencies and organizations as we could rally to our cause. Calling our opposition Stop M, and with the artistry of our next-door neighbor who designed a charming logo for us, we began catching up quickly. For those readers interested in the anatomy of this conflict, I quote here from the "Argument against the Rider Hotel Initiative" in the Voter Information Pamphlet for the General Election November 2, 1982:

> The private developer behind this measure previously asked the City for a big up-zoning of his property to permit building a large hotel in an area zoned for residential use. He was emphatically turned down by both the Planning Commission and the Board of Supervisors. Now he is asking you, the voters, to ask the City to change its policy for his benefit at the expense of others living in the area. His hotel and its bar, restaurant, convention facilities and inadequate parking seem less likely to serve patients and their relatives than conventioneers and tourists. The facts are: The area is already seriously over-congested, with unsolved traffic and parking problems. The adjacent University of California has agreed to limit its own growth. The need is for quiet, reasonably priced accommodations. This proposition asks for spot rezoning that would circumvent the City Master Plan and set a dangerous precedent that would be followed by developers in other residential areas.

Other ballot arguments supporting our position poured in by the dozens. Eventually, we won endorsements from the City Planning

Commission, the Chamber of Commerce, a slew of supervisors, Mayor Dianne Feinstein, the chancellor emeritus of UCSF who lived on our block, UCSF itself, the city's newspapers, its architects, doctors, lawyers, and scores of neighborhood organizations.

I became one of the leaders in this fight and very early in the game took advice from an exceptional lawyer and valued friend and neighbor. He alerted me to the kinds of actions we should expect and ways to deal with them. Almost immediately, a lawsuit was filed against the city by the proponents of Prop M. I played a significant role in its defeat, and I think that early success probably discouraged further attempts at litigation, while encouraging me to trust my judgment.

During the last days of the campaign, we learned of a seemingly innocuous but questionable move by our adversary. So I immediately consulted our lawyer friend and followed his advice, which undoubtedly saved our large margin of victory. Ken refers to this gentleman as a "superlawyer." That experience taught me how vital "super" advice can be, also that important political matters are often settled tactically behind the scenes, knowledge successfully put to use in subsequent battles over the years. We won big—79 percent of the vote—with an outlay of $5,000 against our opponent's reputed half million.

Nothing in the public arena has ever so gripped me or been so satisfying in outcome as the Stop M campaign—my only formal political venture. I learned much of the potent allure of politics and found myself enjoying the process so much that I frequently had to reassure Ken I would *never* go into politics as a career for I could not stand the pace, the scut work, or the compromises one would inevitably face.

Eight days after the election, my mother died in Virginia. I flew east immediately to help my widowed aunt Yine handle the details necessitated by her older sister's death. Mother had once requested, "Please be good to Yine if she is left alone." Nothing could have been easier or more delightful. Mother's death drew Yine and me very close, and during the week spent with her, I was surprised to discover that on appropriate occasions, she had a quick and decidedly unladylike sense of humor, a side of her I had never before witnessed and which made her great fun to be with. Over the next eleven years, the three of us—Ken, Yine, and I—bonded to an extraordinary degree. Our visits were always wonderful. As her eyesight failed, Ken and I drove her on day excursions to favorite places such as Annapolis, where she had lived some of her halcyon years. When no longer able to drive, she gave us her little VW Golf. Upon learning that during our drive west we had successfully negotiated a Wyoming blizzard, chugging past jackknifed big rigs and stranded luxury cars along the way, she remarked, "Little car always *was* surefooted!" A friend who knew Yine aptly summed up our good fortune: "*Every* family should have an Aunt Yine."

Throughout our sons' school years, their best friends had spanned a racial rainbow, so it is hardly surprising that our family soon became, in a neighbor's assessment, "globalized." Steve had graduated from college in 1979 and proceeded to medical school at UC—San Diego on an MSTP (Medical Sciences Training Program) scholarship. In his second year, he met Kim over the cadaver they shared in anatomy lab. A sparkling young lady from Southeast Asia, she became an instant hit in our family. She definitely had the "right stuff," having turned down a similar scholarship two years before to stay home and care for her dying mother. Much later, she helped me through my most serious medical emergency.

Early in Larry's sophomore year of college, he met Carmen. Ken and I learned of this attachment when we returned from a professional trip to Europe that had extended into a two-week driving vacation during which we were out of touch with our sons. Steve met us at the airport with the news that Larry had a new girlfriend. We had kidded both sons about the ethnic range of their friendships, so we jokingly asked Steve Carmen's origins, laughing heartily when he replied, "Transylvania"—which turned out to be true.

Strangely, at first sight, I knew I loved that girl. We flew east to visit, and eager to catch my first look at her before formal introductions, I stood at the top of the stairway in Larry's dormitory, hoping to pick her out from the masses of students trudging up the stairs after morning classes. Presently, I saw an absolute stunner and immediately guessed she was Larry's girl. Never could I have imagined what a sustaining force she would one day become to us. Both of these daughters-in-law have played large roles in our lives ever since.

Larry and Carmen married in December of 1980 in the lovely chapel on the Cornell campus, and in January of 1983, Steve and Kim were wed in San Diego. Like many young American couples, they did much moving about in pursuit of their aspirations, and we enjoyed visits in Pittsburgh and several areas of Florida as Kim and Steve served their internships and their residencies in anesthesiology.

In Florida, their work took them from Gainesville to Leesburg, then Mount Dora, and lastly to Bradenton. The first three of those locales gave us a taste of inland Florida—its parks and lakes and their subtropical wildlife. In the resort town of Mount Dora, there was a small lakeside park maintained in a semiwild state by volunteers. It held its dangers; water moccasins were known to climb to the branches overhanging trails through the jungly woods, and alligators were there too. On an early morning walk, I had the privilege of seeing a legendary local bull alligator, a full fifteen feet long, purported to have many harems in coves around his large lake. While I watched from a dock, he came steaming into the cove looking like a sinuous submarine plated with reptilian scales. His mate was in the rushes with her brood of little ones, which she hastily stashed among the reeds before swimming out to meet their big daddy. In a surprisingly tender gesture, they touched snouts, seeming to commune briefly. Then he turned again toward open water as she quietly returned to her young ones.

Larry and Carmen had farther to go in their careers. Carm had dropped out of college, and Larry surprised us all with a late decision to become a doctor. Their moves took them to Brown University Medical School in Providence, where one of our visits coincided with a major blizzard; Erie, Pennsylvania, where we canoed with Carm as Larry made his sleepless way through internship; and Washington, DC, where he took his residency in ophthalmology. In his payback to the air force, which had financed his medical training, he served in New Mexico and Florida, both locations we especially enjoyed visiting. Their children arrived while their father was finishing his residency, and for the next three years, the family lived in Cedar Crest, a particularly lovely area of the Sandia Mountains above Albuquerque, where Larry was stationed at Kirtland Air Force Base.

Cedar Crest provided the backdrop to one of the most amusing sights it has been our pleasure to witness. Very early one morning we were having coffee on our little balcony over the garage. The normally busy household was still asleep, and the rottweiler puppy the family had adopted was roaming the yard for signs of life. When Binksy spied us, he settled down and began chewing on a large gardening glove he had appropriated. All was peaceful. Suddenly, perhaps showing off to us, he began to savage the glove, standing up, and shaking it wildly. Finishing with an exceptionally vigorous toss, his sharp little teeth were still caught in the heavy glove, and his small body followed it through the air, turning over and falling onto his side. Such a helpless look of surprise and embarrassment! Ken and I burst out laughing, which made him look toward us sheepishly, and we couldn't resist assuring him that this time we were not laughing *with* him but *at* him!

After a quarter-century at UCSF, Ken had gone on partial retirement in 1982, spending the next three years finishing a book for John Wiley & Sons on *Advanced Micropipette Techniques for Cell Physiology*. With such a catchy title, it was bound to sell well—and it did. It covered a number of inventions he and his technician had made in this critical and highly specialized field. One morning, Ken was surprised to find a clipping from the *San Francisco Chronicle*, which his department chairman had placed in his mailbox. It was very brief—just a filler at the bottom of a column—to the effect that he was in the *Guinness Book of World Records* for having made the world's smallest tubes, the *outer* diameter of the tips being only .01 micron (.00001 mm) as well as the world's sharpest manmade cutting edges. Ken was pleased but also amused because he had never thought of his work in terms of world records.

On the eve of full retirement in 1985, we threw a party unveiling our back basement, recently turned into a snug shop for his lifelong hobby of woodworking. He now had time to resume furniture making and knew he wanted to make a cradle as his first project. So he asked if I could give him an idea for an unusual but appropriate design. Deriving inspiration from a whale-shaped wooden cheese board hanging on our kitchen wall, I suggested a cradle with each end in the shape of a whale, so that the cradle rocked on the bellies of the whales. Of course, Ken did all the detailed design and construction creating the prototype, to which I contributed the further suggestion of making it convertible to a "rocking bench" for older children. Together we took out a design patent. Over the next few years, he made a number of these cradles in our favorite wood—cherry. Eventually, one went to each of our children for their babies, plus a few to friends who requested them. We have been asked why we didn't commercialize, and the answer is simple. We were warned we would then become vulnerable to litigation, so would need to take out liability insurance, etc., effectively spoiling the spirit of the enterprise. Instead, Ken made available both the design and construction in an article published in *The American Woodworker* magazine.

During the next several years, Ken created many ingenious and artistic designs that he built for our home and for the homes of our sons and daughters-in-law. Daily we use his lazy Susan made from padouk, an exotic African hardwood that starts out red, oxidizing gradually to a color similar to that of aged cherry. For several friends, and for me, he has made cherry in-and-out boxes for our desks. Family kitchens contain his distinctive cherry bread boxes and cutting boards. My favorites in our home include a slim table hanging beneath our view window that folds out from the wall for meals or drinks. And because I like to cook with wine, he designed a small wine rack for our kitchen. It is unique, for it holds bottles securely without any meshwork of metal or wooden strips. His trick is shelves with a double tilt, lengthwise to keep the cork wet and laterally to keep the bottle secure against the back of the rack. After the quake of 1989, we can attest his wine rack has a Richter rating of at least 7.1.

His pièce de résistance is a hi-fi cabinet so satiny that no woman can resist touching it. Its folding door is cleverly designed to facilitate use in small rooms like ours where the swing of a large door can be a logistical problem. He later turned his hand to stained glass, making three windows for our home, and two for the home of the architect living next door to us. As one whose manual output is pretty well defined by two sweaters, a passel of monogrammed mittens for small fry, and several pillow covers knitted over the years, I stand in awe of the handcrafts produced by this erstwhile retinal physiologist.

Immediately after retirement in 1985, we took the long-awaited trip back to Australia, where we traveled to many desirable places in that vast land which had been beyond our reach on sabbatical. It is well we did for a year later I was diagnosed with a brain tumor called a meningioma—a tumor of the meninges covering the brain and not brain tissue itself. But of course its growth eventually puts much pressure upon the brain.

As with the ovarian tumor removed thirty years earlier, my body harbored this large mass without betraying its presence through expected symptoms. For example, in this case I had no headaches. Neither did any indication show up in a careful ophthalmological exam. Not until I was put on UCSF's new MRI machine was it caught, and by then I was already in decompensation in which the body's support systems begin to fail. As always, Ken and our family rose to the occasion, and I don't see how I would have made it without Ken or Kim. Ironically, her mother's lung cancer a few years before had developed into brain cancer, and Kim had nursed her through that final illness.

When she first offered to fly out to help us, I declined because she was then a few months' pregnant with her first child, our first grandchild, and I did not want to be responsible for jeopardizing the birth. Feeling sure she could help us, apparently Kim then went crying to Steve, who was unable to come himself because he was starting a new job with a difficult surgery on the morning of my operation. He gave her a challenge, "You're not going to accept the word of a lady with a brain tumor, are you?" whereupon she telephoned again to my infinite relief. That time I accepted gratefully, and she came immediately. She was awesomely indispensable—soon caring for Ken at home and me around the corner at UCSF, advising me gently but firmly on what to do at each stage of the proceedings, spending the night after surgery in my room, and answering questions I did not feel comfortable asking my doctors. It was a virtuoso performance, which continued in a different vein as I recovered.

In her inimitable way, she made friends immediately with a hospital nurse just right for me, who looked in on me often. Most impressive was the way Kim, a medical doctor who looked like a teenager, deferentially asked to sit in on my physical-therapy sessions as I was given exercises and taught how to go up and down stairs again. Kim explained she wanted to know so she could help me practice at home. When she wished to underscore something the therapist had said, she would remark, "You see, Mom, that's very good because . . ." thus, making the instruction memorable to me and complimenting the therapist at the same time. At home, she fixed nourishing *pho*, a Vietnamese soup she considered far more nutritious than our canned soups. And she even worked with me to rectify and bring up-to-date our checkbook, which, unbeknownst to me, I had badly botched for several months before my diagnosis. As she straightened our records, she added a little smiling face by each correction, the thought of which cheers me to this day. She was golden. I can never thank her enough.

My surgeon was Charles B. Wilson. Renowned for his surgical genius, some years later, he was singled out as a prime example of "physical genius" in a "Profiles" article in *The New Yorker* sent to me by Steve. There are no words I can add to the accolades and appreciation that have justifiably come his way, except to say that in addition to his medical expertise, he impressed me as a quietly compassionate person.

Four days after surgery, I was sitting in bed when a sudden surge passed through me, and I knew I very much wanted to live. This was interesting in the extreme because until that moment, I had felt unsure whether the effort was worth it. For a number of weeks before diagnosis, I had felt myself dying, which seemed sad, but carried no hint of fear. On one occasion, concerned friends had stopped by to cheer us up, and during their visit, I found myself feeling as though I were existing on a higher plane, looking down upon proceedings that once might have attracted me but now made me wonder why people ever cared about such trivialities. I later learned this is a phenomenon sometimes associated with near-death experiences.

Ken's persistence had finally resulted in the definitive diagnosis on a Friday, leading to surgery the following Tuesday. With the family gathering over the weekend, I had reasoned if this were *really* serious, Steve would have found a way to join us. Assuming his coming would mean all was lost, I had clung to his absence as reassurance.

When Steve did arrive a week later, he was apologetic about not having come sooner, and I quickly assured him his absence was the one thing that convinced me I was *expected* to survive. He taught me much that is worth knowing. As an anesthesiologist, he had experimented with various means of pain control. My type of surgery did not involve much pain, but it can lead to strange mental phenomena—hallucinations and weird sensations. Steve warned me of this, assuring me it "goes with the territory" and should not alarm me unduly. He suggested I put myself on "beautiful beaches" as a means of calming and relaxing my mind during the long hours of recuperation. I followed his advice, reliving our recent Australian trip in my mind.

I imagined myself on the small boat taking us to Green Island where the clear water teemed with colorful tropical fish, mingling in memory with the exotic birds and vegetation of the island to produce what Ken termed "sensory overload." I also tried recapturing the snorkeling on the Great Barrier Reef that had stunned me with its beauty and the uproarious screeches of large bats known as flying foxes as they nightly dropped mangoes onto the tin roof of our cottage. I progressed to Cairns with its lorikeets roosting in the town's trees, its gracious old waterfront speckled with palms, and the Atherton Tableland above it where I saw in my mind's eye the streets lined with lavender jacaranda and pink romagna blossoms in the austral spring.

The fantastic anthills standing stark on the Tableland and an ancient volcanic lake where we swam at a distance from the small freshwater crocodiles inhabiting those same waters were revisited mentally, as were two towering Karri pine trees, natives of New Zealand growing to great height in that one spot far from home. Further material for review was the ancient curtain fig tree, an immensely tall strangler fig grown from seeds thought to have been airborne and implanted on the limbs of a long-departed host tree that was ultimately suffocated and replaced by this vigorous intruder.

The beautiful long beach stretching between Cairns and the sleepy town of Port Douglas brought tears to my eyes. Every bit of that ground was revisited in my mind before flying on to Alice Springs and the wonders of its outback. There, a long pedestrian walkway over the then-dry bed of the Todd River had led us to town, half a mile from where we were staying. And in the light of early morning at Simpson's Gap, we watched rock wallabies at play and lovely little zebra finches, with flashes of red among their gray, black, and white feathers, zipping in and out of pools at our feet.

My determined reveries flew me again above Ayers Rock and the Olga Mountains on our journey to Perth and its lush gardens—Kings Park in full springtime bloom. And there was Rottnest Island, just off the coast of Western Australia in the Indian Ocean. Easily traversing the small island on rented bikes, we took a brief and wild swim from one of its beaches and made friends with an endearing little marsupial native to that island only—the quokka. Resembling a miniature kangaroo, she allowed us to pet her and admire the even tinier offspring empouched within the fur of her soft gray belly. Quokkas are protected and run wild, completely unafraid of humans. Historically they account for the name of the island; when first discovered by the Dutch, the abundant quokkas were thought to be some kind of rat.

The Indian Pacific Railway spans the continent between the Indian and Pacific oceans. Crossing the long stretch of outback known as the Nullarbor Plain, we watched occasional "mobs" of kangaroos lounging around on the north side of the railroad track, their offspring frolicking in the baking sunlight. Colorful springtime resumed for us in South Australia, where our train sped past fields carpeted with a blue flower that is variously called Salvation Jane or Patrick's Curse, depending upon whether the speaker thinks it saves animals during droughts or is poisonous to them. In any case, I can attest that horses grazing in fields of the stuff were a marvelous sight to behold for a person whose favorite color is blue. The entire trip had been magical for me the first time, and its memory became therapeutic.

As my confidence returned after the operation, I volunteered in the Department of Neurosurgery to talk with patients facing surgery similar to mine. I knew the kinds of questions and concerns they would have. Much more importantly, I knew the enormous comfort provided to me by the informed advice and answers I received in friendly informality within my family. I wanted to share that good fortune, and I have been able to help a number of patients through their experiences, daunting at best. In this day of truly remarkable medical advances to which so many of us owe our continuing lives, I often wonder how a patient with no personal connections in the field of medicine manages to thread the modern medical maze. For beyond the awesome new technologies lie new human questions. As my aging mother remarked when she learned our second son had also elected to study medicine, "Wonderful! A family can *never* have too many doctors!"

A few friends have remarked what a shame that I had not been diagnosed and operated upon sooner. Actually, that proved an enormous blessing for which I am most grateful. By the time I was diagnosed there was no time for deliberations and decisions; it was now or never, which relieved us of agonizing over what route to take. But far more important is the fact that I required six pints of blood on an emergency basis, and until a precious few months before my surgery, our Irwin Memorial Blood Bank had probably the highest proportion of AIDS-tainted blood in the nation. The previous spring, reliable tests for analyzing blood had been developed, and on the basis of their results, blood from donors who were likely carriers of AIDS was no longer being accepted by the blood bank. I was a beneficiary of that crucial timing.

Even so, I requested an AIDS test before visiting our newborn grandchild whose existence was a powerful spur to my recovery. When we received the call telling of his birth, Ken and I walked down to a local bakery to celebrate. Discussing this momentous event, Ken remarked, "I don't know why his arrival should make such a difference, but it does. It matters to know that little fellow is in this world." For me, it represented the cycle of life—his mother and I—in our respective lives while being a continent apart, each engaged in personally momentous events.

Hikes at Tennessee Valley soon became a part of my therapy. Just walking the Marin hills again filled me with joy. Returning from one such hike, I commented on the rich mud underfoot as Ken handed me into our car, whereupon he quickly riffled off a couple of pertinent lines from Rupert Brooke's famous poem, "The Soldier." Much impressed, I asked him to repeat the whole poem so I could try to memorize it, and we worked on it together as we drove back across the bridge. This led me back to poetry, first to improve my memory, then for enjoyment. What had begun as mere mental exercise became a hobby that has brought me much pleasure. At one point, I composed a few short poems; especially to my liking was this:

What's in a Word?
Green feather coating
Bright ruby throating

Needle beaking
Sudden squeaking
Iridescing
Evanescing
Summer-blessing
Hummingbird!

Three of my haiku were published in the *Mainichi Daily News*, an English-language newspaper published in Tokyo. The best of these satisfies the classically strict discipline of haiku:

bamboo stand silent
about an unruffled pond
the sun alone moves

Because their guidelines are precise, Japanese forms appealed to me. Moved by our recent trials, I composed a poem that found its way immediately onto Ken's desk where it still resides:

Tanka for Ken

When first we two met
harmony spun about us
like a soft cocoon.
May no gust of ill fortune
unravel its silken threads.

* * *

New doors began opening for me. A decade earlier, we had become friends with a remarkable manual therapist. For some years, Ken had been sporadically plagued with incapacitating muscular spasms in his neck, resulting from an auto accident in which we were rammed from behind by a drunken driver. Customary measures recommended by orthopedists had failed to relieve the pain, and he was finally turned over to a Japanese physical therapist at UCSF who told Ken he could feel the place needing correction but could not make the adjustment because of Ken's fast reflexes. However, he said he knew the person who could and recommended his mentor, Donald K. Swartz in Hayward. Meanwhile, I had developed a condition of "dropped shoulder" that resisted solutions proposed by doctors and osteopaths—adjusting my pillow differently, wearing a lift in my shoe, etc. I seemed on my way to widow's hump, eventual crippledom and/or surgery.

Don largely took care of Ken's condition on our first visit, with a maneuver that caused Ken to yelp but quickly declare it "hurt *good*." Then, after giving me a treatment, which mobilized a spot I had suffered longer than I could remember, Don gave me some exercises he said would be "more helpful than another treatment and, if done daily, will cure your condition." They were—and they did.

Don was a "supertherapist." Blinded in his teens by retinal detachment, a condition then untreatable, over the years, he studied virtually all forms of manual therapy, earning credentials in a great many disciplines including chiropractic and osteopathic techniques. A licensed and registered physical therapist, he has worked with hospitals and doctors in the East Bay for decades. His private practice is in a modest office, and at his recent death, he had an astonishing lifetime list of well over half a million patients, some of whom crossed continents and oceans for his treatments. Often referring to himself as a "body mechanic," he has kept us both "tuned-up" since 1976, and this association blossomed into a rewarding friendship with him and his wife.

Before my brain tumor, I had interviewed Don with the idea of writing an article about his therapeutic methods and the contributions they make to health and quality of life. Afterward, Don introduced me to a physical therapist who could help me resume the project by filling me in on details of their profession. Eddie Guarino was most kind and helpful, as were other physical therapists I consulted, and in 1988, my three-part article entitled "Manual Therapy and Health" was published in the *Physical*

Therapy Forum, a journal of the APTA (American Physical Therapy Association). It took third prize in their annual essay contest—a decided first for me.

For a while, travel took us to visit new grandchildren, and because we had begun shipping paintings to our sons and their wives, we now had the added pleasure of seeing Mildred's works in the light of Florida and New Mexico. We also went again Down Under, visiting Tasmania and friends in the region around Canberra, and in 1991, Ken was guest of honor at the annual Taniguchi Symposium in Kyoto where we spent a strenuous week that proved a further milestone in my recovery.

At home, our neighborhood attracted another threat to its integrity. The target this time was Kezar Stadium. When we moved here forty-five years ago, the 49ers football games were played in the old Kezar Stadium, three blocks directly down our hill. Neighborhood youngsters, including our sons, used to rent out garage and driveway space for parking on game days. About ten minutes before game's end, the sea gulls would begin flying around the stadium, gradually gathering on the high cement rim surrounding the bleachers, where they waited patiently until the stadium emptied and they could move in on discarded food scraps. How they judged the timing is a mystery, perhaps akin to the reputed disappearance of elk just before the opening day of hunting season.

After the 49ers moved to Candlestick Park, Kezar long remained an empty eyesore. Various community and civic leaders, including Mayor Dianne Feinstein, conceived and developed plans for a scaled-down landscaped stadium intended primarily for youthful athletic events. It has functioned admirably since its rebirth, but not without watchfulness on the part of the citizenry.

Early in the '90s, there was a strenuous attempt to fill city-hall coffers by allowing rock concerts in the stadium. Ken joined the Kezar Advisory Council and led a successful fight to prohibit such massively crowded and noisy events in the stadium. Soon afterward, Mayor Art Agnos was defeated for reelection, and his successor, Frank Jordan (another single-term mayor), attempted to introduce alcohol into our youth and community stadium, ostensibly to satisfy the adult spectators at rugby games. At the time, the city was pushing a "Say No to Drugs" campaign and simultaneously sending out the message that Daddy can't watch his rugby without alcohol. This turned into a citywide brouhaha, with youth organizations and neighborhoods uniting to protest the travesty. On this round, I entered the fray. By that time, San Francisco's former mayor Feinstein had become a distinguished senator in Washington, engaged in matters of grave and global significance. But once again, Senator Feinstein demonstrated her devotion to this city. When informed of our efforts to keep alcohol out of the new Kezar Stadium, she took the same attitude toward maintaining the principles of this new Kezar as she had taken years ago in helping to establish them. Thanks largely to her and to the efforts of youth groups and a few other local politicians, Kezar remains a model for community stadiums countrywide.

Grandmotherhood looked to be the big thing for me from then on. Like others of my kind, I quickly discovered its delights and advantages and felt quite ready to submerge other activities to the enjoyment of those pleasures. Ken pointed out a mysterious thing: whereas maternal hormones are well-known, no such easy explanation accounts for what appear to be grandmotherly hormones. Yet the instincts are there and quite overwhelming. Freed from the distractions of running a household, as well as the ultimate parental responsibility for guiding young children into adulthood, a grandparent is able to observe and enjoy them just as children. Through these observations, I have learned far more about child development than I ever knew as a busy parent.

For one thing, a child can understand very well before he can speak as can an adult learning a foreign language. Once on a snowy day, I was asked by my daughter-in-law to help put snow boots on the children, a time-consuming occupation at best with toddlers. For some reason, I could not find the boots in their customary place, and as I walked around looking in unlikely places, the one-year old followed me. In an effort to hold her interest and keep her from toddling out of sight, I began talking as if she could help me, "They're not in the closet. Now where would they be? Where did Mommy put them? Isn't this silly?" She suddenly made a beeline toward a sideboard in the dining room where the good china and linens were kept. Before I could stop her, the cabinet door was flung open, and there stood four little boots in a neat row.

The year 1993 marked a watershed for our family. Late in June, as we were visiting with Larry and family, a call came from Yine's doctor, telling me she was in a coma from a stroke. Ken and I quickly returned home and set out for Vinson Hall, but by the time we arrived, she had died. Steve and Kim had come from Florida to help us attend to her affairs. On the afternoon of our arrival, we learned Steve had become a Muslim. As if in a chain reaction, within a year, he was followed into Islam by his wife and his brother, initiating a momentous new chapter in all our lives, with disruptions in all affected families—ours and those of our daughters-in-law.

The author's photo of Ken while on vacation at Tepee Ranch in the Big Horn Mountains of Wyoming.

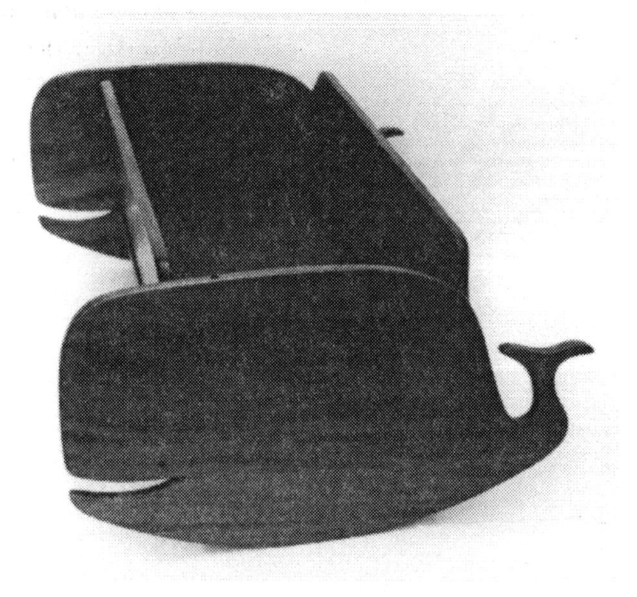

Our first mutual project during Ken's retirement.

Islam in the Family

Steve's startling announcement had an immediate and profound effect upon me. My first thought was thankfulness that Yine escaped this latest development, for she would have foreseen immediately that we faced family upheaval on an unknowable scale. As events of the next year unfolded, we realized our close encounter with Islam was quite rare and possibly unique. While this in no way makes us authorities on the religion itself, we have learned a lot, and our observations provide information important to the understanding of the increasingly bold reach of Islam into all of our lives. The world's population, still predominantly non-Muslim and therefore considered "infidel" by Muslims, has much at stake and should become as well informed as possible. To that purpose, I describe in some detail our experiences and their impacts upon us, as well as the impressions we have drawn from them over a decade of parental connection with this religion.

Islam is an exceptionally demanding faith. From our experience, I have a strong impression its demands account for much of the religion's appeal in Western societies where personal sacrifice is seldom asked for causes greater than ourselves. Simply meeting the seemingly innocuous recommendation of five formalized prayer periods per day imposes immediate challenges not only upon new Muslims but also to their close non-Muslim relatives and co-workers as well, for these requirements conspicuously intrude into established routines. This is only the tip of the iceberg.

Westerners dissatisfied with relativism in our society would do well to give thought to the perils of absolutism before leaping into a fundamentalist faith. Perhaps most important for those considering conversion to Islam is recognition that Islam becomes a lifetime commitment. Once the simple vow has been taken in the presence of a Muslim as witness, the convert is in the religion for life. Converting *from* Islam is defined as apostasy, for which many Muslims consider death the appropriate penalty. Indeed, dissidence of any kind, even disagreement with or criticism of the Muslim religion which guides Islamic enterprise, can be construed as defection and deserving of the same punishment. I know of three individuals in the United States who have successfully put Islam behind them, but in each case, they had to move far away, "leaving no forwarding address" as one of them eloquently put it.

In our case, though we had known our older son was searching, we felt shock and sorrow when his search led him into Islam. His conversion represented such a complete repudiation of the Western civilization that had not only nurtured him but also given him the personal freedom to make such a choice. We knew (though not to its full extent) his disillusion with much in our society, primarily its loose moral values promoted by the popular culture and the secular humanism condoning this. We agreed with this criticism and some others. For example, along with the lack of spirituality he felt in our culture, he also deplored an increasingly evident decline in the ethic of personal responsibility, a problem only now being addressed nationally. In Florida, Steve had witnessed too many wasteful lawsuits charging medical malpractice when none existed—still worse, where none *could* have existed. To my remark that surely such fraudulent cases are thrown out of court, he replied, "They are won every day of the week!"

Seeking remedies for what he perceived as a seriously deteriorating society, he began studying the lives and writings of founders of our American republic, and there he found frequent mention of God and morality. He turned to the Bible, as well as other books of scripture from the world's great religions. He has told me that when he reached the Koran, he "knew" he had been Muslim all his life.

Immediately noticeable upon his conversion were changes in behavior and personality. Humor faded as proselytization took center stage, and humility was replaced by an arrogant attitude of certainty. Some months later, when Larry also became involved with Islam, both our daughters-in-law came under intense pressure, and their children quickly responded to mounting tension in their homes. With Larry's conversion Ken and I felt devastated, bereft. Our family seemed shattered both practically and emotionally in ways hard to imagine except perhaps by those who have lost loved ones to cults.

Indeed, many of Islam's ways resemble those of cults. Name changes, dietary requirements, even codification of bathroom protocols, quickly became manifest. More subtle perhaps, though certainly no less unsettling, are various Muslim beliefs that reminded us of pagan superstitions. I particularly remember one about dogs containing "jinns"—with black dogs likely harboring evil jinns, therefore making them dangerous to touch or even be near. We learned that to keep harmony in the family, not only the convert but also his spouse and children must agree to live by such precepts—alien to us—governing Muslim lifestyle.

In Islam there is no separation between church and state, so theoretically Islamic civilization and governance are inseparable from their defining religion. In recent years, Islam has attracted a growing number of converts in the United States. It is probably no coincidence that in the past few decades there has occurred a quiet revolution of sorts, an unprecedented explosion of Muslim printed materials from the Middle East, translated and distributed worldwide. Many of our large cities also have received energetic attention from Muslim missionaries. And less well known than it should be is the sobering commitment shared by Muslims worldwide, a commitment to continue striving for their god until all the world worships Allah and lives by shari'a (Islamic law). Taken together, these circumstances significantly increase the daunting influence of Islam's presence and importance in today's world.

Undoubtedly the fallibilities of other cultures contribute to this trend. We who live in the West recognize our society is flawed, sometimes grievously. Yet it still represents values of personal liberty and opportunity offered by few other civilizations, past or present. Quite understandably, we do not and should not want to relinquish these ideals to theocratic totalitarianism. By allowing the weakening of spirituality and morality in our culture, our country by default becomes fertile ground for a religion ambitious to impose its own rigid laws governing these values.

I am no stranger to family ruptures caused by religious differences. During World War II, one of my cousins chose to serve in the military while his brother became a conscientious objector. Their strongly held convictions produced a rift within their Quaker family that never entirely healed. Also, my sister found Quakerism lacking and became a Catholic.

Our sons' conversions to Islam, however, represented a different order of magnitude. In contrast to the tolerance and humanitarianism of the Quaker faith, we found a dismaying severity and intransigence in Islam. Its overwhelming emphasis upon dogma was especially alarming. Over the years, I have come to think of doctrinaire religions as strong religions, dependent upon their strong dogma to attract and hold converts. This particular one seemed the ultimate in that category. We were thus confounded by our sons' decisions, within a year of each other, to join such a faith.

While comprehending their interest in "Islamism"—the faith, doctrine, or cause of Islam—we could not imagine making such a comparatively hasty and essentially irrevocable commitment without greater concern for its effects upon loved ones. Surrendering personal autonomy to what was still relatively unknown seemed rash, and we questioned whether they had considered how devastating each unilateral decision would be to the rest of us unavoidably affected.

Initially, our family seemed fractured. Hardly could it have been otherwise, for Islam's demands impacted us all. Energetic proselytization drained us, and the seemingly programmed, robotic talk increased our feeling of unfamiliarity with the sons we thought we had known. Rightly or wrongly, we sensed mind control. Our sons seemed to have become Islam's overnight. For one terrifying period, I found I could no longer enjoy watching children and their mothers in the park. The mere sight struck at my heart, and I felt I could see into their future heartaches. Mercifully, this period was brief and passed as suddenly and unexpectedly as it had arrived.

Islam's already mentioned resemblance to cults was inescapable. Dietary restrictions and name changes cropped up remarkably quickly, and though there is nothing intrinsically "wrong" with either, both raised practical difficulties within an already multicultural family. In our case, dietary changes abruptly deprived young children of favorite foods, and the Muslim names given two of our grandchildren seemed a gratuitous violation of their nascent identities.

Along with these changes came the apparent personality changes in our sons, warmth and lightheartedness giving way to strain and dead seriousness. For us and for our grandchildren, this led to a sense of nervous and artificial austerity creeping into our formerly easygoing familiarity. Sadly, we watched as sparks of romance died out of marriages and coziness fled from their homes. The mosque rapidly superseded both home and family in our sons' lives. Such sudden changes undoubtedly benefit the religion by quickly drawing a newcomer away from past influences, simultaneously binding him closer to the new arbiter in his life, his mosque, while demoting his family accordingly. During that early period I was acquiring information about Islam through reading and inquiry, and the more I learned, the more alien I felt it to be, which led to a very painful and unwelcome sense of alienation from its ardently devoted adherents within our family.

The extreme zealousness of religious converts is well known. A birthright Muslim told me that newcomers to Islam are often afraid they will "make mistakes" and so go to extremes trying to follow all dictates religiously, in every sense of that word. Because Islam's dogma differs so greatly from what the average non-Muslim knows, a switch to Islam comes down especially hard on non-Muslim family members, most particularly wives. With a committed Muslim husband, a non-Muslim wife has two options: she may remain in the marriage on Islam's terms, or divorce.

Islam's terms can be intensely demeaning to wives who find themselves suddenly demoted from equal partnership in a marriage to a seemingly arbitrary subordination in matters affecting themselves and their children. Everything is affected—the foods they cook and consume, management of family finances, scheduling of prayer and familial activities. Especially destructive can be the sudden perception that a body once cherished has automatically become "impure" because its occupant has not accepted Islam. Under such extreme elitist dictates, romance stands little chance, marriage withers, and sanity itself is threatened. For young children, the sudden discontinuation of celebrations of their birthdays and other familiar holidays adds to the hurt and confusion they are experiencing as described later in this chapter.

In Islam, religion and civilization intertwine and realities often deviate from the assurances. On the one hand, we frequently encountered the mantra "Islam means peace," yet there is the mandate to continue struggling until the world becomes Muslim. And Islam claims to be tolerant, while refusing tolerance to four-fifths of the world's population who hold religious views other than theirs. Inevitably, the Muslim religion thus comes across as not only intolerant, but also hypocritical.

Indeed, East and West may turn out to be irreconcilable, since many contradictions exist between our civilizations. Even within Islam there are severe differences of belief between sects, especially between the two major branches, Shiite and Sunni, the latter representing roughly 90 percent of the world's Muslims and the branch to which our sons converted. For the most part, when speaking of Islam I am referring to Sunni Islam, the type to which we have been directly exposed.

Western cultures in the Judeo-Christian tradition have spent centuries trying to improve conditions of temporal earthly life on this planet while Islam seems focused on the eternity of a postulated post-death existence. This dichotomy of outlook threatens to remain an eternal barrier to any basic reconciliation among these monotheistic faiths or the all-important lifestyles they guide.

In our family, early attempts to bridge widening chasms in our family were not successful. Ken and I resented the domination Islam was exerting over us, feeling that in a sense it held us hostage by our love for our children. So much was complicated by rules new to us, and these seemed to pour down upon us in veritable cascades. Initially, we tried to avoid offending by meeting each new rule as it appeared. But in the long run this does not work; accommodation must be a two-way street for a family to maintain its integrity.

In early discussions, Muslim beliefs were being presented as "facts," known by reference to axioms derived from the Koran and/or ancillary writings in the hadith and sunnah. Such sources continue to be studied and debated by Muslim scholars worldwide, as they have been for centuries, and uniformly accepted interpretations of controversial passages continue to appear nowhere in sight. To those theologically inclined, all this may be intellectually stimulating stuff, but for Ken and me, dealing with the pain and practical problems being endured in our family, it held little interest. So we learned to avoid such unprofitable discussions.

Many new Muslims feel their faith helps them become better people by overcoming perceived deficiencies in themselves or their lives. Indeed, Islam brought Steve the answers and peace he sought, so initially—and cautiously—we felt happy for him. Soon, however, we discovered this would not be enough; Islam was declared "right" for all of us. Ken and I lived apart from the epicenter of this tumult, but Kim was alone on the front lines, so to speak. Hence, this good young woman—wife, mother, physician—began worrying and with seeming inevitability she also converted, to her parental family's sorrow. When Kim joined Steve in Islam, so went our oldest grandchildren.

Larry's conversion made us parents of two Abdullahs, replacing the distinct Stephen and well-defined Laurence we had known. In due course, these conversions led to a three-pronged pressure brought to bear on Carmen, the only holdout from their generation to resist conversion. Our converts seemed confident they had acquired an absolute lock on truth because their information came from the Koran. Gone was the humility of "God only knows" when considering debatable religious issues. Young minds once filled with many interests suddenly seemed filled only with newfound certainties derived from theological dogma. Western music and thought gave way to the chanting of prayers and the Koran. Such swift and radical changes cost Ken and me the sense of comfort and ease we had formerly felt with our sons, and also their families, leaving large gaps in our lives that were difficult to fill.

We plagued ourselves with agonizing questions: Why had this happened? What had we not done, or done wrong? Essentially, we had followed the laid-back pattern of our Quaker parents, making no special effort to introduce our children to organized religious observance. Our parents were never regular attenders at Friends' meeting, yet throughout their lives, they had retained and lived by strong Quaker principles. During our period of soul-searching, I once asked Larry if he felt our failure to guide them to a religion had been wrong. He looked genuinely surprised, exclaiming, "Why? Any religion you would have guided us to would have been the wrong one!" Good answer and very comforting to me.

Then along came a single-sentence note from a Swarthmore College classmate who congratulated us on having "raised your children right." This was not only a comfort; it was a quiet affirmation of Quaker values of tolerance by which we tried to live. And it revived my confidence in the essential "rightness" of things. This was important at a time when personal disappointment in the unexpected turn our family life had taken was still acutely painful and confusing.

At times such as those, some solace may be found in the belief that "this was meant to be." Our older Abdullah predicted that someday all of us would feel this change had been for the best, and I think this has come to pass. Certainly, our family's Muslims live admirable lives of honor and service, and they remain fine, principled people.

We are often asked why they took the path they did. Though we can speculate from what we know of them and their lives, perhaps the reasons cannot be fully articulated, even by them. Certainly, the aforementioned sense of having found answers to perceived problems is a factor. But I also have a strong impression that many converts to Islam are seeking an absolutist refuge in a relativistic world.

Of course, arguing religion accomplishes nothing, as said so well in *The Rubaiyat of Omar Khayyam*:

Myself when young did eagerly frequent
Doctor and Saint, and heard great Argument
About it and about: but evermore
Came out by the same Door as in I went.

We appreciate that countless Muslims are salt-of-the-earth people—responsible, peace-loving individuals, leading hardworking and honorable lives, devoted to their families and their faith. I think it likely they comprise the majority of Muslims, who are sometimes referred to as "silent Muslims" because they do not make headlines—a subject discussed later in this chapter.

From our experience, however, I urge Westerners considering conversion to Islam to realize all is not so simple as it may appear. A convert might expect (as did one of our sons) that he may worship privately if he wishes. But in the reality we have witnessed, the local mosque soon takes over much of the convert's life, determining not only where he worships but also how he lives. Communal worship for men is strongly encouraged, which as the world now knows makes mosques easy venues from which to incite Muslims against a predominantly non-Muslim world.

Many of today's problems arise because of the nature of "isms" in general, for they frequently require submergence of their members to an ideology that henceforth calls the tune for the individual. This imposes sudden consequences for the convert, and for friends or relatives who care. In the case of Islamism, many activities formerly shared by a convert and his wife will likely become influenced by determinations made at his mosque. For example, a wife accustomed by mutual agreement with her husband to handling family finances may find herself abruptly denied access even to their records if the husband is thus directed by his religious adviser. For non-Muslim family members, Muslim rules might be acceptable if the convert were willing to leave the non-Muslim partner's lifestyle alone. But therein lurks the rub. Prescribed rules from mullahs are likely to proliferate until they ultimately reduce non-Muslim family members to the equivalent of chattels.

Would-be converts should also know there are practical considerations concerning inheritance. Islamic recommendations include passing twice as much value to a male beneficiary as to his female counterpart, whether sons and daughters, brothers and sisters, or ancillary beneficiaries. Furthermore, Muslim causes and agencies may take precedence over non-Muslim offspring.

Complications also arise with artworks, many of which are required to be buried or destroyed. This matter was important to me, having inherited my aunt's paintings, many of which hung in our sons' homes. With Islamicization, a sizable number of them were in immediate danger of destruction because Islam bans the representational art at which Mildred Miller excelled—landscapes depicting creatures of God's creation: animal and human. We became acutely concerned when told that Muslim rules require burning or burying such paintings. (Sculpture depicting humans or animals must also be buried or destroyed—one does not see such statues in the art of Islam, because they are considered iconic). Our sons were aware of our alarm and, much to their credit and our gratitude, they made responsible accommodation to our wishes. As a result, many of these paintings are now in the art collection at Swarthmore College in Pennsylvania where Mildred had once declined a scholarship in favor of attending the Pennsylvania Academy of the Fine Arts near her home in Philadelphia. Sales of her paintings now benefit the Swarthmore Art Department and its List Art Gallery, and many of Mildred's works have found their way into galleries and homes in the land of her birth and early career.

Not long after our sons' conversions, their marriages dissolved. All three of our Muslims have remarried within their faith and are working and raising families here and abroad. When our sons and their new families moved to Saudi Arabia, friends asked if we planned to visit them there. Our younger son lives in Medina, so visiting him in his home would be very difficult unless we became Muslim. Traditionally, non-Muslims were not even allowed to enter the holy cities of Mecca and Medina, but I have heard recently that some exceptions are now being permitted. However, such travel is uncertain at best, and unlike the situation for employees affiliated with Western or international corporations serving the Kingdom of Saudi Arabia (KSA), American visitors traveling on their own find their American citizenship provides scant official protection. Foreigners going to KSA to visit Muslim relatives put themselves under the control of Muslims, usually the eldest Muslim male in the family and, of course, the Muslim government.

Non-Muslim family members soon learn of the sharp divisions between them and their new Muslims regarding family celebrations. In our experience, traditional American holidays such as Thanksgiving are ignored. And of course Christmas is out and Islamic holidays are in. Our sons' new wives, who had grown up in the Muslim faith, surprised me by having little difficulty wishing us happy holidays just as I wish them the same on their holidays of Eid. Until recently, however, such acknowledgment seemed hard for the newer Muslims in our family, and I imagine considerable time is required to feel comfortable enough in one's new faith to wish happy holidays to those of other faiths. Still, that void seems thoughtless to non-Muslims and further emphasizes the apparent depth of Islamic intolerance toward the rest of the world.

Non-Muslim employees here and in Britain have told me their Muslim co-workers do not like to mix—that they prefer to keep to themselves. This is consistent with the observation that many Muslims immigrating to Western nations resist assimilation into the established schools and cultures of their adopted lands, while attempting to impose Muslim customs such as public calls to prayer upon their host countries. And I understand a few Muslim clerics have even stated that immigration into the West is part of a long-range strategy for continuing their jihad toward eventual religious domination.

Becoming Muslim may result in discontinuing recognition of family birthdays. This caused sorrow to our four oldest grandchildren. Thankfully, the stringency of that early period is relaxing as their fathers mature into their faith, but it has taken the better part of a decade. Unforgettable is the joy expressed by the youngest of those four when, for the first time in years, her daddy sent her a personal birthday greeting!

There is one especially pernicious Muslim tenet we did not discover for some years. That is the belief that if one is introduced to the Islamic religion *and rejects it*, he or she will go to hell. In my experience, such an assertion is unique to Islam.

Surely, thoughtful Muslims must be aware that, regardless of possible scriptural origin ascribed to this assertion, it simply is not provable by mortals, for ultimately it must rest upon God's judgment, not mere wishful thinking or calculated threat. I find it hard to imagine a more intimidating double whammy. In essence, it says "Let us tell you about our religion, and if you don't accept it, you will go to hell." Put another way, if one studies Islam and the Koran, as we non-Muslim family members were being urged to do, he or she must ultimately accept Islam, lock, stock and barrel, or be doomed to hellfire and damnation. What a horrific religious trap! This diabolical twist is the stuff of childhood nightmares, to which it led among our grandchildren.

Regardless of whether or how we articulate our faith, many of us recognize the presence in this universe of forces or powers transcending what is wholly comprehensible to mortals. The fact that these remain mysterious in no way decreases the reality for me. But judging by the tidal wave toward religious extremisms, a great many humans echo our younger Abdullah's assertion when he declared, "That's not enough for me." I wonder, though. How can it *not* be enough, since we can never know beyond the knowable? Humans want to "know," to make sense of life. But life has a "life of its own" going on all around us whether we make sense of it or not—indeed, whether or not it is ever given a thought. Man may be unique in his persistent desire to comprehend the supernatural.

Given humanity's preoccupation with where we go from this life, why is there little corresponding interest in where we have come from? We know nothing about that, and neither do we feel any need to know. Why the inequity? I suspect it is the fact that the latter seems safely in the past whereas the former lies in the unknown future: what lies behind we can do nothing about; what lies ahead we may be able to alter. And this makes the premise of eternal paradise the most powerful persuasion, especially to those whose temporal lives offer little satisfaction. Small wonder, then, that promises of passage to a hypothetically paradisiacal life in the future are effective in determining actions in the here and now.

Muslims currently struggle with embarrassing contradictions. We are told Islam does not approve or condone suicide. Yet Muslims are also led to believe that martyring themselves while fighting for Allah is the highest form of service and devotion, guaranteeing sure and swift passage to paradise. I have heard otherwise peaceable Muslims express the wish that one day they may have the opportunity to die in this fashion. By now, the world knows such aspects of Islamic doctrine make it conveniently malleable to mortal machinations, often with catastrophic results.

One might reasonably ask why a god with the great powers attributed to Allah requires brainwashed adolescents or hate-hardened thugs to fight for him.

We are told Islam means peace, yet in *Islam Unveiled*, author Robert Spencer cites suras in the Koran that read like mandates to continue jihad until the entire world worships Allah and agrees to live by shari'a. These suras emanate from the religion's highest authority, accepted by Muslims as unchanging and unchanged for more than a millennium, although interpretations and translations differ widely. This is a matter of inescapable concern to those categorized by Muslims as infidels—effectively the estimated 80 percent of the earth's population remaining non-Muslim as of this writing.

Ken and I were fortunate that one of our sons' wives retained her former religious views, actually strengthened by her exposure to the Muslim faith. Throughout our adjustment, Carmen helped sustain us emotionally. She and we drew together into a mutually supportive group, exchanging little niceties like holiday greetings and honoring familial traditions as we always had. We cannot imagine how any of the three of us would have made it without the other two. Our feelings deepened into strong bonds of love and admiration, which still strengthen us through continuing reminders of what was lost. Most important of all, these bonds helped us deal with the inevitable hurts and confusions to our grandchildren from the broken marriages and changed lifestyles.

Along the way, there has been a strong attempt to describe a rationale for our sons' adoption of Islam, but I think Carmen put it best: it is entirely a matter of faith—not logic, reason, or dogma imposed by belief systems. Indeed, a lot of spurious intellectualizing always seems to hover over utopian isms, be they humanistic or theologic. In either case, a cadre of interpreters of established dogma stands ready to inform and indoctrinate potential followers, with purportedly rational arguments whose true basis lies in mere human belief or wishful thinking. The world today may not contain more of this than ever before, but surely it is more widely disseminated by modern communication and therefore more readily accessible to those who may be susceptible.

A common consequence of Islamic conversion is moving to a Muslim land. We have the impression that males are encouraged to do so for religious reasons, so they can immerse themselves in the culture and delve more deeply into their religious studies. Sooner or later, most of them return to the West to live. Perhaps a measure of disillusion is involved. Reality of life in most Muslim states diverges dramatically from the ideal that may attract the new Muslim to Islamic ideology. There seems a strong parallel to the terrible contrasts between the communism of promises and the resultant totalitarianism that entrapped early followers of Lenin in the Soviet Union. This is under discussion in literature now appearing in the wake of 9/11.

Those who search are likely to find whatever is out there, be it old ideology or new "con game." On pages 222 and 223 of his book *Inside Al Qaeda,* the terrorism expert Rohan Gunaratna points out that within two decades this new organization, pledged to terror, has gained representation and a degree of acceptance in scores of countries, employing organizational and military methods derived from Leninist and Marxist models that hoodwinked much of the world for a century. There seems a terrible irony that these cynical methodologies developed on behalf of a godless society are now used in the name of a major world religion.

On the brighter side of our personal ledger, we welcome many consequences of our sons' affiliation with Islam. This includes especially their contributions to humanity through medical work that could have been done nowhere else, our two new daughters-in-law in whom I find much wisdom and grace, and of course the blessings and delights from our precious new grandchildren. Ken and I also receive fascinating first-hand information and descriptions from parts of the world essentially closed to us. And high among our blessings remains the rewarding relationship with Carmen and her family, while Kim's remarriage has resulted in a visibly happier, more relaxed family we greatly enjoy. It has been a long road, but we feel we have regained the closeness we used to have with Kim and her children as time continues to smooth the rough edges of suffering.

Fundamentalism imposes intractable conditions, and so there remains between our sons and us an ideological gulf resisting bridges of compromise. I suspect the intransigence of fundamentalism is intentional, for its success is evident, and all sorts of elitists make use of it to empower their movements. In terms of human life and love and mercy, however, this seems ultimately a waste of great gifts. Any bitterness I retain rests almost entirely upon these clever, manmade manipulations that successfully twist faith to serve mortal purpose, erecting earthly power upon the flimsy scaffold of mankind's eternal longings for paradise. But this is not new in human affairs nor limited to the Muslim faith.

During the long life with which I have been blessed, I have encountered many isms. Various utopian schemes have proffered earthly paradise and yielded totalitarian tyranny. At the turn of the previous century, communism reared its head. Marx and Lenin were prophets of that particular secular religion, promising state-dominated heaven-on-earth; Hitler followed suit with his fascistic brand of National Socialism. History has pretty well discredited such attempted utopias. Yet the primitive desire for paradise remains—often bringing political despotism in its wake.

Religious fundamentalism draws its premises and promises from longer ago than socialisms, inviting submission to revelation in the ongoing search for certainty in an uncertain world. Though theological promises of paradise after death are impossible to prove or disprove, we can expect to see more wishful longings and proffered appeasements, for utopian desire seems unlikely to diminish any time soon.

Considering the basic incongruities between our beliefs and those of our Muslim family members, the fact our family survives at all suggests that something beyond our human efforts may play a significant role. The blind manual therapist Don Swartz once remarked, "You sighted people don't know what you're missing!" He had told me of his years of suffering and bitterness, before accepting the reality of his blindness and using it to develop the exceptional powers of concentration and memory with which he was endowed. I once asked him whether he had found these benefits so great that he was glad his blindness had occurred. He thought for a moment then replied he would not go that far, but since it had happened, he had found many advantages in it.

This is much the way I feel about the Islamicization of our sons. I have always felt privileged and amazed that I had been given, on loan so to speak, two such beautiful children to love and rear to the fine adults they have become. Though I could never have envisioned their present lives, I am satisfied they have chosen to live with personal honor and admirable deeds. Close personal exposure to their chosen way has enriched my life with knowledge I could have acquired no other way. And who knows, perhaps one day we shall experience even greater depths of our shared love. It's worth staying around to discover where our various roads will lead us.

* * *

No discussion of Islam today can ignore the events of September 11, 2001, and their ongoing aftermath. Our sons' words eloquently convey some of their feelings about this pivotal occurrence. Steve first learned of the attack when he arrived for work the next morning at his hospital in Saudi Arabia. By then, it was late night on our time, and he called immediately to say he wanted us to know his conviction that "whoever did this was wrong, wrong, WRONG." As things wore on in the Middle East, he wrote in an e-mail, "I disapprove of the bombings, whether you call them suicide, homocide, or combocidal . . . I know the arguments mounted in justification/rationalization, religious (and these are the most tortured arguments) and otherwise, and they just don't add up."

From Larry in Medina came an e-mail registering his shock and concluding with these two paragraphs that Ken taped to the wall beside his desk:

> It is times like this that I feel we need to return to the basics. We need to spend more time with our families. We need to do something nice for the neighbor. We need to remind ourselves that we are the nidus from which the good or evil of our own selves ripples out into the world. So like that beautiful prayer asking The Creator for strength to change what we can, patience to accept what we cannot change, and wisdom to know the difference, we need to concentrate upon what good we can do, what evil we can combat, and patient avoidance of all that which will wear us out, tear our emotions, fracture our hearts, deplete our energy, and in the end, frustrate our honorable purpose.
>
> At the end of the day, have faith in the goodness evident in the hearts, minds, and spirits of those who you have come to trust, seek those whose actions testify to the best of their words, and turn from the uncertainties of this world, for they are a deception and a distraction. And understand that even the tragedies of this life are in some way part of a larger plan, which will not unfold one second earlier or later than what has been specified in the design of The Architect.

From an American Muslim friend came the following note, which I quote in its entirety, hoping its warning will be acknowledged and heeded by Americans of all faiths:

> Among my numerous clippings, notes, articles and letters on the subject of Islam is the following, its origin unfortunately beyond my ability to recapture,

> but I enclose it because it presents a point of view which I believe is accurate, both in its analysis of what the true intention behind the attack on Sept. 11, 2001 was and the likely reaction of Americans whose thinking historically has not been able to accommodate thoughts so alien to those of the West as exist in the East:
>
> Note: whoever engineered the 9-11 attack will not have much trouble raising funds for the next one. There are some very rich private citizens among the 500,000,000 who have a deep grudge against the United States.
>
> We are not dealing with Keystone Cops-vintage idiots this time, the way we were in 1993's bomb-laden van. The 9-11 strategy was not adopted to frighten the United States into submission. It was used to recruit a dedicated army of Islamic terrorists for the next stage. It was used to convince recruits that revenge against the Great Satan is possible—and maybe more than revenge. Maybe even victory over the West, an Islamic goal since 622. We are dealing with a motive that stretches back almost fourteen centuries.
>
> Americans are forgive-and-forget people. Their philosophy is "let bygones be bygones." They cannot conceive of a motive that goes on for 1,400 years.

The above reminder of ancient antagonisms dividing our cultures is chilling indeed, coming from one whose knowledge of these matters far exceeds mine. From where I sit, the danger from these new threats can hardly be overestimated or overstated because the goals of organizations such as al Qaeda are built into the religion shared by all Muslims, and since even constructive criticism of that religion is prohibited, effective dissuasion from within is impossible.

To deny this religious dimension of the threat is awkward and unconvincing at best. Many Muslims deplore terrorism as a means to an end, yet strongly favor the desired end, a pure Islamic state. Recent self-styled "pure Islamic states," such as Iran and the Taliban, are not encouraging to Westerners, nor do they appeal to many of the Easterners caught in their resultant webs of totalitarian theocracy. Somehow, recognition of a connection between pure Islamic states and repression goes largely unremarked within Islam.

The same Rohan Gunaratna, who described time-tested communist military and political techniques effectively used by al Qaeda, also points out (*Inside al Qaeda*, p. 73) that al Qaeda considers "religious indoctrination" to be more important than "battlefield or terrorist combat training." And why not? The power of religion binds its followers to their cause with a fervor exceeding that of any secularism. In today's malevolent case of attempted world domination through terror, terrorist leaders have been quick to capitalize on the uses of dogma by indoctrinating what I have heard described as "false" or "marginal" Muslims—primarily those drawn from the ranks of hopeless and poorly educated masses in their impoverished homelands. They are easily manipulated into action, through exploitation of their emotional zeal, untempered by any of the Islamic precepts intended as moral overrides to emotional extremism. A prominent imam in Medina recently denounced such marginal Muslims, declaring they are working for Shaitan rather than Allah and thus cynically defiling their religion for all Muslims.

Many Muslims appreciate America as a refuge offering a life more closely consistent with their peaceful Islamic ideals than they find in the countries from which they emigrate. And many oppose courageously the terrorist atrocities committed in their name. Yet at the same time many resist assimilation into mainstream American culture, and we can look to ourselves for some of the reasons for that rejection. Undoubtedly, much also stems from their ancient desire to live under shari'a, but there is more to it than that. Much in our culture offends people of high ideals, regardless of religious beliefs or lack of same.

Real problems undermine our society and its morale. We have become preoccupied with image at the expense of substance. We're swamped with advertising and infatuated with the sensational and outrageous. We permit all manner of opportunists to abuse and corrupt our institutions. Malcontents and criminals (including terrorists) can and do roam our society, defying its laws and exploiting the protections those laws provide. Courts that were once our glory have become our shame.

I think many of us loyal to this country sense that we, as a people, have become seriously separated from our nation's defining principles. A young immigrant recently pointed to a red, white, and blue sign proclaiming United We Stand and remarked, "What we really need are signs reminding us Divided We Fall!" In his few years here, he has noted the plethora of special interest groups now demanding privileges as entitlements, regardless of costs to country and citizenry as a whole. Somewhere along the way, we seem to have lost the ethic of pulling together for the common good. In serving the catch concept of "diversity," latest darling in the political lexicon, we are sowing divisiveness and reaping disunity.

Our young people have been surfeited with apparent choices and opportunities without corresponding reminders about the responsibilities accompanying them. Advocacy groups do a serious disservice when they encourage the idea that "you can have it all," thus raising unrealistic expectations that ignore the unavoidable demands of life. In encouraging self-fulfillment above service or sacrifice for a common cause, we cripple ourselves spiritually.

Those who really know this nation see beyond its defects to its clear virtues. Still vital within Americans is a sense of compassion and of moral rectitude, and many still live by the lofty ideals that historically have drawn sufferers to our shores. During the period immediately following the 9/11 attacks, countless largely unpublicized actions were undertaken spontaneously by non-Muslim Americans protecting mosques from vandalism and Muslims from violent backlash. These selfless acts deserve at least as much emphasis as the relatively few inexcusably violent acts of backlash following the September 11 outrage.

An example came my way almost immediately. Concerned about the possibility of such backlash against our Muslim daughter-in-law and her children, I called to suggest they take special care to avoid becoming conspicuous targets. Having twice been driven from their family home by communists in Southeast Asia during her childhood, she was ahead of me in cautioning the children and being watchful herself. Knowing of my concerns, however, she then periodically reassured me. From her I learned that in their city, non-Muslim Americans were turning up voluntarily each morning at Muslim schools to assure the safety of students and their families! Furthermore, bouquets of flowers were left outside several mosques. Some weeks later, following a nasty incident of backlash elsewhere in the country, she and her husband went late to their mosque to pray. There they found a volunteer group of non-Muslims engaged in an all-night vigil to protect the mosque from retaliatory vandalism. As the night was cold and rainy, the protectors were invited inside to warm up, turning the evening into a pleasant social occasion exemplifying some of the best of America and of Islam. Such incidents do more to advance conciliation than any formal pronouncements ever will.

* * *

The world is a political place, and it has become small. The ongoing battles against attempted terrorist takeover of our lives remain real and therefore necessary. Our enemies know and play upon our weaknesses, which we can do little to prevent except by removing as many as possible of the vulnerable ways we conduct our affairs. In a world becoming so dangerously volatile and showing signs of becoming increasingly so, we need not apologize for taking reasonable steps to improve our chances for survival. But we also need to set better examples of conduct. How much do we gain (or lose?) from the in-your-face exhibitionism that has taken hold of our entertainment industry or from the ever-increasing offensive advertising that infests our lives? We coddle our countercultures at the expense of a shared culture and allow degrading "sexploitation" to invade everything from e-mail to Internet. For that matter, how much have we gained by permitting our legal system to advance the rights of lawbreakers beyond those of their victims? We have a seriously fractionated society whose vocal and visible sectors often effectively exploit the laws that protect their voice. Legislation alone cannot substitute for goodwill in men's hearts, for it is in men's hearts that the battles between conscience and exploitation take place.

We must continue to strive especially for high standards in high office, ethical corporate governance, and greater acceptance of individual responsibility for our own welfare and actions, as well as a swift return to realistic attitudes toward risk and entitlement. Only if we improve ourselves will our society improve, and it must do so if we are to survive with our basic ideals intact. Unless we "silent Americans" have the will to live up to our ideals, we are going to suffer more antagonism from those who oppose our way of life. And unless "silent Muslims" speak out to condemn the terrorism conducted in the name of Islam, they and their professed religion will become its principal victims.

I believe the majority of humans want good in this world. Evil may predominate in media coverage of events, but good settles in men's hearts and minds, propelling civilization onward against the tidal rushes of oppression aimed at its destruction. Publicity may focus upon the fundamentalism increasingly evident in mainstream Islam, yet behind these headlines are courageous moderate Muslims participating in ongoing ecumenical efforts to encourage mutual understanding and respect between believers of differing faiths. Furthermore, a few Muslim moderates are now even citing Muslim scripture to justify the existence of a Jewish homeland in Israel—an almost unthinkable challenge to the belligerent propaganda that for decades has preached wiping Israel from the map. In this ever more populous world, a realistic measure of Muslim accommodation to the West becomes necessary to prevent complete stagnation of progressive thought and action in Islam.

* * *

Now a decade down the line from our family's introduction to Islam, our sons clearly have found their milieu. They are devout in their faith, and as they relax into it, Ken and I feel a rekindling of the keen humor that always seemed part of them and their relationships with us. Their professional contributions have become noteworthy: Steve has taken anesthesiology to lands where major surgery was conducted *without* anesthesia. And Larry is advancing the treatment of eye conditions prevalent in third-world countries through research and clinical procedures on patient populations only found there. Indeed, Ken feels that Larry's work on "extreme cataracts" is now becoming the single greatest medical contribution in overcoming one of the greatest limitations imposed by age in primitive and developing countries.

Our new Muslim "in-laws" are similarly dedicated to service—including a teacher from Jordan, a former student from India, and a naturopathic physician from New York. All of them are leading productive lives. We have twice as many families now, and warm feelings extend to them as we gradually meet one another. And as icing on the cake, we have several more grandchildren, precious as can be, so our family globalization project is alive and well. Sincere conciliation takes time, but I dare to think that since it can happen in one family, it might eventually happen upon a larger stage. And I believe such successes demonstrate that love still abounds and exerts an enduring influence in human affairs.

My quarrel is not with Muslims or necessarily with Islam, about which I know little beyond what has impacted our family. We actually share many of Islam's reputed moral values and concerns. My quarrel is with doctrinaire dogma that can, and does, enslave men's minds. Dictatorial fanaticisms capture minds by the million and lives of millions more. Effective methods of enslavement developed by their leaders and successfully copied by imitators are quite evident in this era of religious extremism.

Countless victims of communist repression know the stifling effects of dogmatism upon personal incentive and creativity. This fact should not be overlooked in Islamic lands. Muslims hark back to their glory days a millennium ago when their civilization kept alive through the so-called Dark Ages many aspects of culture that thrive in the West today. But the shoe is now on the other foot. Our western culture offers much that is good, yet spurned by Islam, which leaves rank-and-file Muslims mired in their ancient absolutism.

Many Muslims today envy western achievements, yet see no way of attaining them within their own culture. A quote from the first moon walker, astronaut Neil Armstrong, could serve as a reminder to Muslims yearning for a return to cultural and scientific greatness. Writing of the Wright brothers' attainment of powered flight a century ago, Armstrong points out that since time immemorial, man has been inspired by the freedom of birds. Thus, he posits that the human "predilection for freedom" fuels the motivation necessary for creative accomplishment. Current moderate efforts aimed at liberalizing Islam clearly illustrate this understandable human preference and hopefully will contribute to realizing it within Islam. Not surprisingly, such movements are often initiated by women and one day may enable all devout Muslims to feel God's liberating winds flowing through their hair—insh'allah.

As for the mysterious and endlessly debatable origin and destination of earthly life, I see no reason to consider them more important than the intervening life itself, all of which partakes of mystery and seems to represent a natural continuum. We truly are in transit every moment of our lives, exploring new territories as we go the route all life must go regardless of conjecture about its meaning or its destiny. The nineteenth-century English poet Ernest Dowson, put this well when he wrote the following lines:

Out of a misty dream
Our path emerges for a while, then closes
Within a dream.

Late Larks Singing

When our family life became transformed a decade ago, Ken and I began looking for new ways to find satisfaction and fill our void. Thus began an educational odyssey. A number of activities proved diverting for the short term: performances similar to poetry readings, delivered by enthusiastic young storytellers in Marin County cafes, the acquisition and renovation of an old sailboat, and brief memberships in two clubs—all mere fill-ins for what had fallen out of our lives.

More consistently successful were reunions we began attending. Formerly, Ken had felt no desire to join organizations representing World War II veterans. His present life was rewarding enough. After Islam, however, we began attending meetings of the MHS (B-26 Marauder Historical Society) and his old 391st Bombardment Group. With something akin to joy, we discovered the pleasures of reuniting with people who shared familiar values from the past. We also joined a great minireunion of my high-school classmates held in Vermont where several of them now live. And our fiftieth reunions at Swarthmore College, in 1997 and '99, reminded us there is something to be said for growing old with those we knew when young. A classmate made the apt comment that those surviving to our age are among "the walking wounded." Indeed, to be otherwise might mean we had not done much living.

A poem by William Henley, written upon the death of his wife's sister, became especially inspiriting to me:

Marguerite Sorori

A late lark twitters from the quiet skies;
And from the west,
Where the sun, his day's work ended,
Lingers as in content,
There falls on the old, gray city
An influence luminous and serene,
A shining peace.

The smoke ascends
In a rosy-and-golden haze. The spires
Shine, and are changed. In the valley
Shadows rise. The lark sings on. The sun,
Closing his benediction,
Sinks, and the darkening air
Thrills with a sense of the triumphing night—
Night, with her train of stars
And her great gift of sleep.

So be my passing!
My task accomplished and the long day done,
My wages taken, and in my heart
Some late lark singing,
Let me be gathered to the quiet west,
The sundown splendid and serene,
Death.

Recognizing an element of "whistling in the dark" in our determined efforts to compensate for our hurts, we pinned new hopes on finding some of Henley's "late larks" to ease our transition. Especially beneficial were hatha yoga sessions with a young instructress who was herself an inspiring survivor of traumatic events. We found the quiet thoughtfulness of yoga calming to worn minds, while its stretching exercises relieved somatic pains acquired with advancing age—a decided boost to quality of life when much needed.

We journeyed to restful, exhilarating places. Especially dear to me was a trip to Death Valley, a place I love for its silence. Paradoxically, its below-sea-level air feels to me like the pure air of high mountains. On the drive there, I had an amusing incident with a crow as I walked alone one morning down a small hill to a lake. No one else was about at that early hour, but suddenly, a dog began barking from a deck where he was tied. He stopped after I passed, and I thought no more about it. When I started back up the street, however, I noticed a large crow, most likely a raven, had installed himself on a telephone pole directly across the street from the dog's house, and I wondered why. As I came within range, the dog started barking; and when he stopped, the crow, who had been watching the dog, turned his head directly toward me and, looking down at me, said calmly and deliberately, "*Hoo, hoo.*" I stopped walking, which seemed to excite the dog into another spasm. Together we heard him out, after which my crow again redirected his gaze toward me and repeated his hoo-hoo rather superciliously as if perhaps he and I shared an opinion on the matter. Since there had been no sign of the bird on my way down, and since things did seem awfully boring that early on a frosty morning, I assumed the crow heard the first outburst and, looking for a bit of fun, perched there to see what might happen next. I believe he may have been trying to imitate something he heard in the dog's bark, for I have never before or since heard anything close to such sounds from a crow. In any case, he certainly made sure he got into the act.

* * *

There have been especially satisfying spin-offs from our military reunions. Chief among them is Ken's memoir/history, *Marauder Man*, describing his experience as a bombardier and lead navigator in the B-26 Martin Marauder planes that served him and our country so well throughout World War II. He asked me to read and offer suggestions on the manuscript, and in the process, I became interested in the remarkable achievements of those largely unsung planes and crews. The book was first published by Pacifica Military History in 2001 and already enjoys a modest and appreciative following. Early in 2004, it also went into a softcover edition that is being distributed by Simon & Schuster.

My personal interest in the Glenn L. Martin Company, designer and builder of the B-26, began during World War II when my aunt Mildred interrupted her artistic career to become a draftsman at Martin's main plant near Baltimore. Later, while living in the Midwest, I became fond of the Martin commercial airliners: the 202s and 404s flying us to and from the East Coast. And a decade farther on, Ken and I were delighted to find among Mildred's canvases a small oil painting of a B-26 Marauder in flight over Ken's theater of war.

Shortly before Ken began writing his book, I had been reading *The Codebreakers* by David Kahn, a monumental work documenting the vastly important role of cryptography and cryptanalysis throughout history. I remembered reading there about the Battle of Midway, described by Admiral Chester W. Nimitz as a "victory of intelligence." And I also recalled having heard my father and uncle discussing this American naval victory shortly after it occurred while I was still a teenager.

Describing the preliminaries of that battle, Kahn mentioned "American bombers from Midway" attacking the Japanese fleet. These had to be land-based planes from Midway Island, not carrier-based planes from the U.S. fleet, which was still a considerable distance from the island. Also, from accounts describing Marauder activity early in the Pacific War, I knew the B-26 was then the only Allied plane in the Pacific that could match the Japanese Zero in speed, while greatly surpassing it in durability. So I wondered whether Kahn's "American bombers from Midway" included B-26s. A bit of bibliographic sleuthing soon revealed a fascinating tale that brings forth from the shadows an important footnote to the history of that battle.

From Kahn's references, I found a detailed confirmation of my hunch in *Midway: The Battle That Doomed Japan*, published by our Naval Institute Press in Annapolis. This authoritative book was written some years after the war by Mitsuo Fuchida and Masatake Okumiya. Fuchida was the pilot who had led the air attack on Pearl Harbor six months earlier. He was intended to do the same at Midway, but an emergency appendectomy sidelined him aboard Admiral Chuichi Nagumo's flagship, the *Akagi*. His observations are especially relevant to this account, but Okumiya, an intelligence officer, also observed the battle from another vessel in the Japanese fleet.

For the United States, the weeks prior to the Battle of Midway were grim. When Admiral Nimitz's intelligence indicated Midway Island would be the next Japanese target in an unbroken series of successful conquests since Pearl Harbor, he began beefing up defenses on that distant outpost. Among the aircraft ordered to Midway were four B-26 bombers, hastily armed with torpedoes. In a desperate action, virtually everything the United States could muster was thrown at the Japanese fleet early on the morning of June 4, 1942. Little tangible damage was done until nearly ten thirty when our naval dive bombers struck. But the stage was set irrevocably three hours earlier for one of the greatest and most unexpected victories in naval history.

Admiral Nagumo had steamed toward Midway with every reason for confidence. His naval strength was overwhelming, vastly superior to what was left of ours. His strike force included four aircraft carriers, two battleships, three cruisers, and eleven destroyers, plus major vessels in two other naval units nearby. Aboard *Akagi* with Nagumo were his chief of staff, Rear Admiral Kusaka, and his air-group commander, Captain Fuchida. Together on the bridge of the *Akagi*, they witnessed an attack by American torpedo bombers and torpedo-armed Marauders from Midway Island. None of the six TBF Avengers made it through the

Japanese defensive screen to the carriers, five being shot down. Of the four much faster and sturdier Marauders (two of which made it back to Midway), three reached the carriers through a blizzard of Zeros and antiaircraft fire. These B-26s became the deciding factor in convincing Admiral Nagumo to mount a second attack on the Island of Midway. In Fuchida's words, "the remaining three planes kept bravely on and finally released their torpedoes. Free of their cargo, the attacking planes swung sharply to the right and away, except for the lead plane that skimmed straight over *Akagi* from starboard to port, nearly grazing the bridge. The white star on the fuselage of the plane, a B-26, was plainly visible. Immediately after clearing our ship, it burst into flames and plunged into the sea."

Kusaka watched it heading straight for them and reflexively ducked. As Walter Lord describes, in his stunning recreation of the battle in *Incredible Victory*, "a shaken Kusaka found himself strangely moved. He thought only Japanese pilots did things like that. He had no idea who this steadfast American was, but there on the bridge of the *Akagi* he silently said a prayer for him." That pilot was Herbie Mayes. His friend, pilot Jim Muri, also reached the *Akagi* and dropped his torpedo harmlessly but then strafed low over the entire length of *Akagi*'s deck, killing two Japanese and knocking out a transmitting antenna and antiaircraft gun before he and his injured crew managed to fly back to Midway. Theirs may have been the only physical damage inflicted upon the enemy during those early hours. Although U.S. losses were sacrificially great, the early attacks forced the enemy fleet to take evasive action, significantly disrupting its formations. Furthermore, the all-important Zeros were kept busy near water level, rendering them powerless to interfere with the later successful dive bombers.

Admiral Nagumo, meanwhile, had already been disappointed by the results of the first Japanese bombing attack upon Midway, which found few planes on the ground. Still unaware that our fleet was nearby, the admiral was considering his lead pilot's radioed requests for a second strike on Midway at the very moment the B-26s so narrowly missed his flagship. These land-based B-26s thus became the deciding factor in convincing him to order a second attack on the airfield at Midway from which they had come. As Fuchida states, "Admiral Nagumo needed no further convincing that Midway should be hit again . . . Consequently, at 0715, just as the torpedo attack was ending, he ordered the planes of the second wave, which had been armed for an attack on enemy ships, to prepare instead for another strike on Midway."

Writing of that fateful moment in the chronology of his book *Climax at Midway*, the historian Thaddeus Tuleja italicized only one sentence: "*This is the most critical decision of the battle.*" From that point on, both the flight and the hangar decks of *Akagi* and her sister ship *Kaga* were thrust into considerable disarray. Later, when the presence of our fleet was belatedly discovered and reported to him, Nagumo reversed his earlier decision. Fuchida noted that the crews who had been furiously replacing torpedoes with bombs now "hastily unloaded the heavy bombs, just piling them up beside the hangar because there was no time to lower them to the magazine. There would be cause to recall and regret this haphazard disposal of the lethal missiles when enemy bombs later found their mark in *Akagi*." At 10:25 a.m. American dive bombers caught the Japanese carriers at their most vulnerable, and bomb hits became ship-sinking infernos. In five spectacular minutes, the tide of war turned. The Japanese lost all four of their main aircraft carriers, and their precious cargo of planes and well trained pilots. In Fuchida's words, "the apparently futile sacrifices made by the enemy's shore-based planes were, after all, not in vain."

At Ken's suggestion, I wrote this up for an article, "Marauders at Midway," which appeared in *Marauder Thunder* published by the Marauder Historical Society. My researches had led me to the aforementioned Jim Muri who has become a friend of ours. Ken used the material from my article in his book, and copies of the article are also in the B-26 Archive at Pima Air and Space Museum in Tucson. Subsequently, the article was revised for the International Midway Memorial Foundation.

In 1999 the U.S. Navy hosted an affair at Pearl Harbor and on Midway Island for members of the IMMF. We were able to attend, thanks to Colonel Muri and his late wife, Alice. When they decided not to make the trip for reasons of health, they kindly turned over their invitation to us. Participants in the week-long "IMMF Symposium and Dedication" included veterans of the battle; a civilian military historian; navy and marine officers; officials from the IMMF; and a former chairman of the Joint Chiefs of Staff, Admiral Thomas Moorer. An impressive panel indeed; Ken was the only veteran representing Jim's branch of the service, the Army Air Corps.

Among the groups being honored was the Naval Intelligence Unit at Pearl Harbor. Long before I had any thought of visiting the site, the unit had drawn my admiration when first I read descriptions of its cryptanalysts' amazing exploits in *The Codebreakers*, where I had also seen a picture of its cramped and secret wartime location. At the dedication ceremony, I felt a quiet thrill while standing in that empty insignificant-looking basement room, so critically alive with epochal activity more than half a century earlier. And I felt my father being honored indirectly for similarly covert work in the Mediterranean Theatre half a world away.

Midway is an atoll at the northwestern end of the Hawaiian chain of islands. A strategic outpost halfway between North America and Asia, it consists of a lovely lagoon with two major islands, Sand and Eastern, plus a third tiny island amounting to a good-sized rock. Though the total area of dry land is only three square miles, its history belies its small size, for it was an important way station in the early days of both cable communication and transpacific flights of PanAm Clippers. Our three days there were spent in the small community on Sand Island where we slept in a converted barracks near remains of the old Clipper-era hotel.

Now a wildlife sanctuary as well as a historic site, Midway is a great place for animal and bird observation. The famed "gooney birds"—Laysan albatross—breed there, and during our visit, their fledglings were constantly amusing as they tumbled about trying to fly. There is also a disconcerting "red-tailed tropic bird" that flies backward and a lovely small tern, whose pure white underbody is tinted blue by reflections from the intensely blue ocean over which it flies. The white-sand swimming beach is beautiful beyond words, and gliding on my back, looking up at the fairy terns, was an incomparable experience.

Monk seals and large sea tortoises inhabit the waters as do spinner dolphins and, of course, sharks. When the albatross fledglings prepare to go to sea each season, sharks gather for a feast of those who set out over the world's largest ocean before developing enough endurance to stay aloft.

Large frigate birds cruise high above. One day their sky was shared with some of our most sophisticated jets, flown hundreds of miles from carriers to participate in a memorial ceremony on Eastern Island, now deserted except for wildlife and occasional visitors honoring the sacrifices of World War II.

Our flights between Honolulu and Midway were ethereal. Gazing down upon French Frigate Shoals gave us the most magnificent over-water views we have ever had. Indeed, even the cloud-studded sky held a beauty unlike anything in our experience—so pure, so clear, so peaceful—and such a far cry from what Jim Muri and his crew experienced in the urgent spring of 1942, flying in radio silence at half our speed and altitude toward an unknown, barely perceptible speck located at the limit of their range in that vast and lonely Pacific.

* * *

On the whole, these last years are turning out to be productive and satisfying. Recent activities associated with Ken's book have brought us into contact with people possessing a vigor and directness I sometimes find missing in academics whose expertise seems more inclined toward the abstract. From military veterans and test pilots flying at Mach 3 on the edges of space, to former prisoners of war, the men we meet have lived extraordinary lives; and they exhibit a refreshing humility, integrity, and loyalty to the country we share.

Our renewed associations with World War II veterans have also brought some unusual dividends, rekindling a sense of simple fun so enjoyed in more innocent times. Not long ago, a large national gathering of World War II veterans concluded with a gala evening featuring dancing from our era. There I had the privilege of spinning across the floor with a distinguished and stylish dancer, Lord Earl Jellicoe, second wartime commander of Britain's elite and highly effective Special Air Service (SAS)—a memorable experience. And the evening was topped off by the most exhilarating jitterbug with a partner unknown to me until the following morning when I learned he was the chaplain for our event—an admirably versatile fellow!

We also feel privileged to have shared in some of our children's interesting activities. When our older son was doctoring on southwestern Indian reservations, we were able to visit and become better acquainted with his new wife and their young child, possessor of the broadest "Cheshire cat" grin I have ever seen on a youngster. Likewise, we spent an extraordinarily lovely week at Eglin AFB in Florida with our younger son, wife, and child—plus children from his former marriage with whom I enjoyed one of the greatest of gulf swims. It began quite normally in the afternoon but extended until well after dark—definitely my kind of lark.

Despite gratifying new activities and associations of the last few years, there remains an underlying awareness of loss that occasionally—and unexpectedly—overcomes one or the other of us. In Ken's words, "it rises up and bites us." Especially as we age, we miss the long-ago camaraderie with our sons, but time and circumstance seem finally to be healing many of the most painful wounds. Mercifully, doctrinal differences dividing our family have not conquered us, and we never forget that the losses suffered by millions of this planet's inhabitants far surpass our own. So we count our many blessings, including those ubiquitous blessings in disguise.

Often, I find solace in treasured continuities from the past. In a telephone talk with a schoolmate I have not seen for six decades, I learned that my father's fondness for mathematical puzzles and cryptograms now extends into the lives of *her* grandchildren. And visiting the home of new neighbors brought me face-to-face with an arresting photograph of a palomino stallion, creamy mane and tail flying as he leapt a long-gone hurdle with our host's uncle aboard. The beautiful animal was Sundance from the Montana ranch of my childhood. Thanks to the generosity of our neighbor, the wall in my study now holds a framed photograph of this golden steed, reminding me of a romantic child's Araby.

A dear little lady I have encountered on some of our Canadian vacations pops into my mind more frequently these days. On a particularly scenic walk in Victoria, she and I would often be the only people out walking on cold mornings, and we would smile and greet in passing. After many years, Ken and I spent one night in Victoria, and I took my walk for old times' sake, realizing the old lady very likely would no longer be there. But as I turned back toward our hotel I spotted her on the sidewalk, in front of what appeared to be a senior residence. She was much diminished in stature and was in the care of a nurse. But her gaze remained bright, and as I approached, she smiled and, with noticeable emphasis, stated her usual mantra, "Aren't we lucky?" to which I smiled and made my customary reply, "Yes, we are!"

A decade of wandering in that poorly defined "no man's land," separating East and West, has also seasoned me. Islamic theology interests me less than does the character of those adherents I know best. Increasing closeness with our daughters-in-law—past and present, Muslim and non-Muslim—convinces me all four of them share the age-old desire of mothers everywhere: that their children should enjoy greater security and opportunity than the mothers knew when growing up. Collectively speaking, those childhoods were passed in the presence of war, communist repressions, and traumas from broken and dispersed families. They want better for their children and are working to achieve it. With those enduring aspirations, I am in whole-hearted agreement.

So the beat goes on. These days, Ken and I often round out an afternoon with a walk on our Ocean Beach. Recently, we had an encounter there with a pleasant young woman who had her pet crow and Labrador retriever in tow. After leaving them, I remarked to Ken how astonished I am that, after all our years here, I still thrill to this city, and he replied, "Yes, I know. San Francisco has a lot of weirdos, but where else can you meet a crow in a cage on the beach?"

Always, there will be concern for the future of our grandchildren and their parents. But the future has a way of slipping into the past. I feel proud of them all—of their achievements and the ways they are managing the challenges of their lives, most especially that they have chosen lives of honor and high ideals. I am also profoundly grateful for the richly varied experiences I have been given. In this memoir, my latest lark, I have enjoyed immensely revisiting a life than continues to surpass anything I could have envisioned when embarking upon it. Indeed, it has been—and remains—wondrous.